Sign up for our newsletter to hear
about new and upcoming releases.

www.ylva-publishing.com

Other Books by Jae

Happily Ever After

Standalone Romances:
Paper Love
Just for Show
Falling Hard
Heart Trouble
Under a Falling Star
Something in the Wine
Shaken to the Core

Fair Oaks Series:
Perfect Rhythm
Not the Marrying Kind

The Hollywood Series:
Departure from the Script
Damage Control
Just Physical
The Hollywood Collection (box set)

Portland Police Bureau Series:
Conflict of Interest
Next of Kin

The Vampire Diet Series:
Good Enough to Eat

The Oregon Series:
Backwards to Oregon
Beyond the Trail
Hidden Truths

The Shape-Shifter Series:
Second Nature
Natural Family Disasters
Manhattan Moon
True Nature

Not the Marrying Kind

JAE

Acknowledgments

As always, I'd like to thank my awesome team of beta readers for their help and encouragement—Anna, Anne-France, Christiane, Claire, Danielle, Erin, Laure, Louisa, Melanie, and Trish, you are truly the best!

First and foremost, thanks to my friend Trish for countless brainstorming sessions, overnight beta reading, and for being my American guinea pig to try scenes out on.

Thanks to Melanie for beta reading and for putting food in front of me when I forgot to take a break from writing.

A special thanks to Trish and her mom and to Christiane, Bianca, and her mother Elke for advice on how to run a flower shop and create dazzling bouquets.

Thanks also to my eagle-eyed editor, Amber, and to the rest of the Ylva Publishing team.

Last but not least, I'd like to thank my loyal readers. Writing is a solitary endeavor, so it means the world to me to know that you are out there, reading and enjoying my stories. If you keep reading, I'll keep writing.

Chapter 1

SASHA PUSHED THROUGH THE SWINGING door connecting the kitchen to the front of the bakery and placed the tray of heart-shaped cupcakes into the glass display case. "That's the last tray. Who knew my heart would be such a hot commodity?"

Aunt Mae grinned. "Oh, I knew it all along. There'd be plenty of people interested in capturing your heart if only you'd let them."

"Nah." Sasha wrapped one arm around her aunt. She had to lean down to do so. "Who needs romance when they can have cupcakes?"

Aunt Mae gave her *the* look over the rim of her green-tinted glasses—the one that had gotten Sasha to spill the beans about whatever mischief she'd gotten into as a kid. "Who says you can't have both? Find a good-looking hunk or a pretty gal and eat cupcakes with them." She winked and added, "Or eat other, more interesting things."

Sasha burst out laughing. "No, thanks. There's no one in this town that I want to eat cupcakes with, much less anything else."

The bell above the door jingled a welcome, and Ashley Gaines stepped into A Slice of Heaven.

Sasha never wore a watch when she was working, but she didn't need one to know it was three o'clock. Ashley came in every day at three on the dot, when the afternoon lull hit or, during busy times like today, when she needed a break. She was as regular as clockwork, and she always ordered the same thing. Ashley Gaines was nothing if not predictable.

"Hi, Ash," Kimberly called from where she sat having coffee with her boyfriend.

The other customers sitting at the small tables echoed the greeting, and Ashley returned it with waves and warm smiles, stopping here and there to exchange a few words.

That was the same as every day too. It reminded Sasha of high school, when Ashley, two years ahead of Sasha, had been part of the popular crowd. Back then, she had been class president, head cheerleader—and the quarterback's girlfriend.

Everyone had thought they'd get married right out of high school, but for some reason, that hadn't happened. Maybe Ashley wasn't that predictable after all.

Sasha watched as Ashley finally tore herself away from her fan club and made her way over to the counter. She walked like a dancer, carrying herself with an inherent grace Sasha had envied back in high school. Ashley had skipped that awkward, gangly teenager phase, while Sasha had been the tallest person in her class and had felt about as elegant as a lumberjack.

Even now, at thirty-three, Ashley looked like the nice girl next door in her formfitting, purple sweater and a pair of jeans with a couple of green stains. Sasha couldn't help noticing how nicely they hugged Ashley's curvy hips and showcased her long legs.

Okay, she admitted to herself, maybe what she had felt back in high school hadn't been just envy. Maybe a smidgen of teenage lust had been mixed in too. But now she would rather eat nothing but gas station donuts for a month than get involved with Ashley Gaines, even if Ash weren't the straightest woman in Missouri. If Sasha ever started a relationship, she wanted it to be with a person who was fun and spontaneous, and Ashley was far too focused on her nice-girl image and doing what people expected of her.

"Hi, Ashley," Sasha said. "What can I do to make your taste buds happy today?"

Ashley gave her the same friendly smile she had directed at everyone else. Her strikingly white teeth shone against her face that was still slightly tanned from helping out on her father's farm all summer. "The usual, please."

"Oh, come on. It's Valentine's Day. Aren't you feeling even a little adventurous?"

Ashley hesitated and studied the confections on the other side of the glass.

Sasha couldn't resist teasing her. Ms. Goody-Two-Shoes was always such easy bait. "How about a Sweet Kiss?"

Ashley blinked. "Um…"

"Or would you prefer something hotter?"

"Pardon me?"

Sasha gave her an innocent smile and gestured at the heart-shaped cupcakes as if she had been talking about them all along. "The Sweet Kiss ones are chocolate with salted caramel frosting. Or if you're not in the mood for something sweet, how about a spicy cheddar muffin?"

Ashley brushed back a blonde strand that had escaped her ponytail, but the gesture couldn't hide the blush coloring her cheeks.

Kind of cute. Sasha bit back a groan at the thought. That lingering attraction to Ashley was really annoying.

"Um, no, thanks," Ashley said. "I think I'll go with my usual vanilla cupcake."

Yeah, that was Ashley. Totally vanilla. Sasha suppressed a chuckle.

"Plus two espresso chocolate chip cookies for Brooke and a Beagle Bite for Casper, of course," Ashley added.

"Of course." Ashley never forgot to buy treats for her employee or her dog. Sasha took a paper box with the bakery's logo and reached for one of the vanilla cupcakes with strawberry buttercream frosting.

"You know what?" Ashley said.

Sasha looked up. Would Ashley surprise her after all? "What?"

"Make that two vanilla cupcakes. I think I need the extra sugar today."

Sasha gave her a questioning look, but Ashley didn't elaborate. Not that Sasha had expected her to. They had never exchanged confidences. She placed a second cupcake in the box and put the cookies and the doggie treat for Ashley's golden retriever into two separate bags. "Anything else I can do for you?"

Jeez, why had that come out sounding so flirty?

Ashley didn't seem to notice. "No, thanks." She put the exact change on the counter without having to ask how much she owed Sasha. "See you tomorrow for my cupcake break."

3

"See ya." Sasha took the money without looking at it, her gaze following Ashley as she walked away.

At the door, Ashley nearly ran into Leo and Holly, who had been about to enter.

"Oh, hi, Ash," Holly said. "How are you doing?"

"Um, great. Keeping busy. You know how it is—Valentine's Day is always crazy."

"Is it okay if we add to the craziness? Could you make up a bouquet of gerbera daisies for Leo's mom and some tulips for mine?" Holly asked. "We'll be by to collect them right after we get ourselves a snack."

"Oh, sure. I'll get right on that. See you later." Without waiting for a reply, Ashley hurried down the street toward her flower shop.

Sasha stared after her. For someone who had been close friends with both Leo and Holly at one point, Ashley never seemed completely at ease chatting with them, making Sasha wonder if she was uncomfortable with their sexual orientation.

"Hey, guys," Sasha said as Holly and Leo walked up to the counter. "Are you having a great Valentine's Day?"

"The best ever," they answered in unison.

Sasha playfully rolled her eyes at them. "God, you two are so stinking cute together. You sound like an old, married couple."

They traded a long gaze.

"Um, about that…" Holly sent Leo a questioning look. "What do you think? Should we tell her our news now or wait until later, when she's not so busy?"

"News? There's news in this town, and I haven't heard about it yet?" Sasha opened her eyes comically wide. "Wow. The Fair Oaks rumor mill really isn't what it used to be." She took an apricot-orange cream scone and put it in a bag without asking what Holly and Leo wanted. They, too, always ordered the same. "So, what's the news?"

Holly leaned forward as if about to share a secret. The ear-to-ear grin on her face made Sasha think it had to be something good. "We're getting married."

A second scone and Sasha's pair of silver tongs landed on the counter with a clatter, making several customers look over. Sasha didn't care. She wiped her hands on her baker's apron, rushed around the counter, and engulfed first Holly, then Leo in a warm hug. "That's wonderful. I'm so happy for you guys!"

As soon as she let go, Aunt Mae hurried over and hugged them too. "Did you propose today?" She looked from Holly to Leo and back.

"I wanted to." Holly laughed. "I had it all planned out. A romantic stroll along the creek before heading to Tasty Barn for a candlelit dinner, and when we got to the bridge, I wanted to drop down on one knee and ask her to marry me. But Leo beat me to it last night." She held out her hand, showing off her engagement ring with a single, beautiful diamond.

"I wanted to do it on Valentine's Day too, but then I thought that might be a little too cheesy, even for someone who writes sappy love songs for a living." The corners of Leo's mouth curved up into an embarrassed smile. A ring that looked nearly identical to Holly's sparkled on her finger. "Plus I just couldn't wait any longer."

"Wow. You both planned to propose without the other knowing? Great minds think alike." Sasha had never really believed in all that happily-ever-after stuff, but seeing the obvious love radiating off her friends, she was almost considering changing her mind. "So when's the happy day?"

"We were thinking the first Saturday in May. It's my parents' wedding date, and my mom loved the idea when we told her over breakfast," Holly said. "Plus it's not too hot in May."

Sasha nodded her approval. Elaborate wedding cakes and summer heat didn't mix well.

"We want something small and low-key, not a big, fancy production, so we're not going to have an official maid of honor or bridesmaids with identical dresses or anything like that, but…" Holly traded a look with Leo, who gave her a tiny nod. "We'd like you to be part of our wedding party."

Warmth spread through Sasha, as if she had just taken a bite of a cinnamon roll fresh out of the oven. "I'd be honored."

"And we'd love for you to make our wedding cake," Leo added.

"Of course," Sasha said without even consulting her order book first. "Any idea what kind of cake you want?"

Holly and Leo again exchanged gazes before Holly said, "Not yet. But my mom thinks it's a good idea for the baker and the florist to collaborate closely so the cake and the flowers match both in color and design. Maybe we could all get together at our place in a week or two and talk about the details."

"Yeah, sure. Who'll do the flowers? Blossoms from Kansas City?"

"Um, no," Holly answered. "We want Ash to do it. We haven't asked her yet, but I hope she'll agree."

Ash... It shouldn't have thrown her for a loop. Not only was The Flower Girl the only floral shop in town, but Ashley had also been friends with both brides-to-be in the past. Still, the prospect of having to work with Ashley was more unsettling than Sasha cared to admit, and she couldn't even say why exactly.

"That's not a problem, is it?" Holly asked when Sasha remained silent.

"No, of course not." If Ms. Prim-and-Proper was willing to work a lesbian wedding with her, there wouldn't be a problem at all. Sasha had worked with dozens of other wedding professionals over the years, and it had always gone without a hitch. Why would this time be any different?

"If anyone else walks in here and orders a dozen red roses, I'm going to scream." As the latest in a long string of rose-buying customers disappeared down the street, Ashley sank against the counter and stretched her aching back.

Brooke, her part-time employee, laughed, making the small hoop in her nose vibrate. "Yeah, me too. It's so lame. They all say they want something special and unique for V-Day—and then they order the most cliché thing ever."

"Well, at least we're making good money today." Her little shop really needed that since business was always slow in January.

"Yeah," Brooke said. "It's the day of overpriced chocolates and guilt-trip flowers that people only buy because they're supposed to."

Ash circled the counter to choose the most beautiful gerbera daisies for the bouquet Holly had ordered. "Wow. That's kind of jaded for a nineteen-year-old, don't you think? You sound like—"

"Like you?"

"Me?" Ash shook her head. "I never said anything like that. I merely mentioned that it would be more logical if Valentine's Day were in summer, when roses are actually in bloom. But aside from that practical consideration, I'm a romantic at heart."

"A romantic who hasn't had a date since way before I started working here."

Ash turned away under the pretense of getting sprigs of eucalyptus and some bear grass for the bouquet. This was exactly why Valentine's Day was both a blessing and a curse for her. The most romantic day of the year was a reminder that she was alone and would likely stay that way. She forced a smile as she returned to her workstation and faced Brooke. "Is my mother paying you to say that?"

Brooke grinned and brushed back the long side bang hanging over one eye. "Ooh! You think she would? I need all the money I can get to be able to leave this town and go away to college."

Before Ash could answer, the bell above the door announced another customer.

Barry Clemons, the owner of the grain and feed, stepped into the shop and shook drops of rain and sleet off his coat. "Brr. Hi, Ashley. Can't wait for spring. Bet your dad says the same."

"He does. You know him. Every year after harvest, he swears he'll finally take Mom on vacation, but by the time January and February come around, he can't wait to get back in the fields."

Barry chuckled, then sobered. "How are your folks? Must be a tough time of year for them."

Ash smiled through the stab of pain and sent a glance to the customer who had come in right after Barry. Thankfully, Mrs. Mitchell was busy looking at the orchids and the potted hydrangeas and didn't seem to be listening in on their conversation. "They're okay. Staying busy fixing tractors and doing barn repairs. Dad is even helping me out with deliveries today because we have so many online orders that my driver can't do it all. So, how can I help you?"

"I thought I'd get some flowers," Barry said.

"Captain Obvious," Brooke muttered under her breath.

Ash nudged her behind the cover of the counter. The customer was king, even though it was kind of obvious that he was here for flowers.

"What were you thinking of?" Ash asked.

He looked around the shop, which today wasn't as neat and orderly as Ash usually tried to keep it. The floor was dirty from the many customers who'd come in since seven this morning, when she had opened the shop two hours earlier than usual. She hadn't had much of a chance to tidy up her work area, so trimmings of stems and stripped leaves formed piles behind the counter. One of the adorable plush teddy bears had toppled over on the shelf, as if it had gotten tired waiting for someone to take it home. A heart-shaped balloon had escaped from the flower basket it had been tied to, and now it dangled from the ceiling.

Barry's gaze went from the floating balloon to the bouquets Ash had prepared for walk-in customers. Then he paused on Brooke and looked at her as if he had never seen her before even though she'd worked for Ash since the previous summer. A deep groove formed between his brows as he took in Brooke's nose ring, her kohl-rimmed eyes, and the edgy haircut, short except for a sweeping side bang that almost obscured her left eye.

Brooke met his gaze as if she didn't care what he thought of her.

Ash couldn't help admiring her. At Brooke's age, all she had wanted was to fit in and avoid anything that could make her the subject of gossip again—and that hadn't changed now that she was an adult.

Finally, Barry turned toward the walk-in cooler that took up most of one wall. In it, cut flowers were arranged in metal buckets. "A dozen red roses, please."

Brooke rolled her eyes in that way only teenagers could.

Ash nudged her again. "Why don't you go see if you can help Mrs. Mitchell?" When Brooke trudged away, Ash turned back to Barry. "Roses are always a great choice. I bet Heather will love them. Would you like them wrapped or in a vase?"

"Wrapped, please." Barry watched while Ash pulled a rose from one of the buckets.

She formed a circle with her thumb and index finger and started slotting flowers into it at an angle, constantly rotating the bouquet as she added more roses and some baby's breath. Finally, she created a frill around the bouquet with some leatherleaf fern and held her creation out to Barry for his approval.

He nodded. "Looks great. Thanks."

8

Ash wrapped the stems with floral tape and trimmed them to an even length.

"Could you make up another bouquet and wrap them too?" Barry asked.

Flowers for his mother? How sweet. Ash smiled. "Sure. Roses too?"

Barry shrugged. "Anything will do. You pick." He rifled through his wallet while he waited and put his credit card down on the counter. But then he paused and added a couple of bills. He glanced back over his shoulder at Brooke and Mrs. Mitchell. "Um, I'll pay cash for the roses, if you don't mind."

Ash froze with her hand extended toward a bucket of peonies. Jesus. How much more obvious could he be? She schooled her face and tried to keep smiling, but it wasn't easy.

God knew, she had thoroughly messed up her one and only relationship as an adult, but she had never, ever cheated.

Ash turned away from the peonies and picked yellow carnations and pink snapdragon instead. Heather probably wouldn't know that the flowers in her bouquet symbolized disappointment and deception, but at least Ash could imagine that she was warning her in some way, saying through flowers what she would never dare voice.

A few minutes later, Barry left, cradling the two bouquets and holding the door open for Mrs. Mitchell and her potted hydrangea.

Brooke stared after him. "Did he just...?"

Ash sighed. "Yeah, I think so."

"What an ass. Who do you think it is? The chick he's hooking up with, I mean."

"I don't know, and I don't want to know." Ash really liked Fair Oaks and the people in this little town—well, most people, most of the time—but the one thing she despised was gossip.

"I bet it's Cora. I've seen her head into the feed and grain a couple of times, and I don't think she was there for the corn. She's a postal worker, for fuck's sake."

"Poor Heather," Ash said. "She probably has no idea that he's giving her a bunch of 'anything will do' while sending red roses to another woman."

"Oh, don't worry. She'll find out like this." Brooke snapped her fingers. "This is Fair Oaks after all. Secrets don't stay secret here for very long."

A chill skittered down Ash's spine, making the air in the flower shop appear even cooler. Her own secret had nearly come out a year and a half before, when Travis had told their former classmates about her car being parked in front of Holly's house all night long. But that relationship had ended years ago, and everyone had probably dismissed Travis's suspicions as his dirty little fantasies.

She was safe, especially since she had decided that another relationship wasn't worth the risk. She'd stay far, far away from the women of Fair Oaks...which was easy to do since they were all straight.

Well, all except for the two women who were now entering the shop to collect the bouquets they had ordered.

Holly was the first to step inside, while Leo hung back, her guarded pop star mask firmly in place.

Was she still angry with Ash? There had been a time when Ash could read her well, but that had been back in high school, when they had been best friends. They hadn't exchanged more than a quick hello in the year and a half since Ash had tried to warn her away from Holly. It had been a stupid move, caused by hurt and jealousy; she could admit that now, at least to herself.

She was over it. Okay, mostly over it. She swallowed against the lump in her throat as she watched them walk toward her, hand in hand.

Seeing them together was always a little weird. The first girl she had ever kissed dating the first—and only—woman she'd ever been in a relationship with... It was mind-boggling.

But they looked good together, Ash had to admit. Happy.

Brooke watched them approach with a grin. "Let me guess. You want a dozen red roses?"

Ash sent her a warning glance. She really had to talk to Brooke. If Brooke wanted to keep working for her, she would have to learn to hold her tongue in front of customers.

"Um, no." With her free hand that wasn't holding on to Leo's, Holly pointed at the bouquet Ash was still working on. "Actually, I think this one is for us."

The light caught on a ring glistening on Holly's left ring finger.

The ribbon Ash had been about to tie around the gerbera stems dropped to the worktable. A gasp escaped her, and she stared at Holly's hand. As a nurse, Holly had never been one to wear any jewelry, especially not a tasteful but obviously expensive diamond ring. Her gaze darted to Leo's hand, which sported a similar ring. "Oh my God! Is...is that...? Are you...?"

Holly curled her hand around the ring as if to protect it. A flush of joy colored her cheeks. "I know today is crazy for you. That's why I didn't want to say anything today. But if Brooke could hold down the fort for a minute, maybe we could go and talk in the back."

"Okay," was the only word Ash could get out.

Leo still hadn't said a word as Ash led them around the counter and through the open door into the back room.

Casper, Ash's golden retriever, jumped out of his doggie bed and rushed over to greet them.

Ash was grateful for the distraction so she could get herself together. The low buzz of the flower cooler compressor filled her ears—or maybe it was the chaotic thoughts tumbling through her mind.

Brooke had stared after them, but now she quickly busied herself rearranging the greeting cards next to the counter, affecting a look of sullen teenage disinterest.

Ash didn't buy it for a second. She closed the curtain that separated the workroom from the front of the shop, which she rarely ever did. For once, she wished for a real door.

With trembling hands, she cleared the small, round table in the corner of bows, little packets of flower food, and floral picks with pink hearts and pushed two chairs and a stool over to it. "Please, sit." She took the stool and sank onto it.

Casper settled down at her feet as if wanting to lend support.

Leo and Holly sat across from her without letting go of each other's hand.

Again, Ash's gaze was drawn to their rings. "You...you're getting married?"

A joyous smile lit up Holly's face. "Yes."

"Wow, that's...um..." Finally, Ash's good manners kicked in, and she said, as if on autopilot, "Congratulations. I'm really happy for you." And she was. But at the same time, so many conflicting thoughts and emotions were crashing down on her that she felt as if she were caught in a hailstorm.

"Thanks." Holly beamed, and even Leo's celebrity mask was replaced by a warm smile.

They radiated so much happiness that Ash had to look away. How could they be so happy with their sexual orientation, while Ash still struggled with hers? She couldn't imagine ever getting to a point where she would want to celebrate her love for a woman with a big event that would probably include the entire town.

"We would both really like it if you would come to our wedding and also do our flowers," Holly said.

Ash peered over at them from under half-lowered lashes. "Are you sure?"

"If you'd rather not do a wedding between two women because of what people—or your parents—might say…" Leo said.

That concern had crossed Ash's mind. Her parents and some of her more conservative customers wouldn't be too happy about her being involved in a same-sex wedding, but that wasn't why she hesitated. "No, that's not it." She lowered her gaze to the table. "I mean, after what I said about Holly, I would completely understand if you'd rather use a florist in Kansas City."

For several seconds, no one answered.

Casper let out a low whine as if sensing the rising tension.

Ash looked up. *Oh shit.* Unlike Ash, Holly had never been one to hide her emotions, and now it was written all over her face that she hadn't known about Ash's careless words.

Both Ash and Leo opened their mouths, but before either of them could say anything, Holly lifted her hand. "I don't want to know. It doesn't matter."

"Of course it matters," Leo said, heat in her eyes.

"Leo, after everything that happened—your father dying, you firing your manager, and me finally understanding that I can have a happy relationship despite being asexual—I thought we agreed that we don't want to hang on to any bitter feelings from the past. That's part of why we want to get married, right? To have a new beginning—and that includes a new beginning for you and Ash too."

Tears burned in Ash's eyes. She hadn't expected that Holly of all people would defend her to Leo. It made her feel even worse about the words she'd spoken in anger. "I know I owe you an apology. Both of you." She glanced from Leo to Holly and back. "I was hurt and bitter, blaming everyone else for the way my life turned out. But I made my peace with it, and I'd really like to make peace with you too."

"I'd really like that too," Holly said softly. "I always regretted losing our friendship, and I'd like to work on getting it back."

Ash was speechless. She hadn't expected to be invited back into Holly's life. Maybe she should have known better. Holly had always possessed the biggest heart of anyone she knew.

Holly squeezed Leo's hand. "What do you think, honey?"

Leo looked down at her hand that was joined with Holly's, and when she gazed back up, her tense features had relaxed. "I think you're right." She exhaled and looked Ash in the eyes. "You were once an important person in my life. In both of our lives. I won't lie. It'll take a lot of work to get that friendship back, but we have to start somewhere. Would you be a part of our wedding and also do the flowers?"

Snippets of what her parents and the more conservative people in town would say echoed through Ash's head. She shook off those thoughts. If she wanted to earn back Holly's and Leo's friendship, she had to do something to deserve it. "I would be honored."

Chapter 2

By the time Ash had checked her orders for the next day, cleaned up the shop, and prepped the leftover roses to donate to the local retirement home, it had long since gotten dark outside. Her hands were sore and covered in little nicks, her feet and her back were killing her, and except for the two cupcakes, she hadn't eaten all day. All she wanted was to crash on the couch with a cheese pizza from Casey's.

But before she could pass out from Valentine's Day-induced exhaustion, she needed to walk Casper. The poor boy hadn't even gotten his usual lunch break walk today. Ash's dad had merely taken him outside in between delivery runs.

At least the sleet—part rain, part snow—that had fallen all day had stopped, and she could drop off the money bags in the bank's night deposit box on her way to the park.

Fair Oaks lay in silence as they strolled through town. Casper's softly jingling dog tags produced the only sound around. All of the stores had closed hours ago. Streetlamps threw warm pools of yellow light onto the pockmarked asphalt of Main Street and the cracked sidewalks. Her breath condensed in front of her face, adding to the feeling of being in her own little bubble.

Being out alone at this hour was magical. By the time she reached the bank, Ash could already feel some of the stress leaving her.

A tall figure lurked in front of the night deposit box. A thick coat and a woolen hat made it impossible to even guess the stranger's gender, but the imposing height made Ash's pulse quicken.

She clutched the strap of her purse, where she had stuck the bank bags, with one hand while white-knuckling Casper's leash with the other. God, she was glad she had the dog with her. If push came to shove, she was pretty sure he would defend her.

But Casper didn't growl. He let out an excited woof and bounded forward to greet the stranger—or rather the tiny dog at the person's feet.

The stranger turned, and the light of the streetlamp next to the bank illuminated Sasha Peterson's strong features. Her thick, brown braid stuck out from beneath her woolen hat and hung down in front of one broad shoulder. A sprinkling of flour dusted its tip. Apparently, she was on her way home from work too.

While the dogs began their butt-sniffing ritual, Sasha and Ash stared at each other.

"Jeez," Sasha said. "I didn't hear you walk up. You scared the crap out of me."

"Out of you?" Ash eyed Sasha's muscular six-foot frame. She didn't look as if she had much to fear.

Sasha shrugged. "I do cupcakes, not kung fu." She reached down to pet Casper, who sniffed her and then tried to lick her hands.

"Casper, no." Ash pulled him back.

"Are you dropping off today's cash too?" Sasha asked.

When Ash nodded, she pulled out the handle for her so Ash could drop her bank bag into the deposit box.

"Thanks." With the money safely dropped off, Ash headed toward the park, and Sasha followed.

Ash glanced at the fawn-colored French bulldog scampering after Casper on much shorter legs. "I didn't know you had a dog. Did you just get him or her?"

"Um, yeah, kind of. Snickerdoodle is my aunt's."

"Snickerdoodle?" Ash laughed.

The sound of Sasha's chuckle, deep and full of mirth, filled the night. "Well, my aunt wanted to name her Snatch because she's always snatching up anything edible, but I managed to talk her out of it."

"Sna—" Ash bit back a laugh. "Um, Snickerdoodle is not such a bad name after all. Although it's a mouthful for such a small dog." She watched them out of the corner of her eye. The sight of the tall, solidly built woman walking her aunt's tiny French bulldog with its pink sweater made Ash grin.

"What?" Sasha patted her coat as if believing she had clumps of dough stuck to her clothes.

Ash hid her grin. "Oh, nothing."

They walked along the creek, silence falling between them. Since the creek was frozen, not even its gentle murmur filled the air.

Even though they had mutual friends, Ash had never talked to Sasha, at least not about anything important, so now she didn't know what to say. She had a feeling Sasha would be easy to talk to, but—truth be told—Ash had avoided her for years.

Except for Holly and Leo, Sasha was probably the only person in town who knew that Ash was gay—at least the only person who knew for sure. Not that she and Holly had ever talked about it, but Ash assumed that Holly had told her closest friend about them back when they had first gotten together.

Even worse, Sasha likely knew all the ugly details about their breakup too.

Ash wasn't proud of the way she had handled their problems back then, and she hated that another person knew about it. It made her feel exposed, as if she were strolling through town stark naked.

She shivered and drew her coat more tightly around herself. For a second, she considered telling Sasha that she would prefer some peace and quiet after her busy day and wanted to walk her dog alone, but that would have been rude, so she continued on without saying anything.

Thankfully, Sasha either didn't know what to say to her, or she didn't feel the need to talk.

When they neared the bridge leading to the part of town where Ash lived, Sasha cleared her throat. "So, good day?"

Ash nodded. "Long day too."

"I hear you. I've been baking since three a.m. I think I'm going to need a few days to get my stamina back before we get together."

Stamina? Get together? What on earth...? Ash's foot slid out from under her on a wet patch of grass.

"Whoa!" Sasha caught her before she could fall. "Careful."

Sasha's scent—cinnamon and something else, something spicier—engulfed her. Ash was much too aware of the strong fingers wrapped around her elbow. Annoyed with herself for even noticing Sasha's scent or the way her hand felt on her arm, she pulled away. "W-what do you mean?"

"It's dark, and the grass is wet, so you'd better stay on the path, or you'll—"

Ash waved her hand. "Not that." Then the potential meaning of Sasha's words hit home, and a blush warmed Ash's face. "Oh. You're talking about getting together with the gang on Saturday, right?" *Duh, what else did you think she was talking about? A date?*

That was impossible. As far as she knew, Sasha was straight. Even if she weren't, after everything that Holly had probably told her, Ash was sure that Sasha would rather cut the grass on the high school's football field with a pair of nail clippers than ask her out.

"Um, no, that's not what I meant," Sasha said. "Sure, I'll be at Johnny's on Saturday, but I was talking about just the two of us."

"Just the two of us?" Ash's brain was stuck on repeating the words without understanding them. For a second, she was nearly convinced that she had fallen asleep on her couch after work and this was just one of her crazy reoccurring dreams in which someone outed her in public and the whole town turned their backs on her.

"Well, us and the happy couple, of course." Sasha laughed. "Or do you think Travis, Jenny, and the others will have any valuable input on flowers and cake?"

Ash stopped next to the bridge. "Flowers and cake?" She searched Sasha's brown eyes, which appeared almost black in the light of the nearly full moon. "What are you talking about?"

A line formed between Sasha's brows. "Um, me cake, you flowers? I thought Holly and Leo talked to you."

"You mean about their wedding? Yes, they did. But what does that have to do with…?" Realization struck. "Oh. They want you to do the wedding cake." Of course. Sasha was one of Holly's closest friends after all, so why would they hire someone else?

"Yes. And they want us to work together to coordinate the colors and design. They suggested we all get together sometime next week or the week after to talk about the details."

"Oh."

"Didn't they mention that?" Sasha asked.

Ash scratched her head. Had they? Today had been crazy busy, and finding out that her ex-girlfriend was going to marry the first woman Ash had ever kissed had been a bit of a shock. But she was pretty sure she would remember if anyone had mentioned that. "Um, no, I don't think they did."

Sasha bent her head and studied her closely. "Is that going to be a problem for you?"

"No," Ash said quickly. A little too quickly. "No problem at all. Why would it be a problem?"

Sasha was still scrutinizing her. She folded her arms over her chest. "I don't know. You tell me."

"It's not going to be a problem," Ash said so loudly that Snickerdoodle's bat ears swiveled in her direction.

"Good." It didn't sound conciliatory but rather like a challenge.

"Yeah. Good," Ash repeated.

They stood next to the bridge in a silent stare-down until Snickerdoodle let out a high-pitched whine.

Sasha bent down, picked her up, and cradled her against her chest. "I'd better get her home. Frenchies are pretty sensitive to the cold. See you tomorrow at three for cupcakes."

Ash just nodded, not knowing what to say. With Casper pressing against her leg, she watched Sasha's tall shape disappear into the darkness.

So she and Sasha would be working together to make sure Holly and Leo had the wedding of their dreams. No big deal, right? She had just been caught off guard for a moment.

They would meet a time or two to make sure Sasha's fondant matched the color of Ash's centerpieces at the reception. She had done that before, back when Sasha's aunt had still been running the bakery, so it would be just business as usual. When they met to talk about the details, she would be the model of cool, calm, and collected.

With a decisive nod, she turned away from where Sasha had disappeared and strode across the bridge toward home.

On Friday evening of the week after, Sasha tucked her portfolio under one arm, took the covered tray of cake samples from the passenger seat, and shut the door of her SUV with a firm nudge of her hip.

Only Holly's Jeep Liberty and Leo's BMW X5 were in the driveway as she carried the tray toward the house. No sign of Ashley or her ten-year-old silver GMC Terrain anywhere.

She hadn't shown up at Johnny's last Saturday, and Sasha had been busy in the bakery kitchen all week, so her staff and Aunt Mae had manned the counter, and she hadn't seen Ashley since that weird conversation at the creek on Valentine's Day.

Sasha still hadn't been able to figure out what Ashley's problem was. Why the hell would it be such a big deal for Ashley to work with her? Which it clearly was, no matter what Ashley said.

Sasha might not be the popular girl next door that Ashley was, but she generally got along with everyone, and her friends told her she was fun to be around. So why would Ashley act as if working with her was a huge inconvenience?

She had racked her brain but couldn't think of any reason. Unless...

Sasha paused on the broad veranda. Had Ashley somehow found out about that stupid, little crush Sasha had on her back in high school? Was that what made her appear so uncomfortable any time she was around Sasha?

Nah. That couldn't be it. That had been fifteen years ago. She was no longer that smitten sixteen-year-old who had admired Ashley from afar. Ashley had probably been clueless anyway. She had hung out only with Leo and the popular crowd, without paying Sasha any attention.

But if that wasn't it, what else had made Ashley as twitchy as a long-tailed cat in a room full of rocking chairs?

The front door swung open before Sasha could find an answer or ring the doorbell.

Holly stood in front of her, an amused smile on her face. "Are we having our cake consultation on the veranda?"

"Haha." Sasha gave her a one-armed hug and carried the tray past her into the house.

She'd been a regular visitor since Holly and Leo had moved in, but the house and what they had made of it still took her breath away each time she came by. She especially liked the living room, where Holly led her now. With its high ceiling and the fireplace that dominated one wall, it managed to be both spacious and cozy. Two overstuffed chairs and a tan couch invited you to curl up and relax, and Chance—the red tabby that ruled the house—had done exactly that. He barely lifted his head when Sasha entered.

"Where's your future wife?" Sasha asked as she set down the tray on the coffee table.

An affectionate smile curled Holly's lips. She pointed to the sliding glass doors that led out onto a deck overlooking the large, tree-lined backyard.

A motion-activated light flared on as Leo stepped out of the former guesthouse that they had converted into a music studio. She crossed the backyard, slid open the glass door, and immediately slung one arm around Holly as if she hadn't seen her for weeks. "Hey, Sasha. Sorry. I sometimes lose track of time when I'm composing. Am I late?"

"Just a little," Sasha said. "And so is Ashley. Isn't she coming?"

The sound of the doorbell interrupted them before anyone could answer.

"Speak of the devil," Leo muttered.

Holly nudged her, whispered something that sounded like "New beginnings, remember?" and went to open the door.

Seconds later, Ashley rushed into the living room, holding out what was probably her portfolio as if it were a peace offering. "I'm so sorry, guys. I swear I left on time, but my car wouldn't start, so I had to walk all the way."

She looked more as if she had *run* all the way. Her cheeks were flushed. She must have either lost or forgotten her hair clip, so her nearly waist-long, blonde hair cascaded down her back in loose waves.

Damn if that didn't make her even more attractive. Sasha cursed her libido for even noticing.

"Don't worry," Holly said with a quick pat on Ashley's arm. "We haven't started yet. Sasha just got here too. Take a seat."

Leo and Holly took the two overstuffed chairs, which stood side by side, leaving the couch for Sasha and Ashley.

Sasha folded her frame between Ashley and the cat. Since Chance had somehow managed to take up half the couch, they were forced to sit close, so much so that Sasha could sense Ashley's warmth against her thigh and shoulder.

Under the pretense of putting down her portfolio on the end table, Ashley slid a little to the side, her entire body as stiff as a board.

Jeez. Does she think I have Ebola or that my queerness is contagious?

If Ashley even had a clue that Sasha wasn't straight. Sasha didn't hide her sexual orientation by any means, but since she hadn't dated in years, it wasn't exactly common knowledge in town either. As the owner of the only flower shop in Fair Oaks, Ashley probably heard a lot of gossip, though. Maybe someone had told her that Sasha appreciated a good-looking woman as much as a handsome man, and that was what was making her so uncomfortable around her.

Sasha decided to ignore her and focus on the brides-to-be instead. "So, where will the ceremony and the reception be held?"

"What dresses will you be wearing?" Ashley asked at the same time.

They looked at each other, then away.

"No dress for me," Leo announced. "I've been put into enough sexy dresses and uncomfortable shoes to last me a lifetime. It's a lesbian wedding, so I'm taking full advantage of that fact and will dress comfortably."

Sasha grinned. "Phew. I take it that means no hideous pink taffeta dresses for the women in the wedding party either?"

"Well," Leo drawled, "that depends on how nice you are to us."

"I'll be very nice. I'll even make you the most beautiful wedding cake you've ever seen. Have you thought about what you want?" She slid her portfolio across the coffee table and invited them to take a look at the photos from previous weddings. "Three tiers? Four? Or something completely different? A lot of couples are doing cupcakes instead of a traditional cake right now."

Holly paused on a picture of a three-tiered wedding cake. "I want cake." She looked at Leo, who immediately nodded. "Something traditional, but also something that is just...us."

One thing immediately came to mind. "How about a three-tiered vanilla sponge cake with apricot-orange filling and either vanilla buttercream icing or ivory fondant? It would practically be a wedding cake version of your favorite scones."

"Perfect," Leo and Holly said in unison.

"That was fast. Looks like we won't even have to do a cake tasting. Well, I'll just take my cake samples back with me, then." Sasha pretended to reach for the tray.

With a growl, Leo snatched it away and cradled it protectively against her chest. "Don't you dare."

Sasha laughed, and even Ashley smiled at her antics.

"Let me get us some plates so you two can stay and look at Ashley's flower options." Sasha squeezed past Ashley and walked over to the open kitchen, which was separated from the living room by a U-shaped island. She knew where the plates were kept but had to look around for the forks, which gave her an opportunity to watch her friends and Ashley.

"So where will you have the reception?" Ashley asked while Leo and Holly flipped through her portfolio.

"We booked the ballroom of the country club," Holly said. "Our moms are already up to their necks in wedding planning, eagerly flipping through bridal magazines, so we'll probably be able to give you a good idea of the décor soon."

"And the ceremony?" Ashley asked. "Do we need flowers for the church benches and the altar?"

"No," Leo answered. "Even if the reverend were willing to perform the ceremony, neither Holly nor I are particularly religious. Maybe we'll just go to the courthouse and have someone there perform the ceremony."

"You know that'll start rumors," Ashley said quietly.

Leo chuckled. "Of what? One of us being pregnant, so that's why we're getting married quickly?"

"No, but people might say—"

"Why would they care what people might say?" Sasha put the plates and forks on the table and plopped back down on the couch.

The impact of her heavier weight nearly made Ashley bounce off the couch.

Sasha hid a grin. Maybe it would jostle Ashley out of her constant concern about what people might think. "It's their wedding, so who cares what anyone else thinks?"

Ashley looked down at her hands that lay folded on her lap.

"You know where I'd really like to have the ceremony?" Holly asked before the silence could grow too tense.

Leo grinned at her. "I don't think we can have it up on my mother's roof, sweetheart."

They laughed together.

"No, that's not what I meant. I was thinking of our spot at the creek." Holly looked over at Sasha and Ashley. "That's where Leo asked me out for the first time, where I came out to her as asexual, and where we had our first date."

"And our first argument as a couple," Leo added, but she was smiling and reached over to take Holly's hand. "The creek would be the perfect spot, so yes, let's make that happen."

"I could decorate the railings of the bridge with the flowers of your choice. The classic option would probably be white roses, but if you want a more modern touch, you could also have calla lilies or—" Ashley continued listing options.

Sasha stopped listening because flowers weren't her thing. She reached for the stack of plates, removed the aluminum foil from the tray, and put several of the small samples on each plate.

When she handed Ashley her plate, their fingers brushed.

The slight roughness of her skin was a surprise—and so was the tingle that ran up Sasha's arm. It was probably just because Ashley's hands were rough from working with thorny stems all day, so her touch tickled, Sasha told herself. Or maybe all that wedding talk was making her a bit hormonal. Any good-looking person would have made her react like that, and Ashley was admittedly pretty, even if she did have a stick up her ass.

Sasha pulled her hand away and busied herself with her own plate.

Ashley slid her fork into the first mini-cupcake and took a bite. Her eyes fluttered closed, and her face took on a look of rapture that made Sasha wonder if that was how she looked when she enjoyed the other pleasures of life.

She pushed the thought away.

Then Ashley took another bite, and a low, almost sensual moan escaped her lips.

Not helping, Ashley! How was she supposed to get over the last remainder of her stupid teenage crush if Ashley continued to make erotic sounds like that? Abruptly, Sasha stuffed an entire mini-cupcake into her mouth.

Leo let out a moan too. "Mmm. Good thing we've already decided on our cake. It would be impossible to pick one. They're all so good."

"Better than sex," Holly mumbled around a mouthful of cake sample.

Ashley paused with her fork halfway to her mouth and looked as if Holly had slapped her.

Just because Holly had made a joking remark about sex?

A lot of the people in town were like that—they were fine with their lesbian neighbors as long as they weren't confronted with their sexuality. But Sasha had hoped Ashley wouldn't be like those people. It would make working together uncomfortable.

Finally, after more cake had been eaten and more wedding plans made, Sasha and Ashley packed up their notes and their portfolios and walked to the door. Sasha hugged her friends goodbye, and Ashley followed her example but didn't look exactly relaxed about it.

Come on. Get over yourself, Ashley. Sasha shook her head behind Ashley's back and walked toward her car.

Only when Ashley continued on down the street did Sasha remember her car problems. It was completely dark and cold outside, and while the most dangerous crime being committed in Fair Oaks was a couple of teenagers stealing beer from the mom-and-pop grocery store, Sasha would have felt like an ass if she had made Ashley walk home.

She tossed the empty tray into the back and opened the passenger-side door. "Want a ride?"

Ash turned and looked at Sasha across the roof of the SUV.

Sasha was holding the passenger-side door open invitingly, but her body language and her tone said something else. Clearly, she didn't want Ash to ride with her either. Not that Ash was eager to get into the car with her. The last hour had been uncomfortable enough, since she'd been sitting pressed up against Sasha on the couch.

Sasha had seemed just as awkward. She had jumped at the chance to get the plates from the kitchen as an excuse to get away from her. A few times, she had seemed downright grumpy—but only when she was talking to Ash. Now who had a problem working together?

Ash shook her head. "No, thanks," she called over to Sasha. "It's not that far. I can walk."

"Don't be stupid. It's on the other side of town."

Stupid? Was that what Sasha thought of her? Ash gritted her teeth.

Leo and Holly's neighbor walked past with his dog. "Hi, Ash. Hi, Sasha."

"Hi, Joe." Ash waved, then turned back to Sasha, who still stood waiting, the passenger-side door wide open. If they continued to discuss this for longer than the ride home would take, people would start to wonder what was going on. "Okay, fine. I'll ride with you. Thank you."

She walked around to the passenger side and climbed in.

Sasha closed the door before getting in on the other side.

They rode in silence for a while.

When Sasha braked at the town's only traffic light, she glanced over at Ash. "It's really great that they're getting married, isn't it?"

Ash nodded.

"I'm so happy Holly finally found someone who understands and accepts her. Not like those assholes she dated before."

A wave of heat shot up Ash's chest and made her cheeks burn. She clutched the door handle so tightly that her fingers started to cramp. Was that why Sasha had offered her a lift? So she could finally get her long-held resentment off her chest and accuse her of treating Holly like shit? "Listen." She tried to speak very calmly, but her voice came out sounding like crunching gravel. "I know you don't like me because you think I'm one of those assholes. But what happened between Holly and me is complicated and, frankly, none of your business. So can we please forget about it and just work together like two professionals?"

Sasha stared at Ash. Her jaw moved up and down, but it took several seconds until any words came out. "You...Holly...you were...together? You...you're gay?"

Now it was Ash's turn to stare. She pressed her trembling hand to her stomach. Nausea gripped her. "Oh my God. You mean, you didn't know?"

Sasha slapped the steering wheel with both hands. "No! I had no fucking idea!"

They sank against the backs of their seats. "Holy shit," they said in unison.

Chapter 3

SASHA COULDN'T BELIEVE IT. ASHLEY Gaines, Fair Oaks's darling and the wet dream of every boy in Sasha's high school class, was a lesbian or bi. And not just that. She and Holly had been a couple.

Hell on a stick! No one had told her a thing. She stared over at Ashley and tried to make out her features in the glow of a streetlamp next to the car.

But Ashley had put her elbows on her knees and buried her face in both hands, groaning quietly.

A loud honk from behind made them jump.

Sasha glanced in the rearview mirror.

Brandon Eads, former star quarterback and Ashley's ex-boyfriend, had stopped his car behind them and gestured at the traffic light, which had long since turned green.

Sasha felt as if she were trapped in some bizarre soap opera. She hit the gas a little too hard and sped across the intersection.

Before she could sort her chaotic thoughts enough to ask a question, they reached Ashley's cute, little house at the edge of town.

"Please don't tell anyone," Ashley said, her eyes wide and pleading as if her very life was now in Sasha's hands.

"I won't, but—"

"Thank you." Ashley released her seat belt and opened the passenger-side door. "And thanks for the ride."

"Wait!" Sasha grasped her arm and stopped her from exiting the car. "You can't drop a bomb like that on me and then just leave."

Ashley longingly looked toward the escape that was her front door before slowly turning to face Sasha. Even in the dim light, it was easy to see that her cheeks had taken on the color of raspberry filling. Panic flickered in her eyes. Her gaze darted down to Sasha's hand on her arm.

Quickly, Sasha let go and made a conscious effort to gentle her tone, not wanting to come across like a bully. "So Holly and you…?" She still couldn't believe it.

Ashley closed the passenger-side door before nodding.

"Jesus."

Ashley peered at her out of the corner of her eye. "You really didn't know?"

"How the hell was I supposed to know?"

"I…I thought…" Ashley hunched her shoulders. "I thought Holly might have told you. I mean, you're her best friend."

"That's what I thought," Sasha mumbled. Holly not trusting her cut deep. They had been through so much together—the death of Holly's father, Sasha's father getting remarried, and Holly quitting her job at the hospital to work in home health care. Why hadn't Holly told her?

"I assumed you knew," Ashley said. "I thought that was why you…"

Sasha threw her a gloomy look. "Why I what?"

"Oh, nothing, just… Nothing." Ashley shivered.

Now that Sasha had shut off the engine, it was getting cold inside the SUV.

"Can I come in to talk for a minute?" Sasha asked. "It's getting cold out here, and to be honest, I could really use a drink."

Ashley glanced up and down the street and finally nodded, as if not wanting her neighbors to see her sitting in the dark car with another woman. She got out and led the way to the front door.

Sasha followed and tried not to crowd her as Ashley fumbled with the key, trying to get the door open without any success. Her fingers trembled so much that her key chain jingled, and Sasha had a feeling that it wasn't just the cold affecting her. "Here, let me." She reached around her and took the bunch of keys from her hand.

Their fingers brushed, and Ashley pulled away as if burned.

God, she was a mess. For the first time, Sasha understood that the appearance of perfection that Ashley exuded was just that—merely an appearance, a carefully created illusion.

Sasha unlocked the door and handed the keys back, this time careful not to let their fingers touch.

Casper was waiting by the door. He barked once, tail wagging, and tried to jump up to greet Ashley with doggie kisses.

Ashley bent down to pet him. She buried her face in his fur for a moment but then quickly straightened as if realizing that Sasha was watching. "Come on in." She walked farther into the house.

After giving Sasha a quick sniff, the dog followed.

The hall opened up into a living room that wasn't even half the size of Leo and Holly's. It was clean and tidy and would have looked a bit like the set of a theater production if not for little, personal touches—a small bouquet of some orange flowers on the coffee table, a thoroughly chewed squeaky toy and a tennis ball on the floor, and a paperback with a bookmark sticking out.

"What can I get you?" Ashley asked. Now that she could take refuge in the role of hostess, she sounded less shaky.

"Whatever you're having."

"Except for when we're meeting the gang at Johnny's, I rarely drink. But I have a bottle of wine somewhere, if you want."

Sasha sighed. "Forget the drink. Most of all, I was hoping for some more information. You really threw me for a loop here."

Ash sank into a recliner, looking like a cornered animal. She waved at Sasha to take a seat.

Sasha sat on the couch. She waited for Ashley to start talking, but she just sat there, looking anywhere but at her. Sasha put her forearms on her thighs and leaned forward. "So are you bi, or what the heck is going on?"

"No," Ashley said so quietly that Sasha had to strain to hear her. "I...I'm a lesbian."

Sasha arched a brow at her. It sure hadn't looked like it when she had been making out with Brandon on the bleachers. *Oh, come on. Don't be mean. So what if it took her a little longer to figure out her sexual orientation?* She forced herself to lean back. "How long have you known?"

Ashley still wasn't looking at her. She pulled her legs up and clutched her knees to her chest. "Since I was eighteen."

"Eighteen?" Sasha echoed.

Ashley shrugged. She painted patterns on the fabric of her jeans with her fingernails. "I started to figure it out when Leo..."

"When Leo what?"

"Forget it."

"When Leo came out?" Sasha ventured a guess.

"I said forget it, okay?"

So Ms. Nice had some bite in her after all. Sasha could respect that, even though not getting the answers she wanted was frustrating. "And you and Holly? When did that happen?"

"We started to spend more time together after she got back from nursing school."

"Spend time together," Sasha repeated to give her brain some time to catch up. "But how did you become an item? You're so closeted, and Holly isn't exactly known for chasing after women."

A deep blush tinted Ashley's cheeks. "Remember the party I had when I opened the flower shop?"

Sasha stared, openmouthed. That had been seven years ago! She nodded and waited for Ashley to continue.

"Um, I got a little tipsy, and when Holly drove me home, I complimented her eyes in a way a straight friend probably wouldn't. That's when she found out about...um, me."

Was that why Ashley rarely drank anymore and never more than a beer? Had she gotten even more careful over the years?

"From there, it just...happened, bit by bit." Ashley sighed. "I guess we both needed someone to cling to back then."

Sasha still couldn't believe it. "How long were you together?"

"Not long," Ashley said.

Sasha continued to look at her.

"Three months, two weeks, and a day."

Not a long time, but still it was three months, two weeks, and a day that Holly had been with Ashley without telling anyone. Or had she told other people, just not her? "So no one knew?"

Ashley vehemently shook her head. "No. No one. Well, Travis guessed, but..."

"Oh, yeah. That. I heard him tell the boys about your car being parked in front of Holly's all night and what he thought it meant, but I always put it down to his overactive imagination. Guess you weren't just binge-watching *The Walking Dead* or whatever TV show was popular back then after all."

Ashley didn't answer. She kneaded her folded hands so strongly that Sasha almost expected her to break a knuckle any second. "Sasha, I... Please..." She lifted her head and finally managed to look Sasha in the eyes. "Please, don't tell anyone."

For the first time, Sasha realized that Ashley's eyes were the exact color of the nougat cream Sasha used to fill her famous hazelnut cake. "It's not my story to tell, but is this really how you want to live the rest of your life—always lying and hiding a big part of yourself?"

"Want?" Ashley shook her head. "I don't want that, but I don't have much of a choice in this town. I have a business to think of."

"So do I," Sasha said.

"Yeah, but you're not gay."

"Well, strictly speaking, I—"

The doorbell rang.

Casper jumped up from his spot in front of the recliner and raced into the hall, barking loudly.

Ashley unfolded her arms from around her knees and stood up quickly, as if she was glad to escape further questions. She hurried toward the door, but after just a couple of steps, she paused and looked back. "Please promise me you won't say anything to anyone."

"Jeez, Ashley! I already said I wouldn't tell anyone. Do you think that badly of me? Do you really believe I'd just out you against your will?"

Ashley studied the floor at her feet. "No, I just..."

"I promise, okay?"

"Thank you." Ashley ran her hands over her arms and sides as if trying to wipe away all traces of their conversation before she went to open the door.

"Hey, honey," a deep, male voice came from the hall.

Was that Ashley's father? After what Sasha knew now, it sure wasn't a new boyfriend.

"I brought your car back," he said. "All fixed. It was just the water pump, like I suspected. I replaced the belt too, just in case."

"Thank you, Daddy. How much do I owe you for the parts?"

"Nothing."

"Dad…"

"Nothing," he repeated. "Just bring some flowers for your mother when you come for dinner on Sunday, and we'll be even. You are coming for dinner, aren't you?"

Ashley sighed. "I'm coming."

"How did you get home from that consultation you had?" her father asked. "You didn't walk, did you?"

"Um, no." Ashley paused. "Sasha gave me a ride."

Sasha took that as her cue to announce her presence. One of them constantly hiding was enough. "Hi, Mr. Gaines."

"Oh, I didn't know you had a visitor, honey." A few seconds later, Tom Gaines filled the doorway. At six foot four, he was one of the few people in town who could make Sasha feel small. "Hey, Sasha. How's the bread-and-muffin business going?"

Sasha chuckled. "Can't complain. But I'd better be on my way. A baker's day starts early." She pointed toward the driveway. "If you dropped Ashley's car off, do you need a ride home?"

Ashley pushed past her father into the room. "That's not necessary. I can drive him home."

Sasha studied her. Was she afraid that Sasha would let something slip if she was in the car alone with her father, even though she had promised not to say anything? Knowing Ashley, her family had no clue about her sexual orientation either. Or did she just not want to be indebted to Sasha, even in this small way? "It wouldn't be a bother. But if you're sure…"

"I'm sure." Ashley took the car key from her father.

Clearly, that was Sasha's cue to leave. She followed them to the door. "Guess I'll see you tomorrow at Johnny's, then."

"Um, I don't think I can make it. There's a lot to do at the flower shop."

Her father huffed. "You close at noon on Saturdays, and everything else can wait until Monday. Go meet your friends."

"But I have to send out some invoices and pick up the vases from—"

"Go." Her father's bass echoed through the night. "You don't want to worry your mother and me by working too much, do you?"

Sasha shifted her weight and glanced toward her car. *God, this is awkward.*

Ashley sighed. "Guess I'm going."

So Sasha would see her tomorrow after all—her and Holly. She really didn't know how to deal with either of them after what she had found out tonight.

Chapter 4

THIS TIME, IT WASN'T CAR troubles that made Ash late. She had debated staying home and pretending to be sick, but she knew her parents would find out sooner or later, and the last thing she wanted was to make them worry about her.

Sometimes, being a considerate daughter sucked.

She felt as if her legs were weighed down by lead as she crossed the street toward Fair Oaks's only bar, where her friends met every Saturday evening—if you could even really call them that.

They might know what kind of appetizer she ordered most Saturdays, what her favorite flower was, and how she'd been as a girl in high school, but there was a lot about her that they didn't know…and Ash preferred to keep it that way. Especially after Travis had almost outed her, she preferred to play her cards close to her chest.

When she entered Johnny's, the gang was already seated at the usual corner booth in the back of the room. She spied Sasha immediately; her tall frame was impossible to miss. Ash swallowed hard. She had hoped that Sasha couldn't make it to the bar after all.

But, of course, she was here, just as she had said she would be. As far as Ash could tell, Sasha was a woman of her word. She only hoped that was true for her promise not to tell anyone about her secret too.

"Hey, Ash!" Jenny waved. "There you are. I thought we'd have to go over and drag your ass away from work."

Ashley just smiled and said nothing, content to let them believe it had been work that had made her late. She squeezed in at one end of the horseshoe-shaped booth. Zack's wife, Lisa, had joined them today, so it was a tight fit at the table. Once again, Ash found herself pressed against Sasha's side. The warmth emanating from her engulfed Ash like an electric blanket, and the scent of cinnamon teased her nose.

"Hi," Sasha said, her voice low and much too intimate for Ash's liking. "I take it your dad made it home okay last night?"

Ash squirmed. The question seemed to be aiming at so much more than just her father, and she worried about what the others might be thinking. "Um, yeah. He got home safe and sound. Thanks."

"What does everyone want to drink?" Leo asked. "Holly and I are paying. We have something to celebrate."

"I never say no to free beer." Travis waved the waitress over, and they ordered drinks as well as chips and salsa for everyone to share.

"So, what are we celebrating?" Chris asked. "Another album that went platinum?"

"Better." Leo exchanged a loving look with Holly. "We wanted to tell you last week, but Ash and Chris couldn't make it, so we decided to wait."

"They're here now, so tell us. What's the big news?" Travis grinned. "One of you is pregnant?"

Jenny swatted her husband, and Sasha threw her coaster at him. It bounced off his forehead, skidded across the table, and slid to a stop in front of Ash.

She picked it up and handed it back to Sasha, careful not to let their fingers brush.

Travis rubbed his forehead and glared at them. "Hey, I'm just repeating what I was told. Marv said Izzy told him Jess overheard it in the bakery last week. According to Jess, Holly and Leo came in to ask Sasha if she'd do the cake for the baby shower or something."

Oh Jesus. Ash shook her head. What a game of telephone, Fair Oaks-style, with everyone adding to the rumor until the initial story was completely distorted!

"You should know by now that you can't believe everything people say, honey," Jenny said.

"Well, they aren't completely wrong," Leo said. "We did go to the bakery to ask Sasha if she would—"

Jenny let out a cheer and pressed her hands to her mouth. Her gaze flew back and forth between Leo and Holly. "Oh my God, you're pregnant?"

"Um, no." Leo took a big breath. "We're getting married."

For a second or two, even Travis fell silent.

Ash tensed. Their friends had seemed very accepting of Holly and Leo's relationship so far, but she had seen firsthand that some heterosexual people reacted in unexpected ways when it came to same-sex marriage, as if two women or two men tying the knot would somehow take away from their own relationships. Would one of them say something stupid and spoil their friends' happiness? If that happened, Ash hoped she would be brave enough to stand up for them.

Then everyone was talking at the same time, shouting their congratulations.

"Wow, that's wonderful!" Jenny hugged Holly, who sat next to her, and reached across her to pat Leo's shoulder. "I'm so happy for the two of you."

Her husband nodded. "Yeah, that's great. Will there be an open bar at the reception?"

Ash stared at him. Two women had just announced that they would be getting married, and all Travis wanted to know was if there would be free booze? Maybe she had misjudged their friends, and people in Fair Oaks were far more open-minded than she had expected.

The waitress came over with a tray full of drinks. "What's the happy occasion?"

"They're getting married." Travis reached for his beer.

"They?" The waitress looked at Ash, then at Chris.

Travis snorted. "Not them. I don't think these two will get married anytime soon. They're both still hung up on one of the brides."

Heat shot up Ash's neck. She tried to hide her face behind her beer, but she could feel Sasha's gaze rest on her.

"Would you finally stop that nonsense about Ash and Holly?" Jenny glared at her husband with a look that warned him that he would sleep on the couch tonight if he didn't stop.

"Wait. Did you just say...o-one of the brides? You mean...?" The waitress stared at Holly and Leo.

Leo nodded. "Holly and I are getting married."

"Oh." A frown settled on the waitress's face. "Well, that's...um... different."

The hope Ash had harbored about the people in town being more open-minded than expected was snuffed out like a candle in a hurricane. Being seen as different was not a good thing in Fair Oaks; she had experienced that firsthand.

"No, it's not," Sasha said firmly. "It's just two people who love each other and want to spend the rest of their lives together, just like any other wedding." She stared at the waitress until the older woman averted her gaze and retreated behind the bar.

Ash couldn't help admiring Sasha for speaking up without any hesitation.

"Don't mind her," Jenny said. "She'll come around quick once she sees how much business a celebrity wedding will bring to Fair Oaks."

Leo sputtered into her beer. "It's not going to be a celebrity wedding! It's just going to be Holly and me and our families and friends."

Ash had to smile at the indignant expression on her face. "I hate to tell you, but you are a celebrity."

"Am not," Leo grumbled.

"Are too."

They grinned at each other, and for a moment, it was almost as if the fifteen years since prom night had disappeared and they had their friendship back.

Jenny interrupted by lifting her beer bottle. "To Holly and Leo and wedded bliss!"

They all clinked bottles and glasses.

"Now we only have to find someone for Ashley, and everyone in our high school class will be happily married," Jenny added.

A sip of beer went down the wrong pipe. Ash started coughing and fended off Sasha's hand as she tried to pat her back. "Thanks. I'm fine. I, uh, I'm not sure I want to get married. I'm happy on my own, and the shop keeps me too busy for a relationship anyway. You know how it is." She sent Sasha a gaze that practically screamed for help.

"She's right," Sasha said. "Owning your own business isn't exactly a nine-to-five job. I don't know many people who'd be very understanding of having a date cut short because I have to get up at three the next morning."

Ashley nodded a silent "thank-you" in her direction.

"Hmm, that's right. It's been pretty quiet for you in the romance department too, hasn't it, Sasha? I haven't seen you with a guy since..."

Lisa paused and seemed to think about it. "Since you went out with Ethan, and that was years ago, before he met Cait."

Zack grinned at Holly. "Our brother spoiled her for all other men."

Sasha snorted. "Ethan's great. Don't get me wrong. But we realized not even halfway through our one and only date that we're better off as friends."

Ash had to agree. She couldn't see Sasha with Ethan, who had a tendency to step back and let other people deal with his problems. He would never have an equal relationship with someone as confident as Sasha.

"Plus it's kind of hard to work up any kind of sexual spark after you've seen a person eat an earthworm back in kindergarten," Sasha added with a grin.

Jenny shrieked, while everyone else laughed.

"Yeah, the joys of dating in a small town." Chris sighed and took a big swig of his beer. "Hard to maintain an air of mystery and coolness when you've all grown up together."

"Oh, I don't know." Holly grinned and gave Leo an affectionate look. "I've had to listen to the story about how Leo shoved a pebble up her nose when she was three about a million times, and it didn't stop me from falling madly in love with her."

"Didn't stop me and Travis or Lisa and Zack either," Jenny said. "So that can't be it. I also don't think it's just your job. I mean, look at you." She gestured at Sasha with her beer bottle. "You're strong and fiercely independent, and I bet you can still beat up most of the guys in town, like you did when you were ten and Joey made that comment about your mother running off to—"

"Yes, thank you, Jenny," Sasha grumbled. "I think we all remember what he said."

"Sorry." Jenny reached across the table and squeezed her arm. "I just meant that women like you can come across a little...well, intimidating to most guys."

"Maybe you should try dating a woman, then," Leo quipped.

Sasha looked at her. A slow smile spread over her face. "Who says I haven't? Didn't go all that well either."

"What?" Holly's bottle slid from her grip and clattered onto the table. She quickly righted it before more than a few drops of beer could spill out. "You've been with a woman?"

"More than one, actually," Sasha murmured and shrugged.

Everyone stared at her.

Ash couldn't believe it—not just that Sasha was queer but how casually she had revealed it. As if it wasn't a big deal at all. Then, when her stunned brain started to work again, anger bubbled up inside of her. Just yesterday, Sasha had been on her ass about lying and hiding a part of herself, judging her for not coming out to the entire town, and now it turned out she'd been in the closet herself. What a hypocrite!

"You never told me that!" Holly stared across the table at her best friend.

Sasha held her stare without flinching, a silent accusation in her eyes. "It's not like you talked about your relationships before Leo either."

Holly looked away and started to peel off the label on her bottle.

Oh, please, please, shut up. Ashley dug her nails into Sasha's arm beneath the table. Strong muscles bunched beneath her fingers.

Their gazes connected. Sasha's brown eyes, normally so full of good humor, reflected nothing but hurt.

Ash gentled her grip.

"Oh come on!" Travis thumped his bottle onto the table. "You seriously expect me to believe you're a lesbian too? The whole world can't be gay!"

"I never said I was a lesbian."

"You said you've been with women."

"So?" Sasha looked him in the eyes. "That doesn't make me a lesbian. If you need to have a term for it, I guess you could say I'm pansexual, but personally, I think labels are for bread and cupcakes, not for people. If they are hot and kind and fun to be around, I don't care about a person's packaging."

Oh yeah? For someone who didn't care for labels, Sasha had been pretty insistent on finding out whether Ash was gay or bi. But Ash couldn't very well point that out without drawing attention to her own sexual orientation.

"Pansexual. Man, I need another beer." Travis waved the waitress over and ordered another round for the table.

"Not for me," Sasha said. "I have to get up early tomorrow to make the cake for Mr. Gillespie's birthday, so I'd better get going."

Jenny reached across the table and grabbed her hand.

Ash marveled at that casual touch. She'd never been able to act so carefree around women and just allow herself to touch them without thought, even in such an innocent way.

"I'm sorry, Sash," Jenny said. "I didn't mean to put you on the spot and chase you off."

"Nah. You didn't. I'm fine with who I am." Sasha gave her hand a squeeze, then waved at the others before facing Ash. "Could you please let me out?"

Ash got up. "I should be leaving too. I, um, have to get up early. Invoices and stuff, you know?" It wasn't a lie, but, of course, it wasn't the full truth either. Mainly, she didn't want to stay behind, afraid to have the attention turned toward her once Sasha was gone and everyone was talking about sexual orientations.

Holly stood too. "I'm coming with you. I'll walk you home, Sasha."

Sasha shook her head. "This is practically your engagement party. You should stay and toast marital bliss again. We'll talk another time, okay?"

Holly sank back into the booth and leaned against Leo's shoulder. "Okay."

Ash wanted to put some money on the table, but Leo waved her away. "I've got it."

"Thank you." Then she walked to the door, with no idea what she would say to Sasha once they were outside.

Sasha closed the door behind them and looked around in search of Ashley's SUV. Finally, she discovered it a bit down the street. "Come on. I'll walk you to your car."

While they walked, Ashley kept glancing at her out of the corner of her eye. Twice, she opened her mouth as if to say something, but both times, she stayed silent. The disapproval radiating off her spoke volumes, though.

A quiet sigh escaped Sasha. *Okay, let's get it over with.* Even though she suspected the invoices Ashley had to prepare tomorrow had been just an excuse, Sasha really had a cake to bake first thing in the morning.

She turned around to Ashley. "Want to come home with me?"

Ashley nearly stumbled because she was staring at Sasha instead of watching where she was going.

Sasha snorted. "I didn't mean it like that. I meant you might as well come in with me to talk. Clearly, there's something you want to say to me, and we wouldn't want the good people of Fair Oaks to see you talking to a queer woman."

It came out a lot harsher than she had intended. Her anger—or maybe more hurt than anger—was really directed at Holly for not telling her about their relationship. Taking it out on Ashley wasn't fair, so she tried to rein herself in.

But this time, Ashley didn't back down or flinch from her anger. She put her hands on her curvy hips and held Sasha's stare for the very first time. "Oh, that would only be a problem if anyone knew you're..." She cut herself off and then finished in a whisper, "...not straight."

"Fine, if you want to discuss this here, I can do that."

"Um, no. Can we...?" Ashley pointed down the street, toward the bakery.

Wordlessly, Sasha led her to her apartment and up the stairs. She unlocked the front door and held it open for Ashley.

Compared to Ashley's very tidy house, her apartment looked like the typical bachelorette pad, with mismatched furniture, this morning's empty coffee mug still in the sink in her tiny kitchenette, and an unmade bed. Not that Ashley would ever get to see the latter, and Sasha decided she didn't care what Ashley thought about the rest.

She took off her boots and coat, padded across the burgundy-and-tan area rug, and dropped down on the couch. "Want to sit down?"

Ashley paced back and forth before finally sitting on the other end of the couch. She hadn't taken off her coat, either because she didn't intend to stay long or because she felt she needed its protective layer.

Sasha watched her silently. With her flushed cheeks and her flashing eyes, Ashley looked kind of attractive. *Yeah, about as attractive as a Doberman who's about to tear into you.*

"I really can't believe you," Ashley finally burst out as if her emotions had reached a boiling point. "You're...you're pansexual?"

"What? You of all people have a problem with that? That's pretty hypocritical, don't you think?"

"Oh, you are one to talk about hypocrisy!" Ashley glared at her. "I don't have a problem with you being pansexual. I have a problem with you judging me for not being out and proud, while you're a total closet case yourself!"

Sasha vehemently shook her head. "I'm not in the closet. Never was."

"Come on! Not even your closest friend knew!"

"That doesn't mean I'm in the closet. I never hid my sexual orientation. I just never had a reason to talk about it. Why would I when I haven't met anyone I clicked with since culinary school? I'm not the one who had a relationship and hid it like a dirty little secret."

"I didn't! She wasn't… I just… I couldn't handle it. The stares…the whispering…people talking about me… I just can't." Ashley sank back against the couch. She shoved her hands beneath her thighs, but Sasha could tell they were trembling.

At the sight of Ashley's distress, Sasha's annoyance deflated like a punctured cream puff. She pinched the bridge of her nose. "Okay, listen. This isn't getting us anywhere. We have to work together. Can we agree to try and get along?"

"If you promise to stop judging me all the time. You've been doing it for years, and I'm sick of—" Ashley's mouth snapped shut midsentence, and she narrowed her eyes. "Wait a minute. I always thought you were judging me because of Holly and the way we broke up, but if you didn't know about that… What is it that you dislike about me so much?"

"I like you just fine," Sasha mumbled. In fact, there had been times when she had liked Ashley a little too much. Well, not *liked* liked, of course, but her libido had been stuck in high school mode for a while. Who could blame her? Pretty much everyone in her class had had a crush on Ashley, male or female, gay or straight. It didn't mean a thing, even though it was still annoying as hell.

"Could have fooled me."

"No, really." *Shit.* She couldn't very well tell Ashley that she wasn't angry with her as much as she was angry with herself for having had a crush on someone who, personality-wise, wasn't her type at all. "I like you…well, most of the time. I guess sometimes, that prim-and-proper routine can be a little much."

Ashley sat so straight you could have put a level against her back, and it would have been perfectly balanced. "It's not a routine," she said, her voice quiet, but firm. "I honestly care about doing what's right."

"Yeah, about what's right for people, not for yourself or for Holly."

Ashley's nougat-colored eyes flashed. "Is this really the best you can do at not judging?"

Christ. Ashley was even more infuriating when she was right. Sasha held up her hands. "Okay, okay. I'll try harder."

"Good," Ashley said. "And can you please try not to hold it against Holly either? She wanted to tell you about…about us, but I asked her not to. I just didn't think she'd honor my wishes even after we broke up." She sounded deep in thought, as if she was talking more to herself than to Sasha. "I thought for sure she had told you."

"Then you don't know Holly very well." Sasha was starting to understand that Ashley didn't know anyone very well—and that she didn't let anyone else close enough to know her very well either.

Ashley sighed but didn't answer. She withdrew her hands from beneath her thighs and stood. "I'll let you get some rest now since you have an early start tomorrow."

Sasha walked her to the door and opened it for her.

Ashley stepped outside but then paused and turned back around. "Do you think we can do this? Work together without all this tension?"

"Yeah, sure. No problem." She wasn't a kid anymore and could easily ignore those momentary flashes of attraction that added to the tension. "We're both adults after all. Should be a piece of…"

"Wedding cake?" Ashley finished for her. The first real smile all evening curled the corners of her mouth, drawing Sasha's attention to her full lips.

She cleared her throat and forced herself to look away from that smile. "Yep. A total piece of wedding cake."

Chapter 5

TUESDAYS WERE USUALLY ASH'S QUIETEST days, with not that many customers and no fresh flower deliveries. But for some reason, today had been unexpectedly hectic...and slightly awkward. A beaming, freshly engaged couple had come in to order flowers for their wedding just as Ash had been showing different options for funeral wreaths to a grieving widow.

It wasn't until she had closed the shop for the day that she finally got around to taking the small sample bouquet she had created over to the bakery. At first, she had considered having her driver drop it off but quickly rejected the idea.

She and Sasha had agreed to work together, so she couldn't avoid her, as much as she wanted to.

Her fingers were a bit clammy around the paper-wrapped bouquet as she reached out to pull the front door of the bakery open. It was silly, really, but now that Sasha knew she was gay, Ash felt like a knight whose shield had been ripped away. Strangely, knowing Sasha wasn't straight either made her even more nervous.

Determined to get over it, she gave the door a sharp tug.

It didn't budge, jerking Ash back.

She leaned forward and peered through the glass.

The *closed* sign dangled at eye level, but there was still light in the bakery. Ash could make out the fox-red hair of Mae Peterson, Sasha's aunt.

When Ash knocked on the glass, Mae looked up from wiping down the counter. A smile spread over her lined face. She gave a wave, rounded the corner, and unlocked the door. "Evening, Ashley. You missed your three o'clock cupcake, didn't you?"

"I did. Brooke wasn't working today, and the shop got unexpectedly busy, so I didn't have time for a break."

"Well, we're closed already, but I'll see if there are some left over, just for you."

"Oh, no, that's not necessary. They are delicious, but I'm actually not here for the cupcakes. Is Sasha still here?"

Mae lifted her green-tinted glasses that hung around her neck on a chain of colorful beads and squinted at the flowers as if seeing them only now. "Oh, how lovely! Flowers for Sasha? She'll be delighted."

Warmth crept up Ash's neck. "Oh, no, no, they are not for Sasha." She got it out so fast that the words nearly ran into each other. "I mean, they are for her, but just workwise, so she can make the cake match the flowers."

"Aww, that's too bad. It's been much too long since my girl got any flowers." Mae marched back into the store and waved at her to follow. "Come on. She's still here, but she's got a bun in the oven, so you'll have to talk in the kitchen."

Ash nearly inhaled her own spit. Dear God, Sasha's aunt was something else.

Mae pushed through the swinging door at the back of the room. "Sasha, you've got a visitor."

Ash peeked into the kitchen. The scent of yeast and rosemary greeted her. "Um, hi. Sorry for dropping by after hours. I brought some flowers. To show you for Leo and Holly's wedding," she added quickly.

Sasha looked up from the dough she was kneading on a huge worktable. Her sun-bronzed skin was flushed from the heat in the kitchen. Flour sprinkled down when she lifted her hand in greeting. "Hey. Come on in."

"I'm heading home," Mae said. "Unless you girls need me to chaperone?"

Ash froze in the doorway. "Uh…"

"Don't mind her. Thanks, Auntie Mae, I think we can manage just fine."

With a wave, Mae let the door swing closed, forcing Ash to step fully into the kitchen to avoid getting hit. "You didn't tell her about…me, did you?"

"Nope. I didn't say a word," Sasha answered. "But even if I did, Aunt Mae couldn't care less."

That might be true for Mae, but not for the rest of town.

Ash unwrapped the bouquet and held it out as if she needed that barrier between them. "I made up a sample of the flowers Holly and Leo want in their bouquets, and I thought maybe you'd like to see it so you'll know early on what design and colors I'm planning."

"Good thinking. Let me finish this real quick and we can talk." Sasha nodded down at the dough. "I'm trying out a new recipe—rosemary cheese bread—and if I stop now, I'll have to start over."

"No problem. Finish your bread." Ash took up position in an out-of-the-way corner of the large kitchen, careful not to touch anything, and looked around. She had bought cupcakes at A Slice of Heaven nearly every day for years, but she'd never been in the kitchen.

A bread machine was whirring in the back of the room, where its hooks were going around and around. Shelves lined two walls, each one filled with cupcake pans, mixing bowls, storage bins, and other baking equipment Ash didn't recognize. An industrial-sized dishwasher shared space with a big stainless-steel sink and several ovens, which, judging by the heat in the kitchen, were still running.

Two long wood-topped worktables formed the center island. Sasha stood bent over one of them.

The black bandanna she wore to hold back her hair made her look a bit like a swashbuckling pirate. Her flour-flecked, white apron covered a pair of jeans and a gray T-shirt. She lifted the dough, sprinkled a handful of flour onto the worktable and the mound, and smacked it back down.

Wow. No wonder Sasha had all those muscles. Her hands were strong from years of kneading and rolling dough, and the muscles in her arms stood out in sharp relief as she pushed the heels of her hands into the dough in a rhythmic motion. Like Ash's own, her fingers were bare of any jewelry.

Now that she knew Sasha was pansexual, Ash found herself viewing her differently. Or maybe it was just that she had never seen Sasha like this before. She always appeared to be completely comfortable in her skin, but she was clearly in her element when working in the bakery kitchen.

"Excuse me. I need that bowl." Sasha's voice right next to her startled Ash.

Boy, she had to be really tired to let her attention drift like that. "Oh, sorry." She stepped out of the way so Sasha could get the giant bowl from the counter behind her.

"No problem." With nimble fingers, Sasha formed a dough ball, set it into the greased bowl, and turned it over once. She placed the bowl on top of an oven and covered it with a dish towel, probably to let the dough rise.

"You're very good at that," Ash said.

Sasha gazed away from where she was washing her hands at the sink. For a moment, she looked just as surprised as Ash felt. She hadn't meant to say that out loud.

Then Sasha chuckled. "Well, I'd better be. I own a bakery after all. I've always enjoyed doing things with my hands. I suspect you do too."

The comment made Ash flush, even though she knew Sasha hadn't meant it like that. She pretended it was just the heat of the ovens staining her cheeks red. "Um, yeah. It seems our jobs have that in common."

"That and the shitty work hours and the not making much money part." Sasha laughed.

"There's that too. But at least we get to make people happy with flowers and delicious treats."

"True. Speaking of flowers..." Sasha pointed at the bouquet Ash had tucked under one arm. "This is what our brides-to-be wanted? Roses and... what are they?"

"Alstroemeria. They symbolize friendship and devotion, while the roses mean pure love and fidelity."

Sasha studied the white-and-pink blooms that formed a nice contrast to the white roses and the smaller, apricot-colored spray roses. "They're beautiful, but they look a little delicate. Are you sure they won't wilt in the heat of an outdoor wedding?"

Ash stroked her fingers along the stems. "They'll be fine. They may look delicate, but they're actually pretty hardy."

A grin tugged on Sasha's lips. "Kinda like you, huh?"

"Me?" Ash bristled and straightened to her full five foot eight. "I'm not delicate."

"Compared to me, you are."

Well, Ash couldn't deny that. Sasha was at least four inches taller and what Ash's mother called big-boned. It wasn't a compliment in her mother's book, but Ash had to admit that she found Sasha's broad shoulders and her sturdy build appealing. Quickly, she steered the conversation back to work. "So, you think you can work with these?" She held out the bouquet.

"I thought apricot-colored spray roses would be a good fit since the cake is going to have an apricot-orange cream filling."

"Great thinking. We could decorate the cake with some fresh roses and alstroe…"

"…meria," Ash supplied. "They're also called Peruvian lilies."

Sasha nodded. "But truth be told, I'm not really a fan of that option. Fresh flowers on cake can trigger allergies, not to mention that some of them are toxic. Plus if we go with option number two, I get to really work my magic." She wiggled her fingers, drawing Ash's attention to her strong hands.

Quickly, Ash forced her gaze away. "Which is?"

"I could incorporate some floral elements into the cake design," Sasha said. "Make sugar paste roses and lilies. What do you think?"

"I like edible flowers, but I'm not the one who has to like it."

"Oh, I'll ask Holly and Leo, of course, but they both have quite the sweet tooth, so I don't see a problem there. Let me take a couple of photos of the flowers so I have something to work with when the time comes." Sasha dried her hands on her apron, took her phone from one of the shelves, and tapped the screen twice before lifting it to eye level. "Smile."

Ash smiled reflexively, even as she said, "You don't have to do that now. Why don't you keep the flowers? I made the bouquet for you. Um, I mean, for you to take home, so you can take photos in better light."

Sasha tilted her head and grinned down at her. "Oh my. Ashley Gaines sending flowers home with another woman! Whatever will people say?"

A flare of defensiveness seared through Ash. She raised the bouquet as if it were a sword used to parry an attack. Then she looked into Sasha's eyes, which crinkled at the edges as she grinned down at her, without even a hint of malice.

"Hey, relax." Sasha stepped closer and nudged her lightly. "I'm just teasing, not judging."

Ash forced herself to give up her defensive pose. Just teasing. That would take some getting used to. Her sexual orientation had never been a laughing matter to her.

"Okay, you win," Sasha said. "I'll take them home. But don't say I didn't warn you. I'm not good with flowers. I have a black thumb, or whatever the opposite of a green thumb is. I killed the only plant I ever owned—and it was a cactus."

Ash had to laugh, and the tension drained from her body. "How on earth did you manage that?"

Sasha shrugged. "Guess I watered it too much or something."

"Well, that can't happen with these." Ash held up the bouquet. "You just put some flower food in the water, change it every other day, recut the stems at an angle, and make sure none of the leaves are under water. Then they'll last you well into March—as long as we get them out of this heat and into some water now."

"Oh. Yeah, sure." Sasha pulled a huge measuring cup from the shelf, filled it with water, and carried it to the front of the bakery, where she set the improvised vase on one of the small café tables.

Ash followed with the bouquet and handed it over.

Sasha lifted it to her face. Her eyes fluttered shut in expectation as she sank her nose into the flowers and inhaled deeply.

For a moment, strong and tough Sasha Peterson looked strangely vulnerable so that Ash couldn't help staring.

Then Sasha looked up with a wrinkle on her forehead. "Um, there's no scent."

"Sorry. Most modern roses are bred to last longer, and they lost their scent in the process. It's the same for the alstroemeria."

Sasha wrinkled her nose. "So much for stopping to smell the roses."

For a person who insisted on not being the flower type, she looked surprisingly disappointed.

Ash had to smile. "Well, not all flowers have had their fragrance bred out. Any time you want to smell the flowers, you could just—" She cut herself off before she could extend an open invitation to come over to her flower shop any time. If she hung out with Sasha too often, people would start to talk, especially if Sasha's sexual orientation became common knowledge. In fact, she was surprised that she hadn't heard any gossip about it yet.

"I could just...what?" Sasha prompted.

"Um..."

A knock on the glass door saved her from having to answer.

Ash jumped and looked up.

Holly stared at them from the other side of the glass, clearly surprised to find Ash at the bakery.

God, when had her life become so complicated? Now she felt as if she had to justify all of her actions, even though absolutely nothing was going on between her and Sasha. Ash tugged on the end of her ponytail. Maybe agreeing to do the flowers for Holly and Leo had been a mistake. But now there was no way out.

For a second, Sasha looked just as hesitant to let Holly in, but then she smiled warmly and unlocked the door. "Hey, Holly. Come on in." She spread her arms wide, and after an almost unnoticeable hesitation, Holly stepped into her embrace.

It was just a hug between two friends, but for some reason Ash still squirmed as she watched them. *Oh please. You got over Holly years ago.*

Finally, they let go, and Holly surprised Ash by greeting her with a short hug too.

It had been years since Ash had shared a close hug with anyone who was not family. Holly's warmth felt good, but at the same time, Ash couldn't fully relax into the embrace. Not in public and not with Sasha's gaze resting on her.

She stepped back. "I brought Sasha a sample of your bridal bouquet." She gestured toward the flowers. "Don't worry. This is just a mock-up. Your bouquet will be bigger and a lot prettier."

"I'm not worried." Holly looked at the flowers with a pleased smile. "They are gorgeous. Plus I promised myself that I wouldn't obsess over any wedding-planning details. Yes, I want a wonderful celebration with all the people I love, and I'm looking forward to beautiful flowers and tasty cake, but what's really important is that I get to spend the rest of my life with Leo."

A mix of happiness for Holly and pain at the thought of never getting to experience a love like that coursed through Ash. It was starting to become a familiar feeling. She covered it with a smile. "I'm happy to hear that you're not going to turn into Bridezilla anytime soon."

"Not planning on it." Holly turned toward Sasha. "Do you have more flower/cake coordinating to do, or would now be a good time to talk?"

Sasha's easygoing grin disappeared. If Ash wasn't mistaken, she even paled a little beneath her tan.

Ash couldn't help feeling sorry for her, even though just three days ago, she had been the one who had lashed out at Sasha for keeping her sexual orientation a secret.

"Now's good," Sasha said.

Ash had realized before that Sasha wasn't one to shy away from tough conversations. *That makes one of us.*

"I'll go so you can talk." Ash hastened to the door. "Casper's waiting for his dinner."

Sasha stayed next to Holly, but her gaze followed Ashley. "I'll come over and show you some sketches of the cake design I have in mind once I have them."

"Sounds good. Have a good night, you two." Ash stepped outside and let the glass door close between them. As glad as she was to escape the situation, she would have liked to be a fly on the wall during the conversation about to take place.

A lump the size of the bread dough formed in Sasha's throat as she turned toward Holly, even though she told herself she had done nothing wrong.

Holly put her hand on Sasha's shoulder. "Relax. I'm not angry."

Sasha arched her brows.

"I'm not," Holly said. "Not really. I'm mostly hurt."

Great. That was actually worse. Sasha wasn't really the relationship type, but she prided herself on being a pretty good friend. The thought of having hurt Holly made her queasy.

"Take a seat, and let's talk." Sasha grabbed the container of cookies from behind the counter, where she'd set it earlier, and placed it on one of the small tables. Her aunt had taught her that a sweet treat made conversations like this one easier. "Help yourself."

Holly sat and reached for one of the cookies, then paused. "These aren't new doggie treats you want to try out, are they?"

Sasha laughed and took a seat across from her. "No. They are macadamia chocolate chip cookies. I set them aside for you because I had a feeling you'd be by."

"Yum." Holly chose a cookie but then held it in her hand without eating.

They looked at each other across the table.

"Why didn't you tell me?" they said at the same time.

They smiled, easing the tension in the room a little.

Sasha decided to get it over with and answer the question first. Ripping off the Band-Aid fast had always been her style. "Because there wasn't anything to tell. Except for a date or two—which I always told you about—I have pretty much been single since I came home from culinary school. I figured I'm just not the relationship type, so why tell people about something that doesn't play much of a role in my life?"

"Okay, I get that. But before that, when you were in a relationship with a woman, why didn't you ever mention it? It's not like you to keep something like that from me."

"I didn't consciously keep it from you. The topic just never came up. You barely ever talked about your relationships either, so why would I?"

"I told you about Dana."

"Because you needed to get it off your chest. And that's completely fine," Sasha added quickly, not wanting Holly to read it as an accusation. "You can talk to me any time, about anything, you know that. But I never got my heart broken like that, and figuring out my sexuality wasn't a big deal for me."

"You still could have told me."

"I know I could have. But I enjoyed the fact that we always had so many other things to talk about. Not like some of the other women in town, who seem to have nothing besides their significant other to talk about when they get together with their friends."

Holly nodded. "I always enjoyed that about our friendship too. Especially when everyone else nudged me to start dating again and, at the same time, I didn't think I'd ever find a woman who would accept me just the way I am. Spending time with you was like a vacation from all that pressure."

Sasha had always sensed that, but it felt good to hear it.

"Is that why you never told me?" Holly tilted her head. "Because you thought I didn't want to talk about relationships?"

"That's just it, Holly. What I had with those girls in college…that wasn't a relationship. Both of us knew it wouldn't last. It was just some fun dates and sex—really hot sex. I wasn't sure you would want to hear about that."

Holly wrinkled her nose. "I don't. Well, not about the sex part anyway. But I'd still like to know what's going on in my best friend's life."

"All right. I promise if there is ever something interesting going on, I'll tell you—if you promise to do the same."

"Oh please! I probably talk too much about Leo as it is."

Not *too* much, but she did talk about Leo a lot; that was true. "So why didn't you ever say a word about you and Ashley?"

Holly looked away. "So I wasn't just imagining things at Johnny's. You do know about me and Ash."

"Yeah. It still boggles my mind—not just that you were together, but that you didn't tell me. I wouldn't have said anything to anyone, if that was the problem."

"I know," Holly said immediately. "And that was a big part of it—Ashley wanting to keep it quiet."

"But that's not all, is it?"

Holly took a big bite of her cookie and chewed thoroughly, as if buying herself time to think about her answer. "I guess I was mostly embarrassed."

"Embarrassed?" Sasha echoed. What was there to be embarrassed about? Surely not the fact that she'd been with a woman. Holly had known that Sasha was completely fine with that, even back then. And while Ashley was complicated, she was also friendly and good-looking, and Sasha had a feeling she could be fun to be around if she ever allowed herself to relax and just be herself, without that constant fear of being judged. So why would Holly be embarrassed?

"It was such bad timing." Holly sighed. "Dana had just broken up with me, trampling all over my self-esteem, and then I got home from college and immediately got involved with the first gay woman around. Okay, the *only* gay woman around, as far as I knew. I didn't want anyone to think that it was just a rebound thing."

"Was it?" Sasha asked.

Holly picked a nut out of her cookie and crunched it. "Maybe a little. Not that I was aware of it at the time. I mean, you know Ash. She's beautiful, and once you crack her shell, she's also incredibly nice, and I just wanted someone like that. Someone who wouldn't treat me the way Dana did, making me feel like there was something wrong with me just because I didn't desire her, um, sexually."

"And did you find that someone in Ashley?" Sasha asked.

"I thought so at first. She never wanted any sleepovers—for different reasons, obviously, but it worked for a while."

"Then why did you break up?"

Holly sighed. "In the end, we couldn't give each other what we wanted. I wanted a partner who would be proud to hold my hand in public, and Ash wanted someone she could love without restrictions—but only in the privacy of her own home."

"That must have been tough," Sasha murmured.

"Yeah, especially since it was my second breakup within six months." Holly cradled her half-eaten cookie as if it were a good-luck charm that could ward off pain. "I just wanted to forget it and move on, so I never talked about it with anyone…until I met Leo."

Sasha reached across the table and squeezed her hand. "I get it. I'm still not happy you didn't tell me, but I understand why you didn't."

"Thank you," Holly said quietly.

For a while, they ate cookies in companionable silence.

"So," Holly finally asked, "how did you find out about Ash and me? You always seemed to dismiss it as wishful thinking when Travis started talking about us."

Sasha snorted. "Forget Travis. He would have thought you were doing the horizontal mambo even if all you had been doing was painting each other's toenails."

Holly laughed, spraying cookie crumbs over the worktable. "Oops. Sorry." She wiped them off with her sleeve. "If it wasn't Travis…"

"Ashley," Sasha said. "I found out from her."

Holly stared at her as if she had just told her the town had been taken over by pink-dotted Martians. "Ash told you about us? Just like that?"

Sasha chuckled. "Not exactly. She somehow got the impression that I already knew, so she accidentally outed herself."

"Holy shit!"

"That's what I said—and what Ashley said when she found out I hadn't actually known about the two of you."

"I can imagine. I bet the fact that you know makes her want to jump out of her skin." Now it was Holly who reached across the worktable and squeezed Sasha's hand. "I'm sorry. That's probably going to make working together on our wedding uncomfortable as hell. If you'd rather—"

"Don't even say it," Sasha said firmly. "We're both adults. We'll be fine. And who knows? Maybe being around me will make Ashley more comfortable with herself too. She might even come out at some point."

"Been there, thought so, and I can tell you it won't happen. If anything, I think the way our relationship ended made her even more determined to stay away from women. Hell will freeze over and our high school football team will win the Super Bowl before Ashley will ever come out."

Sasha shrugged. "Well, maybe you should hire a lesbian stripper for your bachelorette party. That might nudge her out of the closet."

Holly threw the last piece of her cookie at her.

Chapter 6

Ben, the owner of Under the Hood, the local auto repair shop, looked up from the tire he was changing out front. "Hey, Sasha! Are you doing deliveries now?" Laughing, he gestured at the bakery box she carried.

"Nope." Sasha gave him a teasing grin. "Your wife would hate me if I did."

"Are you saying I'm fat?" He patted his belly.

"Nah. That would be bad for business."

He gave the box a longing look. "So who are they for?"

God, small-town curiosity. The phrase *none of my business* never seemed to enter anyone's mind. Sasha chose her words carefully so she wouldn't get Ashley in trouble. "I'm meeting Ashley to discuss a wedding collaboration, and I thought I'd bring some cupcakes."

The grin disappeared off his face. "Oh right. I heard. Holly and Leo are getting married…or whatever you call it when it's two women."

"Marriage, Ben. Same thing as when you married Amber." *Just that they don't have to tie the knot because one of them is pregnant,* she wanted to add but held back the words. No sense in stirring trouble.

"I guess." He didn't look convinced. "Are you sure you don't want me to take that box off your hands? No need to carry it all the way to Ash's shop."

A minute ago, Sasha had been about ready to give him one of the cupcakes, but his less than tolerant attitude didn't make her eager to hand out free treats. "Pretty sure. Have a nice weekend, and say hi to Amber for me."

She continued down the street without looking back.

Clearly, Ash was already preparing her flower shop for spring—no wonder since March had started off like a lamb, with temperatures into the mid-fifties. The blue-and-white-striped awning looked as if it had recently been cleaned. The colors in the sign above the door—reading *The Flower Girl*—were bright, as if it had been freshly painted. Yellow narcissi in little baskets gave the two display windows a friendly air.

Sasha transferred the box to her left hand and pulled the front door open. Moist air swept over her, along with the scent of soil and fresh blooms. Since she hadn't been in a relationship where flowers were required as a romantic gesture in ages, wasn't in contact with her mother, and her aunt preferred presents of the edible kind, Sasha had never had a reason to visit Ashley's flower shop before. She looked around curiously.

The shop resembled Ashley's house in a way; it was just as tidy and warm. The walls were painted a soft peach and adorned with watercolors of sunflowers and some purple blooms Sasha couldn't identify. A large, glass-fronted walk-in cooler took up one wall. Vases, pots, and gift items filled a tall shelf. Potted plants and flowers in wicker baskets were neatly arranged on a long, three-tiered stand.

Ashley was behind the counter, inserting flowers into some green, foamy material that had been fitted into a large pot. At the chime of the bell above the door, she looked up and gave Sasha a friendly smile. "Hi, Sasha. Come by to smell the flowers?"

Sasha laughed. The nearly teasing tone was a surprise—but one she liked. It was good to see that Ashley wasn't distant and guarded around her. "That too. I thought I'd drop by and show you my wedding cake sketches, if you have a minute. And I come bearing gifts." She lifted the bakery box.

As if on cue, Casper rushed out from the back room, nose in the air. He sniffed eagerly, as if he wanted to inhale the entire box through his nose.

Sasha pulled the paper bag with the Beagle Bite from her coat pocket and gave Ashley a questioning look. "I brought a treat for him too. Can I give it to him?"

"Sure. If you're prepared to make a friend for life."

Sasha grinned. "You can never have too many friends, right?"

Ashley paused with an orange gerbera daisy in her hand.

It was only then that Sasha realized her words could be read as an offer of friendship that extended to Ashley as well. Oh well. Despite her many layers, Ashley seemed like a good person, so why not? She held her gaze until Ashley nodded.

Casper jumped around her and tried to get the treat as she pulled it out of the paper bag. Despite his eagerness, he was gentle as he took the Beagle Bite from her hand. It was gone in less than two seconds.

"Ooh. Did I hear the word *treats?*" Brooke stuck her head out of the back room. "Oh, hi, Ms. Peterson. Is there something in there for me too?"

The bubblegum pink hair she had sported the year before had grown out, but Sasha was glad to see she still had her nose ring.

You go, girl. Don't let this town tell you what you can and can't do with your body.

"Call me Sasha, please, or you'll make me feel old." Sasha grinned and opened the lid of the bakery box. "Well, there are two espresso chocolate chip cookies in here."

"My favorite!"

"I know. I know everyone's secret cravings."

Ashley dropped the bundle of floral wire she'd been holding.

Sasha bit back a grin. She hadn't meant her remark like that, but it was kind of fun to tease Ashley.

Brooke giggled.

Not for the first time, Sasha wondered why someone as uptight as Ashley had hired Brooke, who wasn't afraid to stand out from the crowd. Maybe Ashley did have her moments of standing up to public opinion after all.

"Why don't we go into the back room, and I'll take a look at your sketches," Ashley said, as if trying to get Sasha away from Brooke and anyone else who might drop by and witness their conversation.

"Let's eat first." Sasha put the box down on the counter so Ashley and Brooke could help themselves. "My motto is pleasure before business."

Brooke dove in without having to be asked twice. "Yum, these are so good," she mumbled with her mouth full of cookie. She devoured her treats faster than Casper had.

Ashley, however, seemed more hesitant. She wrapped another gerbera daisy with green wire and inserted it into the foamy material before she even glanced into the bakery box.

Sasha studied the centerpiece that was taking shape. She was no expert on flowers by any means, but even she had to admit that the arrangement was beautiful, with the orange gerbera and some other, white flowers standing out nicely against the green of the fern around the edges. Ashley really had an eye for colors. "You're very good at this."

She said it because it was true but also because Ashley had told her the same when she had watched her bake earlier in the week, and Sasha wanted to see if she would answer with the same joke Sasha had made about being good with her hands.

Ashley sent her a look that made it clear she knew exactly what Sasha was doing. "Thank you. I really enjoy it."

"Working with your hands?" Sasha quipped.

Ashley peered at her like a librarian reprimanding someone who had been talking too loudly. "Helping customers pick just the right flowers to express their feelings and then putting them together into a beautiful arrangement."

So that was what she enjoyed about her job. Sasha could empathize. But at the same time, she couldn't help finding it a little ironic. Ashley was helping her customers express their feelings with flowers, while so much was left unsaid in her own life.

Finally, Ashley dried her hands on her green florist's apron and reached inside the bakery box.

Sasha had filled it with the two cookies for Brooke and three different kinds of cupcakes, and of course, Ashley picked a vanilla one with strawberry buttercream frosting. She took a bite and chewed while making little humming sounds of pleasure in the back of her throat. Her tongue darted out and licked a crumb off her bottom lip.

Unexpected heat flickered low in Sasha's belly. What the hell? Maybe she had been single for too long and should consider dating again. Yeah, just not Ashley, of course.

"What?" Ashley dabbed her face. "Am I making a mess of myself?"

"Oh, no, no, you're fine. It's just... You've got a leaf in your hair." Fortunately, a bit of greenery was indeed clinging to Ashley's hair above her ear. Sasha pointed. "There."

Ashley took the hair tie out of her ponytail and ran her fingers through her hair to loosen any fragments that might be stuck there. "That's what happens when you work in a flower shop. Some days, I look like an extra from *The Walking Dead*."

"You watch TWD?"

"Sure, why not?"

Brooke reached for a red velvet cupcake. "I got her hooked on it."

With her ponytail back in place, Ashley closed the lid of the box before the girl could help herself to the last cupcake too. "Let's take a look at your sketches before people get off work and come in to buy flowers for their weekend dinner invitations."

Sasha took off her coat and followed her through an open doorway into a workroom filled with greenery, buckets, pots, and all kinds of other material. A big worktable reminded her of her setup in the bakery. Not for the first time, it struck her how much their jobs had in common.

Ashley led her to a small table in the back of the room.

Both of them sank onto their chairs with a sigh of relief.

Sasha grinned. It seemed their jobs had that in common too: they were on their feet for most of the day. "Long day?"

"Long week. And you?" Ashley leaned forward, and her gaze went through the open door to where Brooke was hovering next to the bakery box. "How did the conversation with Holly go?" Her voice was so low that even Sasha could barely hear her. "Was she angry with you?"

"No, not really. She can't blame me too much for not telling her about my past relationships when she herself didn't tell me about—"

Ashley loudly cleared her throat, drowning out the end of Sasha's sentence. Her gaze was still on the door, and her shoulders were as tense as if she were about to bungee jump into a crocodile-filled lake. "Um, yeah. Guess she can't. So the two of you are okay?"

"We're fine. We talked things out."

"Good. I'm happy to hear that." She looked away from the door and into Sasha's eyes. Her gaze was sincere. "So, sketches? If I leave Brooke alone with my cupcake for too long, she'll eat it. She's worse than a golden retriever—and that's saying something."

"Hey, I heard that, boss!" Brooke managed to sound indignant. "And it's not my fault that these are so fucki...um, very delicious."

Ashley smiled affectionately, and the tension drained from her features. "Go ahead. Eat it."

"Really?" Brooke squeaked. The paper box rustled before she had gotten a confirmation.

Sasha wryly shook her head. Apparently, it would take a minor miracle to get Ashley to try one of her other cupcakes and not just the vanilla ones. Next time, she'd have to bring a dozen.

"Yeah, sure," Ashley said to Brooke. "You're probably doing me a favor anyway. Once you're over thirty, those evil creations go straight to your hips."

Sasha let out a snort. "Oh please." She bit her lip before she could say more and assure Ashley that she was beautiful and didn't need to watch what she ate. "Sketches." She opened her sketchbook and flipped through it to find the correct page.

Instead of waiting until Sasha passed her the sketchbook, Ashley slid her chair around the round table until it was next to Sasha's.

Her unexpected closeness distracted Sasha. She leafed past the page, then had to flip back. "This is what I had in mind."

Ashley leaned closer. "Oh wow. That's incredible. May I?"

"Sure."

Ashley reached out and touched the paper, tracing the flowers cascading down the side of the three-tiered wedding cake. Sasha had started with the biggest flower, a rose in full bloom, at the edge of the top tier and then drawn each flower progressively smaller as they spiraled down the cake. It gave the design a three-dimensional effect.

Two brides—one in a traditional dress, the other in an elegant, white pantsuit—held hands in the center of the cake. Their faces weren't the nondescript faces of most cake toppers but actually looked like miniature versions of Holly and Leo.

"Wow," Ashley said again. "If you manage to make the cake look even half as good as this, everyone will be completely blown away."

Over the years, Sasha had gotten a lot of compliments for her sketches. Normally, she didn't like it when people made a big deal of her drawing skills, but now she couldn't help feeling pleased. "You like it?"

"Like? I love it! This is good, Sasha." Ashley gently tapped the page. "Really good. If you ever get tired of being a baker, you could be an artist. You are incredibly talented. You probably got that from your mother."

The warm glow that had filled Sasha only moments ago fizzled out. "I prefer to think that it's a talent I developed all on my own. She certainly wasn't there to nurture it."

Ashley withdrew her hand from the sketchbook. "I'm sorry. Sorry that she wasn't there for you and that I brought the subject up. I didn't mean to…"

"It's okay," Sasha said. But even after all these years, it really wasn't. Having her mother walk out on them when Sasha had been six was a wound that would never fully heal, and the compassionate look in Ashley's eyes revealed that she could sense it.

Ashley ducked her head. Her gaze flicked back and forth between the table and Sasha's face. "Do you…?" She stopped herself. "Sorry. It's none of my business."

Sasha knew she should leave it at that, but she found herself saying, "You can ask. I don't mind."

Ashley hesitated. She rubbed at a small, green stain on the tabletop. It didn't come off. "Do you ever hear from her?"

"I get the obligatory card on my birthday, and she calls every now and then, but really…what is there to say? She can't relate to my life. Never could. She especially doesn't understand why I'm still living here. Apparently, she hated every minute she spent here. That's why she left. She said life in Fair Oaks was suffocating and choked her creativity." Sasha snapped her mouth shut. Wow. She hadn't meant to say so much, but once she had started talking, the words had bubbled up from somewhere deep inside.

"Oh, so that's why she left? I heard people say…" Ashley blushed. "Forget it. I should know better than to listen to gossip."

Sasha knew exactly what people were saying. The stories about her mother leaving her father because of another man had been circulating for decades, no matter how often her father had tried to set the record straight. Maybe that had been part of the reason why he had moved away years ago.

"Sorry to disappoint. There was no hot French lover who swept her away to Paris. At least that's something to be said for her, huh? The only person she ran off for was herself. Apparently, real art can only be created when you live as a hermit in a beach house, with no husband and kid around." Gently, Sasha closed the sketchbook, as if to confirm that this chapter of her life was closed for good.

"You proved her wrong." Ashley's voice was soft, yet full of conviction. She slid the sketchbook out from under Sasha's bigger hand and opened it to the last sketch. "Because this..." She caressed the flower cascade on the page with a tenderness that made Sasha shiver. "...this is art."

Sasha swallowed against the sudden tightness in her throat. Where the hell was this coming from? It had been years since she had gotten so emotional over her mother. She forced a smile. "If you think that's art, wait until you see the actual cake."

"Can't wait." Ashley's eyes held a knowing look, as if she understood the need to change the subject. "Just one tiny thing for when you make the sugar flowers... The filaments on the variety of alstroemeria I'll be using for the bridal bouquets are actually a soft pink, not white."

"Filaments?" Sasha repeated, not sure what part of the flower that was.

"The flower penis, basically," Brooke called from her position at the counter.

"Christ, Brooke!" Ashley wrinkled her nose. A light pink dusted her cheeks.

Sasha had noticed that she blushed easily. Was it wrong of her to find that charming?

"What?" Brooke answered. "It is, kind of."

"The stamens are the part of the flower that carries the pollen." Ashley looked around as if searching for the right kind of flower to show her. "See those Stargazer lilies over there? The thin parts sticking out from the center of the blooms are the filaments. They support the anther, where the pollen is produced."

Sasha got up from her chair to take a closer look at the large, pink blooms.

"Don't get too close," Ashley said, just as Sasha bent over the flowers. "They look like they're about ready to explo—"

A blast of orange powder burst from one of the lilies, dusting the front of Sasha's shirt.

"Oops." Sasha looked down at her stained shirt with a lopsided grin. "I think your flower just threw up on me or something."

"Oh my God!" Ashley jumped up. "I'm so sorry. That's why I had the lilies back here. I always remove the stamens from all the lilies as soon as they open, especially since the pollen is toxic to animals and I need to be careful because of Casper."

"No big deal." Sasha lifted her hand to brush off the pollen.

"No!" Ashley raced over and grabbed her hand. Her fingers were warm and unexpectedly strong. Then, as if only belatedly realizing what she had done, she let go. "Don't touch it. It won't wipe off. If you touch it, your fingers will be stained orange for days."

"Yeah," Brooke said from the doorway. "That stuff is bad. Gives you Cheetos fingers. Good thing human semen is not—"

"Brooke!" Ashley spun around to her. "You know what? It seems to be a quiet afternoon. Why don't you take off early?"

"Really? Wow, thanks. See you next week!" Brooke didn't hesitate. Within seconds, the bell jingled as the front door closed behind her.

Ashley groaned. "Sorry. That's what I get for employing a teenager. She's normally pretty mature for her age, but sometimes…"

"Don't worry about it. She's all right just the way she is." Not to mention the fact that her interaction with Ashley was pretty hilarious. Sasha looked down at the orange dust on her shirt. "Is there something we can do about this? Or do I just go home with a Cheetos chest and try to soak the shirt?"

"That wouldn't help. The only way to get it off is this." Ashley stretched her arm past Sasha and dragged a massive Scotch tape dispenser closer.

"Tape?"

"Yeah." Ashley tore off a long piece, held it between both hands with the sticky side down, and stepped closer, right into Sasha's personal space. "Like this." She gently pressed the tape onto the pollen—which covered the top of Sasha's left breast. Then, obviously realizing her hand was on Sasha's chest, she froze.

Sasha's heartbeat sped up beneath her hand, and a tingle went down her body, but her feet seemed to be rooted to the spot, so stepping back wasn't an option.

"Oh my God!" Ashley snatched her hand away and jumped back as if she had burned herself. "I wasn't… I didn't mean to…"

Sasha cleared her throat. "Well, it worked."

"Um, pardon me?"

"The tape trick. It worked." Sasha nodded down at her shirt, then wanted to slap herself. *Yeah, sure, draw attention to your breasts, why don't you? Idiot.*

Ashley stared down at her chest, but Sasha wasn't sure if she was looking at the strip of fabric where the pollen had been lifted off or at her hardened nipples that were clearly visible through the shirt.

"Oh. That's nice," Ashley mumbled. "I mean, good that it worked. Wouldn't want you to have to throw away the shirt. Here." She pushed the Scotch tape dispenser toward Sasha.

Sasha tore off a strip of sticky tape and lifted the remaining pollen off her shirt. Her breasts felt achy and strained against the fabric. Why the hell was a simple, accidental touch affecting her like this? Had to be pre-menstrual hormones or something.

Ashley turned away and walked to the table, where she stood with her back to Sasha. "You know, I've been thinking about these little buds of yours."

Sasha paused with the tape in hand. Her gaze went to her nipples that were currently tenting the fabric of her shirt. At Ashley's words, they seemed to get even harder. "Um, you have?"

"Yeah. They just look so mouthwatering."

Heat flared through Sasha. She swallowed but couldn't get her vocal cords to work. Finally, she managed to croak out, "They do?"

"Yes! Don't you think so?"

Ashley's voice was so casual, it finally dawned on Sasha that she couldn't possibly be talking about her nipples. Ashley wasn't the type to comment on a woman's anatomy, no matter how obvious it was. "Oh, you mean the sugar roses?"

"Yes. What did you think I—?"

"Oh, nothing. Absolutely nothing." Sasha exhaled sharply and ordered her breasts to behave as she tossed away the tape and dropped down into her chair. "So, what about my...the roses?"

"Do you think you could make some more of the little ones that you're planning to put on the bottom tier of the cake? I was thinking we could decorate the cake table with gum paste flowers instead of real ones and maybe even put some onto each table at the reception."

Sasha's body temperature slowly went back to normal as she focused on work. "Yeah, sure. I could totally do that. Do you want some of the Peruvian lilies too?"

"If it's not too much work."

"Depends on how many weddings guests we're talking about," Sasha answered. "I have a feeling Holly and Leo might not end up with that small, intimate wedding they wanted. Leo's mom came in to get some scones yesterday, and the guest list she has in mind sounded like Fair Oaks's phone book."

Ashley laughed.

The doorbell from the other room announced the arrival of a customer.

"I'll be right out," Ashley called through the open door. She got up and whistled for Casper so he wouldn't bother the customer.

"Take your time," the customer answered. It sounded like Regina Beasley, whose husband owned the local funeral home. "I'll be looking around. I want something special today."

Casper loped into the back room.

Sasha got up too. "Oh, that reminds me. Do you have plans for this weekend? I need someone to experiment with." She couldn't help teasing Ashley but lowered her voice so Mrs. Beasley wouldn't hear. "Interested?"

Ashley looked nearly as stunned as she had when she'd realized she had her hand on Sasha's breast. "Uh…"

Sasha burst out laughing. "I want to try out some new dog treat recipes on Sunday morning, and since my aunt put Snickerdoodle on a diet, I was thinking Casper might want to taste-test."

"Dogs aren't allowed in a bakery, are they?"

"No, but I was thinking you could keep me company and maybe taste-test some snacks of the non-doggie kind and then take the dog treats home to Casper." Sasha took her coat and gave a one-shouldered shrug. "As exciting as trying out new recipes is, sitting around on my own, waiting until the timer goes off, can get a little boring."

"And you're sure Casper is the right dog for the job? His tastes aren't very discerning. He eats anything."

"My favorite kind of customer," Sasha answered. "Maybe he'll inspire you to finally try a different type of cupcake."

"I'm not committing to that," Ashley said, but Sasha noticed that she hadn't said no to the invitation.

"So you're coming? Sunday at ten?"

Ashley walked to the doorway. "I'll be there," she said just before stepping through to the front of the store.

Sasha watched her greet Mrs. Beasley and tried to rein in her grin. She didn't even know why she had spontaneously asked Ashley to come over on Sunday, yet alone why her agreeing had made her so happy. They would merely bake doggie treats, and there would be no more touching of breasts, accidental or otherwise.

Chapter 7

"WHAT ON EARTH ARE YOU doing?" Ash mumbled to herself as she drove across town on Sunday morning. Dropping by the bakery for a wedding collaboration was one thing, but keeping Sasha company while she baked doggie treats was something entirely different.

Well, it wasn't as if she had a lot of other options, she admitted to herself. Or maybe she did have options—God knew she got a lot of invitations from church groups, the bowling league, the book club at the library, and even her mother's knitting circle to join them—but none of these offers appealed to her. She had certainly tried, but making it seem as if she fit in with the rest of them took too much of an effort, so she had slowly let these activities die away.

Now Saturday nights at the bar with the gang and lunch with her folks on Sunday were the only outings she had all week. Admittedly, weekends could get a little lonely these days. Once all the work in the shop was done, all that remained was Netflix and long walks with Casper.

"And I'm perfectly happy with that," she said out loud, as if that would make it true.

She parked her SUV across the street from the bakery but didn't get out or shut off the engine. White-knuckling the steering wheel, she debated with herself about whether she should actually go in or call Sasha and make up some excuse about why she couldn't make it after all. *Yeah, like a sudden bout of idiocy.*

Movement drew her attention. Ashley turned her head.

Sasha was sitting on the steps of the bakery, waving at her.

Damn. Now leaving was no longer an option. With a sigh, Ashley turned off the engine and got out of the car.

"Morning," Sasha called over to her. "This isn't too early for you, is it?"

"God, no. I'm used to getting up before sunrise."

Sasha nodded and got up. "Another thing our jobs have in common. Come on in. I have coffee."

When they stepped inside the bakery, the scent of cinnamon hung in the air.

Ashley's mouth watered. "That's not the doggie treats I'm smelling, is it?"

"No, that's yours." Sasha walked over to the back counter and pressed a few buttons on the chrome espresso machine, which came to life with a hiss. "I made cinnamon rolls as a reward for you helping me."

"Helping? I thought I was just supposed to keep you company." Ashley chuckled nervously. "Trust me, you don't want me to help with the baking. I've never baked anything more challenging than a brownie mix."

"There's a first time for everything." Sasha handed her a paper cup of coffee without having to ask how she took it. She probably remembered her preferences from when Ashley had ordered a coffee with her daily cupcake.

"Thanks." Ash inhaled the aroma of the freshly brewed coffee. "But I think I'll stick with keeping you company. I've really got the baker's equivalent of a black thumb."

Sasha shrugged. "Fine. Be a pillow princess."

The first sip of coffee Ashley had just taken shot out of her nose. "Jesus, Sasha! You can't say things like that!" She wiped her nose and chin and then automatically glanced over her shoulder, but, of course, they were alone in the bakery.

Sasha grinned unrepentantly. "Oh, I can. My bakery, my rules. Come on." With her hand on the small of Ashley's back, she guided her toward the kitchen.

That big, warm hand rested there as if it was the most natural thing in the world. To Ash, it was everything but. The touch wasn't unpleasant, though. When Sasha finally took her hand away, Ash's back felt strangely cold. She shivered.

"You cold? Don't worry. That'll change in a second." Sasha preheated one of the ovens and then slung an apron around her hips with practiced movements.

"So, what are we making?" Ashley asked when they both washed their hands at the sink.

"We?"

"You."

"I was thinking of doing both doggie cupcakes and muffins." Sasha's hair disappeared beneath her black bandanna. Her pirate look made Ashley smile. "You up for that?"

"Sure. As long as I'm out of here by noon to have lunch with my folks, we're good."

"Then let's get started." Sasha handed Ashley an apron, set a cupcake pan onto the worktable, and lined it with paper liners. "Could you get me two eggs from the fridge and two bananas from that bowl over there?"

"Um, didn't we agree that I wouldn't be helping?"

"We agreed you wouldn't be baking...which you aren't. You're just handing me the ingredients. Strictly speaking, that's not baking."

Ashley regarded her with a shake of her head. "Has anyone ever told you that you should have been a lawyer?"

"My dad. He always wanted me to follow in his footsteps."

Ash put on the apron, went to the giant fridge, and took out two eggs, which she carried over to Sasha along with the requested bananas. "But practicing law held no appeal to you?"

Sasha spread her arms wide.

Her impressive wingspan made Ash stare for a moment. God, she probably gave amazing hugs. She shoved the silly thought away.

"Look around." Sasha gestured at the kitchen. "Would you trade this for a lawyer's office?"

"No," Ash said without having to think about it. "There's just something so satisfying about..."

"Working with your hands," they finished together and grinned at each other.

Sasha nodded. "Yeah. You get it. My father never did. Does yours?"

"Oh yeah. I'm lucky, at least in that regard. Both of my parents were completely supportive from the moment I first told them I wanted to open a flower shop. Guess it comes with the territory, my dad being a farmer and all."

"That makes sense." Sasha mashed up the bananas and cracked open the eggs on the edge of the bowl with just one hand. Her motions were efficient and elegant at the same time. It was like watching a ballet dancer performing a familiar routine.

She added freshly ground peanut butter and a little milk, then sifted flour on top, with Ash handing her each of the ingredients.

They worked unexpectedly well together, and to her surprise, Ash found that she enjoyed helping.

In what seemed like no time at all, Sasha spooned the batter into the paper liners, slid the pan into the oven, and set the timer. "I still need a name for them." She pointed at the oven. "*Peanut butter and banana cupcakes for dogs* might be pretty boring. Any ideas?"

"Oh God. You're asking the wrong person." Ash took a sip of her coffee that had gone lukewarm. "I nearly named my shop Ashley's Flower Shop. It was my mom who suggested The Flower Girl. I'm afraid I'm not very creative."

Sasha leaned against the worktable and folded her strong arms across her chest. "I don't believe that for a second. I've seen the bouquets and centerpieces you design. You're very creative."

Ashley looked down at the black-and-white tiled floor. "I don't know."

"Come on. Just make a suggestion. It doesn't have to be spectacular. Just something to get the brainstorming going."

Ash allowed a tiny smile to curve her lips. "You know, my brain always thinks best if I feed it some sugar."

Sasha laughed. "Is that your not-so-subtle way of asking for one of the cinnamon rolls I promised?" She opened a big container and held it out to Ash, who took one of the fragrant sticky buns.

It was still warm, and the first bite nearly melted on her tongue. "Oh, yum."

Sasha got started on the cream-cheese-and-banana frosting for the cupcakes while Ash devoured her treat. "So?" Sasha finally asked. "Did that put your brain into working order?"

Ash swallowed another bite of cinnamon roll. "Let's see… Doggie cupcakes… How about Pupcakes?"

"Yes!" Sasha pumped her fist. "That's genius. I knew you'd be good at this."

It was stupid, really, but Sasha's praise warmed her more than the bakery oven. She hoped she wasn't blushing. "Nah. It's your cinnamon roll doing its job."

"We also need a name for the carrot muffins we're making next. How about...hmm... Oh, I have it! Woofins!"

"Ooh, I love it. Now who's the creative one?" Ash nudged her with her elbow. "And you haven't even had a cinnamon roll."

Sasha grinned broadly. "What can I say? I'm a woman of many talents."

"But modesty is not one of them."

"Nope. Can't say that it is."

"If you need a name for the entire doggie treat line, how about..." Ash licked sugar and cinnamon off her fingers. "...Sasha's Barkery Treats?"

"Huh?" Sasha gave her a dazed look, as if something had distracted her.

"Barkery... Like bakery, only..."

"Oh, I get it. That's great too." Sasha gestured with her hands as if unrolling a banner from which she read. "Sasha's Barkery Treats... Good enough to howl."

They burst out laughing.

"We make a great team." Sasha held her hand out for a high five.

Ash reached up, once again very aware of how much taller Sasha was, and tapped her palm with her own. Without her meaning to, her fingers lingered against Sasha's warm hand.

Sasha didn't pull away either.

The oven timer went off, startling them apart.

Ash withdrew to the other side of the worktable. It was much safer there. "Sorry."

"What are you apologizing for?" Sasha asked, her tone light.

So she hadn't noticed that moment of...well, Ash wasn't even sure what to call it. *Insanity,* a voice in her head supplied. *You wanted to stay far, far away from women, remember? Especially women who aren't straight.* She cleared her throat. "Um, just my fingers being sticky. From the bun and all."

Sasha shrugged. "Don't worry about it. I'm a baker. I'm not afraid of getting my hands dirty." She pulled the cupcake pan from the oven and set it on a cooling rack.

Ash forced herself to focus on the cupcakes, not on the way Sasha's jeans tightened over her butt as she bent over the oven. "Wow, they smell good. If Casper doesn't want them, I might eat them instead."

"You could," Sasha answered. "They aren't as sweet as my regular cupcakes, but the Pupcakes are safe to eat for dogs and humans alike. Let's start on the muffins...pardon me, the Woofins while we wait for the Pupcakes to cool enough so we can ice them."

Ash quickly washed her hands and then moved back in place to play baker's assistant again, handing Sasha the ingredients as she asked for them. She nearly dropped an egg when her phone chimed, announcing an incoming text message. After giving Sasha the eggs, she pulled it from her back pocket. Several more messages arrived before she could even glance at the small screen.

They were all from the same sender: her mother. Each of them contained a photo: a sleeping baby, the same baby with its foot stuck in its mouth, the baby crawling across a carpet toward a huge pile of toys.

Ash tapped the screen to type out a teasing reply about her mother adopting a sister or brother for her but then paused and deleted the two words she had already written. She didn't want to remind her mother of Melissa and make her sad by mentioning the word *sister*.

Another picture arrived, making her phone vibrate in her hand.

This one finally gave her a clue as to whose baby it was. Vicky, who she had gone to school with, was holding the baby in this photo. Instead of wearing a baby-spit-covered sweatshirt as Ash had expected, Vicky wore a silk blouse and pearls, and she held the baby as if it were a fashion accessory she wanted to show off on Instagram.

The phone chimed again.

Isn't she cute? I ran into Vicky at the hair salon yesterday, and she invited me over for coffee. What a darling little girl, don't you think?

Sasha looked up from where she was sifting flour into the shredded carrots and the applesauce. "You got a hot date later on?"

Ash snorted. She hadn't had a date in years, and it had been even longer since she'd had one she could call *hot*. "No." She held out the phone and showed Sasha one of the photos.

"Um, isn't she a little young for you?" Sasha sent her a teasing smile.

"Oh, you!" Ash reached across the worktable to playfully slap Sasha's shoulder.

Laughing, Sasha danced out of the way. For a woman with such a solid build, she sure was light on her feet.

Yeah, and for a woman who vowed to stay away from women, you sure are very touchy-feely with her. That wasn't like her at all. As a child, Ash had loved physical closeness. Her mother had always called her *my little cuddle bug.* But as she got older and realized why she loved to hug some of her female friends in particular, Ash had become more careful about who she touched. Even though she still loved hugs, she avoided initiating them more often than the other person, if at all.

"You okay?" Sasha looked at her with an expression that almost resembled concern.

"Oh yes," Ash said quickly. "I'm just not too crazy about getting messages like these."

"Don't you like kids?"

"No, that's not it at all. I like them just fine. What I don't like is my mother sending me these subtle reminders that I'm not getting any younger and my biological clock is ticking."

Sasha huffed out a breath. "Jeez. So that's why she's sending you a whole photo album of the kid."

"Yes. Give it a second, and she'll start in on my love life...or lack thereof."

As if on cue, the phone chimed again.

Ash read it out loud: "Did I tell you that Sheryl's oldest son is back in town? He's taking over as the branch manager of our bank, and I heard he's divorced."

"Wow." Sasha filled the last of the paper liners with the Woofin batter and slid the pan into the oven. She turned and gave Ashley her full attention. "What are you going to say to that?"

"The same thing I'm always telling her. That I'm too busy to date and that he's nice but not my type." She typed it in and sent off the message.

The answer came fast.

Oh, honey. I don't understand you. Handsome and gainfully employed men are not your type?

Ash sighed and rubbed her face with her free hand.

"I take it she doesn't know men aren't your type, period?" Sasha's tone was gentle, with no hint of judgment.

"God, no! I could never tell her that."

"But wouldn't it be easier in the long run?" Sasha asked. "Otherwise, she'll keep shoving every unmarried, divorced, or widowed man within a two-hundred-mile radius at you."

Ash tightened her grip on the phone until her fingers started to cramp. "Easier? No. There'd be nothing easy about it, trust me." No matter how hard she tried, she could never imagine a conversation in which she would come out to her parents.

"Okay, maybe *easy* wasn't the right word to use, but at least you could live your life without having to hide and to lie all the time."

"I'm not." Ash struggled not to raise her voice as she felt herself getting defensive. "I'm not dating anyone, so there's nothing to lie about. I learned that lesson with Holly." That last bit slipped out before she could censor herself.

Sasha studied her, and those chocolate brown eyes seemed to look far too deep for Ash's comfort.

"What about you? Are you out to your family?" Ash asked, just to turn the topic of conversation away from herself. "I mean, your aunt obviously knows. But what about your parents?"

"Oh yeah, they know. The rest of my family too."

How calmly she had said that! As if it were the most normal thing in the world, with no pain and heartbreak involved. "And they are fine with it? They accepted it...just like that?"

"More or less. I have a couple of cousins and an uncle who stopped talking to me for a while, but most family members were fine with it. Half of my mother's friends are gay men. My father wasn't overjoyed but finally came to accept it. I think Aunt Mae might have kicked his ass. She's—and I quote—more supportive than an underwire bra."

That made Ash smile, despite the tension settling around her ribs like an iron band. "God, you don't know how lucky you are."

"Trust me, I do know," Sasha said quietly. "I learned not to take unconditional love for granted early in my life."

Ash bent her head. She hadn't meant to be so egoistical to imply that she was the only one struggling, while Sasha had always had it easy in life. "I'm sorry. I—"

"It's okay. But don't you think there's a chance your parents might be like my dad, maybe struggle a bit at first but then come around? Who knows? They might surprise you."

"No." Ash held up her phone, which at that moment chimed again. "They're already not too happy about me being unmarried and childless. If I told them why…" She squeezed her eyes shut because she didn't even want to imagine it. "They'd be devastated."

"So what will you do?" Sasha asked. "Date some poor, unsuspecting man to please your parents?"

"No. I'm done with that. I did it in the past, just to keep up appearances and maybe because I was hoping there'd be a spark with one of them if I tried hard enough."

"But there wasn't." Sasha made it a statement, not a question.

Ash sighed. "None whatsoever."

"But if there is with women, do you really not want to—?"

"No," Ash said firmly. "I'm okay being alone and letting my parents think it's because I'm too picky or because the shop keeps me too busy. If I'm lucky, my mother will forget about Vicky and her baby in a couple of days and stop bugging me for a while. At least until she runs into the next person who's just had a new baby or recently got engaged. Any time I tell her I'm working a wedding, she starts asking me when it'll finally be my turn. Always the florist—"

"Never the bride," Sasha finished for her. "I've heard that a time or two from my aunt too. Just that she wouldn't care whether it's two brides on my wedding cake as long as she gets to make it."

Ash couldn't imagine what it must be like to have an aunt like that. None of her aunts and uncles would react like Mae if they ever found out she was gay. "Would you ever do that?" She knew it would have probably been better to keep things between them completely professional, but Sasha seemed like such an interesting person, and she couldn't help being curious.

"Let her make my wedding cake?" Sasha asked.

"No. Get married to a woman."

"Nope. I don't think so." Sasha held up her hand before Ash could say anything. "Not because of the same-sex thing. I can't see myself marrying a man—or a nonbinary person—either. Guess I'm just not the marrying kind."

"That's what my mother always tells her friends—that I'm just not the marrying kind because I'm too focused on my shop."

Sasha chuckled. "She probably has no idea that 'not the marrying kind' used to be a euphemism for being gay."

"God, no. She has no clue."

"So what did she say when she found out Holly and Leo are getting married?" Sasha asked. "Did that start the entire 'when is it finally your turn' thing again, or was she too outraged about it being two women?"

"I don't think she's heard yet."

Sasha arched her expressive eyebrows. "Really? The whole town is talking about it."

"I'm pretty sure my mother would have called me right away if she knew. My parents are starting to become really busy on the farm, ordering seed and fertilizer and getting things ready for tilling and planting, so they're not coming into town that much. And I guess at the hair salon Vicky's baby and Sheryl's divorced son were the big news."

The phone chimed again. Now three messages from her mother were waiting for her reply.

Ash quickly sent her a message, telling her they would talk when she came over for lunch.

"Or maybe your mother does know, and that's why she keeps sending you all these photos that are supposed to make your ovaries ache, none-too-subtly nudging you toward a heterosexual lifestyle." Sasha formed air quotes with her fingers.

Ash clutched the edge of the worktable with both hands. "Oh God. I hope that's not it. Did I mention that I'm going over to my folks for lunch right after this?"

"Hey, I didn't mean to worry you." Sasha's hand hovered over Ash's fingers clamped around the worktable, but then she withdrew it without touching her. "You're probably right. Your parents are too busy on the farm to keep up with all the town gossip."

"Yeah, I'm sure of it."

But when the doggie treats were done an hour later and Ash helped fill a bakery box with Pupcakes and Woofins for Casper, she couldn't push the thought out of her mind. She was in for one nerve-racking lunch.

Sasha got a second bakery box and piled cinnamon rolls into it. "Here." She folded down the lid and held out the box. "Take these to your folks."

Ash reached out to accept it but then pulled her hands back. "Uh, I'm not sure that's a good idea."

"Why? Your parents aren't diabetic or on any health-related restrictions, are they?"

"No. It's just… They know the bakery is closed on Sundays, so if I show up with freshly baked cinnamon rolls…" Ash trailed off, not wanting to say the words.

Sasha stood with the box still extended toward her for another moment. Then she abruptly pulled it back and turned away to set it on the counter behind her. "They would know you spent time with me. You're right. We wouldn't want that."

Ash stared at Sasha's broad back that was taut with tension. She took one step toward her, and her hand rose as if on its own volition, about to touch that tense back. *Are you crazy? Keep your distance from her, dammit!*

But she couldn't ignore the hurt in Sasha's voice and her stance. It surprised her how much she wanted to soothe that away. "I'm sorry. I'm probably just being paranoid." She took a deep breath. "So what if they know I spent the morning at the bakery? I just helped you make treats for Casper. That doesn't mean anything, right?"

The tense set of Sasha's shoulders relaxed. She turned around and regarded Ash with a serious expression. "You don't have to take them. I don't want to get you into trouble."

"It's fine." Ash stepped around the worktable and took the box. "There won't be any trouble." She could only hope that was true.

"All right. Then I hope your folks enjoy them." Sasha walked her to the door. Again, her hand came to rest on the small of Ashley's back.

Did she do that with all of her female friends and acquaintances?

What? You think you're special to her? Please! If she had been Brooke, she would have rolled her eyes at herself. But she had to admit that she liked that bit of human contact.

At the door, they both paused and turned to face each other.

"Thanks for the barkery treats and the cinnamon rolls," Ash said. "That was really nice of you." Okay, that sounded lame. But what else was she supposed to say?

"My pleasure." Sasha tried to shove her hands into the front pockets of her jeans, then seemed to realize that she was still wearing an apron and hooked them into her back pockets instead. "So…it's been fun. We should do this again sometime."

Was it just her being paranoid again, or did that sound a little too much like something you might say at the end of a date? Ash decided that it was all in her head. After all, Sasha had just told her that she wasn't the marrying kind either, and she didn't seem eager to start a relationship with anyone.

"Definitely," Ash said. To her own surprise, it wasn't just a polite response that she didn't really mean. Baking—or at least helping Sasha while she baked—had been unexpectedly fun. She glanced at her watch. "Oh shit. I need to go, or I'll be late. I need to pick up Casper before I head out to my parents'."

"Okay. Drive carefully." For a moment, Sasha looked as if she was debating hugging her goodbye.

Ash's pulse started racing. She found herself leaning forward, toward Sasha, even as she firmly told herself to pull back quickly if Sasha really hugged her.

But then Sasha just opened the door and held it for her.

Ash pressed the two boxes to her chest and walked past Sasha. "See you tomorrow at three."

"See ya."

Ash marched to her SUV and put the boxes on the passenger seat. She wasn't disappointed that she hadn't gotten a hug. Absolutely not. She was actually relieved about it. Right?

Absolutely. Yep, very, very relieved.

She would be even more relieved once lunch with her parents was over and her mother had mentioned neither Sheryl's eligible son nor Holly and Leo's wedding.

Ash barely had time to put down the bakery boxes on the side table in the hall before her father engulfed her in a warm embrace. Casper jumped around them, demanding to be greeted too. She couldn't help thinking of the hug she hadn't gotten from Sasha. How ridiculous! So what if someone she was supposed to work with hadn't hugged her?

"You okay, honey?" Her father released her and held her at arm's length to study her. Concern flickered in his blue eyes that stood out against his fading farmer's tan and his graying hair.

"I'm fine, Dad." She squeezed his hand that rested on her shoulder.

He still regarded her carefully, as if not wanting to miss anything that might be going on with her.

Ash bit her lip. With Melissa, they had all missed the signs, and she knew that, deep down, her parents harbored the fear of making the same mistake with her. That was part of why she had become so good at playing the role of the perfect daughter over the years.

"How's the shop doing?" her father asked.

"Wonderfully." That was a bit of an exaggeration, but business was indeed picking up. Spring was in the air, and that put people in the mood to buy flowers.

Finally, her father seemed to be convinced that she was doing okay. He dropped his hand from her shoulder and bent to lavish attention on Casper.

Her mother stepped out of the kitchen, wearing the really ugly red-and-white-checkered apron that Ash had made her in middle school. "Hi, sweetie." She engulfed her in a tight embrace. "So good to see you."

Jeez, her mother made it sound as if they hadn't seen each other in months, even though Ash came over for lunch every Sunday. Her mother always told her that she should come over for dinner more often, but Ash rarely took her up on it. Coming home was a double-edged sword for her.

She glanced at the stairs leading to the second floor. She knew what she would find should she ever venture upstairs—which she never did unless she had a very good reason. Her parents had left Melissa's room exactly the way it had been, as if she would one day come home. Maybe it was soothing to her parents to be able to step into her room any time, but for Ash, it just kept the pain alive. That was one of the reasons she had moved out as soon as she could.

She hugged her mother tightly and breathed in the familiar gardenia aroma of her favorite perfume and something else that she identified as frying oil after a second. "Yum." Ash licked her lips. "Are you making fried chicken?"

Laughing, her mom released her. "Are you sniffing my hair to find out what we're having for lunch?" She, too, studied Ash with an imploring parental gaze. "Are you eating enough? I know you're skipping lunch when the shop gets busy. I could always bring you some lunch, you know? A nice, home-cooked meal every day..."

"Mom, I'm fine. I'm eating plenty." That reminded her of the two boxes she had put down on the hall table. She picked up the one on top and handed it to her mother. "Dessert."

Her mother opened the lid and sniffed. "Oh, they smell heavenly. Like fresh out of the oven."

"They are," Ash said before she could stop herself. To distract her parents, she walked into the kitchen and started to carry the bowls and platters of steaming food into the dining room.

Her mother followed, set the box down on the counter, and tapped the logo on the top. "Since when is A Slice of Heaven open on Sundays?"

"They aren't. Sasha wanted to try out new doggie treat recipes, so Casper volunteered to be a guinea pig."

Her mother laughed and pointed at Casper, who was busy gobbling up some morsels that had dropped on the floor while she'd been cooking. "Oh yeah, I bet he did. He's about as food-motivated as you were when you were a toddler. God, I had to watch you like a hawk, or you would shove anything into your mouth. Once, you bit into an onion, peel and all."

For once, Ash didn't mind the embarrassing childhood story. At least it got her mother away from the topic of Sasha and why she was spending time at the bakery on a Sunday morning.

She settled Casper down in the giant dog bed her parents had bought him, pointing out that he was their only grandchild, so they should be allowed to spoil him.

They washed their hands and then took a seat at the table in the dining room, with Ash choosing the same chair she had sat in all of her life.

Her father held out his hands. "Let's say grace."

Ash had to stretch her arms to both sides of the table in order to take their hands. The painful gap in their family was never as obvious as during mealtimes. She tightly held her parents' hands—her father's big, calloused one and her mother's smaller one—and they gripped hers just as firmly.

Her father bent his head. "Lord, thank you for the food before us, the family beside us, and the love between us. Amen."

At least he always kept it short, as if not wanting to prolong the moment of missing the feel of Melissa's hand in his.

Her mother passed her the bowl of mashed potatoes, then the peas and the sweet corn, which she had canned from their own fields and garden last summer. She nodded down at the heaping platter of golden-brown chicken pieces. "What would you like, honey?"

For Ash, the answer was a no-brainer. "Breast, please."

Her mother pierced a chicken breast and put it on Ash's plate.

Her father chuckled and picked up a drumstick. "You always liked breasts best. I'm more of a leg man myself."

The forkful of peas Ash had just taken nearly went down the wrong pipe. Coughing wildly, she lunged for her water glass.

Her father didn't seem to realize what he'd just said. "You okay, honey?" He patted her back.

Ash nodded but couldn't yet speak.

Her mother paled. "Oh no. Did I use too much pepper in the peas?"

Ash shook her head. "No," she finally gasped out. "They're fine. I just inhaled at the wrong moment." She picked up the chicken breast from her plate and took a big bite so they'd stop staring at her with those concerned gazes. Yum. Her mother's fried chicken was the best. It was crispy on the outside and tender on the inside.

A lot like Sasha, she suspected.

God, where had that thought come from?

But it was true. With her sturdy six-foot frame and that pirate bandanna, Sasha might have looked tough, but her reaction when Ash had refused to take the cinnamon rolls had revealed that she was a big marshmallow on the inside.

"Great as always." Her father wiped his fingers on his napkin and reached across the table to squeeze his wife's hand.

Her mother beamed. "The trick is to soak the chicken in buttermilk overnight. That makes it much more tender. Karen told me she does the same." She turned toward Ash. "Oh, speaking of Karen, isn't her granddaughter adorable?"

With her mouth full of chicken, Ash just nodded. She had wondered how long it would take for her mother to bring that up.

"She didn't cry at all when Vicky let me hold her. Such a sweet girl. I bet your children will be the same. When you were little, you never went through that stranger anxiety phase either."

Ash let her mother's talk about babies wash over her without really paying attention.

Predictably, she hadn't made it even halfway through her piece of chicken when her mother started talking about Sheryl's son. "I bet you'd barely recognize Derek, honey. He had LASIK a couple of years ago, and Sheryl says he started working out when he went through the divorce."

Ash sighed. She hadn't been attracted to him in high school, and a six-pack and the lack of glasses wouldn't change that. "Good for him," she said, hoping her mother would move on.

"I told Sheryl that he should join you and your friends at Johnny's on Saturday."

Ash dropped her half-eaten chicken breast onto her plate. "You did what?"

"Why is that a problem? Derek went to school with the rest of you, didn't he?"

"Yes, but everyone else goes to the bar just to hang out with friends, not to pick up a date."

Her mother put down her chicken wing. "So what if he asks you out? What would be wrong with that?"

Ash clamped her greasy fingers around her napkin. "Nothing, but—"

"I don't understand why you're being so stubborn. If you don't want to go out with Derek, fine. There are other men out there. But you refuse to even meet any of them. You're thirty-three, honey."

Ash let out a groan, but her mother continued.

"I don't want you to end up alone. You need to—"

Her father tossed the bone of his drumstick onto an empty plate. "Leave the poor girl alone, Donna. You can't force things like that. Don't you worry." He patted his wife's hand. "She'll find someone and fall in love, probably when she least expects it."

The lines of concern on her mother's forehead didn't ease. "But what if that doesn't happen because she's not putting herself out there, always hiding behind work?"

"I'm not hiding behind work," Ash said. "Running my own business really leaves me with little time to date."

"Oh, but you seem to have plenty of time to spend with Sasha Peterson. Betty from the hair salon said you hang out with her a lot these days."

What? Ash stared at her. "That's not true! The time we've spent together was mostly for the wedding, and it was hardly a lot."

The moment the words left her lips, she regretted them. First, because she knew her passionate denial would come across as over-the-top, and second, because it sounded as if spending time with Sasha would be bad. The truth was, she did enjoy spending time with her. She was just so easy to be around. That rarely happened to Ash. And what definitely didn't ever happen was her opening up the way she had with Sasha this morning. If she found the courage to continue hanging out with her, Sasha could become the first female friend she'd made since Holly.

"Wedding?" Her mother paused with a forkful of mashed potatoes an inch from her lips. "What wedding?"

Oh shit. Now she'd done it. She had steered the conversation directly to the topic she'd wanted to avoid. "Oh, you know…" She waved her fork in a vague gesture. "Several, actually. Now that her aunt has handed over the bakery completely, we'll probably work together a lot during wedding season. Sasha is making a name for herself as an excellent wedding cake designer. You should see some of her sketches. She's really, really good."

"That's wonderful, honey," her mother said. "Maybe she'll do your wedding cake one day."

Now they were back to her mother's favorite topic. If her fingers hadn't been so greasy, Ash would have covered her face with her hands and groaned.

Thankfully, her father steered the conversation to his newest tractor and the best time to start planting corn.

Ash breathed a sigh of relief, but she knew she'd bought herself only a little more time. At some point, her parents would find out about Holly and Leo's wedding—and it would probably be sooner rather than later.

Chapter 8

THE DOOR TO JOHNNY'S OPENED, letting in a gush of spring air.

Sasha looked up from the beer bottle she was cradling and craned her neck to see who it was.

Just Phil Eads and his son.

She slumped against the back of the booth.

Holly leaned across the table. "You okay? You're not thinking about leaving already, are you? We just got here."

"What? No. I can stay for a while." It was only then that Sasha realized what she had been doing. She had been on the lookout for Ashley any time the door opened, but it had always been someone else. "Isn't Ashley coming tonight?"

Zack shook his head. "I ran into her at the grocery store earlier, and she said she wouldn't be able to make it tonight. Something about having to finish a wreath."

A pang of disappointment flared through Sasha. *What, now you suddenly can't have a fun night out without her?*

In the past, she had never paid much attention to whether Ashley made it to their Saturday night get-togethers. But now that she had spent more time alone with Ashley, away from the gang, she was starting to realize that Ashley was different from Sasha's high school image of her. While she clearly had some issues and cared a little too much about what people might be thinking, she wasn't the superficial, egoistical person that would do anything to be popular, as Sasha had thought.

The door opened again.

Sasha couldn't stop the reflex of looking up, even though she now knew Ashley wouldn't be coming.

A man entered and walked up to their table. "Hey, guys. Good to see you."

Sasha stared at him. Was she supposed to know him? He did look kind of familiar, but she couldn't put her finger on it.

Travis jumped up and gave the stranger a man hug, thumping his back repeatedly. "Derek Hatchfield! Man, it's great to see you too. I didn't know you were in town. Visiting your folks?"

"No. I'm back for good. Mr. Mitchell is retiring, and I'm taking over as the branch manager of the bank."

Travis let out a piercing whistle. "Wow. I bet you make good money."

Derek shrugged. "Can't complain."

Sasha recognized him now. He'd been a year ahead of her in school, but he had changed a lot—and definitely for the better.

Derek pointed at the horseshoe-shaped booth. "My mom said that this is where you all hang out on Saturday night. I guess not much has changed, has it?" He laughed and looked at Leo. "Well, except that you're famous now."

"Not here," Leo said firmly. "Here in Fair Oaks, I'm just boring, old Leo Blake."

"Please." Holly, who sat next to her, lightly bumped her shoulder. "You couldn't be boring if you tried."

"C'mon, join us." Travis waved at Sasha to slide over in the booth to make room for Derek.

When he sat next to Sasha, his broad shoulder brushed hers, and the scent of his aftershave or cologne teased her nostrils. With his athletic body, wavy, dark hair, and kind smile, he might have normally been her type, but now she couldn't help thinking how much nicer it would have been if Ashley had been sitting next to her instead.

Derek ordered a beer. Once he had it, he let his gaze sweep over his former schoolmates. "Where's Ashley? My mom mentioned that she still lives in town."

"Yes, she does. Never left," Zack said. "But she's working late tonight."

"Oh." Derek might have been a good banker, but he would have made a lousy poker player. His disappointment was obvious.

Truth be told, Sasha was a little disappointed too. She had seen Ashley a couple of times during the week, when she had come in to get her three o'clock cupcake, but with other customers in line behind her, they hadn't been able to have much of a conversation.

"Well, I guess I'll catch up with her later." Derek looked from one to the other. "So, catch me up on what's new with you guys. Marriages, babies, divorces?"

"No divorce yet, but sometimes, it's tempting," Jenny said with a teasing grin.

Travis frowned. "Hey!"

Jenny leaned her head against his shoulder. "Just kidding, hon." She straightened. "As for marriages… You probably heard already that wedding bells will be ringing for Fair Oaks's most famous daughter."

Derek swiveled to face Leo. "What? You're getting married?"

A happy smile lit up Leo's face as she nodded.

"Wow." Derek shook his head. "Not that I read the tabloids or anything, but why didn't I hear about this before?"

"Oh, you know how people in Fair Oaks are," Holly said. "They might gossip, but they're not talking to outsiders about one of their own…well, two of their own."

"So your fiancé is a local?" Derek asked. "Who's the lucky guy?"

Silence settled over the booth for a moment.

"Man, you really don't read the tabloids, do you?" Travis slapped Derek's shoulder. "It's a lucky gal, not a lucky guy."

Derek put his beer down with a thump. "I knew it! It's Ashley, isn't it? That's why she wouldn't go out with me in high school."

"Oh please." Lisa rolled her eyes. "Why do men always think if a woman refuses to go out with them, she must be gay, like that's the only reason she could possibly resist you?"

"Yeah," Sasha mumbled into her beer. Talking about Ashley behind her back didn't sit well with her. "Ashley probably didn't go out with you because you behaved like an idiot every time you talked to her."

Derek let out an awkward chuckle and rubbed his neck. "Yeah, well, there's that."

"No, it's not Ashley," Leo said. "I'm marrying the most beautiful, intelligent—"

Holly blushed and covered Leo's mouth with her hand. "She's marrying me."

Leo kissed her hand and then entwined their fingers. "Lucky me."

Playfully, Zack covered his eyes with his hand. "See? That's what Ethan and I are currently having to live through every Sunday, when the family gets together at Mom's. PDAs at the dining table and endless talk about wedding invitations, guest lists, and the color of table linens at the reception."

Holly and Leo groaned.

"Hey, cut us some slack, big brother. We're the ones who are having to suffer through most of that." Holly looked at her friends. "Our moms have caught the wedding-planning fever. They want everything to be picture-perfect."

Leo sighed. "They don't get that it'll be perfect because we get to marry each other. Everything else will be just…"

"Icing on the cake," Sasha finished for her.

"Exactly. It might be fun for our moms, but personally, I find all that wedding-planning stuff more stressful than my last world tour. Booking a concert at Madison Square Garden was less complicated than booking the country club for our wedding reception!" Leo gave Holly a pleading look that was only halfway kidding. "Are you sure you don't want to elope? Think about it… Just you and me on a remote beach, exchanging vows in white bikinis as the sun sets against a cloudless, blue sky…"

"Don't tempt me," Holly muttered.

Lisa flicked a tortilla chip at them. "Oh no! You two are not eloping. You can't deny the people who love you the chance to see you get married."

Sasha nodded her agreement. "Plus don't you want to show the homophobes that not only can we get married now, but we refuse to do it quietly to avoid offending their small-town sensibilities?"

No one reacted to the way she had phrased the sentence, using *we* instead of *you*. Either her friends didn't care, or they hadn't paid attention to her choice of words.

Leo chugged down the rest of her beer. "I want to get married, not make a political statement."

Sasha gave her a sympathetic look. "Well, if you're one of the most successful recording artists of the decade, who happens to be gay, you can't do one without the other."

Jenny reached over and patted Leo's shoulder. "Just wait and see. It'll be the best day of your life. Once you see Holly in her dress, you'll forget about all the stress."

"God, and here I thought getting divorced was bad," Derek said.

Everyone laughed, and the conversation turned to Derek's failed marriage and his life since they had last seen each other.

Sasha didn't really listen. She started peeking at her watch. It wasn't that late yet, but she had gotten up early and after Derek's remark about Ashley and why she hadn't dated him in high school, she wasn't too interested in his love life. She finished her beer and tucked a couple of bills beneath the empty bottle. "All right, guys. See you next week. Mr. Sandman is calling my name."

"Ooh, new boyfriend?" Travis drawled.

She gave him the finger but didn't grace his remark with a verbal reply.

Derek stood to let her out, and she squeezed past him. A chorus of "Night, Sasha" followed her as she walked toward the door. The air outside smelled like spring, but the temperature had cooled down after sundown. She paused on the sidewalk to zip up her jacket and gazed across the street.

A light was still on in Ashley's flower shop.

Sasha walked down the street, but instead of climbing the stairs to her apartment, she unlocked the door of the bakery.

What are you doing?

She knew she should go home and get some sleep. But she didn't stop. She went to the walk-in cooler and looked at the leftover cakes.

A piece of orange cheesecake with a bittersweet chocolate glaze seemed like the perfect choice for a late-night-at-work snack. Plus the complex, contradicting flavors were a perfect fit for Ashley's personality.

Oh, now you're a cake psychologist? Eat the damn cake yourself and go to bed!

Again, she didn't listen to that inner voice. Gently, making sure not to chip the glaze, she placed the piece of cake into a bakery box, put a Pupcake for Casper into a separate box, and locked the door behind herself.

The light in the flower shop drew her toward it like a moth.

Soft music came from inside, and Sasha recognized "Crazy in Love" by Beyoncé, a song that had been in the charts the year she'd been a junior in high school. In fact, she had heard Leo and her band perform that song at school parties, with Ashley at the keyboard. But after Leo had left, she had never again seen Ashley play or heard her sing. Maybe she had given up music the way she had given up women.

Sasha paused in front of the flower shop and peered through the glass door.

Ashley wasn't working on a funeral wreath. Well, she held a carnation in her hand, but at the moment, it served as a fake microphone that she sang into as she danced through the shop as if it were a stage.

God, this was the cutest—and the hottest—thing she had ever seen.

Laughter bubbled up, and Sasha pressed her free hand to her mouth to stifle it. No way did she want to end this performance by making her presence known.

Her heartbeat thudded in her ears, nearly drowning out Ashley's singing. The way Ashley shimmied her hips was doing dangerous things to her pulse.

Ashley danced around a potted ficus tree, circling it as if it were a lover she was trying to seduce.

Oh sweet Jesus! Sasha's free hand came up to steady herself against the glass door while she clutched the two bakery boxes with the other. The temperature outside no longer felt cool at all.

She knew this was stupid, not to mention creepy, but she couldn't make herself stop watching. The chance to watch Ashley act so unrestrained might never come again.

Finally, the song ended, and Ashley lowered her carnation microphone and stopped dancing. She went back to her work area, trimmed the stem of the carnation, and inserted it into a half-finished wreath as if she hadn't just given Beyoncé a run for her money.

Sasha exhaled the breath she'd been holding and gave herself a mental kick. *Stop acting like a smitten creep!* She would just give Ashley the cake, pretend she hadn't just witnessed this little erotic dance interlude, and then go home. Yeah. Piece of cake—literally.

She lifted her hand and knocked on the glass.

Ash inserted the carnation into the wreath and forced herself not to glance in the direction of the bar for the hundredth time. She had already wasted too much time staring out the window and letting the music playing in the back transport her to her high school years, when she had played keyboard in Leo's band. If she hurried up, she might be able to join the gang at the bar before everyone went home.

But knowing Sasha, she had probably already left, so even if she went to Johnny's now, she might not see her.

Regret tightened her throat. Well, she had only herself to blame. She didn't really have to finish the wreath tonight; she had just wanted to avoid running into Derek when he joined the gang at the bar.

It was stupid. Why had she let herself be kept from seeing her friends, on the off chance that Derek might be there and try to ask her out?

She wanted to know how the wedding preparations were going, if Jenny had finally told Travis about the dent in his car, and most of all how Sasha's canine customers had taken to the Woofins and the Pupcakes.

Now she'd have to wait another week to find out. Being in the closet really sucked sometimes. If she were as out and proud as Leo and Holly, Derek would never even think of asking her out.

She sighed, took another carnation, and picked up her knife to trim the end.

A knock on the glass nearly gave her a heart attack.

The sharp edge of the knife grazed her finger. Pain flared up her hand and made her drop the knife. "Ouch! Dammit!" Clutching her finger, she looked up to see who had knocked on the door so late.

Sasha stood on the other side of the glass, an embarrassed grin on her face and two small bakery boxes in her hand. She waved and mouthed, "Sorry."

She looked so much like a little kid who had accidentally smashed a window with a baseball that Ash had to smile despite the burning pain in her finger. She curled her left hand into a fist to stop the bleeding, crossed the room, and unlocked the door.

"Sorry," was the first thing Sasha said as she stepped inside. "I didn't mean to startle you."

"It's okay. I was—"

"Shit, you're bleeding. Did you cut yourself?"

Ash hid her hand behind her back. "It's just a little nick. I get them almost every day. It comes with the job."

Sasha strode closer with the determination of a superhero on a rescue mission. She set the bakery boxes on the counter and stepped close. Concern darkened her chocolate-colored eyes. "Let me see."

Slowly, Ash pulled her hand out from behind her back and held it out to her.

They stood close together, gazing down at the injured hand.

Blood was trickling out of a cut on her index finger.

Sasha sucked in a sharp breath as if she were looking at a deadly wound.

Ash had to smile. "It's not so bad. Won't even require stitches."

"Are you sure?"

"One hundred percent. Trust me. I've had my fingers stitched up twice. I would know if this were lucky number three." Ash went to the sink in the back room to run her finger beneath ice-cold water that would clean the wound and help to stop the bleeding. She felt more than heard Sasha follow her. Sasha's presence always seemed to fill every room she entered.

"Where's your first aid kit?" Sasha asked.

"First aid kit? All I need is a Band-Aid." With her unharmed right hand, Ash pulled open the drawer where she kept Band-Aids of all sizes. She fumbled with the paper wrapper that proved difficult to remove with just one hand.

"Let me." Sasha carefully dried off the injured finger with a clean tissue, then took the Band-Aid from her and removed the wrapper. She curved her hand around Ash's, positioning it the way she needed it.

Ash held very, very still. Not so much because putting on the Band-Aid hurt but because the gentleness in Sasha's strong hands made her breath catch. The way Sasha's fingers moved over her skin seemed to put her in some kind of trance.

"You okay?" Sasha asked, her voice so soft it was almost a whisper. "You're not going to pass out from what you insist is just a nick, are you?"

Ash shook her head. If she passed out, it wouldn't be from this little cut.

Sasha smoothed the edges of the Band-Aid down, careful not to apply pressure on the wound. "There. Good as..." She looked up, and their gazes met.

Warmth flooded Ash that had nothing to do with her harmless little injury. She had a feeling she was flushed from head to toe.

"Um, new." The look on Sasha's face made Ash almost think—or maybe wish—she would lift her hand to her lips and kiss it all better. But, of course, she didn't. Sasha stepped back, finally awakening Ash from her trance.

Under the pretense of throwing away the wrapper, Ash turned away because she needed a moment to get herself together. *What the heck was that?* Sasha was becoming a friend, and that was all it could ever be. Her short-lived relationship with Holly had nearly destroyed the tentative friendship they had built after Holly's return from college. She wouldn't allow her goddamn libido to do that a second time.

Sasha walked away, toward the front of the shop, as if she needed to put some distance between them too.

But that was probably just wishful thinking.

"I brought you some cake," Sasha called. "I thought since you're working late, you might need a snack."

God, good-looking *and* considerate. Sasha Peterson might just be the kryptonite of closeted lesbians.

"Where's Casper?" Sasha asked. "I brought something for him too."

"He's having a sleepover at my parents'." They had offered to take Casper so he wouldn't be home alone all evening while she hung out with her friends at the bar, and Ash hadn't wanted to tell them she wasn't going.

"Well, then he can have his Pupcake later. But you can have your snack now."

When Ash joined her in the front of the shop, Sasha slid one of the bakery boxes over and opened the lid.

Ash stared at the huge piece of cake, covered by a dark chocolate glaze. Her mouth watered, and her stomach rumbled, reminding her that she had forgotten to eat dinner. "Wow. That looks positively decadent. I'll need to start working out if we keep spending time together."

"Do you want to?"

"Eat the cake?" Ash chuckled. "As if I could resist." At least not the cake. She could resist the baker just fine…right?

"No. I meant, continue to spend time with me."

Was Sasha asking her to be friends? Or was there something more behind the question? To buy herself some time, Ash rummaged through another drawer and dug out a plastic fork that had been left over from ordering taco salad last week. When she turned back around, Sasha stood looking at her, waiting for her answer.

She really shouldn't hang out with Sasha too often; Ash knew that. Betty Mullen from the hair salon had already told her parents that she'd been spending a lot of time with Sasha when it wasn't even that much. If they began to hang out more often, rumors might start.

Stupid rumors that wouldn't be true, but still.

She opened her mouth to tell Sasha that she didn't have time to hang out very often, but what came out instead was "I'd really like that."

The smile spreading over Sasha's face stopped her self-reprimanding instantly. "Great."

"Just as friends, of course," Ash added quickly.

"Of course." Sasha nudged her gently. "Jeez, someone thinks very highly of herself. What makes you think I'd want to date you?"

A flush rose up her neck so fast that Ash was sure Sasha could follow its path. "I…I didn't think that. Of course I didn't. I mean, you… I…"

"Relax." A smile crinkled the edges of Sasha's eyes. "I'm just teasing. Well, I'm not teasing about not wanting to date—you or anyone else. I'm not looking for a relationship right now."

"Me neither."

"Then we're on the same page. Friends." Sasha stuck out her hand as if to seal the deal.

Ash took her hand and felt Sasha's long fingers cradle her palm. "Friends," she repeated and ignored the tingle going through her body.

They held on a couple of seconds too long for a simple handshake.

Finally, Ash pulled away and picked up the plastic fork to try the cake, trading in one temptation for the other, safer one. The dark, bittersweet chocolate melted on her tongue and blended with the tartness of the orange cheesecake. "Oh my God," she mumbled even as she took a second bite. "Why have I never had this before?"

Sasha chuckled. "Because you always order the same thing. Every now and then, you should really take a risk on something new."

Ash looked up from the bakery box. Were they still talking about cake?

Sasha held her gaze but didn't say anything else, so Ash continued to eat.

"How's your finger?" Sasha asked once the last crumb of cake was gone.

"Much better already." Ash smiled and licked the last bit of chocolate off the plastic fork. "Must be the cake."

Sasha cleared her throat. "Yeah, never underestimate the power of cake." She leaned one hip against the counter and hooked her thumb into the front pocket of her faded jeans that clung to her strong thighs.

God, why did she have to be so damn sexy? Ash tossed the used fork away with more force than necessary.

"So, why are you working so late on a Saturday evening?" Sasha pointed at the nearly finished wreath. "Last-minute order?"

"Um, yeah." With anyone else, Ash would have left it at that. She was so used to telling only selective parts of the truth that it would have been easy to do. But to her surprise, she didn't want to do that with Sasha. "But truth be told, I didn't really have to do it tonight."

"Oh." Sasha's face was so expressive she couldn't hide her dismay. "Then why did you tell Zack you couldn't make it to Johnny's?"

"Derek," Ash said as if that would explain everything. But then again, she didn't even know if he had actually shown up, so Sasha might have no clue what she was talking about. "My mom invited him to join us at the bar."

"Yeah, he was there."

Well, at least she hadn't missed the get-together with the gang for nothing. "Did he ask about me?"

"Did you want him to ask about you?" Sasha asked.

"God, no! That's why I didn't go to Johnny's tonight. My mom thinks he might be interested in asking me out, and I wanted to avoid that awkward moment when I have to tell him no without being able to offer an explanation."

Sasha gave her that quiet look that always made Ash wish she had the same inner peace. "Since when do you need an explanation? A simple no should be enough."

Ash swiped a couple of trimmed stems into the garbage can with her arm. "I guess."

"He isn't just in town to visit his folks, you know?" Sasha said. "He's here to stay."

Ash sighed. "I know."

"Sooner or later, you'll have to face him. Or are you planning to avoid the bar—and your friends, not to mention the bank—for the rest of your life?"

"No, of course not." Ash knew she had to stop running from her problems, at least a little. She held Sasha's gaze. "I'll be there next week."

"Good." Sasha brushed her shoulder with a fleeting touch that Ash felt all the way down to her toes. "If he doesn't accept a simple no, you know you have backup."

The protectiveness she radiated warmed Ash. "Thanks."

Sasha nodded at her. "No need to thank me. You've got friends in this town who'll have your back—if you let them."

Ash didn't know what to say to that. It happened often when she was around Sasha.

"So," Sasha said after a while, "was your little workout earlier enough to burn off the calories from the cake, or—"

"Workout? What workout?" Ash looked around the shop. What could she possibly m—? Oh shit. She remembered what she had done just before Sasha had knocked. Heat shot up her neck. She covered her overly warm face with her hands and peeked through her fingers. "Please tell me you didn't see that!"

Sasha sported a big grin. "I saw." She pulled Ash's hands down but was careful not to squeeze her injured finger. "Hey, come on. It was cute and—"

"Cute and what? Embarrassing?" Was it just her imagination, or was it now Sasha's turn to blush?

"No. Cute and, um, impressive. I mean, it looked and sounded like you belong on a stage, not in a flower shop."

Ash waved dismissively. "God, no. Leo is the musical genius in our group, not me. I was always just mediocre, and now I'm totally out of practice. These days, I only sing in the shower."

Sasha studied her with one of her intense gazes. "Why did you give it up?"

"Showering?" Ash laughed, but even to her own ears, her joke sounded lame. "I didn't."

"You know what I mean. I haven't seen you at the keyboard since you graduated. Why did you give up music?"

"You know how it is when you're no longer in school," Ash said as lightly as possible. "I didn't have time to keep up with it."

Sasha crossed her arms over her chest. "That's your favorite excuse, isn't it?"

Ash's gaze snapped up to her face. Anger stirred in her belly. "Excuse me?"

"You heard me." Sasha didn't back down from Ash's glare. "It's the same excuse you give your mother when she asks why you aren't dating."

"It's not an excuse. Well, maybe it is about dating, but not when it comes to music. All those gigs and band practices take up a lot of time. Just ask Leo."

"I'm not talking about aiming for perfection so you can make a career of it. I'm talking about playing every now and then, just for fun."

Ash kicked at a stem that had dropped to the floor. "It stopped being fun when Leo left. Without her..." How could she explain that playing the keyboard and not hearing the notes mingle with the sound of Leo's guitar had been just too painful? She couldn't tell her that.

When Ash didn't finish her sentence, Sasha reached out and gently nudged her chin up with the touch of one finger, making Ash look her in the eyes. She regarded her for a while as if searching for answers on her face. Then her mouth dropped open. "Holy...! Why didn't I realize before? Leo and you...?"

"Sssh!" Ash's gaze darted to the display windows, but, of course, there was no one outside.

"So it's true?" Sasha pressed one hand to her mouth and blew air through her fingers. "What Derek said earlier wasn't complete bullshit after all?"

Ash's stomach spiraled out of control. She clutched both hands to her belly. "What did he say?"

"Nothing that bears repeating. Just some stupid nonsense about why you wouldn't date him. Forget it." Sasha shook her head back and forth as if that would help the thought sink in. "Wow. I can honestly say that I didn't see that coming."

"Neither did I," Ash muttered.

Sasha cocked her head. "What do you mean?"

Shit. She should have kept her mouth shut, as she had for the past fifteen years. So far, she had never told anyone about what had happened on prom night, not even Holly when they had been together. Chewing on her bottom lip, she hesitated.

"If you'd rather not talk about it, that's okay. I'll try to forget I ever found out. But, frankly, it'll be hard because... Jesus! You and Leo? Wow, wow, wow. Now I get why she seemed to avoid you for a while. Ugly breakup?"

"No, nothing like that. We were never a couple."

"But I thought you said...?"

Ash hesitated again. But she had already started to talk about it, so she might as well tell Sasha everything. She realized that she trusted her to keep quiet about it. "Leo and I...we got a little buzzed on prom night."

Sasha shrugged. "Like the rest of the seniors. It's a yearly tradition."

"Yeah, but I did it to talk myself into finally sleeping with Brandon."

"Did you?" Sasha lifted both hands. "Sorry. You don't have to answer that. That's way too personal."

A sigh escaped Ash. She picked up a carnation and inserted it into the wreath. She could finish it while they talked. At least that way, she didn't have to look Sasha in the eyes. "It's okay. I didn't sleep with him. Because it turned out the only reason Leo was drinking was to work up the courage to kiss me—and when she did, all thoughts of Brandon went out the window."

"Must have been quite the kiss." A hint of amusement entered Sasha's tone. "You're blushing, even fifteen years later."

Was she? Ash touched her cheek with the back of her hand. Yeah, she was definitely flushed. "It was. I mean, in hindsight, it was clumsy and awkward because I'm pretty sure I was the first girl—the first person—she'd ever kissed, but... God, her lips were so soft and—"

"Okay, okay. TMI. Holly is like a sister to me, so that makes Leo my sister-in-law. I don't need those images about her in my head."

Neither did she. Ash slid in another carnation between bits of greenery.

"What happened then?" Sasha asked.

"Nothing."

"Nothing?" Sasha's tone was skeptical.

Ash nodded firmly. "Not a thing. I, um, I ran. I just... I couldn't deal with it. I didn't sleep a wink that night, and when Leo searched me out the next day..."

"More kisses?" Sasha asked, a twinkle in her eyes.

"No. I told her I was straight, and when she asked why I had kissed her back, I blamed it on the alcohol. Told her the kiss didn't mean a thing to me. She left for New York the next day."

"Ouch," Sasha mumbled.

"I know, I know. I wanted to make it right so many times, but what was I supposed to do? By the time I could get up the courage to talk to her, she was a superstar, and I would have come across like one of her little groupies."

"But you've talked to her now, since she came back, right?"

Ash inserted a ribbon on a wooden pick into the wreath and slid her fingers over the silky material. "Yes, I did." She drew the line at telling Sasha she had been stupid enough to ask Leo out. She had already embarrassed herself enough for one night.

"So all is well between the two of you now?" Sasha asked.

Ash hesitated. Was it? Leo had agreed to move on and let go of any bitterness, but maybe she had made that promise more for Holly's sake than because she really meant it. "I don't know. I think so. I mean, I just received an invitation to their wedding, and they hired me to do their flowers, so I assume—"

"You *assume*? Don't you think you should know? You should talk to her, Ash."

It was the first time Sasha had ever called her anything other than Ashley, and it distracted her enough for her not to get defensive. "I know. I will. At some point."

Sasha regarded her for a second longer. "Okay."

A breath escaped Ash when Sasha didn't pressure her further but just accepted her answer.

"So, are you done?"

"With Leo? Absolutely." Yes, she had tried to ask her out, but truth be told, she didn't know what she would have done if Leo had said yes. She wasn't ready to come out, even if she had thought so for one crazy moment. "Besides, she's marrying Holly, in case you've forgotten."

Sasha smiled. "I didn't mean with Leo. I was talking about the wreath."

"Oh." She tugged on the ribbon to turn it a little to the side. "Um, yes, I'm done."

"Then let's get out of here. It's getting late."

"I have to put the wreath in the cooler and clean up first," Ash said.

Sasha's gaze swept the shop as if assessing what had to be done. "You put the wreath away and do whatever else you have to do, and I'll clean up."

"You don't have to do that."

"I know." Sasha straightened from where she had leaned against the counter. "Come on. Point me in the direction of a broom so we can get out of here."

Ash gave up her resistance and handed her the broom. "Thank you."

They worked together as if they had been a team for years. While Ash put the wreath in the cooler and changed the water in the buckets of the remaining flowers, Sasha swept the shop, wiped down the worktable and the counter, and even disinfected the knife and the other tools.

"If you are ever sick of getting up at four a.m., let me know," Ash said, meaning it. "I'd hire you on the spot."

"Nah." Sasha grinned and wiggled her fingers. "Your tools of trade seem even more dangerous than mine, and I'm too fond of keeping my fingers in full working order."

No, no, no. Don't think about it. Think about...world hunger, taxes, stepping into a pile of dog poop. But, of course, images of what those capable fingers might be able to do flashed through her mind anyway. She forced her gaze away from Sasha's hands.

Sasha put the broom back where it belonged. "Ready?"

"Oh yeah. Um, I mean, yes. All done." Ash took her keys and the garbage so she could toss the latter into the dumpster on her way out.

Once again, Sasha's hand came to rest on the small of Ash's back as they walked to the door.

It was starting to become a familiar feeling, but that didn't stop the tingle of excitement that rushed through her any time Sasha touched her like this.

While Ash locked the door and took the garbage to the dumpster, Sasha waited next to her and then walked her to her SUV, which was parked a few steps away.

When Ash pressed the fob, the taillights flashed, illuminating Sasha's tall, broad shape for a moment. She looked like a bodyguard hovering next to the person she had promised to protect.

Ash opened the driver's side door, but instead of getting in, she faced Sasha. "Want me to drop you off in front of your apartment?"

"Nah." Sasha waved her hand. "It's just a few steps. Walking will do me good. Oh, speaking of… That's what I was about to ask you earlier, before you dropped that Leo bomb on me. Want to get together tomorrow? You, me, Casper, and maybe Snickerdoodle and a nice, long walk in the park. Oh, wait, Casper will still be at his grandparents', won't he?"

Ash hesitated. She should have just confirmed that Casper wouldn't be there and instead offered to meet next weekend to space out their get-togethers. Hopefully, that would stop people from talking about how much time they were spending together. But the thought of walking side by side with Sasha, seeing her interact with her aunt's tiny dog, and maybe even making her laugh a time or two was just too tempting. She had already missed spending time with her friends tonight, and she didn't want to miss out on what promised to be a nice Sunday morning too. "Actually, my parents will drop him off on their way to church tomorrow morning. A long walk might be a good idea. He needs to work off some calories if you keep supplying him with barkery treats."

A smile made Sasha's teeth gleam in the dim light of a streetlamp. "Great. Nine o'clock at the bridge?"

"Can we make it nine thirty? My parents will drop Casper off around nine."

"Sure," Sasha said. "Nine thirty is perfect."

Ash shifted her weight. Her gaze went back and forth between the SUV and Sasha. *Come on. Get in. It's late.* But she stood rooted to the spot.

Sasha was the first to move. She stepped closer and leaned down.

Ash's pulse hammered in her ears. Her breath caught. Was she…?

Then Sasha's long arms went around her in a hug.

A hug. Just a hug. Of course. Not that she had expected or wanted anything else. Nope, not for a second. Her eyes fluttered shut. God, the heat Sasha emanated was incredible—and so was the way her taller body felt against Ash's. She had daydreamed about what a hug from Sasha might feel like, but this was even better than anything her imagination had come up with.

Sasha gave a soft squeeze and released her.

Quickly, Ash opened her eyes and put on a nonchalant expression, as if she hugged good-looking queer women several times a day.

"Night," Sasha said. "Drive carefully."

"Will do. See you tomorrow." Ash slid behind the wheel and closed the door between them. Safely behind that barrier, she blew out a breath. That Sunday morning walk with Sasha had sounded like such a nice idea a few minutes ago, but now she was no longer sure.

Maybe she should call her tomorrow and tell her something had come up.

But Sasha would see right through that; she had called her on her excuses earlier already. Nope. There was no way out—and Ash wasn't sure she wanted one. That was even scarier.

She started the engine. Without allowing herself to glance over her shoulder to see if Sasha was still there, she sped down the street a little too fast.

Chapter 9

SASHA WAS EARLY. WAY EARLY. Even though she had to adjust her long stride to Snickerdoodle's tiny steps, it wasn't even a quarter past nine o'clock on Sunday morning when she approached the park.

She had gotten bored at home, and there was only so much scrolling through Instagram for cake inspiration she could do.

Yeah right. You're bored when you have at least a dozen unread books on your nightstand, half a season of Killing Eve *to watch, and decorations for Easter cupcakes to think about.*

Okay, she admitted to herself, maybe she'd been a little excited for her Sunday morning walk with Ashley and had left home too early because she was eager to meet up with her. Nothing wrong with looking forward to seeing a friend, right?

Sasha chuckled to herself. Especially when the friend in question was easy on the eyes and surprisingly pleasant company.

When she rounded the bend in the path and the bridge came into view, Sasha caught sight of the lone figure leaning against the railing of the bridge.

Ashley. Sasha didn't have to see her face to recognize her immediately. The dog sitting at her feet was a dead giveaway too.

Had Ashley been just as eager to see her, so she had rushed off as soon as her parents had dropped off the dog?

Ashley stood with her back toward Sasha, her elbows on the railing and her head tilted back, letting the rays of the morning sun warm her face. For once, her long hair wasn't pulled back into a ponytail. The wind blew through it, giving Ashley a carefree look. Sasha knew that it would lighten to the color of wheat come summer, but now it gleamed like a jar of the finest wildflower honey.

Like honey? Please! That was cheesier than Leo's love songs. She really had to get over that leftover crush from her high school days.

Her gaze was drawn back to Ashley's hair, though. Would it be as soft and silky as it looked if she buried her fingers in it and drew her closer to—?

Snap out of it! She shoved her hands into her jacket pockets. She wasn't looking to start anything with anyone, least of all a closeted woman—even if that closeted woman looked damn cute in pink tennis shoes and a tight pair of jeans that hugged her long legs and curvy hips.

Casper had spotted them now. He let out a bark and tried to pull Ashley toward them.

Ashley straightened and turned. A smile spread over her face, and for once, Sasha had the feeling it wasn't her automatic girl-next-door-who-is-friendly-to-everyone smile but a genuine one.

"Good morning." Sasha stepped onto the bridge and walked toward her.

"Morning," Ashley answered.

Snickerdoodle and Casper strained toward each other with excited yips.

Knowing how fragile the Frenchie's neck and spine were, Sasha loosened her grip on the leash.

The dogs greeted each other with tail-wagging, butt-sniffing, and muzzle-licking.

Sasha wished it was that easy for her and Ashley too. An image of her licking Ashley's face and sniffing her butt flashed through her mind. She bit back a smile and paused in front of Ash, not sure how to greet her. Should she hug her? The memory of how Ashley had melted into her last night—like delicious chocolate glaze—was still imprinted on her body.

But now Ashley's body language practically screamed her hesitance. She looked as if she would rather be staked to a fire ant hill, naked and covered in honey, than accept a hug in public.

The words *naked* and *covered in honey* started an NC-17-rated slideshow of images in Sasha's head. The whiff of Opium, Ashley's signature perfume, trailing on the wind didn't help with that either.

Maybe it was a good thing that the dogs performing their greeting ritual created some kind of barrier between them.

Ashley shuffled closer and lightly grazed Sasha's forearm with her fingertips. "Hey, you're early."

"You are too." Sasha bent to greet Casper, who rolled onto his back to get his belly scratched, while Ashley knelt to pet Snickerdoodle.

Since the dogs acted like long-lost siblings who couldn't stand to be apart, Sasha and Ashley ended up with their faces just a hand's width apart.

Ashley got up quickly. "Um, shall we?" She gestured toward the path that led along the creek.

Sasha nodded and followed her across the bridge. Okay, she definitely had to get a grip on this attraction. Even if Ashley hadn't been so clearly ambivalent, getting involved with her was a bad idea. At the first hint of trouble, she would do what Sasha's mother had done: run for the hills. Being left behind once was enough.

"I think this is the spot, by the way." Ashley pointed at a large, flat rock along the edge of the creek.

"Spot? What spot?" Had she missed something Ashley had said?

"Leo and Holly's spot," Ashley said. "Where they want to have the ceremony."

Sasha caught up with her so they could talk. "Oh, that spot. How do you know?"

A blush dusted Ashley's cheeks. "Um, I saw them here more than once."

What had they been doing to make Ashley blush like that? Sitting at the creek with their feet in the water, kissing? "Is it weird for you?" Sasha asked. "Seeing them together?"

"It used to be, but I think I'm over it. They fit so well together. Much better than I ever did with either of them." A hint of sadness vibrated in Ashley's tone. "Anyway, they could set up folding chairs here and here, forming an aisle that leads toward this rock, where they could exchange vows." She described the shape of the aisle with her hands, painting a vivid picture. "Maybe they could make it a sunset ceremony. The rays of the setting sun would bathe the creek in colors, making it look like bronze. Wouldn't that be nice?"

Sasha couldn't help smiling. Who knew? Ashley Gaines was a romantic.

"What?" Ashley asked. "Why are you smiling like that?"

"Can't I just be enjoying a peaceful Sunday morning stroll with a—" Sasha stopped herself before she could say *beautiful woman*.

Ashley sent her a questioning gaze. "With a what?"

"With a friend at my side."

That didn't get her the blush she knew her intended sentence would have evoked, but the shy smile curling Ashley's lips was even better.

Sasha wasn't sure how long they stood at Holly and Leo's special spot and smiled at each other.

Rapid steps crunching over the gravel path interrupted their eye contact.

When Sasha turned, Holly and Leo were jogging toward them, keeping perfect pace with each other despite Leo's longer legs.

"Good morning." Holly paused in front of them. "You're not stealing our spot, are you?"

Now Ashley did blush. "What? No, no, we were just..."

Holly chuckled. "I'm just kidding, Ash." She gave Ashley a quick hug and then nudged Leo to do the same while she embraced Sasha.

Over Holly's head, Sasha watched Leo and Ashley hug. After what she had found out about the kiss they had shared on prom night, Sasha saw their interaction in a new light. They made a striking couple, but she couldn't see them in a relationship with each other, and neither could she see Ashley with Holly.

Once everyone had exchanged hugs and the dogs had gotten their share of attention, Holly gestured toward the creek. "So, what are you really doing here? You're not working on a beautiful Sunday morning, are you?"

Working? How could what they were doing look like work? "Um, what do you mean?" Sasha asked.

Holly wrapped one arm around Leo and pulled her close so they were touching from hip to shoulder.

Ashley watched them with a stony expression. Emotion darted through her eyes like clouds across the sky on a windy day. Not jealousy exactly, but Sasha could sense that she was mentally chewing on something.

Wow. When had she gotten so good at reading Ashley?

"Are you checking out the place for our ceremony to plan the flower decorations and other wedding stuff?" Holly asked.

Neither of them had even mentioned flowers, but Sasha wasn't sure if Ashley wanted their friends to know that they had started to hang out together without the rest of the gang present. She bit her lip and waited for Ashley to answer.

"Um, that too," Ashley finally said.

God, she was incredibly good at not telling the truth without lying outright. It was a talent that Sasha never wanted to develop. Being denied like that left a bitter taste in her mouth, so she could only imagine how Holly must have felt when she and Ashley had been in a secret relationship.

The leather of Casper's leash creaked as if Ashley was gripping it too tightly and then she added, "But mainly, I'm just enjoying a peaceful Sunday morning stroll with a friend."

The bitter taste disappeared from Sasha's mouth as if it had never existed. She had a feeling she was grinning way out of proportion for such a simple statement. But she knew it had been anything but simple—or easy—for Ashley.

"Well, then..." Holly and Leo exchanged a gaze, clearly both not sure what to say to that.

"We'd better continue before we cool down too much," Leo finally said.

"Are you going to be in the bakery later, Sasha?" Holly asked. "We might drop by if we need a little break from our mothers obsessing over party favors, hors d'oeuvres, and wedding dresses."

"Yeah, sure, come by any time you need a wedding-free zone. We'll be there."

Holly gave her a strange look. With a wave and a "see you later," the two disappeared around a bend in the path.

"Did I say something wrong?" Sasha wondered out loud.

"You said *we*," Ashley murmured.

Sasha ran what she had said through her mind again. "Oh. I didn't mean to say that or to make any assumptions. I just thought maybe you might want to come to the bakery with me and replenish some of the calories we burned."

"All twenty of them?" A teasing twinkle entered Ashley's nougat-colored eyes.

Now that it was just the two of them again, she seemed a lot more relaxed.

Sasha laughed. "Yeah. So? Want to join me?"

"What about Casper?" Ashley pointed at the dog, who was sniffing at a tuft of grass. "He can't come into the bakery."

"He can hang out with Snickerdoodle at my aunt's until you're ready to leave for your parents'."

Ashley looked back and forth between Sasha and the dog. A wrinkle formed on her brow. "Are you sure Mae won't mind? Casper isn't exactly tiny, like Snickerdoodle."

"Mind?" Sasha laughed. "You might have to fight her to get him back."

"Okay, then let's go. But just so you know: If my mother complains about me not having much of an appetite at lunch, I'm sending her to you."

Would she really, Sasha wondered as they set off toward A Slice of Heaven. Would she tell her parents where she had spent the morning, or would she carefully avoid mentioning Sasha's name during lunch?

Sasha had a feeling it might be the latter. But maybe, just maybe, Ashley would surprise her, the way she had when she had told Holly and Leo she was here to enjoy a stroll with a friend.

They hadn't even made it five steps down the path when another person out for a Sunday morning walk approached them.

Ash instantly recognized Regina Beasley, one of her regulars, who was walking her yappy Chihuahua.

The older woman looked as if she was ready for church, dressed in a black wool coat and a black below-the-knee skirt. Dressing in black was probably a side effect of being married to the man who owned the local funeral parlor. Or maybe it was an indication of Mrs. Beasley's mood. The corners of her mouth pointed downward as if she had just bitten into something sour.

Casper bounded toward the Chihuahua, tail wagging, but the tiny dog barked at him so fiercely that the pink bow nearly slipped out of her fur, so Casper backed off.

Snickerdoodle plopped down on a tuft of grass and ignored the yapping.

"Did you hear about them?" Mrs. Beasley said, not even bothering with a good morning. She pointed down the path.

"Um, who?" Ash asked.

"Leontyne Blake and Holly Drummond. They are getting married."

Ash nodded carefully. "I heard."

"Well, by now, probably everyone's heard." Mrs. Beasley tsked. "I really don't know why they find it necessary to rub people's noses in their lifestyle. Don't get me wrong. I have nothing against homosexuals."

Ash bit the inside of her cheek to keep quiet. She couldn't afford to annoy the wife of one of her most important customers.

"No, of course not." Sasha's tone was dripping with sarcasm.

Ash couldn't help admiring her for fearlessly standing up to Mrs. Beasley in a way that she couldn't. At the same time, she prayed that she would let it go. She fought the urge to grip Sasha's arm and drag her away from this fruitless discussion. Nothing good would come out of arguing with Mrs. Beasley.

Mrs. Beasley gave Sasha an icy stare. "I'm not. One of my nephews is… like that, and I helped pay his college tuition. I just never understood why they have to flaunt their personal business like that."

"Flaunt it?" Sasha echoed. "If getting married is considered flaunting your lifestyle, why did you get married?"

"That's hardly the same! It's not like they could have children and start a family."

"They could, if they wanted," Sasha answered calmly. "But you probably think that's wrong too."

"And you don't?" Mrs. Beasley looked honestly baffled. Her gaze went from Sasha to Ash. "Don't tell me you're part of this wedding."

Ash gathered her courage and struggled to look her in the eyes, bolstered by Sasha's solid presence next to her. "It's our job, Mrs. Beasley. We can't just turn them away."

"So you are doing their flowers? Are you sure that's a good idea, dear?" Mrs. Beasley gave her a look of fake motherly concern. "Aren't you afraid it will harm your business?"

Ash sputtered. "Why would it harm my business? I'll be able to say I did the flowers for Jenna Blake's wedding. That will bring me a lot of business from out of town, from people who want to be able to say they used the same florist as the famous pop star."

"Be that as it may, but after that dies down, you'll once again be dependent on local customers, and I can't imagine anyone in Fair Oaks liking that kind of thing. I'm sure they would rather get their flowers from someone who supports traditional values."

Ash's mouth went dry. Was Mrs. Beasley threatening her? She definitely had the power to do that since she was incredibly well-connected. Not only did her husband own the only funeral parlor in town, but she was also the head of the Fair Oaks improvement committee and hosted a Bible study group and a quilting club. Nothing happened at the Fair Oaks community center without Mrs. Beasley knowing about it. If she got her husband and her friends to boycott her flower shop, Ash would be in trouble.

"Oh, the two of us are the biggest supporters of traditional values you can imagine," Sasha said before Ash could get her vocal cords to work.

Ash hoped she would leave it at that, but she knew her well enough by now to suspect she wouldn't.

A pleased smile spread across Mrs. Beasley's face.

"I mean, two people in love wanting to spend the rest of their lives together..." Sasha added. "You can't get much more traditional than that, right?"

Mrs. Beasley's smile disappeared as fast as chalk being wiped off a blackboard. "I guess I can't blame you for thinking like that, having been raised without a mother and all. It's not your fault no one instilled family values in you."

Sasha staggered back a step as if Mrs. Beasley had hit her with the huge purse slung over her shoulder.

Ash's mouth dropped open. Wow, what a low blow. She couldn't believe Mrs. Beasley had just said that. She raised her arm to wrap it around Sasha, but under Mrs. Beasley's observant gaze, she pulled back at the last moment.

Sasha straightened to her full six-foot-plus height and stared down at the older woman. "I can assure you my father and my aunt instilled plenty of values in me—including not being mean to people or talking about them behind their backs."

Mrs. Beasley's mouth moved, but nothing came out. She looked like a fish that had been pulled out of the water. It would have been comical if the situation hadn't been so tense. "I can't believe I thought so highly of you. Come on, Princess." She tugged on the leash, pulled the Chihuahua past them, and marched down the path.

Oh shit. Ash stared after her. That was bad. Really, really bad.

Casper whined, pressed against her leg, and tried to lick her hand.

She buried her fingers in his fur and then turned toward Sasha, who was watching Mrs. Beasley storm off too. "Are you okay?"

"Yeah. I don't let mean biddies like her get to me. Well, not much." Sasha's eyes narrowed, and she took a step toward her. "But are you okay? You're shaking like a leaf."

Ash wrapped her arms around herself and tried to get her emotions under control, but another tremor ran through her limbs.

"Hey." Sasha pressed against her side and wrapped one arm around her.

Her warmth seeped into Ash, and she leaned in to her without much thought.

"Don't let her spoil our morning, okay?" Sasha wrapped her other arm around her too. Her breath stirred the hair at the top of Ash's head, making her shiver in a different way.

Ash sighed. "Easier said than done. The funeral parlor is one of my most important customers. If she convinces her husband to use another flower shop from now on..." She looked up into Sasha's eyes from only inches away. "She could do serious harm to my shop. To the bakery too."

"Don't worry. We'll be fine." Sasha's hands were on her hips and squeezed gently. "Most of the town will still buy our flowers and baked goods, no matter what Mrs. Beasley says."

Despite the pleasant feelings coursing through her, Ash couldn't let go of her despair. "How do you know? Unlike Mrs. Beasley, most people keep their prejudices to themselves, which makes it hard to know how many think exactly like her. How many of the people we have known since we were children would reject us if they knew we're not straight?"

"Well, you'll never know unless you come out."

"I don't *want* to find out." Another tremor went through Ash.

Sasha held her more tightly. "This isn't just about your shop, is it? What are you so afraid of?"

Ash rested her forehead against Sasha's strong shoulder for a moment. She wanted to stay in that embrace for the rest of the day, but she forced herself to pull away. It wouldn't be too long before someone else came around the bend in the path. "I don't want to talk about it right now. Can we just go and get some cake?"

Sasha slid both hands into her coat pockets as if they suddenly felt empty and led the way toward the bakery. "Cake it is. But you know that you can talk to me any time, don't you?"

Ash couldn't imagine ever wanting to talk about her fear of coming out but nodded anyway. If she ever talked to someone, it would probably be Sasha. The realization made Ash's step falter. Wow. After a lifetime of living in the same town and barely talking, how had that suddenly happened?

"Come on, slowpoke." Sasha had lengthened her stride and was now several steps ahead of her. "First one to the bakery gets the last piece of orange cheesecake with dark chocolate glaze."

Ash set off at a run, and Casper immediately caught up with her, enjoying this new game.

"Hey, not fair!" Sasha called when they ran past. "Snickerdoodle is a Frenchie, not a racehorse!"

"All is fair in—" Ash cut herself off. "Um, in the fight for cake."

"Yeah? Then watch this!" Sasha sped past her with Snickerdoodle securely cradled to her chest.

Barking twice, Casper gave chase and pulled Ash after them.

Ash broke into an all-out sprint, but she knew no matter how fast she sprinted, she wouldn't be able to outrun her fears.

After running into Mrs. Beasley, Ash had thought her day couldn't get any worse. That theory was proven wrong when her mother chased her pulled pork around on her plate without really eating.

Finally, she put her fork down and looked over at Ash, who swallowed hard, sensing that something unpleasant was coming. "We were talking to Sheryl and her son after church this morning."

Ash made a noncommittal sound and gripped her fork more tightly.

"He mentioned how disappointed he was not to see you at Johnny's last night."

Ash's stomach seemed to shrivel into the size of the corn on her plate. "Um, yeah. Something came up. Last-minute order for Mr. Miller's funeral. You know how it is."

Now it was her mother who let out a noncommittal "Hmm."

"By the time I was done with the wreath, I was just too tired to go over to the bar," Ash added.

"He also mentioned that your friends Leontyne and Holly are getting married—to each other."

Oh shit. Ash pretended to chew a piece of pulled pork to buy herself some time. "Um, yeah."

"Did you know?" Her mother waved away her answer before Ash could even open her mouth. "Of course you knew. They are your best friends."

"They *were* my best friends," Ash said quietly. "We haven't been close in years."

"I remember. You never told me what happened. Is it because they are…gay?"

"No, Mom." Ash shoveled a forkful of corn casserole into her mouth, even though the food suddenly tasted like sawdust. "I guess I got busy trying to establish the flower shop, so I stopped hanging out with Holly. And Leo… That was a long time ago. I barely remember what made us stop talking. Just some crazy teen stuff, I suppose."

"I just hope you won't do anything crazy now," her mother said.

Ash stared at her with alarm. "Um, like what?"

"Like becoming too involved."

"I-involved?" Ash's fork clattered onto her plate.

Her mother nodded. "With the wedding. People talk, you know? I don't want you to be associated with that."

Part of Ash's tension lessened. Her mother was just talking about her involvement in the wedding planning, not about her involvement with Holly or Leo—or Sasha. She picked up her fork. "I can't turn away customers who want me to do the flowers for their wedding." Then she let herself be inspired by Sasha's courage when facing down Mrs. Beasley and added, "Not that I'd want to. Even though we aren't as close as we used to be, they're still my friends, and I want them to have a beautiful wedding."

"That's very kind of you, honey, but…" Her mother wrinkled her nose. "Don't you think it's a little strange? Two women getting married?"

Before Ash could be forced to voice an opinion, her father cleared his throat. "Pass me the coleslaw, please."

Ash was quick to comply, glad for the distraction. "Here, Daddy."

"Thanks." He heaped coleslaw onto his plate.

"Don't you think so too?" Her mother faced him with a questioning look.

"I think this coleslaw is amazing," her father said. "Other people's... um...preferences are none of our business."

Wow. Ash stared at him. She had never heard him say even one word that indicated he was accepting of gay people. It was like being buried beneath an avalanche of rocks and then hearing the search party approach. A heavy weight seemed to be lifted from her chest, and she breathed freely for the first time in many years.

"They aren't our daughters, after all," her father added.

The ton of rocks clattered down on Ash's chest again. So other people's children were allowed to be gay, but when it was his own daughter, it stopped being okay.

"But if they were, would you be able to go along with all of it, the way Beth and Sharon are doing? There was even talk about them walking the bride down the aisle! Or brides, I guess. Good heavens, this is all so confusing." Her mother shook her head. "Could you do something like that?"

Her father shrugged between bites of coleslaw. "Lord, no. That would be just weird. But it's a moot point. Just because our Ashley is as picky as a spoiled toddler with a plate full of veggies doesn't mean she's...like that." He chuckled and continued to eat.

"No, of course not," her mother said. "I just don't want people to think so."

"Nah. She's just doing her job, creating beautiful flower arrangements. Right, honey?"

Ash just nodded because she was sure her voice would tremble and betray her. She didn't dare tell them that she had also been invited to the wedding. While her parents finished their lunch, she pushed her plate away. She had lost her appetite, and this time the piece of cake Sasha had served her earlier had nothing to do with it.

Chapter 10

BROOKE LOOKED UP FROM THE order of large hybrid tea roses she was conditioning and let out an exasperated sigh. "Want me to go over to A Slice of Heaven and get you some cupcakes?"

"No, thanks." Ash continued to scrub the metal bucket with disinfectant, putting her full body weight into the task. She hadn't been to the bakery all week, and sending Brooke instead didn't seem right.

"Oh, come on. You know you want it."

Ash gazed over at her. "Excuse me?"

Brooke put down her floral clippers. "You've had this restless energy all week, cleaning like a maniac. At the pace you're going, we'll run out of disinfectant by tomorrow."

"You know how important hygiene is in a flower shop. If there are bacteria in the water—"

"The flowers won't last. I know," Brooke said. "But you're taking hygiene to a whole new level. Why don't you just admit that you're on some crazy diet and having the worst sugar cravings ever?"

So that was what Brooke thought was going on. Ash gave a tired smile. It wasn't sugar she was craving; it was not talking to Sasha that was making her restless—and realizing that made it even worse. It told her that Sasha was already way too important to her. Maybe keeping her distance for a while was indeed a good idea, even if it didn't feel like it.

Lunch with her parents on Sunday had once again proven that staying in the closet was the right thing for her to do, and spending too much time with Sasha would make that harder.

With a sigh, Ash brushed a strand of hair that had escaped from her ponytail out of her face. She was just about to clean the next bucket when movement from beyond the display windows drew her attention.

Her heartbeat seemed to falter for a moment, then drummed in a faster rhythm.

Sasha was crossing the street, heading straight for the flower shop.

Ash dropped the brush into the bucket and reached up to redo her hair but then stopped herself. *What are you doing? You don't need to pretty up for her.*

Before Sasha could reach the front door, Barry Clemons stopped her and apparently started to chat.

Ash narrowed her eyes. What were they talking about? Was the old Casanova trying to flirt with Sasha?

Brooke's voice filtered into her consciousness as if from far away. "… Isn't she lovely?"

"Yes," Ash murmured, her gaze still on Sasha. "She certainly is." Although *lovely* wasn't the word she would choose to describe Sasha. It was too soft, too weak for a strong woman like her. *Striking* fit her much better. Ash had never before allowed herself to have a type—and maybe she truly didn't have one. The only two women she had ever kissed were nothing like Sasha, yet to her, Sasha's tall, solid body and her strong hands were as appealing as her confident, easygoing personality.

Brooke gave her a confused look. "Um, I was talking about the tea roses. You said that's what they are called, right? Isn't She Lovely?"

Oh God. Heat rushed through Ash from head to toe. "Oh. Of course. That's their name. Isn't it just perfect for them with their beautiful creamy hues? I love how the outer petals are almost white and then the colors turn a soft peach toward the middle. It's like they were created to draw the gaze into the heart of them." She knew she was babbling but couldn't help it. Hopefully, Brooke would blame it on her sugar withdrawal.

"Uh, yeah. They're nice, I guess. So, where do you want them? In the cooler or are you using them for an arrangement right away?" Brooke's gaze went to the door, and she pumped her fist. "Cupcake delivery! Awesome! Guess these go into the cooler." Without waiting for a reply, she carried the roses past Ash, who stood frozen as the front door swung open.

"Hi, Brooke. Nice flowers." Sasha stopped to sniff one of the blooms. "And they even have a fragrance."

For someone who insisted she didn't know a lily from a dandelion, she sure had an appreciation for flowers. It was one more thing that made her endearing—as if Ash needed any more reasons to like her.

Sasha walked over. When she paused in front of Ash, she shuffled her feet once, revealing the tiniest hint of insecurity. "Hi."

The moment Casper heard her voice, he rushed out from the back room, whining and jumping around her as if he hadn't seen her in years.

Yeah, buddy. I know the feeling. Ash watched them greet each other and drank in the way Sasha's face lit up and her long fingers scratched behind Casper's ears.

Finally, Sasha straightened and held out the bakery box she was carrying. "I thought if the mountain won't come to Muhammad... You haven't been in all week. You okay?"

It was tempting to just nod and say that she'd been busy spring-cleaning in preparation for Easter next month and then Mother's Day and the wedding season starting the month after. But when she looked into Sasha's warm brown eyes, she couldn't lie—not even a lie of omission.

"It's been a bit crazy." More quietly, she added, "And not just in here." She looked pointedly in Brooke's direction, knowing the teenager was listening to every word they said.

"Oh. Anything I can help with?" Sasha asked, her voice pitching lower.

"Not right now. But these will help." Ash tapped the bakery box.

"I understand." Sasha's gaze revealed that she really did. She wouldn't ask any more questions—at least not here. "Good thing I brought four different kinds." She opened the lid and pointed at each of the cupcakes in turn. "Chocolate chip with espresso buttercream frosting..."

Brooke let out an excited shriek that nearly deafened Ash.

Sasha laughed. "I thought you might like that. I also brought banana walnut with maple frosting and chocolate with salted caramel frosting."

Ash peered into the box. "No vanilla one?"

"How did I know you would ask that? Yes, there's a vanilla one with strawberry buttercream too." Sasha pointed at the fourth cupcake and then held up a paper bag. "And a Woofin."

Casper and Brooke crowded her and looked up at her with equally pleading gazes. Brooke wolfed down her treat in about three seconds, and Casper gobbled his down so fast that Ash barely had time to remove the paper liner before he could eat that too.

Sasha's gaze remained on Ash. "You don't want yours?"

"I do, but I need to wash my hands first." Ash went to the big sink in the back room and felt Sasha follow.

"You okay?" Sasha asked quietly while the water gurgled down the drain, covering her low voice. Her hand came to rest on Ash's hip for a moment, then Sasha withdrew it before Ash could say anything.

She wasn't sure she would have. That warm touch had been too comforting, and Brooke was probably busy devouring the rest of the cupcakes, so there was a good chance she wasn't watching them.

Ash started to nod, then stopped herself. "Not really. Can we talk later?"

"Sure. Tonight? I got an overnight order for two hundred cupcakes for the fiftieth anniversary of Eads Plumbing, so I'll be in the bakery. You could come over and keep me company again, if you want."

Somehow, the thought of talking in the bakery kitchen, surrounded by soothing scents and the heat from the ovens, was comforting. "I close at five thirty."

"I know," Sasha said.

Why did Sasha keep track of when the shop closed? But then again, Ash knew the bakery's hours too. *Yeah, well, pretty much everyone in town does, right?*

Ash dried her hands and turned toward Sasha.

Their gazes met and held.

"Can I have the chocolate one too?" Brooke called from the front, reminding Ash that they weren't alone.

"Yes," she answered. "But don't you dare touch the vanilla one."

"Wouldn't think of it, boss. I'm not into vanilla stuff anyway."

Sasha laughed. "You walked right into that."

"Guess I did." Ash smiled. She hadn't even taken a bite of cupcake, yet she already felt better. "Brooke is too young to appreciate that vanilla stuff can be very," she lowered her voice to an intimate drawl, "very satisfying too."

Sasha's eyes widened. She gulped audibly. "Did you just make a joke about...?"

"Cupcakes," Ash said. "I was just talking about cupcakes." She couldn't believe she had said that.

"Yeah, right."

The bell over the front door chimed, announcing the arrival of a customer.

"Guess that vanilla stuff will have to wait until later," Sasha said. "I'm talking about your cupcake, of course." She squeezed Ash's arm. "You take good care, okay?"

Ash nodded.

Then Sasha was gone, but at least Ash had a cupcake and an evening at the bakery to look forward to. So much for her plan to stay away from Sasha for a while.

Sasha squeezed the pastry bag and piped a swirl of frosting onto the last cupcake. Then she stepped back and wiped her damp brow. She'd been running the ovens nonstop since this morning, so it was warm and steamy in the kitchen. Even though she'd stripped down to her tank top beneath the apron and had propped the back door open, she was still sweating.

But at least she was almost done. She'd worked without a break, so once she finished whipping up the last twenty lemon cupcakes, the order for Eads Plumbing would be complete. Maybe she would even be done by the time Ashley arrived, and they could talk over a beer at home.

From the way Ashley had looked earlier, she might need a drink or two before she started to talk about whatever was bothering her.

Sasha set the four types of cupcakes she'd done so far into airtight containers and put them into the walk-in cooler. When she stepped back out, the scent of melting cheese seemed to trail through the kitchen.

Her stomach rumbled.

Oh God. She was so hungry that she was apparently hallucinating already. With her nose in the air, she circled the bread machine—and found herself face-to-face with Ashley, who stood one step into the kitchen, two pizza boxes in her hands.

Sasha jumped and pressed one hand to her chest. "Jesus! You scared the hell out of me!"

"Sorry." Ashley took a step back. "I parked around the back and saw that the door was propped open, so I thought…"

Sasha's heartbeat settled. "It's okay. I just wasn't expecting you to come from there." Why had Ashley parked around the back anyway? Had it just been more convenient because she knew the front door would be locked, or had she wanted to avoid anyone seeing her car parked in front of the bakery?

Ashley held out the pizza boxes like a peace offering. "I thought I'd return the favor and bring you something to eat for a change. I took a guess that you'd like something savory after making cakes and other sugary treats all day."

The mere thought of pizza made Sasha's mouth water. "You guessed right. After a day like today I've been known to have a jar of pickles for dinner. For a while, Jenny was convinced that I was pregnant because I kept buying them."

Ashley laughed, and that carefree sound made Sasha smile in return. Making Ashley laugh was as special as being served pizza after a long day of baking.

"Come on. Let's sit at one of the tables and enjoy the pizza." Sasha got them plates from one of the cupboards and led her out front. "What kind did you get?"

Ashley put the boxes down on one of the small, round tables. "I didn't know what you like, so I got one cheese and one taco pizza."

"Oh yum. My favorites. I could kiss you."

Ashley froze with the lid of one pizza box halfway opened.

Sasha's gaze darted to Ashley's full lips. The Cupid's bow of her upper lip was a work of art, and she wondered how it would feel to trace it with her tongue. She shook off the thought. "Don't worry. I didn't mean it literally. The only one who'll get up close and personal with my incredibly talented lips is this pizza."

Ashley chuckled. "Well, then, I wouldn't want to keep you from the love of your life." She deposited a slice of each pizza on a plate and handed it to Sasha.

"Nah. My true love is apple pie. This is just a hot fling." Sasha took a big bite of the taco pizza—and promptly burned her tongue. "Ouch. A very, very hot fling," she mumbled around a mouthful of gooey cheese and crunchy tortilla chips. She strode behind the counter, got them each a bottle of cold water from the fridge, and took a big gulp of hers. Before she took a seat at the small table again, she stripped off her frosting-smeared apron and hung it on a chair behind her.

"Thanks." Ashley accepted her water and took a swig. Through the clear plastic bottle, she watched Sasha with the intensity of a polar bear eyeing a baby seal.

Something in her gaze made Sasha's mouth dry, even though she'd just taken a sip of water. "Um, what is it?" She followed Ashley's gaze and peered down at her tank top to see if she had gotten frosting or flour on it too.

Nope. The tank top was clean, even though it clung to her damp body.

Oh. Was that why Ashley was staring at her like that? A grin crept onto Sasha's lips. Even though nothing would ever happen between them, it was good to know that Ashley wasn't completely unaffected by her either.

"Is that how you handle your love life?" Ashley twisted the cap back on, avoiding Sasha's question, and kept her gaze on the bottle as if it required her full concentration. "You said you're not the marrying kind either, and you haven't dated in years. So do you just…?"

"Eat pizza every now and then?" Sasha finished with a grin, impressed that Ashley had dared to ask her a question like that.

Ashley peeked at her. "Um, yeah. Something like that."

"Not really. Don't get me wrong. I've had my fair share of pizza—all kinds of pizza—in college. At the time, it met my…um, nutritional needs just fine." Sasha flashed her a grin.

"But?" Ashley reached for a slice of the cheese pizza but held it in her hand without eating it.

"It's never really come up here, but I would have pizza again if I was in the mood for it." Sasha picked a piece of tortilla chip off her pizza and crunched it, then froze. "Uh, are you just curious, or are you trying to, um, invite me over for pizza?" She held her breath while she waited for Ashley's reply, not sure what she would say if Ashley did want a one-night stand or a fling with her.

Ashley dropped her slice back onto her plate and held out both hands. "Oh, no, no, I was just... I don't know. I guess, relationships and what is and isn't possible for me are on my mind a lot lately, and there aren't many people I can talk to about it."

"So you're not into pizza." Sasha made it a statement, not a question. She had already sensed Ashley's answer, and yet a hint of disappointment flickered through her.

"Only into this one." Ashley held up her slice of cheese pizza. She took a bite and chewed thoroughly as if she needed time to think about what else she wanted to say. A tiny bit of tomato sauce dribbled down the corner of her mouth, and she flicked out her tongue to lick it off.

Sasha resisted the urge to press her cold water bottle to her overheated face. How could Ashley make a simple thing like eating pizza look so damn sexy?

"It would probably be so much easier if I were into pizza," Ashley said after a while. "But it just isn't my thing. Too many empty calories, I guess."

Sasha nodded slowly and nibbled on her crust. "I know what you mean. Every now and then, I wonder how something more substantial would taste. I mean, the, um, regular steak dinners that Holly and Leo have look pretty good, don't they?"

"They sure do." Ashley let out a quiet sigh.

"But then I think that it's probably not worth the risk of food poisoning for me," Sasha said. "Plus the food around here isn't that appealing."

Oh yeah? a little voice in her head piped up. *Then why do you keep looking at her as if she were dessert?*

"Hmm." Ashley ate the rest of her slice and then reached for a piece of the taco pizza.

Sasha studied her. It appeared as if Ashley had something else on her mind. "Your question about pizza...does that have anything to do with the craziness that you said has been going on this week?" She tried to think of what might have happened. The first thought that came to mind made her put down her second slice as she lost her appetite. "Did you meet someone you want to have pizza...or a steak dinner with?" *Okay, I think you need to stop using this analogy.* It was getting confusing, especially since they were having pizza together.

"No." Ashley pushed her plate away and leaned back. "My parents found out about the wedding."

She didn't need to explain whose wedding she meant. "Oh. I take it they don't think two women getting married is a reason to celebrate?"

"Not at all. My mother doesn't even want me to do the flowers or attend the wedding because she doesn't want me to be associated with it in any way."

Was that where Ashley's fear of being judged was coming from? Had she learned it from her mother? "What about your father?" Sasha asked quietly.

Ashley, who normally had the posture of a ballet dancer, hunched her shoulders. "He didn't seem as bothered."

"But that's good, isn't it? I mean, it's a start."

Ashley shook her head. Her expressive, nougat-colored eyes held a world of hurt. "He isn't bothered—as long as it's not his own daughter walking down the aisle with another woman. If he found out I'm gay, he would never accept it. Neither of them would."

Sasha opened her mouth to tell her that she needed to be true to herself and find her own way, no matter what her parents or other people thought. But Ashley didn't need a lecture right now. She needed a friend. Sasha reached across the table and took Ashley's hand.

Ash jumped as if she hadn't expected that, but she didn't pull away. Her fingers were cold, even though she had held the hot pizza up until a few moments ago.

"I'm sorry." Sasha looked deeply into her eyes. "You deserve so much better. They should just love and support you, without putting conditions on it."

Ashley said nothing, but she held Sasha's hand firmly, as if it were a lifeline tethering her to dry land.

Instinctively, Sasha put her other hand on top and cradled Ashley's smaller hand in both of hers. If only she could shield her from her parents' and everyone else's prejudice as easily.

They sat in silence, just holding hands, the pizza forgotten next to them.

"The pizza's getting cold," Sasha murmured after a while.

"I don't care. I lost my appetite anyway. But you go ahead and eat." Despite that offer, Ashley didn't let go, so Sasha had no hand free to eat.

"You know what? I think I've had enough pizza too." Then, realizing Ashley might think she was talking about the metaphorical pizza, she added, "Taco and cheese pizza, I mean. Want to help me burn off some of the calories we've just consumed?"

Ashley arched her brows.

"I'm talking about exercise of the non-fun, non-naked kind. Well, I'm hoping it will be fun too, just less sexy. Want to help me bake the last bunch of cupcakes for Mr. Eads?"

"Sure, I can hand you what you need," Ashley said.

Sasha shook her head. "No. I think it's time you really try your hand at baking."

"I don't think that's a good idea."

"Come on, Flower Girl." Sasha squeezed the hand she still held. "I helped out in the flower shop last weekend; now you get to be a baker."

"You helped clean up," Ashley said. "You didn't actually handle the flowers."

Sasha had to give her that. "Let's make a deal: I'll come over sometime and play florist if you bake with me now."

Ashley hesitated. "What if I do something wrong and completely mess up your order?"

"So what? Then we'll just start over. We're baking cupcakes, not doing brain surgery."

That got her a smile, and Ashley's hand relaxed in hers. "Okay. Let's put the pizza away for later and go bake."

They got up, and their hands slid apart.

Sasha didn't know what to do with her hands, which felt empty now that she wasn't holding on to Ashley's, so she put her apron back on, picked up the pizza boxes, and carried them to the kitchen to put them in the cooler.

With the back door still open and the ovens not running, the temperature in the kitchen had cooled down. *Yeah. Cooling down. Might be exactly what you need.*

Shivering, she closed the door and preheated the oven.

"Where do we start, boss?" Ashley asked as they washed their hands at the sink. The sadness from earlier was gone from her eyes, as if she had decided to focus on the here and now and enjoy this new experience.

"First, we get you the right outfit."

Ashley glanced down at her purple, soft-looking V-neck sweater, a pair of fitted jeans, and pink sneakers with a few green stains on them. "What's wrong with what I'm wearing?"

"Nothing at all." In fact, Ashley looked great. Sasha liked her style: feminine, but in a low-maintenance kind of way. "But you are missing an apron and a hairnet."

"Can't I have a bandanna like you?" Ashley pointed at the one Sasha was wearing. "I like them."

It wasn't really a compliment for the way they looked on Sasha, but it warmed her anyway. "Yeah?"

Ashley nodded.

"Then let's get you one." Sasha opened one of the cupboards and got out a clean apron and one of her bandannas.

Ashley took off her sweater, revealing a white T-shirt that was thin enough to hint at the black bra cradling full breasts.

Don't stare, pervert. Quickly, Sasha averted her gaze and focused on lining up the ingredients. Once Ashley had put on the apron over the T-shirt, Sasha raised her gaze back up.

"How does this work?" Ashley pointed at the bandanna.

"Let me show you." Sasha folded it into a triangle, then folded down the top two inches. Her body buzzed with awareness of their closeness as she stepped behind Ashley and tied the bandanna around her forehead so the triangle part was hanging down over her face.

For a moment, Ashley was blindfolded. She stiffened. "What are you…?"

"Trust me and relax," Sasha whispered into her ear. "This really is the best way to do it."

Ashley blew out an audible breath and held still. "Okay."

Gently, Sasha flipped the top layer of the triangle back, over the top of Ashley's head, and pulled it through the knot. She walked around to her front and slid the whole thing back a little, uncovering Ashley's eyes.

When their gazes connected, Sasha forgot the next step for a moment.

"Done?" Ashley asked, staring into her eyes.

Sasha tucked in the corner of the second layer and rolled the front up until it was in the middle of Ashley's forehead. "Done."

"Do I look like a pirate?" Ashley reached for the measuring cup, lifted it as if it were a saber, and lowered her brows in what she probably thought was an intimidating expression.

Sasha tried to suppress her smile but knew she was failing completely. Ashley was much too cute to be a pirate. Sasha liked this playful side of her. She had a feeling not a lot of people ever got to see it. "Oh yeah. So, is the Terror of the Seven Seas ready to begin?"

"Aye, aye, Captain. What are we making?"

"Lemon cupcakes with raspberry buttercream frosting." Sasha threw a lemon in the air, caught it, and set it down on the worktable. "And just so you know, as the baker, you're obligated to try one."

"Ah, I see! So it's all just part of your evil plan to make me try one of your other cupcake flavors."

Sasha shrugged. "Trust me. It won't be a hardship. They're delicious."

"Maybe not when I make them," Ashley muttered. "I'm the woman who can ruin a brownie mix, remember?"

"Have some faith. You just have to follow my lead, and they'll turn out great." Sasha wrapped one arm around Ashley's shoulder and pulled her over until they were side by side at the worktable. She slid the laminated recipe with her aunt's messy handwriting closer so Ashley could read it. "First step: measure out the flour, the sugar, and the other dry ingredients."

Ashley looked back and forth between Sasha and the recipe. When Sasha gave her an encouraging nod, she dipped the measuring cup into the flour bag.

"Oh, no, no. Not so fast. Spoon the flour into the cup. If you scoop it out, the flour will become packed, and you could end up with too much flour."

Ashley spooned the flour into the measuring cup. "Wow. This is more of a science than an art, isn't it?"

"It's both, and that's what I love about it. It pays off to be precise with things like measuring the flour, but with some of the other ingredients, you can get creative."

Once Ashley had measured out the flour, she moved on to the next ingredient on the list, filling the measuring cup with the sugar spoon by spoon.

It wasn't necessary for the sugar, but Sasha said nothing, not wanting to spoil her fun by correcting her at every turn. She watched Ashley as she added baking powder and a pinch of salt.

Her face was a study in concentration. She looked as if she were calculating the flight path of a space rocket instead of baking—well, except for the fleck of flour dusting her cheek.

Sasha's fingers itched to wipe it away. Instead, she handed her the first of four eggs. "The eggs go into a separate bowl please. We'll need them in a second. Do you know how to crack them?"

"Um, I just hit the egg on the edge of the bowl until it cracks?"

"Kind of. You tap it onto the edge lightly until you have a crack. Then you put your thumbs in the crack and pull the shell apart. That way, there won't be any bits of shell in the bowl." Sasha demonstrated with an egg. "See?"

Ashley imitated her. When the yolk and the egg white slid neatly into the bowl, she beamed at her.

"Great." Sasha patted her shoulder. "You'll be a master baker in no time. Don't get me wrong, but I'm a little amazed that your mother never taught you how to bake. I tried her apple pie at a church sale once, so I know she can bake. Why didn't she show you?"

"Oh, she wanted to." Ashley let out a sarcastic laugh. "After all, how am I supposed to catch a husband if I can't bake?"

"But you weren't interested—in finding a husband or in learning to bake?" Sasha asked.

"Definitely not the former. When I was little, I looked forward to learning how to bake, but..." Ashley cracked the other two eggs and stared down into the bowl. "It was something that Melissa and my mom shared. They used to spend entire days in the kitchen around Christmas time, and the house smelled so amazing." She paused as if getting lost in the memory. Then she shook her head. "After Melissa...after she was gone, my mother asked me to bake with her, but I couldn't. It felt so wrong. Like I was trying to take Melissa's place."

Shit. She shouldn't have asked and reopened old wounds. Her sister might be the reason Ashley had been so reluctant to help her bake. "I'm sorry. I shouldn't have nudged you to do this. If you'd rather just watch while I—"

"No," Ashley said firmly. "In here, it doesn't feel like I'm trying to fill Melissa's shoes. With you, I'm all me."

Sasha's throat tightened. Wow. What a powerful statement. It seemed to include so much more than just baking. She cleared her throat. "Good. I wouldn't want you to hide or be someone you're not when you're with me."

"I'm not."

They looked at each other.

Hey, baking, remember? Those cupcakes won't make themselves. Sasha reached for the hand mixer and held it out to her. She normally used a stand mixer, but she wanted Ashley to have the hands-on experience.

Ashley gulped but gamely took the mixer.

The simple gesture had taken on a whole new meaning now that Sasha knew why Ashley had been so reluctant to try baking. She had to move even closer to add ingredients when needed. The mixer was loud, so she shouted her instructions directly into Ash's ear, and Ashley did the same to her whenever she had a question. Since she was shorter, her breath tickled Sasha's neck, sending shivers through her entire body. Was it just her, or was it getting really hot in here?

Sasha wasn't sure if she was relieved or disappointed when they had added the lemon juice and some zest as the last ingredients and the batter had a nice, smooth consistency. She reached up to turn off the mixer. Her fingers brushed Ashley's, making her breath catch.

When the mixer stopped, silence filled the few inches of space between them.

Because Ashley had trusted her—not just by talking about her sister, but also by being willing to bake with her—everything between them seemed more intimate now.

"What now?" Ashley asked.

"Yeah, that's a good question," Sasha mumbled. She had no idea where to take it from here.

"Um, what?"

Sasha gave herself a mental kick. "Now we scoop the batter into the cupcake pans." She carried the bowl over to where she had prepared the two pans with cupcake liners. "Only fill them a little more than halfway, or you'll end up with muffin tops."

"Me or the cupcakes?" Ashley's eyes twinkled.

Sasha chuckled, enjoying Ashley's relaxed mood. "Both."

Ashley spooned the batter into the paper liners, again with that very focused, very cute expression on her face.

When she was done, Sasha slid the pans into the oven and closed the door.

They turned to face each other.

"Let's get started on the frosting while they bake," Sasha said before Ashley could ask "what now?" again. She still had no clue how to answer that question other than with baking instructions.

The handle of the mixer vibrated beneath Ash's fingers. At least she could blame the tingle going through her arm on the mixer, even though she knew that it had been caused by Sasha's hand brushing hers whenever she added an ingredient.

Baking with Sasha was fun, she had to admit—and not just because of those accidental brushes of their fingers. Sasha was a patient teacher, and as a result, Ash felt more confident by the second. This time, she hardly needed any assistance.

Sasha only had to show her how to run the pureed raspberries through a fine-mesh strainer to remove the seeds, and Ash took it from there.

In what seemed like no time at all, they had a smooth, delicious-looking frosting. Normally, Ash preferred strawberry to raspberry buttercream, but she was tempted to stick her finger in the bowl and try some.

Sasha peeked into the bowl. "Ooh, that looks yummy."

When she looked back up, Ash discovered that Sasha had managed to get a pink streak of frosting on her cheek. In combination with the pirate bandanna on her head, it looked almost like a scar from a saber fight.

Before Ash could stop to think about it, she had reached out, gently wiped it away, and licked the frosting off her finger. It was only when the sweet yet tart taste of the raspberry buttercream spread across her tongue that she fully realized what she had done. *What the hell...?* Her finger slid out of her mouth.

Surprise, amusement, and something else—something that made Ash want to fan herself—mingled in Sasha's gaze. "Hungry?" Her voice was low and husky.

You've got no idea. Ash felt as if she'd been starving all of her life.

"Because if you are, you can have a little more." Sasha ran her finger along one of the beaters and smeared a glob of frosting across Ash's face, then wiped her finger on the edge of Ash's apron.

Ash reached up and touched the sticky substance on her cheek, then looked at her fingertips with wide eyes. "I can't believe you did that!"

Sasha grinned. "New bakers have to be christened. You and your pristine white apron looked way too clean. We can't have that."

"Hmm. You and your apron are missing a bit of pink color too." Ash ran her finger along the second beater and swiped a bit of frosting across Sasha's apron, right where a brownish streak ran across her chest already. *Her really soft chest. Oh shit.* Heat flooded her face. *What is it with me and her breasts?*

Sasha stared down at the pink smear on her apron. Clearly, she hadn't expected Ash to do that.

Ash hadn't either. When she was around Sasha, she found herself doing things she never could have imagined doing. "I'm sorry. I didn't mean to—"

Sasha didn't let her finish. She grabbed a beater with each hand and wiped them up and down Ash's apron.

Little specks of pink frosting landed on Ash's white T-shirt.

Oh, just you wait, my friend! Ash dipped two fingers into the bowl and scooped out more of the frosting.

Sasha stood her ground, her eyes flashing a challenge. "You wouldn't dare."

That had been the wrong thing to say. Ash had been underestimated her entire life, and she wanted Sasha of all people not to see her in the same way. She flicked the frosting right into Sasha's face.

A loud gasp echoed through the kitchen, and Ash wasn't sure if it had come from her or from Sasha.

Slowly, Sasha opened her eyes, which she had reflexively closed, and wiped her face. "Oh, you are so going to pay for this!" She snatched the bowl away from Ash, stuck her whole hand in there, and threateningly lifted her handful of pink goop.

Uh-oh. Ash slowly backed away. After a few steps, the counter stopped her retreat. Her gaze darted left and right, looking around for escape routes, but there were none.

Sasha towered over her with a triumphant grin. "Got you now!" She rubbed her handful of frosting in Ash's face as if it were snow.

Sputtering, Ash tried to get away. She licked off a bit of frosting that ran down her face. God, it was delicious, possibly even better than strawberry buttercream—not that she'd ever admit that. But that attack still called for revenge. Since Sasha was much stronger and still had the frosting bowl firmly in her grip, she needed new ammunition.

The bag of flour sat on the worktable.

Ash lunged for it, reached inside, and flung a handful at Sasha.

In retaliation, Sasha lopped more frosting at her.

Soon, they were laughing and screaming and pelting each other with flour, powdered sugar, and every other food item within reach.

Sasha skidded through a puddle on the tiled floor, slid to a stop in front of the giant fridge, and wrenched the door open to take cover behind it. With a triumphant cry, she located something inside.

Oh no. It was a container of eggs. If Sasha got her hands on them... Ash dove across the kitchen and tackled her.

"Uff!" Sasha dropped the eggs. They both went down.

They ended up on the tiled floor, with Ash on top and Sasha stretched out beneath her.

"Give me the eggs or...!" Ash tried to reach the container Sasha held out of reach.

"Or what?" Sasha drawled.

"Or I'll have to do something drastic."

Sasha flashed a challenging grin. "Like what?"

"Like...like..." Ash paused. Her ribs and cheeks ached from laughter. She hadn't laughed so much in years. She stared down at Sasha, who was still laughing unrestrained. The sound of it vibrated through Ash's body.

Pink frosting dripped down Sasha's nose. Her bandanna had slipped off, and her hair was dusted in flour. Powdered sugar clung to her face and to her tank-top-and-apron-clad body, and Ash had the sudden urge to lick it off. God, she was beautiful.

"Like...like this." Ash bent down and kissed her.

Sasha froze for one thudding heartbeat.

Oh, shit. I—

Before Ash could retreat, Sasha's mouth opened beneath hers. Sasha dropped the container of eggs and wrapped her arms around Ash, pulling her even closer. Her lips caressed Ash's, slowly at first.

Ash's eyes fluttered closed, and all of her other senses sparked to life. Sasha's taste, her scent, the heat of her skin made her head swim.

Then Sasha experimentally touched the tip of Ash's tongue with her own, sending a jolt of pleasure down Ash's spine, and the kiss turned urgent.

Their tongues slid along each other with long, sensual strokes.

God, she tasted so good—of raspberries and a hint of taco spice and something that was just Sasha. Ash couldn't get enough of her. She fanned her fingers over Sasha's strong jaw, holding her against her with both hands, and tilted her head to deepen the kiss.

Sasha cupped the back of her neck with one strong yet gentle hand while her other came to rest in the small of her back.

Oh God. More. Need swirled through Ash. She pressed closer, pushing her hips into the V of Sasha's muscular thighs.

Sasha arched up into her. A low moan escaped from deep in her throat as they continued to kiss.

At the sound, a trill of desire raced down Ash's body. She melted against Sasha and let go of her face with one hand to explore her shoulder, left bare by her tank top. She wanted…needed to feel her warm, soft—

A shrill ringing penetrated the thick fog of desire.

What…? Ash dragged her mouth away from Sasha's and gasped for breath. For several seconds, she stared down at her without comprehending what had happened and how they had gotten into this position.

They were lying on the floor, in a sticky mess of flour, powdered sugar, and frosting. The container of eggs was leaking yolks onto the tiles next to them, and the oven timer was going off.

Sasha's hand slipped from the back of Ash's neck, but her other palm stayed where it was, resting in the small of her back. Her lips were red from their kisses, and her pupils had widened, making her eyes look like the dark chocolate glaze of her orange cheesecake.

They stared at each other, their bodies still pressed together and their faces only inches apart.

"Ashley, I—"

In the front of the bakery, a key jangled in the lock. "It's just me, Sasha," Mae called.

"Shit, shit, shit." Ash jumped up, slipped in a puddle of frosting, and nearly fell.

Sasha sat up and gripped her thighs to steady her.

As Mae's steps approached the swinging doors, Ash freed herself from Sasha's gentle grasp. Her heart slammed against her ribs in a fast staccato. "I have to go."

"What?" Sasha blinked up at her. Powdered sugar clung to her lashes. "Now? Come on, Ash. Let's—"

Ash backed away. "No, Sasha. I…I can't." She whirled around, wrenched open the back door, and rushed outside into the cool night air.

"You haven't even tried the cupcakes!" Sasha called after her.

Ash didn't stop. The only craving she had wasn't for cupcakes; it was for more of Sasha's kisses—and that scared her. As she fled to her car, she reached up and touched her tingling lips. *Sweet Jesus.*

Her world titled on its axis, and there was only one thing she knew for sure: She had never been kissed like that…had never kissed anyone like that.

Moments from earlier flashed through her mind's eye like scenes from a movie. God, had she really started a food fight, like a teenager? Had she really tackled Sasha to the floor? Had she been the one to initiate that kiss? That wasn't like her at all.

Or maybe it was. And that was the scariest thing of all, because she didn't know what to do with this new version of herself.

"Fuck." Sasha stared after her.

Now that her body was no longer in contact with Ashley's, the cold from the tiles started to seep in, and she realized the back of her tank top was drenched with a mixture of egg and frosting.

She slowly got to her feet and shook out her apron. A cloud of flour and powdered sugar rose in the air.

The double doors swung open, and her aunt paused in the doorway as if she had run into an invisible wall. Wide-eyed, she took in the kitchen.

Sasha looked around too. Pink frosting was spattered all over the worktable, the cupboards, and the fridge. The counters and the floor were covered in a dusting of flour and powdered sugar. The only spot where she could see the black-and-white-checkered tiles was where she and Ashley had strained against each other in a passionate kiss, as if the white layer had been snow that had melted from the heat of their bodies.

Jesus. Sasha wiped her sticky face.

Her aunt pressed a hand to her mouth. "Good heavens! What happened to the kitchen?"

Ashley happened. To give herself some time to answer, Sasha opened the oven, pulled out the two pans, and set the cupcakes onto the cooling rack. "Just a little accident," she said with her back to Aunt Mae.

Was that what they would put it down to—an accident? Just a moment of mutual confusion that would never be repeated?

Judging from the way Ashley had run out, that was exactly what would happen.

Maybe it would be for the best. Sasha wasn't looking to get involved with anyone and certainly not with someone as complicated as Ashley.

But after that kiss, her body had difficulties remembering that. God, the way Ashley had leaned down and just kissed her had been so incredibly hot. Ashley had surprised her, first with her playfulness during the food fight and then with her passion. If that fucking timer hadn't gone off and her aunt hadn't come over, they would probably still be stretched out on the floor, making out in a layer of flour and powdered sugar.

"Accident?" her aunt repeated. "With an elephant? Because that's what my kitchen looks like. As if a herd of elephants had stampeded through here."

"*Your* kitchen?" Sasha chose to focus on that part of the conversation because she didn't know what to say to the rest. "I thought we agreed that you'd buy a rocking chair and finally enjoy retirement?"

Aunt Mae shrugged. "Rocking chairs make me nauseated, and retirement is for old people. I thought I would come over and see if you needed help." She eyed the eggs forming a puddle in the middle of the kitchen. "Apparently, you do."

"No, Auntie. You don't need to help. This is my mess to clean up."

"If you'd rather do it yourself..." Aunt Mae gestured at her to go ahead but didn't retreat from the doorway.

Sighing, Sasha ran hot water into the sink and began to wipe down the sticky counters.

"So," her aunt said after a while, "do you want to talk about the elephant in the room? Or rather, the elephant who ran out of the room?"

The cleaning rag splashed into the sink. Sasha stared at her. "Um, how do you know...?"

A smile deepened the wrinkles on her aunt's face. "There are footprints all over the kitchen, all the way to the door, and they aren't a size eleven, like yours."

Sasha looked down. Sure enough, a trail of yolk and raspberry-colored footprints led to the back door. *Damn.* For a moment, she felt the way she had when she'd been caught kissing Travis's cousin, Kristi, who'd been visiting from New York. But she was no longer fourteen, and Ashley wouldn't be leaving town at the end of the week. They would have to deal with what had happened between them.

"Let me guess." Aunt Mae pointed at the footprints. "These were made by Ashley Gaines's cute, pink sneakers."

"Um..." Sasha had never kept secrets from her aunt. Auntie Mae had practically raised her, so she deserved better than to be lied to. "Yeah."

Her aunt's eyes twinkled behind her green-tinted glasses. "Does this," she swirled her finger through the air, indicating the mess, "mean you finally kissed her?"

Sasha, who had just picked up the cleaning rag again, dropped it a second time. "How did you know that I...? That she is...? That we...?"

"*Fried Green Tomatoes,*" her aunt said as if that would explain everything.

Sasha leaned against the sink and shook her head from side to side, feeling as if she had some frosting stuck in her brain that was slowing down her thinking. "Um, what?"

"The movie," Auntie Mae said. "Haven't you watched it?"

"Of course I have." She had watched it a dozen times or more—even knowing the ending always made her cry—mainly for Mary-Louise Parker's cute smile and for the way Idgie rocked a pair of suspenders. "But what does that have to do with anything?"

"Did you know that the food fight scene was intended as a symbol for them having sex?" Her aunt gave her a knowing look and a wink. "That's how I knew."

Sasha sputtered. "What? But Ashley and I...we weren't... We didn't have sex!"

"But you kissed her," Aunt Mae said with a triumphant I-knew-it tone.

"No, I—"

"Come on, honey! You don't expect me to believe that you have been taking almost the entire inventory of the bakery over to her shop this past month because the orchids have discovered their fondness for vanilla cupcakes, do you? You're sweet on her! Just admit it."

"No, that's not..." Sasha snapped her mouth shut. Who was she kidding? "Okay, maybe I do have a tiny bit of a crush on her." She held her thumb and index finger half an inch apart. "But for the record, she kissed me."

Auntie Mae whistled through her dentures. "I didn't think she'd have the guts to do that."

"Me neither," Sasha murmured. "Surprised the hell out of me."

"But you kissed her back, right?" her aunt asked.

Sasha laughed. "Hell, yeah! I'm not stupid. I mean, she's beautiful, totally cute, and a lot of fun once she drops her guard. She's also one heck of a kisser." She trailed her finger over her bottom lip as she flashed back to the way Ashley had kissed her, then stopped when she realized what she was doing.

"Just a tiny crush, huh?" Her aunt gave her a teasing grin. "Are you sure that's all it is?"

"Pretty sure," Sasha said. She was, wasn't she? The way Ashley had run out of there proved that she was like Sasha's mother—not someone she could tie her heart to, even if Sasha were the tying-her-heart-to-someone type. "Neither of us are the marrying kind."

"I don't know about Ashley, but I think you could be." The teasing tone was gone from Aunt Mae's voice now. "I don't want you to end up with regrets one day because you didn't challenge the assumptions you made—about her or about yourself."

Sasha studied her aunt's familiar face. "Do you have any? Regrets, I mean. You never had a serious relationship. Not after I practically moved in with you. I hope you never felt like you had to give up your own happiness to be there for me."

Her aunt entered the kitchen, ignoring the mess on the floor that would likely stain her shoes, and wrapped her arms around Sasha. Her head came only to Sasha's shoulder. "You and the bakery are my happiness. I hope you know that."

Sasha swallowed against the lump in her throat. She squeezed her aunt softly. "I do. But you could have had both, you know?"

"Hey, I still can. I'm hotter than apple pie fresh out of the oven." Aunt Mae fluffed her dyed hair.

They both chuckled, then sobered.

"I never met anyone I could see myself growing old with," her aunt said. "But if you ever do, promise me you won't run from it."

"Me?" Sasha looked at the back door. "I'm not the one who ran out of here like a bat out of hell."

Her aunt patted her shoulder. "There's more than one way to run. Sometimes, not moving an inch is the worst kind of running." She stared at her hand and rubbed her fingers together, which were now sticky too. "My God, what did you do? Roll around in frosting? Are you sure you didn't have sex right here on the kitchen floor?"

"I think I would remember that." As it was, the kiss they had shared on the kitchen floor would probably be seared into her brain for the rest of her life.

"Yeah, you probably would. It's always the quiet, innocent-looking ones like Ashley who are real tigers in bed—or on the kitchen tiles."

Sasha gaped at her aunt. After knowing her for all her life, she should have been used to the things she sometimes said. "Thanks a lot, Auntie. I really didn't need those images in my head." She gave her aunt a somber look. "You know you can't mention this," she gestured around the kitchen, then vaguely in the direction where Ashley had fled, "to anyone, right? Ashley is scared to death of being outed."

Her aunt gave her another pat on the shoulder. "Don't worry, honey. You know I'm not in the habit of discussing your private life at the dog park or with the ladies from the bridge club. Come on. Now that my shoes are already sticky, I might as well help you clean up and make a new batch of frosting, or you'll never get out of here at a reasonable hour. Four a.m. comes mighty early, and you need to get some sleep."

Sleep? Sasha had a feeling she wouldn't get much of it, no matter when she left the bakery.

Chapter 11

FOUR O'CLOCK, THE TIME WHEN the bakery closed, came and went. Not that Ash was watching the clock or anything.

Okay, maybe she was. She hadn't been thinking of anything but that crazy kiss for the past twenty-two hours and eighteen minutes. She had been so distracted all day that she'd even mixed up two orders, which had never happened to her before. Thank God her driver had wondered why the funeral home would order an arrangement with a floating balloon saying, *It's a girl.*

Ash could only imagine what Mr. Beasley would have made of that mistake.

Even Brooke appeared distracted today. Every few minutes, she paused in the middle of sweeping the shop and glanced out the window.

The bell above the front door jingled.

Ash looked up, half hoping, half afraid to see Sasha in the doorway with a bakery box full of lemon cupcakes.

But it was only Travis who burst into the shop as if his pants were on fire.

"Just Mr. Bonnett." Brooke sounded as disappointed as Ash felt. "I don't think she's coming to bring us cupcakes today." She stuck out her bottom lip like a pouting toddler.

Travis rushed up to the counter. "Thank God. I thought you might be closed already."

Ash looked at the clock on the wall again. Their shop hours had officially ended two minutes ago, but she never locked the door until she was leaving. That way, she could help out last-minute customers and earn some extra money. "Still here. What can I do for you?"

"You can save my life."

"Um, if you're in a life-threatening situation, wouldn't you rather go to the ER?" Ash chuckled. "My flowers are powerful, but they are not that powerful."

"I don't think the ER docs can help me. Well, unless maybe by surgically removing my head from up my ass."

Ash gave him a sympathetic look. "Ouch. What did you do?" She bit back a *this time*.

Travis sighed. "I made some dumb-ass comment about the price of the outfit that Jenny bought for the wedding. And the shoes. And the purse."

"Oh, I see. So it's a flower emergency."

He nodded. "Do you have a flower that says 'I'm sorry for being an ass'?"

Ash had a feeling she needed that kind of apology flower too. "Sure. Do you want a bouquet or a potted plant?"

"Potted plant," Travis said without hesitation. "Probably won't be long before I mess up again, and a potted plant will last longer."

Ash stepped out from behind the counter and walked him over to the shelf that held plants in colorful pots. "How about a white orchid? White is the color of peace and agreement after all."

"Peace. Yeah, that's what I need at home. I'll take it." He grabbed the biggest white orchid off the shelf and tucked it under his arm as if it were a football.

"Um, want me to wrap it in some tissue paper?"

"Oh. Yeah. I guess." He handed over the plant, and she wrapped it for him while Brooke rang up his purchase.

He slid his credit card back into his wallet and again tucked the orchid beneath his arm. "Wish me luck. I'll let you know how powerful your plants are when I see ya at Johnny's."

Ash nodded. "See you Saturday." She would also see Sasha at the bar. But that was two days away. Was it really fair to wait that long? Ash knew she couldn't expect Sasha to always be the one who came to her. She had been the one to start the kiss, and she had been the one who ran and left

Sasha to deal with the mess in the kitchen. Now she would also have to be the one to seek her out and apologize.

Maybe she should take a page from Travis's book and give her an apology flower.

Once Travis was gone, she glanced at the leftover white orchids.

No. Orchids were out, since they also symbolized passion.

What's wrong with that? a little voice in the back of her head piped up. Her mind immediately flashed back to the way Sasha had kissed her. That little flutter thing she did with her tongue would have made her knees buckle if she hadn't already been on the kitchen floor. Those had without a doubt been the most passionate moments of her life.

"No," Ash said loudly to drown out that other voice inside of her. "No orchids."

Brooke looked up from where she was cleaning up her workstation. "Um, no orchids for what?"

"Oh, nothing. Just thinking out loud. I might take a flower to a...uh, a friend, and I was wondering which one would be the right one." She looked over their stock as she changed the water in the buckets for the flowers in the cooler.

The lavender roses were especially beautiful today, but they weren't an option either since they represented love at first sight. Pink camellia were out too because they told the recipient *I long for you.* The message of lathyrus—*Thank you for a lovely time*—seemed a little ambiguous given how they had spent their last evening together.

Too bad there wasn't a flower that said, *Sorry for kissing you and then running for the hills.*

"You're letting all the cool air out of the cooler," Brooke said. "Must be a super special friend if it's taking you this long to decide."

"She is," Ash said in a whisper not meant for Brooke's ears. More loudly, she added, "Picking a flower with exactly the right meaning isn't easy."

Brooke shrugged. "Most people wouldn't know what they mean anyway."

"*I* would know," Ash said quietly.

"I think you're making this way too complicated. Why don't you get them something else?" Brooke suggested. "Like, I don't know, cupcakes or something."

Ash chuckled nervously. "I don't think that's a good idea." Cupcakes were what had gotten them into this mess in the first place. She took the remaining alstroemeria and closed the cooler. The Peruvian lilies symbolized friendship, and Sasha had seemed to like them when she had seen them in the mock-up of the bridal bouquet. "Why don't you take off now? All that's left to do is closing out the cash register and dropping off the money at the bank."

Brooke reached for her jacket and slipped it on. But then she paused in the middle of the shop. "I was wondering if you could pay me early this week. I'm going to St. Joe for dinner and a movie with Logan tomorrow night, and I'm kinda broke." She turned the front pockets of her jeans inside out as if to prove it.

"Logan?" It was the first time Brooke had mentioned him. "Wait, you're dating the Beasleys' son?"

"Hell, no." But Brooke was blushing to the roots of her hair that she'd dyed blue last week. "We're just hanging out. That's why I need the money. I don't want him to pay and assume...you know?"

Ash could only wish she'd been so insightful about what she wanted and didn't want at Brooke's age. "I think that's really good."

"So you think dating him would be a bad idea? Not that I want to. Just...in general and everything."

The knowing grin on Ash's lips died away. Oh jeez, why did Brooke have to ask her of all people for dating advice? That was like going to eighty-nine-year-old Mr. Gillespie for tips on how to write a rap song. "I don't know, Brooke. I only talk to his parents, but I don't really know him well enough to say."

Brooke stuffed her hands into her jacket pockets. "Yeah. Never mind. It's totally hypothetical anyway."

Ash didn't believe that for a second. She tried to think of something helpful to say. What kind of advice would Sasha give if she were here? "How does he treat you?"

"Depends. When it's just us and a bunch of friends, he's great. Really listens to me, you know? Like my opinion matters."

"That sounds great." Ash knew Brooke didn't get that at home. Most of the time, her parents' idea of communication was to shout at her.

"Yeah, but he doesn't want his parents to know that he hangs out with me." Brooke's shoulders slumped, and she sank into her jacket up to her chin, like a turtle withdrawing into its shell.

Ash's stomach bunched into a tight ball. Her first instinct was to tell Brooke how stupid he was for not being proud to have her as his friend—or even date—but who was she to say that when she had run out on Sasha so her aunt wouldn't see them together?

"I'm sorry, Brooke. I wish I had some real advice to give you. The only thing I can tell you is that I don't think it's about you. It's about him and his own insecurities."

Brooke didn't look convinced. "How do you know?"

Ash sighed. "Because I've been there."

Brooke let out a snort. "Yeah, right. Everybody's always talking about how you dated Mr. Homecoming King when you were my age. I bet he proudly paraded you around every chance he got."

Ash's gaze went to the door. "Promise you won't repeat what I'm about to tell you to anyone. I don't want to hurt anyone by making this public knowledge."

"Cross my heart." Brooke drew an X on the left side of her chest with her finger and leaned forward eagerly so she wouldn't miss a word.

Shit. Now she had put herself into a situation where she had to maneuver carefully so she wouldn't say too much. But helping Brooke was worth it. "Brandon did parade me around, and I did the same to him. But that's all it was. We were with each other for all the wrong reasons—because it was kind of expected of the head cheerleader and the star quarterback, not because we cared deeply for each other."

"So that's why you broke up?" Brooke asked.

"Yeah, basically." There was a lot more to it, of course, but she couldn't tell Brooke that. Not without coming out to her.

"Are you saying that if Logan and I really care for each other—totally hypothetically, of course—it doesn't matter if he keeps it from his parents?"

"No, that's not what I meant at all." She had seen what hiding their relationship had done to Holly. It had slowly suffocated that joy she now saw back in Holly's eyes. She didn't want that for Brooke. "Maybe you should talk to Logan and try to find a solution together."

Brooke sighed. "What if there is no solution? You know his mother. She wants him to bring home someone like you. Not...this." She gestured at her blue hair and her nose ring.

God, the irony of it. "Trust me, Mrs. Beasley would be lucky to have someone like you, not someone like me, as her potential daughter-in-law."

"Whoa!" Brooke's kohl-rimmed eyes widened. "Hey, we're talking hypothetically! No one said anything about daughter-in-law."

"Oops. Sorry. Of course. Completely hypothetical." She opened the cash register, handed Brooke her money for the week, and added a little extra. "Gas money," she said at Brooke's questioning gaze. "Wouldn't want Logan to think it's a date because he's driving."

Brooke chuckled. "Right. Thanks. For the money and, you know, the advice."

"You're welcome." Ash watched her leave. When the door closed behind Brooke, she arranged the alstroemeria into a hand-tied bouquet. It was time to take her own advice and go talk to Sasha.

Sasha lay stretched out on her couch, cradling a bottle of beer. *The Great British Baking Show* was on TV, but even the 3D novelty cake the contestants were making couldn't capture her interest today.

Snap out of it. So she kissed you, and now she's avoiding you. Big deal. Ashley hadn't come by the bakery today, but that was hardly a surprise. Avoidance was how Ashley dealt with problems, and that was why Sasha never should have kissed her back.

Sasha snorted. She couldn't not have kissed her back even if her life depended on it. Back in high school, she had wondered a time or two—okay, maybe two hundred—what kissing those soft-looking lips would be like. For once, reality didn't just live up to her fantasies but even surpassed them. Never in her wildest dreams had she imagined that Ashley would kiss with such intensity, as if she wanted to crawl inside Sasha's skin to experience her even more closely.

Just thinking about it now made her body temperature shoot up. She took a swig of beer and then grimaced because it had gone lukewarm.

When the doorbell rang, she nearly dropped the bottle.

Ashley! She scrambled upright and shoved the beer onto the coffee table, then stopped herself from dashing to the door. It would probably be Holly or one of the neighbors, not Ashley.

But her heart was still beating faster as she walked to the door. *Idiot.* She peeked through the peephole.

The first thing she saw was a bunch of flowers—Peruvian lilies, if she wasn't mistaken. Then they were lowered, and Ashley's face appeared.

Wow. She came. That was the third time in twenty-four hours that Ashley had surprised her—first by starting a food fight and then... She shoved the thought away. It was better not to think about the last time Ashley had surprised her.

But...flowers. Ashley had brought flowers. What did that mean? Was it just a florist thing, or was there more behind the gesture?

Ashley leaned closer, as if trying to see through the peephole. Her shoulders lifted and fell beneath a long sigh before she turned and disappeared from view.

No! Sasha wrenched the door open. "Wait!"

Ashley froze, already halfway down the stairs. Slowly, she turned. "Oh. I thought maybe you weren't home."

"I'm home." Sasha grimaced inwardly. *Yeah, genius, obviously you are, or she wouldn't be able to talk to you.*

Ashley scraped the tip of her pink sneaker along the concrete step beneath her. "Um, can we talk?"

With her heart hammering in her ears, Sasha nodded and opened the door wider. "Sure. Come in."

The Great British Baking Show was still blasting from the TV. It took her a minute to find the remote to switch it off.

Silence filled the living room.

"Oh." Ashley thrust out the flowers as if only now remembering them. "For you." Her hands were shaking.

It eased Sasha's own nerves to know that Ashley hadn't been able to just brush off the kiss either. "Thank you. I'll try my best not to let them die right away." She took the flowers, carried them to her tiny kitchenette, and rooted through the cupboards for anything resembling a vase.

"I think...um, I owe you an apology," Ashley said, as if finding it easier to talk while Sasha wasn't facing her.

With her largest jug in hand, Sasha turned. She studied Ashley's pale face. Dark shadows beneath her eyes revealed that she hadn't slept much either, but to Sasha, she still looked lovely. "What exactly are you apologizing for?"

"Kissing you." A blush brought color to Ashley's cheeks. "I shouldn't have done that. And I especially shouldn't have run out of there and left you to deal with the mess in the kitchen all by yourself."

Sasha looked her in the eyes. "I won't lie. That hurt."

Ashley glanced away.

"Well, not the kiss." Sasha cracked a smile to ease the tension. "That didn't hurt a bit, even though it did leave some parts of me aching."

Ashley's blush intensified.

Sasha was sure it extended all the way down to her toes. She tried to focus on the conversation instead of imagining what places the blush might be touching in between. "You running. That's what hurt. It's what my mother did to me and my dad when I was little."

"I know. That's why I'm here." Ashley lifted her gaze with obvious effort. "I don't want to hurt you like that."

Sasha needed a moment to process all the different emotions that statement brought. Appreciation won out, but only by an ounce. She removed the tissue paper from the flowers, put them into the jug she'd filled with water, and carried them to the coffee table. "Come on. Let's sit."

Ashley followed her to the couch. Without taking off her jacket, she settled down on the opposite end of the couch and rearranged the bouquet in the improvised vase. It probably helped calm her, so Sasha let her do it.

"Friendship," Ashley said when she looked up from the flowers. "Um, I mean, the Peruvian lilies. That's what they symbolize."

So the flowers were more than an apology. They were a message—one Sasha wasn't entirely sure she was happy with.

"I've known you practically all of my life," Ashley added, "and for the past nine or ten years, I've seen you nearly every day in the bakery, but I never really *saw* you, if you know what I mean."

Sasha nodded, even though it had been different for her. She had noticed Ashley a little too much back in high school, but what she had admired back then had just been Ashley's good looks and the way she got along with everyone. Now she was getting to know the person behind that mask.

"Now that I finally do, you're turning out to be an amazing friend. Someone I can be myself with, and that's rare for me." A look of almost desperate intensity flashed across Ashley's face. Sasha had only seen that look once before—when she had kissed her. "I need that kind of friendship in my life, Sasha. I don't want to do anything to endanger that."

"Friendship," Sasha repeated. The word tasted bittersweet on her lips. "But you kissed me."

Ashley swallowed. "Yes. I did." Her fingertips fluttered over her lips as if she wasn't even aware of it. "I admit I find you attractive. I mean, look at you. Who wouldn't?"

Maybe Sasha should have been flattered, but at the moment, she couldn't have cared less about other people finding her attractive.

"But we're adults," Ashley said. "It doesn't have to mean anything."

The kiss hadn't felt as if it didn't mean a thing. But maybe that had just been her. "So that kiss was just…what? A meaningless bit of chemistry?"

Ashley leaned back heavily, pulled the hair band from her ponytail, and let her hair tumble down around her face, like a curtain that was supposed to hide her feelings. "That kiss…" Her voice was a whisper. "…was one of the most amazing things I've ever experienced."

Her words settled on Sasha, heavy with meaning. Immediately, she had to fight the urge to crawl across the couch and show her even more amazing things. Instead, she sought refuge in a joking remark. "Just *one* of the most amazing?"

Ashley reached over and lightly pinched Sasha's thigh. "Oh, don't get cocky."

They smiled at each other, and Sasha tried her best to ignore the tingle shooting up from the place Ashley had touched.

Ashley sobered, pushed her hair back behind her ear, and regarded her with a serious expression. "As amazing as the kiss was, it doesn't change the fact that I can't start a relationship with you."

"Relationship?" Sasha echoed. "Who's talking about a relationship? I'm not sure I'm ready for the entire steak dinner either. But you said you're not the pizza type, so maybe we could…I don't know…just start with the appetizer. Maybe go on a date or something and see where that takes us."

Ashley looked just as startled as Sasha felt.

Wow. Had she really just suggested that? And had she meant it? Was she ready to date, especially someone as complicated as Ashley, with the option of it becoming more? *Appetizer,* she reminded herself. *Just think about the appetizer, not the entire meal.*

"Sasha..." Ashley sighed. "Even if that was what we both wanted, where would we go?"

"Go?"

"Yeah. On our date. We can't go anywhere without people talking."

"Um, I don't know. Where did you take Holly when you were dating?"

"That's the thing. We never went on a real date. I knew if we did, my parents would find out." Ashley took a shuddery breath. "I can't do that. I can't lose them too." She tugged on one of the lilies and removed a leaf that had been beneath the waterline. "That day...when Melissa...when she killed herself, it was my mother who found her. It was the week before Valentine's Day, and she had taken me to the store to get card stock and glitter glue so I could make my own cards. When we got back, the house was strangely quiet. My mom went upstairs to check on Melissa. It took so long for her to return that I headed upstairs too."

Sasha knew the end of that story, of course, had heard it at least a dozen times from various people over the years. But hearing it from Ashley made her stomach hurt.

"My mother urged me out of the room before I could see Melissa. But from the look on her face, I knew something horrible must have happened." A tremor went through Ashley. "I still see that look on my parents' faces sometimes, when they think I'm not paying attention. Not knowing why... why she killed herself, never finding any kind of closure...that keeps the pain alive, you know? I don't want to cause my parents the same kind of pain."

The urge to take Ashley into her arms and to shelter her from that pain gripped her, but she wasn't sure it would be welcome. "Do you...?" She had to clear her throat before she could continue. "Do you really think having a gay daughter would be the same for them as having a daughter who...a daughter who died?"

"The same?" Ashley shook her head. "Nothing could ever come close to that. But they would still have to wonder what they did wrong, and they'd have to pretend they don't hear what people are whispering behind their backs. One stigma against the family name is enough. I can't make my parents go through it again."

As much as Sasha wanted to, she couldn't argue against that. Not when she could feel the pain radiating off Ashley almost like a physical wave. "Where does that leave us?"

Ashley brushed her finger along the bloom of a Peruvian lily. "At a point where we can be friends, I hope."

Okay, so no dating Ashley. It shouldn't have been a big deal since a little more than a month ago, she had still assumed Ashley was straight. But somehow, she felt as if she had lost a chance at something that could have been great. "Sure," Sasha said, trying to sound casual. "I'd like that."

Ashley smiled, but the sadness clung to her like a cloak.

Was it all about her sister and her parents, or did she, too, regret that they wouldn't get the chance to see what could have happened between them?

"So, what did you tell your aunt when she saw the kitchen?" Ashley asked after a while.

Sasha's smile became more authentic. "That an elephant had trampled through it."

"Excuse me?" Ashley patted her shapely hips. "Are you calling me an elephant?"

"Actually, I think we were talking about an entire herd of elephants—because that's what the kitchen looked like after you left."

Ashley's cheeks flamed red. "Well, I guess it's better than telling her what really happened."

Sasha hesitated, but she didn't want to lie to Ashley. "Actually, she has a pretty good idea of what happened."

"You told her?"

"She guessed."

Ashley's face went from cherry red to chalky white. "She...she guessed about me being gay? About us...?" She gestured helplessly. "Do you think other people can tell too?"

"No," Sasha said quickly. "Aunt Mae has the best gaydar I've ever encountered. She knew I was interested in girls and boys long before I had a clue. But don't worry. She won't tell or judge. She couldn't care less who you sleep with."

"That's the thing—I'm not sleeping with anyone."

"Yeah, your loss." Sasha gave her a teasing wink. "Because just so you know, I never had any complaints."

Ashley's face switched back to a fiery red color. Finally, the corners of her mouth twitched up into a weak grin. "You're impossible."

"Part of my charm," Sasha drawled.

They smiled at each other, but it felt a little shaky.

"Are we okay?" Ashley asked quietly.

Sasha bit back a sigh. "Yeah." They would be. At some point, those hot images flashing through her brain any time she handled frosting would fade…hopefully.

Chapter 12

ASH HAD DECIDED TO STOP seeing Sasha for a while, at least until she could look at her without constantly thinking about their kisses and what it would feel like to press her lips to hers again. But on Saturday morning, she found herself crowded into Beth's big SUV, on their way to a bridal shop for wedding dress shopping in Kansas City.

She hadn't expected to be invited, but apparently, Holly and Leo had been serious about including her in their wedding and working on getting their friendship back.

Of course, Sasha had been invited too. As the tallest person in the car, she was in the passenger seat next to Holly, while Ash was in the back seat, squeezed in between Beth and Sharon—Holly's and Leo's moms—who were chatting a mile a minute about wedding dresses, shoes, and the veil-vs.-no-veil issue.

Sasha turned her head and gave her a sympathetic smile.

Now she understood why Holly had practically begged her and Sasha to come along and not leave her alone with the wedding-obsessed moms. Leo's offer to join them had been met with an outcry from Beth and Sharon. Apparently, the spouses-to-be weren't supposed to see each other's outfit before the wedding, as it was considered bad luck.

Ash still couldn't believe how supportive the two were being. They had thrown themselves into the wedding planning as if they had waited all their lives for their daughters to get married to each other. If Ash ever announced she was getting married to another woman, her mother's outcry would not be about the wedding dresses; that was for sure.

"...wedding, Ashley?" Beth's voice startled her from her thoughts.

Ash looked over from where she'd stared out the window. "Um, pardon me?"

"I asked what you'll be wearing to the wedding," Beth said.

"Probably one of my summer dresses, since it's going to be an outdoor ceremony."

Beth shook her head. "I still can't believe Holly and Leo aren't going with identical dresses for the bridesmaids. You girls would have looked so cute in them."

"They're women, Mom, not girls," Holly said from the driver's seat. "And we're not even having bridesmaids, so they can wear whatever they want. What we want from our wedding is a relaxed day sharing our joy with friends, not a fashion event where everyone can't wait to get out of their uncomfortable shoes and stuffy clothes."

"Besides," Sasha added with a laugh, "can you imagine me in one of those cute little bridesmaid dresses?"

Beth chuckled. "Oh, I don't have to imagine it. I still have a photo of you at Travis and Jenny's wedding."

Sasha let out a long groan.

Had Sasha been one of the bridesmaids when Jenny and Travis had gotten married? Ash honestly couldn't remember, but she definitely couldn't imagine her in a bridesmaid dress. Now, Sasha in a custom-tailored suit, like the one Holly said Leo's costume designer would be making for her...

Ash discreetly touched her chin to make sure she wasn't drooling—and promptly missed another question directed at her, this time from Sharon.

"Sorry." She hoped she wasn't blushing. "What was that?"

Sasha turned and peeked at her through the gap between the front seats. "You okay?" she asked quietly.

Ash nodded. Now she was definitely blushing. "Just haven't had my morning coffee yet."

"Ooh, coffee." Holly drove a little faster. "Let's stop at the next Starbucks."

Sharon reached over and patted Ash's knee. "So, what about that plus one? Are you bringing anyone to the wedding?"

It got quiet in the car as everyone waited for Ash's reply.

Ash felt Sasha's gaze on her, so she avoided looking in that direction. "You know I'm single—happily single. I'll just go alone."

"Why don't you ask Derek?" Sharon asked. "I'm sure he'd love to go with you."

"Yeah, I'm sure," Ash mumbled under her breath. "Um, I guess, I just…" She gestured helplessly.

"Coming alone is fine." Holly met her gaze in the rearview mirror. "I went to weddings on my own for years."

"She did," her mother said. "I had almost given up hope of her ever finding anyone."

Holly groaned. "Mom!"

"Okay, okay." Beth turned toward Sasha. "So what about you? Are you taking anyone?"

Ash found herself holding her breath. It was stupid. She shouldn't care if Sasha went with anyone, man or woman.

"Nah," Sasha said. "I'll have to keep an eye on the caterers to make sure they aren't ruining the cake anyway, so I wouldn't be a fun date."

Ash very much doubted that. Being around Sasha was always fun, even when she was working. She bit her lip.

"I think you two are pretty much the only unattached people going to the wedding," Beth said. "Why don't you go together?"

An image of walking into the ballroom of the country club on Sasha's arm flashed through Ash's mind. Her breath caught with a strange mix of panic and joy.

"They don't have to go with anyone, Mom." Holly came to her aid. "Like I just said, attending without a plus one is just fine. I never understood this need to pair up just because it's a wedding."

"There's a Starbucks coming up." Sasha tapped the window.

Ash noticed that Sasha hadn't responded to Beth's suggestion. Would she have wanted to go with Ash, just as friends, if that had been an option?

Holly took the exit and pulled up in front of the coffee shop since the line for the drive-through was much longer.

"I got it." Sasha swung the passenger-side door open and waved at the others to stay in the car. "I know what everyone wants."

Did she really? Ash let her head sink against the backrest. At the moment, she wasn't even sure if she knew what she wanted.

A few minutes later, they continued their wedding dress road trip, and it wasn't long before they reached the bridal shop.

"Oh, it looks smaller than I expected," Beth said as they got out of the car and walked toward the shop. "Do you really think you'll find something here? Maybe you should have taken Leo up on her offer to fly you to Kleinfeld in New York."

Ash nearly spat out the last sip of her coffee. Fly her to New York, to buy a dress at the most famous—and probably the most expensive—bridal boutique in the country? Most of the time, Leo was just her former best friend, one of the locals, to Ash. Since Leo possessed such a down-to-earth personality, it was easy to forget that she was a superstar who could treat her fiancée to a trip to New York and a designer dress.

Anxiety gripped Ash. Could her modest little flower shop produce beautiful bouquets and centerpieces to contend with the big-name florists Leo could have hired?

A warm touch to the small of her back stopped her momentary panic.

Sasha had paused next to her to hold the door open for Ash. She didn't even seem to notice that she'd touched her.

"Thanks." Ash meant mainly the soothing touch but knew Sasha would assume she was talking about the door.

"You're welcome."

"This will be fine, Mom," Holly said. "They might be small, but they do one-of-a-kind dresses, not just mass-produced stuff. I'm sure I'll find something beautiful."

Ash followed Holly and the two moms into the store, very aware of Sasha's presence behind her.

The shop might have been small, but it was filled with rows of wedding dresses in lace, crepe, satin, and taffeta. Strategically placed mannequins showed off more dresses in various styles.

"Oh, aren't they all beautiful?" Sharon stopped at the threshold of the store to marvel at the dresses. "Doesn't that sight just make you want to get married too?"

Ash and Sasha traded gazes. "No," they said in unison, then grinned at each other.

A saleswoman of about fifty, with chubby cheeks and a happy smile, greeted them and offered them flutes of champagne.

Ash declined. Sasha's presence next to her was enough to make her head spin.

"Any idea what kind of dress you'd like?" The saleslady pointed at different styles of dresses. "Something modern and sexy or something charming and traditional?"

"Something traditional," Holly said. "I'd love to have a dress that is simple, yet elegant."

"How about something like this?" the saleswoman pulled out a dress and held it up.

Holly scrunched up her nose. "Not quite. No giant bows, no ruffles, and no train, please. Oh, and I'd like a dress that doesn't make me spend the entire ceremony worrying about my breasts popping out."

The saleswoman laughed and led her farther into the shop. "A bride-to-be who knows what she wants—and what she doesn't want. I love that. What is the groom wearing?"

Apparently, Holly hadn't mentioned whom she would be marrying when she'd made the appointment. That was typical of her. She probably hadn't wanted the extra attention the salesclerks would have given her if she had told them the other bride was Jenna Blake.

Ash tensed. Would the saleslady's friendly mask transform into a disapproving frown when she found out there was no groom?

"Oh, didn't I mention that on the phone? The other bride will be wearing a gorgeous cream-colored suit with a vest." A dreamy smile lit up Holly's face, but the steely glint in her eyes revealed that she wouldn't allow anyone to spoil her day or treat her relationship with anything but respect.

The saleswoman paused for less than a heartbeat, then nodded. "So should we be looking for a cream-colored dress for you too?"

Ash couldn't help staring. That was all the reaction they were going to get?

Sasha nudged her softly. "You know, you have to stop always expecting people to hit you over the head with their Bibles or to hurl homophobic slurs at you," she said in a whisper.

Had it been that obvious? Ash ducked her head. "Yeah, but sometimes, they will react like that."

Sasha tilted her head in acknowledgment. "Sometimes. But most of the time, people take their cues from you. If you act like two women getting married is the most normal thing in the world, they will too."

Ash didn't believe that it would be that easy, at least not always, but she was glad for Holly that it had been like that this time.

The saleswoman grabbed a couple of dresses to get a feel for what Holly liked and led her to the changing room. The rest of the group settled down on two short couches to either side of the dressing room, prepared to wait while Holly tried on dress after dress. Since the two moms sat together, Sasha and Ash took the other sofa.

The couch dipped beneath Sasha's weight, making Ash slide toward her. Their shoulders brushed, and Ash caught a whiff of Sasha's cinnamon scent. She forced herself to move away from her warmth. "Sorry," she mumbled.

Sasha turned on the couch to face her. "I don't mind."

Ash's body didn't mind at all either, and that was part of the problem. She was very much aware of the two moms sitting in full view of them.

"God, Ash, relax, will you? You'll bruise a vertebrae or something if you keep sitting there so stiffly." Sasha bounced up and down on the sofa, throwing Ash into her.

"Sasha! Stop it." Ash threw her a rebuking gaze, but a giggle bubbled up from deep inside of her. Sasha's fun-loving nature and that carefree grin were hard to resist.

Thankfully, the two moms didn't pay them any attention because, a moment later, Holly stepped out of the changing room with a self-conscious look on her face. She slid her hands down her hips and studied herself in a giant mirror. "What do you think?"

The cream-colored dress formed a striking contrast to Holly's rich auburn hair. A sweetheart neckline with halter straps showed off her generous curves without displaying too much of them. The lace flared out from the waist and reached all the way down to the floor.

"Wow." Ash was the first to find her voice. "You look beautiful."

"Yeah. I'll have to hold on to Leo so she doesn't topple into the creek when she sees you," Sasha added.

Beth and Sharon were both rooting through their purses for tissues.

The saleswoman laughed. "If you make your mother and your mother-in-law cry, you know you've found the right dress."

Holly beamed and again looked into the mirror.

"But the most important question is: Do you like it?" Sasha asked.

Ash wasn't surprised; it was such a Sasha thing to say.

"I love it," Holly said quietly. She stroked her palms down the dress, caressing the fabric as if in awe of its beauty. "But I can't buy the very first dress I try on...can I?"

Sasha shrugged. The movement made her arm brush Ash's. "Sure you can. Sometimes, you just have to trust your heart if it tells you it's right."

Holly looked at her with an affectionate smile. "You're such a romantic. Remind me again why you're still single?"

"Guess my heart hasn't pointed me to the right person yet."

Ash looked down at her shoes and tried not to imagine Sasha finding someone else.

Holly turned toward the saleswoman. "I'll take it."

The saleslady blinked several times. "Just like that?"

Holly pointed to the bottom of the dress. "I think it'll have to be taken up a little, but other than that, I can't imagine a more perfect dress."

"Well, far be it from me to mess with perfection." The saleswoman pinned the bottom of the dress and set up an appointment for a final dress fitting. Within less than twenty minutes of first entering the store, they were on their way back home.

"Wow, that was fast," Sasha said as she settled into the passenger seat. "If only finding an outfit for me would be as painless."

Ash had never really thought about it, because Sasha always looked great in whatever she wore, but since she was so tall, finding something nice to wear was probably a nightmare.

Holly reached across the middle console and patted Sasha's arm. "Want me to go outfit shopping with you next weekend?"

"Nah. I know you and Leo have your hands full with wedding prep stuff. I'll be fine."

Ash couldn't bear the thought of her out shopping alone, going from store to store and becoming more discouraged with each one. "I could go with you." The offer was out before she could think twice about it.

Sasha turned and searched her face. "Are you sure?"

"Yes. I mean, it's just an afternoon of outfit shopping, right? It'll be fun."

"I wouldn't go that far," Sasha muttered. "But if you help me find something I like, I'll spring for dinner afterward."

"Deal."

Sasha stuck her hand through the gap between the seats, and they shook on it.

Just an afternoon of outfit shopping, Ash repeated to herself. *Completely harmless.* All she had to do was to ignore that almost magnetic pull she felt any time Sasha came within inches of her and the tingle making its way up her arm right now.

Much earlier than expected, Holly pulled the big SUV into her mother's driveway, and they all climbed out.

"Want to come in for some coffee?" Beth asked.

Ash had a feeling that her offer translated to several hours of going through bridal magazines, browsing online stores to find the nicest place cards, and discussing the best way to organize RSVPs. The two moms had talked about nothing but the wedding the entire way home.

"I'd love to," Sharon said immediately.

"Um..." Ash traded gazes with Sasha and had to smile when she realized Sasha was also looking for a polite way to refuse.

"No, thanks," Ash said. "If I have coffee in the afternoon, it keeps me up all night."

"Oh, I have tea too," Beth countered.

"Sorry, Mom. I need to go home and check on Leo and the costume designer. She came all the way from New York to make sure Leo's measurements are the same as during her last concert. If you can drive Sharon home later, I'll drop these two off on my way home." Without waiting for a reply, Holly herded Sasha and Ash to her Jeep, which was parked next to her mother's SUV.

They climbed in faster than bank robbers rushing into their getaway car.

As they pulled out of the driveway, Sasha wiped her brow and chuckled. "Phew. Thanks for the rescue, Holly."

"Sorry, guys. I hope they go back to normal after the wedding."

Ash laughed. "The moment you say 'I do,' they'll probably start planning the baby shower and the baptism of their first grandchild."

A snort escaped Holly. "Aren't you forgetting something? Even if we do have sex on our wedding night, neither of us can get pregnant."

An almost physical jolt went through Ash every time Holly talked so openly about sex—or the option of not having sex. That was one of the many reasons they hadn't worked out as a couple. They had never talked openly about what happened or didn't happen between them in the bedroom.

"Oh, don't worry," Sasha said. "Knowing your moms, they'll come up with a solution for that little problem too."

Holly stopped the Jeep in front of the bakery.

Sasha unfastened her seat belt and turned to look at Ash. "So, you and me have a hot date next weekend?"

"Um…what?"

Sasha laughed. "All that talk about making babies has put your mind in the gutter, hasn't it? I was talking about hunting for my wedding outfit."

Heat rose up Ash's neck. For the millionth time in her life, she cursed her tendency to blush easily. "I knew what you meant. Yes, we're still on for outfit shopping."

"Great." Sasha's teasing grin gentled into a warm smile. "Thank you." She said goodbye to Holly and got out of the Jeep. As she loped up the stairs to her apartment, Ash caught a glimpse of Sasha's nice butt.

Holly cleared her throat.

Ash jerked her gaze away and met Holly's questioning look in the rearview mirror.

"Aren't you going to move to the front?" Holly asked.

"Oh, yeah, of course." Cursing herself for getting distracted, Ash got out and climbed into the passenger seat, which was still warm from Sasha's body heat.

As Holly drove across town, it got quiet in the Jeep. Only Jenna Blake's new, award-winning album broke the silence as it quietly played in the background.

Ash had to smile. How cute was that? "She makes you listen to her songs?"

"Makes me?" Holly shook her head and glanced away from the street to give her a quick look. "Leo doesn't make me do anything I don't want to do. I love her music, especially now that she has returned to her roots."

Ash dug her teeth into her bottom lip. "Sorry. I didn't mean it like that."

"It's okay," Holly said, and Ash realized she no longer knew her well enough to tell if she really hadn't been offended. Maybe she had never known her that well.

Holly stopped the Jeep in front of Ash's house.

"I hope you never felt like I made you do things you didn't want to do," Ash blurted out. Wow. Where had that come from? She hadn't meant to say that. But now that she had said it, she realized it had been on her mind for some time.

Holly sucked in a sharp breath. She turned off the engine and pointed toward the house. "Want to go in and talk? I think it's time we finally cleared the air."

Ash swallowed against the lump in her throat. "Are you sure?"

"Of course. Or are you afraid that people will talk if my car is parked in front of your house for too long?"

A certain bitterness resonated in her tone, proving that they indeed did have a lot to talk about.

"No, that's not why I… I just meant, you said you needed to check in with Leo and the costume designer."

"Nah. Leo can handle the costume designer. I just said that so Mom wouldn't drag me in and make me look at a thousand permutations of the table plan for the reception."

"Oh." So they were actually going to talk. Ash's fingers trembled as she undid her seat belt and opened the door.

"Where's Casper?" Holly asked as they stepped into the house and no excited barking greeted them. "Getting spoiled at his grandparents'?"

"Yeah." Ash went to the kitchen to make some tea, mainly to give her hands something to do. The cinnamon scent instantly calmed her nerves a little.

When she walked back into the living room, Holly was reacquainting herself with the space, looking at the photos on Ash's bookshelf—pictures of Ash's parents, Melissa unwrapping presents on her last Christmas, and Casper romping through the snow when he'd been a puppy.

Even during the short time they had been a couple, there had never been any photos of her and Holly on the bookshelf. Those were safely tucked away in an album, where no one could see them.

When Ash placed the two mugs on the coffee table, Holly sat on the couch next to her and took a sip of tea. "Oh, this is good." She looked at the tag dangling from the cup. "Hot Cinnamon Sunset. New favorite?"

Ash nodded and cradled her mug with both hands to stop her fingers from trembling. She blew across the tea to avoid looking at Holly. "I've been wanting to talk to you for a long time, but I always chickened out."

"Yeah, I wanted to talk too, but then I thought maybe it doesn't matter anymore."

"I don't know if it still matters to you, but I feel like I need to say it," Ash murmured.

Holly nodded at her to go on.

"I…" Ash forced herself to look up and into Holly's eyes. "I'm sorry for how things ended between us. I could have…should have been more understanding."

"How could you when I didn't even fully understand it myself back then?"

Ash was grateful for the out Holly offered, but it wasn't that simple to her. "It wasn't just you or your asexuality that I didn't understand. It took me some time to figure myself out too."

"And now you have?" Holly asked.

Ash nodded. "I realized that it wasn't just about the sex—or lack of sex."

Over the rim of her mug, Holly gave her a disbelieving look.

"No, really. I mean, yeah, sex was important to me. But not really for the sex itself but because it felt like the only kind of intimacy I could have. My home…my bedroom was the only place where I could be myself without fear of being judged."

Holly stared into her tea. "And I took that away."

"I know you didn't mean to. That was my issue, not yours. But…" Ash lifted her hand and dropped it into her lap. "Not being able to fully express myself and my feelings for you… It made me feel pretty alone and ridiculed."

"Ridiculed?" Holly pressed a hand to her chest. "By me?"

Ash clutched her mug to hold back all the old hurt that wanted to bubble up. "You touched me so rarely. Um, and I don't mean in a sexual way, just little loving touches. It got to a point where you only showed me any kind of affection when we were out in public, when you knew I couldn't enjoy it or return it. Sometimes, it seemed like you did that just to spite me or to get back at me for being in the closet."

"What? No! I didn't even realize I was doing that."

Now it was Ash's turn to give her a doubtful look.

"I swear I wanted to be affectionate with you, Ash, and not just out in public. But I guess I was afraid that if I touched you when we were alone, you'd…"

"Afraid? Of me?" The blood rushed from Ash's face so fast that she grew dizzy. She put the mug on the coffee table before it could slip from her grasp. "I would never have forced you to—"

"I know." Holly put her mug away too and took her hand.

Ash stared at their fingers, tangled together in a tight grip. "This," she whispered. "This is what I missed most."

Holly nodded. "I missed it too, but I was afraid that any kind of touching would inevitably lead to you wanting sex."

"Jesus, Holly! You make me sound like a sex addict!" Ash tugged on her hand, but Holly didn't let go. "I've lived without sex for the past seven years just fine." Okay, maybe the *just fine* was a bit of an exaggeration, but she had gotten used to it.

Holly's eyes widened. "You seriously haven't been with anyone since…? I thought you and Sasha might have hooked up."

"No!" Ash finally freed her hand. "Why would you think that?"

"Because I have a rearview mirror," Holly said with a grin.

"Um, what?"

"Earlier, when we dropped Sasha off, I saw you watch her walk away in the rearview mirror. I'm usually pretty oblivious to stuff like that, but even I couldn't miss that hungry look in your eyes."

Ash's ears began to burn with heat. God, she really had to be more careful. If anyone other than Holly had seen that… She wanted to cover her face with her hands, but she knew she had to play it cool. "Yeah, well, she's pretty easy on the eyes. And, um, like I said, it's been seven years. But we're just friends. I'm not looking to get involved with anyone. If there's one thing I learned from us, it's that I can't have a happy relationship while I'm in the closet."

"Is that really how you want to live your life?" Holly asked quietly. "Just because we didn't work out doesn't mean you don't deserve to be happy. I want you to have what I have with Leo."

"I tried to ask her out." God! Ash slapped both hands over her lips. What the hell was coming out of her mouth today? She definitely hadn't meant to tell her that. She eyed the tea as if it contained truth serum.

"Sasha?" Holly asked. "Don't tell me she rejected you. I'm not the best at judging these things, but if I'm not mistaken, she looks at you the same way you look at her."

Ash tried not to listen or think about the way Sasha looked at her and what it meant. "No, not Sasha. Leo."

"Oh." Holly reached for her mug and gulped down half of the tea as if it were liquor. Then she looked into Ash's eyes. "I know."

Good thing Ash hadn't picked up her own mug. It would have crashed to the floor at this point. She gaped at Holly. "You…she…she told you that?"

Holly nodded calmly. "We try not to repeat the mistakes from past relationships, so we tell each other everything."

Everything except for Ash calling Holly's sexual orientation an "issue." Leo had kept that from Holly to protect her, but Holly probably had a pretty good idea of what Ash had said anyway. Ash wanted to crawl behind the couch and never come back out. "It's not because I'm still in love with her." Oh Christ! Now she had basically admitted to having been in love with Leo in the past.

But Holly didn't react to her confession, as if she had already known that too. She calmly nodded at her to go on.

"It wasn't really her I wanted. I wanted what she had: a happy relationship and fans who adore her. No one seems to mind that she's gay."

"She didn't get there without a struggle, Ash."

"I know that now," Ash said. "I just wanted to apologize in case…in case I created any problems between you two."

Holly patted her arm. "Don't worry. You didn't."

"Good. Because I want you to be happy. Both of you."

"Thank you. We are." The quiet glow radiating off Holly confirmed her words. "I want you to be happy too."

Ash waved her hand. "I'll be fine."

"That's not the same as being happy," Holly said.

Ash sighed. "Maybe not, but I'll have to settle for it. As long as I have my shop, my family, my friends…and Casper, it'll be enough."

"Aren't you afraid of what people will say about you being friends with the only two lesbians in town? Oh, and let's not forget the only pansexual too."

Ash decided to be completely honest. "I can barely remember a time when I haven't been afraid of that. But I have already sacrificed so much. I'm not willing to give up my friends too, so I guess I'll have to live with that fear."

Holly softly squeezed her arm.

For a while, they sipped their teas in amiable silence. Ash's chest…her entire body felt lighter, and she realized how heavily the things they had left unspoken had rested on her for years.

"I'm really glad we talked," Holly said.

"I was just thinking the same thing."

They smiled at each other.

"Oh, there's one more thing I wanted to talk about," Holly added.

Part of the tension returned to Ash's shoulders. "What is it?"

"It's about the bachelorette party," Holly said. "We'll send out invitations with all the details on Monday, but now that I have you alone, I thought maybe I should check to make sure you're okay with it."

"Okay with what?" Ash let out a chuckle. "You're not dragging us to a lesbian strip club or something, are you?"

Holly snorted. "No. Leo and I talked about what to do for our bachelorette parties, and we decided we don't want to do separate things. At first, I didn't want a bachelorette party at all. I don't feel like I need one last hurrah before I get married. I want all of my hurrahs to be with Leo."

"Aww. That's so great. So, what were you thinking?"

"Instead of a girls' night out, we want to make it an entire weekend," Holly said. "We want it to be an opportunity for our friends to get to know each other, so we've rented a beach house in Key West for the weekend a month before the wedding."

"That's in three weeks, isn't it?"

"Yeah." Holly gave her a sheepish smile. "I know that's not much notice, but we didn't want it to get too close to the wedding. Otherwise, it would be a lot of travel within a short time for our out-of-town guests. We are, of course, paying for the beach house and everyone's flights."

"You don't have to do that," Ash said. "I'd be happy to come even if I have to pay my own way."

Holly shook her head. "No. I'm a nurse, remember? I know what it's like to live on a limited income. Making you pay when Leo has millions in her bank account doesn't feel right."

Ash swallowed her pride. "Then thank you. I accept the invitation."

"Um, maybe wait until you hear the snag before you decide."

"A beach house all to ourselves in Key West." Ash laughed. "How bad could it be?"

"Not bad, but… We've invited my sisters-in-law, Jenny and my cousin Nicole, my friends Jo and Meg, Leo's friend Lauren and her wife, and you and Sasha."

"Sounds great. I'd love to meet your friends."

"Um, the snag is there's only six bedrooms in the beach house."

Ash did the math. Her breath caught as it dawned on her what Holly was saying. "That means…"

Holly nodded. "You'd have to share a room with Sasha."

Ash swallowed against her dry mouth.

"I had no idea it might be a problem when we booked the beach house," Holly added.

"It's not," Ash said quickly. "No problem at all. Why would it be a problem?"

"Um, because you looked at her as if she's a yummy chocolate cake and you're on a diet, struggling not to fall off the wagon."

"No, no, I didn't… I wasn't… I'm not struggling. Seriously. It's not a problem."

Holly laughed. "The lady doth protest too much, methinks."

"No, really. It's fine." Ash finally managed to sound so believable that she almost convinced herself.

"If you're sure. I don't want to make you uncomfortable."

"You're not. Like I said earlier, Sasha and I are friends." Friends who had shared the most passionate kiss of her life not even a week ago. She pushed away the thought.

Holly got up. "Great. I'm really looking forward to that weekend."

"Yeah," Ash said, hoping she didn't sound too lame, "me too."

She walked Holly to the door.

"Thanks for asking me in to talk." Holly opened her arms, offering a hug.

After a moment's hesitation, Ash allowed herself to sink into her embrace. There was no spark, no magnetic pull, no urge to tackle her to the floor and kiss her. This was how it should have been between them. They had always made much better friends than lovers.

Ash watched her leave. When the door clicked shut behind Holly, Ash leaned against it from the other side and rubbed her face with both hands. She had three more weeks to get herself together before she would spend an entire weekend at a beach house with Sasha. Well, Sasha and ten other women, she reminded herself.

"So what?" she said out loud. They were both adults. They could share a room without a problem...in a romantic beach setting...with possibly a party with lots of alcohol being consumed...for two nights. *Oh God.*

Chapter 13

THE NEXT SATURDAY, SASHA AND Ashley were back in Kansas City. Ashley had left Brooke in charge of the flower shop, while Aunt Mae and Tammy—Sasha's part-time employee—were manning the bakery so Ashley and Sasha could go outfit shopping. Unfortunately, their expedition wasn't very successful so far.

Sasha looked down at the borderline too-short slacks, then in the mirror at the blazer she was trying on, and finally at Ashley.

"No," they said in unison.

Sasha squished the shoulder pads. "I look like a linebacker in this."

Ashley snorted. "Nonsense. You don't. It's just that you have such nice, strong...I mean, really strong shoulders, so you don't need any shoulder pads."

A smile tugged on Sasha's lips. So Ashley thought her shoulders were nice? That almost made up for the stress of shopping. She slipped out of the blazer and gave it to Ashley to hold while she ducked back into the dressing room, where she had already tried on and discarded several outfits.

Everything had either been too businesslike, making her look like a CEO going to a business meeting, or not available in her size, and she hadn't felt comfortable in the one dress she had tried on.

"Why don't we head to dinner now?" Sasha said through the curtain separating them. "I have a nice pair of slacks and a blouse at home that I can wear to the wedding."

"Oh, no. That wasn't our deal. We'll go have dinner only once you have found something to wear."

Sasha sighed. "That could take us until Leo and Holly's first wedding anniversary."

"One more stop, okay? I want you to look good. Um, I mean, not that you usually don't, even in your frosting-smeared apron, but..." Ashley cleared her throat.

Even without seeing her, Sasha knew she was blushing. Was she thinking about the last time she had seen her in a frosting-smeared apron?

"If you don't find anything you like in the next store, you can wear whatever you have at home," Ashley said.

Back in her comfy jeans, Sasha stepped out of the dressing room. Truth be told, spending time with Ashley made the shopping experience bearable, so she nodded and steered them toward the escalator.

Ashley wanted to continue on to the ground level, but Sasha pulled her to a stop on the next level. "I think this should be our last stop."

"Um, this is the men's section."

Sasha shrugged. "So? Half of my wardrobe is from the men's section."

"Really?"

"Yeah, why not? Clothes don't have a gender. Shopping in both sections doubles my chances of finding something that actually fits. Plus the stuff in the men's department is cheaper."

"Which is so unfair. If clothes don't have a gender, neither should price tags."

"Preaching to the choir." Sasha waved toward the men's section. "So? Want to look around?"

Ashley's gaze went to the single salesclerk and several shoppers milling around, most of them men. She dragged in a long breath, then nodded and strode forward as if she owned the place.

Sasha stared after her. Shit. Confidence looked damn sexy on her. She hastened after her.

No one gave them any weird looks. Sasha had a feeling they all assumed they were shopping for a boyfriend or a male relative. Frankly, she didn't care what anyone else thought, but she knew Ashley did. It meant the world to her that Ashley was braving the men's department for her.

Ashley headed toward a row of suits at the back wall, pulled out one outfit, shook her head, slid it back in, and then repeated the process. Since she seemed to know exactly what she was searching for, Sasha just let her proceed and watched her with a smile.

It wasn't long before the salesclerk walked over. "Can I help you, ladies?"

Ashley turned. "Yes, thanks. We're looking for a suit for a wedding."

"What size is your boyfriend or husband wearing?" the salesclerk asked.

Sasha opened her mouth, about to step in.

But before she could say anything, Ashley spoke up. "We're actually looking for a suit for her." She put her hand on Sasha's shoulder.

The simple touch of support felt better than anything Sasha had experienced since…okay, since the kiss on the bakery kitchen floor.

"The women's section is upstairs." The salesclerk pointed to the escalator.

"We know." Ashley held his gaze, even though Sasha knew it was probably a struggle for her. "That's where we just came from, but nothing really fit, so we're trying our luck here."

The salesman turned toward Sasha and let his gaze trail over her from head to toe.

Ashley's hand on Sasha's shoulder tightened.

Finally, the salesclerk gave a slow nod. "So let's find you a suit."

Sasha blew out a breath—more for Ashley than for herself. She was used to all sorts of reactions, good and bad, but she hadn't wanted Ashley's bravery to be rewarded by an asshole comment.

"What were you thinking of?" For some reason, he looked at Ashley, not at Sasha.

Ashley ran her gaze up and down Sasha's body as if imagining the clothes on her.

The intense perusal heated Sasha's skin.

"Dark gray pants and vest, no jacket, and a white dress shirt." Ashley's tone was so decisive as if she'd had weeks instead of just seconds to think of the perfect outfit.

"Be right back." The salesclerk marched off to do her bidding.

Sasha stared from his retreating back to Ashley. "Wow. What was that? You kind of took over there."

Ashley's cheeks colored. "Sorry. I didn't mean to—"

"No, no. Don't apologize. It's ho—um, I mean, it's great. I just didn't expect you to get even one word out, to be honest."

"I'm trying out your advice to act like this is the most normal thing in the world, hoping he will take his cue from that," Ashley said with a small smile.

Sasha pointed to the salesclerk, who was returning with several suits and shirts for her to try. "Seems to be working."

"I didn't think it would, but maybe you're right—at least some of the time."

The salesclerk handed over his bounty. "The changing rooms are over there, but, um, they're the men's dressing rooms."

Sasha took the hangers from him. "That's fine. There's a curtain, so it's not like I'm performing a striptease in the middle of the store."

This time, the salesclerk and Ashley competed for the fieriest blush.

Chuckling, Sasha walked over to the changing room.

An older man gave her a startled look, but no one said anything.

Sasha slid the curtain closed and changed into the first outfit. The pants were an amazingly good fit, and for a change, even the men's shirt wasn't too tight at the waist. But when she buttoned up the vest, the fabric was straining against the top two buttons. She stepped out of the fitting room to show Ashley.

Ashley jumped up from a padded bench next to the dressing rooms. She stared at Sasha with a slack jaw.

Sasha peeked down at the straining buttons. "That bad?"

"Bad? No, you look great. Really, really great. You were right. We should have looked in the men's section from the start." Ashley's admiring gaze left no doubt that she meant it and wasn't just being polite.

Sasha's chest inflated under her gaze, making the buttons groan almost audibly. She quickly opened them before they could pop off. "Yeah, but this," she pointed at the vest, "isn't tailored with a woman's breasts in mind. That's usually my problem with men's vests."

"Can you take it off for a second?"

Sasha removed the vest and dangled it from her index finger.

Ashley studied her, then stepped closer and rolled up the shirtsleeves.

Her fingers grazed Sasha's forearms, setting off tiny explosions all along her skin.

"You know, I think you don't actually need a vest. Could you get us a bow tie and a pair of suspenders?" Ashley asked the salesclerk without looking away from what she was doing.

He hurried off.

"A bow tie?" Sasha asked. "Isn't that a bit too formal for the kind of wedding Leo and Holly are planning?"

"I don't think so, especially if you're not wearing a vest or a suit jacket with it. I'm sure a lot of people will dress up a little, no matter what they say. Plus…" Ashley stopped herself and busied herself putting the discarded vest back on its hanger.

Sasha gave her a gentle nudge. "Plus what?"

"A woman in a bow tie is kind of…" Her voice got lower with every word until she whispered, "Sexy."

Sasha grinned. She had assumed Ashley would be scared of what people might say about a woman dressed in traditionally male garb. Sasha knew she would definitely wear a bow tie now, even if that meant being a bit overdressed. "Oh, you think so, hmm?"

The salesclerk returning with a pair of suspenders and several bow ties saved Ashley from having to answer.

Ashley went into full fashion designer mode. She took the suspenders and clipped them to Sasha's waistband, then slid them up over her shoulders.

Sasha had no clue why she wasn't just handing them over and letting her do it, but frankly, she didn't care. If she had ever experienced something hotter than being dressed by Ashley Gaines, she had forgotten about it the moment Ashley had rolled up her sleeves. She would be Ashley's personal dress-up doll any time.

She held her breath as Ashley closed the top button of her dress shirt, turned up the collar, and looped the tie around her neck. An image flashed through Sasha's mind—of Ashley pulling on the ends of the tie to tug her down, raising up on her tiptoes, and kissing her.

Instead, Ashley tipped Sasha's chin up with one finger and tied a bow with practiced movements.

"You've done this before." Sasha hoped she didn't sound jealous, but she really disliked the thought of Ashley doing this for anyone else.

"Many times." Ashley turned down the collar and arranged the wing tips the way she wanted them. "For my father. He says my mother ties it too tight."

"Ah." The claws around Sasha's stomach loosened their grip.

Ashley straightened the bow tie and smoothed her palms along Sasha's shoulders. "Done."

Shock waves of sensation spiraled down Sasha's body, even after Ashley had stepped back. Taking Ashley outfit hunting had either been her most genius idea ever or the most masochistic one.

"Don't you like it?" Ashley asked when Sasha just stood frozen in front of the store mirror.

Sasha hadn't even taken a look at herself, too distracted by the intimate act of Ashley helping her dress. Quickly, she glanced into the mirror. *Wow.* She ran her thumbs beneath the suspenders and let them snap back against her shoulders. She loved how they looked with the purple bow tie Ashley had picked.

"I think it looks great," Ashley said, as if she had to convince Sasha.

"Yeah," the salesclerk added. "I didn't think so at first, but the suspenders were actually a good idea. Your girlfriend looks very dapper in them."

Oh shit. Sasha glanced at Ashley. She'd been doing great so far, but this was definitely out of her comfort zone.

"I...she..."

Sasha put a hand on her back, stopping the stammered explanation. "Just because two women are shopping in the men's section doesn't necessarily mean they're gay or a couple," she told the salesclerk, not unkindly.

The guy's Adam's apple bobbed up and down as he swallowed. "Oh. Sorry. I didn't mean to offend you."

"Oh, I'm not offended," Sasha said. Quite the opposite. Having him assume that someone as beautiful as Ashley was her girlfriend was actually very flattering. "Thanks so much for your help. You've been great."

He gave them a tight smile and hurried off.

"So," Sasha tugged on both ends of her bow tie, "I assume I'm buying this?"

"You're buying this," Ashley said with a decisive nod.

Sasha undid the bow tie and stepped back into the dressing room to get changed.

"You didn't have to tell him we're not gay." Ashley's quiet voice filtered through the curtain. "I don't expect you to lie or hide in the closet just because I—"

"I didn't," Sasha said. "I just told him that because two women are shopping in the men's section doesn't automatically mean they are gay. There's plenty of straight women who prefer a more androgynous style."

"Hmm. I guess you're right." Ashley was quiet for some time.

Sasha had a feeling she had a lot to digest today. She slid out of the dress shirt and back into her button-down. "Are you ready for some food? The restaurant is keeping our table all evening, so we can go whenever you want."

"No," Ashley answered.

Sasha paused with the suit pants halfway down her thighs. "No?" Had Ashley changed her mind about the dinner invitation afterward? Was she afraid that it would be too much like a date?

"No," Ashley repeated. "Before we can have dinner, you need shoes to wear with your new outfit. Or do you have a pair at home?"

Sasha sighed. "Shoe shopping it is."

"Come on. It'll be fun."

Maybe—but not half as much fun as trying on the suit since Ashley probably wouldn't help her put her shoes on. Chuckling to herself, Sasha buttoned up her jeans and grabbed the new outfit. After one last soft touch to the bow tie Ashley had declared sexy, she slid back the curtain and joined Ashley outside.

Ash had assumed Sasha would take her to one of the many barbecue restaurants in Kansas City. Instead, Sasha parked in the River Market neighborhood, and they walked down the historic street, past a bookstore bar and other quaint little places.

A streetcar rattled past, and Sasha held on to Ash's elbow, as if protecting her from trying to cross the street at the wrong moment.

With other dates, Ash had felt patronized in similar situations, but with Sasha, she only felt cared for.

Other dates? This isn't a date, she told herself firmly.

Once the streetcar had passed, Sasha led her across the street, to a late-nineteenth-century building and held open the door to The Meadow, one of the trendiest restaurants in town. Sasha's hand rested in the small of her back, warming Ash from head to toe, as Sasha guided her inside.

When Sasha gave her name, the hostess led them to a corner table in a small room that was separate from the main dining room. The restaurant was elegant but cozy, with subdued lighting and candles flickering on tables for two. The exposed brick walls were covered by artwork and a huge chalkboard listing the farms where the food was coming from. An open kitchen took up half of the room. Behind a broad workstation, Ash caught glimpses of two chefs who were busy chopping vegetables, frying meat, and preparing dessert plates with amazing efficiency. The scent of roasted garlic, tomatoes, and sage made Ash's mouth water, and soft live music drifted over from the main room, where a pianist was playing jazz.

"Wow," Ash said as the waiter left them with the menus. "This is great. How did you manage to get a table, much less have them reserve it for us the entire evening? I heard you have to make reservations at least a month in advance."

Sasha gave a mysterious smile. "I have my ways. So you haven't been here before?"

Ash laughed. "It's a little out of my price range." She sobered and looked at Sasha across the small table. "You didn't have to take me somewhere this expensive. I would have been happy with a burger or some pizza."

"Nah. You deserve to be treated. In fact, you deserve dinner for a month for helping me find an outfit. God, you had the patience of a saint."

Patient was the last thing Ash had felt when she had seen Sasha in her chosen wedding outfit. Who knew women could look so hot in suspenders and a bow tie? Or maybe not women in general, but Sasha had definitely looked hot. Ash had wanted to slide those suspenders down Sasha's strong shoulders, unbutton the dress shirt, and kiss a path down the skin she laid bare.

"You okay?" Sasha leaned forward and studied her in the candlelight. "You spaced out there for a minute."

Ash was grateful for the low lighting that hopefully hid her blush. She shook her head to clear it. "Oh yeah. I'm fine. Just listening to the piano player. He—or she—is really good."

"They have live music every night, mostly up-and-coming local jazz artists," Sasha said. "I thought you, as a former musician, would appreciate it."

"I do." Sasha was so thoughtful, Ash had to remind herself again that this wasn't a date. The romantic atmosphere didn't exactly help, though.

Sasha opened the menu. "Pick whatever you want. If you look at the prices, I'll be insulted."

Ash studied the list of dishes, determined to not go overboard, no matter what Sasha said. It wouldn't be hard to pick something in the middle of the price range since everything sounded delicious.

"They prepare all their dishes with farm-to-table, locally grown ingredients, and their meat is from happy cows and pigs only," Sasha said.

Ash looked up from her menu. "How do you know so much about them? Did you research the restaurant before deciding where to take me?" She could see her doing that to make sure they had a good time.

"That too." Sasha lifted the menu as if hiding a bit of a blush herself. "But mostly, I know because I went to culinary school with one of the co-owners. She's The Meadow's pastry chef, responsible for their yummy breads and desserts, while her business partner is the head chef."

"Have you ever thought about working in a restaurant like this?" Ash asked.

Sasha shook her head immediately. "Not for a second. It's not that I'm not a team player, but I like doing my own thing."

"I know what you mean. That's what I like about having my own shop too." Ash returned her attention to the menu. "God, this is hard. It all sounds so good. What will you get?"

"The Meadow Caesar salad, for starters," Sasha said without hesitation. "They serve it with walnut bread fresh out of the oven. So good."

Ash laughed. "You're such a bread geek."

"Oh, you're laughing now, but try it, and you'll be addicted for life."

Ash looked into Sasha's sparkling brown eyes. A woman could easily get addicted to gazing into those dark eyes. *Stop it. This is just a thank-you dinner, remember?* She focused on the menu again. "What are you thinking for an entrée?"

"Their hanger steak is to die for." Sasha let out a moan that nearly convinced Ash to take the steak too. "It's so tender it nearly melts in your mouth."

Ash ran a finger beneath her collar as the temperature in the cozy room seemed to skyrocket. "Steak?" Her chuckle sounded a little husky. "I thought you weren't ready for a steak dinner?"

"I'm ready for their steak dinner any time." Sasha lowered her voice to a seductive burr that made shivers run through Ash.

Thankfully, the waitress chose that moment to step up to the table and ask for their order.

Still preoccupied with the things Sasha's voice had done to her, Ash chose the salad with the yummy bread Sasha had recommended and decided on the first entrée that caught her attention—gooseberry-glazed duck with mashed sweet potatoes and sherry-pickled beets.

The waitress delivered their orders straight to the chefs working in the open kitchen.

One of them looked over, and a broad smile dimpled her cheeks. She gave a wave and abandoned her workstation to stride over. She took off her white chef's hat as she walked, revealing wavy, raven black hair piled up into a stylishly messy bun on top of her head.

Wow. She was striking. Ash tried not to stare. Was that Sasha's friend from culinary school?

The woman didn't even glance at Ash or anyone else in the restaurant. She went straight for Sasha like a heat-seeking missile. "Hey, stranger." She had a hint of a French accent that made her even more attractive. "Long time no see!"

Sasha got up and wrapped her arms around the chef in a bear hug, practically lifting the slender woman off her feet in the process.

The chef let out a delighted laugh, apparently not caring at all that every guest in the room was now looking at them, and wrapped her arms around Sasha's neck.

Ash's body went cold. She clenched her hands into fists beneath the white tablecloth. The delicious scents wafting through the room suddenly lost their appeal. Was the woman really just a friend from culinary school, or was there more going on? Was she why Sasha was so intimately familiar with the restaurant's menu? Did she drive to Kansas City every now and then to see her—or have "pizza" with her?

"Okay, okay, enough." The woman lightly slapped Sasha's shoulder. "Let me down now, or your companion will think I'm a bad hostess for not even saying hello to her."

Sasha gently set her back on her feet.

The woman kept one arm wrapped around Sasha's waist as she turned toward Ash.

Years of living in a small town where everyone seemed to constantly watch her had made Ash perfect a polite mask, and now she put it to good use as she slowly rose too. "Hi," she said with a friendly smile and stuck out her hand.

"Ash, this is Nadia Jamison, one of the owners of this culinary marvel of a restaurant. Nadia, this is Ashley Gaines."

No qualifier for her, Ash noticed. She wasn't sure whether she liked that or not. Deep down, she had been curious as to how Sasha would introduce her—as a friend? Someone she worked with? *Yeah, well, what is she supposed to say? Someone she kissed in the middle of a food fight?* At least that might get Nadia to back off.

Nadia shook her hand. Her grip was confident, but she didn't try to turn the handshake into a show of strength, and Ash grudgingly liked that. "Great to meet you, Ashley." She clapped Sasha's shoulder. "I've been telling this one to bring a date for ages, but she never has—until now."

Sasha shifted her weight. "Uh, this isn't a date, Nadia."

"Oh. I thought…" Nadia looked back and forth between them and then grinned. "Well, in that case…" She lifted Ash's hand to her lips and hinted at a kiss to the back of her fingers. "…dessert is on me. I'll be out to chat later, but now we need to get cracking on your dinner." A wink and a wave and she walked back to her workstation.

Ash sank back onto her chair and stared after her. "Did she just…flirt with me?"

Sasha frowned. "She did. I can tell her to cut it out, if it makes you uncomfortable."

"It doesn't." To her own surprise, it was the truth. Kansas City was a lot bigger and more anonymous than Fair Oaks. No one knew her here, and if Nadia was flirting with her, that meant she hadn't set her sights on Sasha.

"Oh." The line between Sasha's brows deepened.

Was she interested in Nadia? Ash softly cleared her throat. With most other people, she would shy away from asking personal questions, afraid that the other person would want to ask about her private life too, but with Sasha, she was beyond that already. "So you and Nadia… Back in culinary school, were you…did you…go out?"

"Yeah." Sasha laughed. "Well, there actually wasn't much going out involved. I nearly flunked the Human Nutrition course because we were busy, um, staying in, if you know what I mean."

Ash had already gotten the impression that there was more than friendship between them, but hearing it confirmed still made her back stiffen. "She seems great," Ash said, a bit lamely.

Sasha nodded. "Yeah. She is." Something seemed to be bothering her too, because her usual easygoing smile was absent.

For a minute or two, they waited for their starters in silence. Ash realized that silence between them had been rare. They always seemed to have something interesting to talk about.

"It's been over between Nadia and me for years," Sasha said after a while. "So if she asks you out—and I'm sure she will—please don't feel like you have to say no because of me."

Ash stared at her. "A-ask me out?"

"Yeah. I know Nadia," Sasha muttered. "She'll dazzle you with her dessert creation, and instead of having the waitress bring you the bill, she'll send over her phone number at the end of the evening."

Ash looked over at Nadia's workstation.

Nadia gazed up from the bread she was cutting and sent her a smile.

Ash ducked her head back down. Jesus. How had she gotten herself into this situation? "She's beautiful, and I'm sure she's very nice."

Sasha's brows lowered. "Yeah."

"But I don't want to be dazzled with dessert creations or anything else," Ash added firmly.

"No?" Sasha asked.

"No. You know my situation. I'm not into, um, pizza, and eating steak in secret doesn't work for me either."

Sasha nodded thoughtfully. "So you'll tell Nadia you're…um, on a diet?"

"If she really asks me out, I guess I will."

Sasha seemed relieved. Was that because she wasn't completely over her ex and didn't want Ash to get in the way, or because—?

Whoa. Thinking like that wouldn't do her any good.

It didn't take long until their salads arrived, so either they were getting special treatment or the chefs were always this fast.

Ash took a bite of the walnut bread, which was still warm. "Oh my God," she moaned around a mouthful of bread. "This is so good."

Sasha laughed. "Told you. Just tone down the moaning a little."

"You don't like moaning?" Ash couldn't help putting just the tiniest bit of flirtation in her tone.

"Oh, I like it just fine—as long as I...I mean my breads...are causing it."

"Jealous?" Ash asked with a grin.

"Nah. I'm confident in my superior skills." Sasha winked at her. "My baking skills, of course."

God, flirting with her was fun, but Ash knew she had to cut it out. It was a fine line to walk. "Since we're speaking of exes," she said quietly. "I talked to Holly last weekend. About us...her and me...and how it all ended. Talking to you about it made me realize that it was long overdue."

Sasha pierced a bit of romaine salad with her fork but didn't eat it yet. "How did it go?"

"Really well. I actually think we can be friends now."

"That's great. I'm happy to hear that." Sasha reached across the table with her free hand and squeezed Ash's fingers.

A rush of warmth spread through Ash. She stared down at her hand, amazed at the strength of her reaction at such a simple touch.

Sasha followed her gaze and quickly withdrew as if only now becoming aware she had touched her. But she continued to smile at her.

She radiated such sincerity that Ash beamed along with her. "Me too." Then she remembered what else she and Holly had talked about. "Um, did you get the invitation for the bachelorette weekend?"

"Yeah. A weekend in the Keys and a beach house just for us. Isn't it great?" Sasha grinned and then chewed her forkful of salad.

Hadn't she heard about the sleeping arrangements yet?

Ash slid to the edge of her chair as her tension grew. "Uh, yeah, it is, but…"

"You might have to stop me from making a fool of myself." Sasha playfully pressed her water glass to her forehead. "Just think! We might get to see Grace Durand in a bikini."

"Grace Durand?" Ash stared at her. "What are you talking about?"

"Didn't they mention that Leo is friends with her wife, and they are both coming to Florida?"

"Grace Durand is coming to the bachelorette weekend? *The* Grace Durand?"

"Yeah. The one and only." Sasha playfully fanned herself. "Four-time Golden Globe winner, *Esquire*'s Sexiest Woman Alive, and the crush of my teenage years."

Ash frowned at her. "Maybe you want to share a room with her instead of with me, then," she muttered and stabbed at her salad.

Sasha chuckled. "Oh, I think her wife wouldn't apprecia…" She froze and stared at her. "Uh, did you just say we'll be sharing a room?"

"Yeah. That's what I was trying to tell you before you went all gaga over Grace Durand. There are only six rooms in the beach house, so we'll all have to double up and share with someone—and you get me."

Sasha mumbled something.

"Pardon me?"

"Um, I was just asking if that's okay with you."

"Of course it is. Why wouldn't it be?" Ash studied her across the table. "Are you okay with it?"

"Oh yeah. No problem." Sasha gulped down her water and flagged down a passing waiter for more.

Ash watched her throat move as she swallowed. How could anyone look so sexy drinking? She took a big gulp of her own water and was glad when the waitress brought their entrées.

Both the duck and Sasha's steak looked fantastic.

Sasha's eyes fluttered shut as she took the first bite. "Yum. This is so good. Want to try?" Without waiting for a reply, she cut off a square, spread a bit of blue cheese butter over it, and held it out to Ash, inviting her to eat it right off her fork.

Very conscious of Nadia and anyone else who might be watching, Ash reached for the fork instead. As Sasha handed it over, their fingers brushed. A shiver went through Ash. Her skin felt hypersensitive, as if trying to soak up the fleeting touch.

"You don't like it?" Sasha asked.

"Oh, no. I love it." Ash quickly chewed and swallowed the forgotten bite of meat. It was juicy and tender, with just a hint of Dijon mustard, rosemary, and garlic. "Yum. That might be the best steak I've ever tried—and that's saying something since my dad is a grill master."

Sasha grinned. "You'd better not tell him, then."

No, Ash definitely wouldn't. If she told her parents she'd been to The Meadow, that would only lead to questions about who she had been with and why she was spending so much time with Sasha instead of going out with Derek or some other man.

"Want to try some of mine? It's pretty amazing too." She held out a forkful of her gooseberry-glazed duck for Sasha to try.

Instead of taking the fork, as Ash had, Sasha leaned forward and wrapped her lips around it.

The waiter should have left the pitcher of water at their table because Ash's throat went dry again.

"Enjoying your food?" Nadia's voice right next to the table made Ash wrench her gaze away from Sasha.

"Oh. Yeah, very much so," Ash said. "It's wonderful."

"That's what I like to hear." A pleased grin formed charming dimples on Nadia's cheeks. "Listen, don't order dessert. I'll create something especially for you."

She seemed to be speaking more to Ash than to Sasha, and Ash wasn't sure how to handle that—other than by being polite. She smiled up at her. "Thank you. That's really nice of you."

Nadia touched her finger to her chef's hat and wandered back toward her workstation.

Sasha put down her fork, her gaze following her ex. "Unless you're ready to eat pizza with her, I wouldn't encourage her."

"Encourage her?" Ash echoed. "How did I encourage her?"

"You smiled at her, and you praised her food. That's a total aphrodisiac for us culinary types."

A couple of beets that Ash had just pierced with her fork splashed into the mashed sweet potatoes. "Um, I always smile and tell you how good your cupcakes are every time I come into the bakery."

"That's different." A lopsided grin curled one corner of Sasha's mouth. "Or are you saying you've been flirting with me?"

"No! And I'm not flirting with Nadia either. I was just being polite."

"Good." Sasha dug into her steak with gusto.

Ash watched her. Was Sasha jealous…and maybe not because she was still interested in her ex but because she didn't like Nadia's interest in her?

"Why are you grinning?" Sasha asked.

"I'm not grinning." *Am I?* Ash touched her lips. Okay, she was. "Just enjoying my meal."

Sasha watched Ashley dig into the cinnamon apple crisp on her dessert platter with a smile. It was good to see her enjoy the simple pleasures of life instead of always keeping herself in check.

Unfortunately, Nadia seemed to enjoy Ashley's enthusiasm for her apple crisp, her chocolate swirl cheesecake, and her passion fruit mousse just as much. She was watching Ashley from behind her workstation with an enchanted grin. God, had she been such an incorrigible flirt when they had gone to culinary school together?

Well, back then, Nadia had flirted with *her*, and Sasha hadn't minded at all.

Finally, Ashley admitted defeat and put her dessert fork down to press both hands to her belly. "If I eat another bite, I'm going to explode."

When the waitress came over to whisk away the half-empty plates, Sasha requested the bill.

Instead, the waitress returned with two boxes of their uneaten dessert. "No bill. Dinner is on the house."

Sasha handed her a generous tip. "Tell the chefs thank you, please." She would find a way to pay her friend back.

The waitress nodded. The box she set down in front of Ashley had a familiar phone number scribbled on the side.

Ashley stared at it, clearly unsure of how to handle this situation.

She'd spent her life in the closet, Sasha reminded herself, so this might be the very first time a woman had openly hit on her. Sasha's protective instincts flared. She reached across the table and squeezed her hand. "Do you want me to talk to her?"

Ashley turned her hand beneath hers and returned the gentle squeeze before withdrawing. For a moment, she looked tempted, but then she shook her head. "Thanks, but I can handle it." She sounded as if she wanted to convince herself as much as Sasha. "Be right back."

After a steadying breath, Ashley rose and walked over to the open kitchen, where Nadia was leaning against her workstation, watching her approach. The expression on her face revealed that she appreciated Ashley's girl-next-door good looks as much as Sasha did.

Ashley paused in front of her.

Sasha couldn't hear what she was saying over the din in the restaurant, but she could read Ashley's body language loud and clear. Her awkward stance screamed how uncomfortable she was.

Nadia answered, and whatever she said, it got Ashley to relax a little.

Watching them with each other was weird, like two worlds colliding that had never mingled before. Sasha had to admit that they would have made a striking couple. Nadia's messy black locks, her slim figure, and her French accent, which stemmed from spending part of her youth in her mother's native country, formed an attractive contrast to Ashley's flowing, blonde hair, her graceful curves, and her—at least to Sasha's ear—lack of an accent.

Once upon a time, Sasha hadn't been able to take her gaze—and her hands—off Nadia long enough to study for an important exam, but now she found herself ignoring Nadia to watch Ashley instead.

After a minute or two, Ashley's gestures became more animated, and the bright, clear sound of her laughter drifted over.

Sasha loved hearing her laugh so unrestrained, but at the same time, she wondered what Nadia had said. Was she trying her French charm on Ashley—and was it working?

Finally, Nadia gave her two kisses on the cheeks.

Cassidy, her business partner, watched them with a frown that probably resembled the one Sasha was sporting. Her knife slid through a bundle of leeks with more force than necessary.

Ooh. Sasha's mood brightened. *Am I sensing a little kitchen romance?* Interestingly, the usually suave Nadia seemed clueless.

Ashley returned to the table and picked up her dessert box—the one with Nadia's number on it. "All right. I'm ready to leave."

Wasn't she going to say anything? Sasha kept waiting as she guided her outside and back to the car. When she started the engine, she couldn't take it anymore. "Nadia isn't used to being rejected. How did she take it? Um, you did turn her down, didn't you?"

"Of course I did. What did you think?"

"I don't know. Those two little kisses looked awfully friendly." Sasha peeked over at her, then back at the traffic. "So?"

"I thanked her for dinner."

"And...?" Sasha nudged her. "Tell me."

"I told her that I'd definitely be back for more of the great food, but that I wouldn't be calling her for anything else."

"Wow." Sasha knew such frank words weren't normally Ashley's style. "That's great. Uh, I mean, it's good that you're making yourself clear. How did she take it?"

Ashley shrugged. "Didn't bat an eye. She made a joke about losing her touch and then told me to get you to make your famous hazelnut cake with caramel mousse for me."

"Huh." Sasha hadn't thought Nadia would take it so well.

"What? You expected her to be heartbroken?" Ashley laughed. "I'm not that irresistible."

Sasha's libido thought otherwise—which was why she was equally looking forward to and dreading sharing a room with her in Florida.

"So," Ashley said as Sasha got onto Interstate 35, "will you?"

"Um, will I...what?"

"Make your famous hazelnut cake for me."

Sasha chuckled and rubbed her neck, which felt overly warm. "That's what I sometimes made for Nadia after we had...um...burned a lot of calories together."

"Burned a lot of... Oh!" Ashley turned her head to stare through the side window as if trying to hide her blush.

God, she's cute. Sasha grinned and admitted to herself that she really liked making her blush. Then, when she took her gaze off Ashley to focus on driving, she froze. *Wait a minute...* If Nadia had suggested Sasha make her hazelnut cake for Ashley, did that mean she thought they were sleeping together—or would be sleeping together sooner or later?

So what if she thinks that? She's wrong. There would be no hazelnut cake for Ashley and especially no caramel mousse that could be licked from interesting places.

But apparently, her brain hadn't gotten the *no* in that message. It immediately showed her snapshots of her licking caramel mousse off Ashley's nipples and then swirling her tongue along the mousse trail on her belly. *Jesus.* She turned up the air-conditioning and directed the vents at her face.

Ashley let out an embarrassed chuckle. "Well, maybe hazelnut cake isn't such a good idea after all. I'd better stick to your vanilla cupcakes."

Sasha bit her lip and said nothing. After that kissing incident in the bakery kitchen, she wasn't so sure cupcakes would be safer.

Chapter 14

"GODDAMN MOTHER-FUCKING BASTARDS!" LEO'S FAMOUS pop star voice even sounded good when hurling curses across the Hy-Vee parking lot.

Uh-oh. Ash, who had just stepped out of the supermarket, slowed her step. That sounded as if Leo was having a bad day. Maybe she could help. She deviated from her course and carried her watermelon over to Leo's BMW X5 instead of continuing to her own car. "You okay?"

Leo whirled around. She gripped her phone so tightly that Ash thought the screen would shatter. "Did that sound like I'm okay?" she snarled.

Ash took a step back and clutched her watermelon. "Um, no, not really."

Leo sighed, shoved the phone into her pocket, and rubbed her face. "Sorry. I didn't mean to take it out on you. It's just so damn frustrating."

"Music industry trouble?" Ash asked.

"I wish. At least then I could pretend to be a diva, knock some heads together, and be done with it."

"Then what is it?" Ash stepped closer. "Can I help in any way?"

Leo's grim expression softened. "That's nice of you to offer, but unless you have a reception venue in your back pocket, I don't think you can."

"Reception venue? Why do you need another one? I thought you booked the ballroom of the country club."

"Yeah, that's what I thought too." Leo slumped against the rear of her car. "But they just called and said they've double-booked the ballroom on that day, so they can't give it to us after all."

Ash stared at her. "Is this some kind of," she glanced left and right and lowered her voice, "homophobic bullshit?"

Leo sighed. "I don't know. I'll give them the benefit of the doubt and believe that it's really just a mistake. They apologized profusely, but that doesn't do us any good."

"Even if it was an honest mistake, how can they kick Jenna Blake out?" Someone with a brain the size of a pea must have made that decision.

"I guess that's what I get for not wanting to play the superstar card and insisting they kick out the other couple."

Ash smiled at her. That was what she liked about Leo. Even after four Grammy Awards and five platinum albums, she never assumed her own needs were more important than those of everyone else.

"Looks like I'll have to make a few calls. It shouldn't be too hard to find something else, but probably not in town. Not at this late notice." Leo kicked a pebble across the parking lot. "Shit. My mother had her heart set on a Fair Oaks wedding. We already disappointed her when we refused to get married in the church where my dad played the organ every Sunday for over thirty years. And now this…"

Growing up, Ash had spent almost as much time at the Blakes' as she had at home. Leo's father had taught her how to play the piano, and Leo's mother had held her after Melissa had killed herself and her own parents had been too overwhelmed with grief to really be there for her. "What if…?" She hesitated. If she let this particular Pandora out of the box, there was no way back. *Do it. Come on. It's for Leo and Holly.* She inhaled deeply, then blew out a breath through her nose. "What if I have a venue you could use?"

Leo gave her a tired smile. "It's a lovely offer, Ash, but I don't think all of our guests will fit in your tiny backyard."

She hadn't called her *Ash* in years, and Ashley only now realized how much she'd missed it. Hearing it strengthened her resolve. "I'm not talking about my backyard. Do you remember the old barn where we used to have band practices?"

"You mean the one where you broke my little heart when I caught you kissing Brandon?" Leo's eyes twinkled, indicating that she had long since gotten over it.

A blush warmed Ash's cheeks. "Um, yeah, that one." He had been kissing her, not the other way around, but that didn't matter now. "My dad isn't really using it anymore. He keeps some tractor parts and other equipment in there, but that's all. Maybe I can talk my parents into letting you use the barn for the reception."

Leo stared off into space as if she could already see the barn set up for the wedding. "Hmm, that could work. According to my mom's bridal magazines, old barns and their rustic charm are all the rage for weddings right now. I bet Holly would love it." She turned her gaze on Ash. "But are you sure you want to ask your parents to let us use it? Knowing them, they won't exactly be overjoyed to host a lesbian wedding on their land. Do you really think they'll say yes?"

"I have no idea," Ash said honestly. "But asking won't hurt, right?"

Leo looked at her as if she knew it wasn't that easy for Ash. Asking *would* hurt, but Ash was willing to do it anyway. "Thank you," Leo finally said.

"They haven't said yes yet, and I can't guarantee they will." Ash didn't want Leo to get her hopes up too much.

"Thank you anyway." Leo reached across the watermelon in Ash's arms and patted her shoulder. "Can you let me know by the end of the week? If it doesn't work out, I'll need to start looking for other options."

Ash gave a grim nod. That would give her four days to talk to her parents. "We're having a barbecue on Sunday. I'll ask them then and call you right after."

Ash left Casper with her mother in the kitchen, not stopping to chat beyond saying hello, and went outside to where her father had set up his beloved charcoal grill. She knew she had to talk to him first, since he usually handled all decisions regarding the farm buildings.

When she slid open the glass door, the tantalizing aroma of sizzling steaks wafted over. Usually, it would have made her mouth water, but now she was too nervous to be hungry.

Her father placed the lid on the grill and waved his long-handled barbecue fork in welcome. "Hi, honey. Good timing. The steaks should be done in a few minutes."

"Hi, Dad." She walked over and kissed his cheek.

He wrapped one arm around her and didn't let go as they talked, keeping her next to him at the grill. "I hope you're hungry. Your mother is baking enough potatoes to feed a team of football players. Maybe you should call some of your friends and ask them over."

"Um, I'm sure they all have plans for lunch already."

Her father shrugged. "Then invite them over another time. It's been ages since you brought anyone home."

Ash suppressed a groan. Clearly, her mother had talked to her father about her lack of dates, and that was what he was hinting at. But his invitation had also opened the door for what she wanted to talk about. "Um, actually, I was thinking of having some friends over. But not just for a barbecue."

"If you want to throw a big party for your birthday this year, sure. We've got the space."

"Not for my birthday." Ash shuffled her feet. Her father's arm around her shoulders suddenly felt heavy. "I was more thinking of a wedding."

A screeching cry and the crash of glass interrupted her father before he could say anything.

Ash turned her head.

Her mother stood in the doorway of the sliding door. A bottle of barbecue sauce had escaped from her grasp, and now little shards of glass and spatters of sauce covered half of the patio. "You're getting married? That's…that's…wonderful, but…who…?"

Ash pressed her hand to her forehead. Oh Christ. She was making a mess of things. "No, Mom. I'm not getting married. My friends are."

"Oh." Her mother's face fell. "Who's getting married? I didn't know we'd have another wedding in Fair Oaks. Why am I always the last one in town to find out? We're spending too much time on the farm, Tom."

"Um, it's not another wedding, Mom. I'm talking about Leo and Holly's wedding." Ash forced herself to continue before she could chicken out. "The country club just canceled their reservation, so now they don't have a space for their wedding reception. I was thinking maybe they could use the old barn."

Her father lifted the lid of the grill and flipped the steaks without saying anything.

"Dad?"

Her father took his time replacing the lid. "Why would you want them to celebrate that kind of wedding in our barn?"

Ash tried to keep her voice from shaking. "Because they're my friends."

He rubbed his neck. "I don't know about that, Ashley."

A spark of anger smoldered hotter than the charcoal in the grill. "When we were growing up, Leo spent a lot of time helping out at the farm. She walked beans as much as I did, and she never complained about the blisters on her hands, even though her father gave her hell about them because they interfered with her violin playing. You told her to call you Tom because she was almost like a family member…and now you don't care that she won't have a place to celebrate her wedding?"

"That was a long time ago," her father mumbled. "She was different then."

"No, Dad. She wasn't. She was gay back then too. You just didn't know it." The words bubbled out of Ash like a flooded river in spring.

"I'm not talking about," he waved his barbecue fork, "that. She got too big for her britches. Ms. Famous Singer thinks she's too good for little people like us, and now she wants our barn for her wedding? Hell, no. Either she is one of us, or she isn't. Can't have it both ways."

"Yeah," her mother added as she picked up the biggest glass shards and started to clean up the mess. "Don't think we didn't notice that she didn't call—not even once—all the years she was gone. Not even a card to say congratulations when you opened the flower shop. It was out of sight, out of mind, and she of all people should have known how much it would hurt you to lose anyone else after Melissa…after losing your sister."

Her father stabbed at the steaks. "Yeah. Leontyne also barely talked to you the first year after she got back. What kind of friend does that?"

Oh shit. Her parents had noticed but had completely misjudged the reason. "That had nothing to do with her thinking she's too good for us. Yes, we stopped talking for a while, but that's all on me. It was my fault. I…" How could she explain what she had done to make Leo stop talking to her?

She couldn't—not without outing herself.

"I did some stupid things that hurt her. That's part of why I want to make it up to her by helping her find a place for the reception." She gripped her father's sleeve. "Please, Daddy. Let her use the barn."

She rarely asked him for anything; they both knew that.

Their parents exchanged gazes across the grill.

"The steaks will burn if we don't take them off now," her mother said.

Her father reached for the platter and piled inch-thick steaks on it.

Ash gritted her teeth. Maybe a month or two ago, she would have just ducked her head and respected her parents' silence, but spending time with Sasha was teaching her to speak up for herself. "So you're not even going to give me an answer? Are we going to pretend I never said anything? I thought what happened with Melissa taught us better than that." As soon as the words were out, she regretted them.

The lid fell onto the grill with a loud *clunk*.

Her mother flinched as if Ash had hit her.

"Mom, I'm sorry. I didn't mean—"

Her father lifted his hand, interrupting her. "No, you're right. We should have kept digging to find out what was bothering your sister instead of thinking the problem would solve itself if we just didn't speak about it. If we had, at least we wouldn't have to live with this horrible pain of not knowing why...or we might have even been able to prevent it." His gaze sharpened. "But if you ever throw it in your mother's face again..."

"I won't. I'm sorry. It's just..." Ash's eyes burned, and she blinked rapidly to fight back the tears that threatened. "This is important to me, and I didn't know how else to get through to you."

One arm wrapped around his wife, her father carried the platter of steaks inside.

Without saying a word, her mother got a new bottle of barbecue sauce from the pantry.

They took their seats at the table, and her father held out his hands.

Ash joined hands with her parents and lowered her gaze to her empty plate, waiting for him to say grace.

"They can have the barn," her father said instead.

Ash's head flew up, and she stared at him, then at her mother, who sighed and nodded her agreement.

"But let's be clear: We're doing this for you, not for Leontyne or Holly," her father added.

Ash jumped up and threw her arms around him, then around her mother. "Thank you." She gave her an extra squeeze and whispered, "I really am sorry."

Her mother squeezed back. "I know." She wiped her eyes with the back of her hands.

"Now let's eat," her father said gruffly. "The steaks are getting cold."

Ash sat back down and exhaled. She had asked, and her parents had said yes. The conversation had been too hurtful for her to be happy about it, but at least she had managed to stand up for her friends this time. She removed the foil from her baked potato and ignored the trembling of her hands.

On Monday morning, when Ash went to work, she was still a little shaken. Deep in thought, she walked up to the flower shop's front door and almost stumbled over the box sitting in front of it.

"What the...?" Frowning, she bent to pick up the box. It wasn't until she held it in her hands that she remembered it was April 1. *Oh shit.* Was this a practical joke someone was playing on her?

But the box didn't explode or give off any awful smells, so she carried it inside and flipped on the lights.

A Slice of Heaven's logo on the lid smoothed out the line on her forehead. The box was from Sasha. Despite her sense of humor, she didn't seem the type to play practical jokes on April Fools' Day. Had she sent some delicious treat to sweeten Ash's start into the workweek?

Her thoughtfulness put a smile on Ash's face. Whenever Sasha was ready to have a real steak dinner, some woman would be damn lucky. The thought made her smile falter.

She opened the lid and lifted out a single cupcake—vanilla with strawberry buttercream frosting. No cookies for Brooke today. This was all for her. A tiny, red sugar flower stuck out of the frosting. Sasha had recreated the ruffled petals of a carnation to perfection. Carefully, Ash pulled the carnation from the buttercream, wiped off the frosting, and admired the sugar flower from all sides. She already knew that she wouldn't be eating this little piece of art.

Then her gaze fell on the card taped to the inside of the lid. She recognized Sasha's bold handwriting from her wedding-planning notes.

Ash,

I heard what you did for Holly and Leo. Wow. I can imagine that must have been hard for you. I googled the meaning of flowers online, and the website said red carnations mean pride and admiration.

They also symbolized love, but apparently, the website hadn't mentioned that. Ash gave the sugar carnation another look, then continued reading the card.

You certainly have mine. Well done! Enjoy your cupcake.
Sasha

For the second time in as many days, Ash had to blink back tears. To have Sasha be proud of her meant a lot and warmed her like a mug of hot chocolate on a cold winter day.

She carefully pulled off the tape, removed the card from the box, and put it into a drawer with the sugar carnation so she could reread it later. With a grin, she lifted the cupcake, removed the paper liner, and took a big bite.

Chapter 15

THE NEXT FRIDAY, AFTER DAYS of not sleeping much and constantly thinking about how they would manage to share a room, it was finally time for the bachelorette weekend.

Ashley leaned out across the railing of the boat that was taking them to a private island and watched Key West grow smaller behind them. Her blonde hair blew with the ocean breeze, drawing Sasha's gaze.

"Careful." She stepped next to Ashley and wrapped one arm around her. "I don't think Leo and Holly want to lose anyone overboard on their bachelorette weekend."

Ashley pulled back from the railing, but not from her embrace, so Sasha lightly kept her arm around her. They were in Florida, far from home and most people they knew, and Ashley already seemed much more relaxed.

"This is so beautiful, it's almost unreal, isn't it?" Ashley stared out across the turquoise water.

Sasha looked at her instead, charmed by the wide-eyed wonder on her face. "Yeah, it is. I take it this is your first time in Florida?"

Ashley tore her gaze away from the water to glance left and right. Holly, Leo, and their other guests were on the other side of the boat, where the tiny island off Key West was now appearing. Ashley leaned closer, as if not wanting anyone else to overhear. "It's actually my first time to see the ocean."

Now it was Sasha's turn to stare with wide eyes. "Any ocean?"

A hint of red dusted Ashley's cheeks. She nodded and averted her gaze.

"Hey, nothing to be ashamed of. I know your parents couldn't leave the farm to go on long vacations, and with you now running your own business, it's hard to get away. Honestly, it's not often that I get any time away from the bakery either, so this is quite a treat for me too." She gently bumped Ashley's hip with her own, still keeping her arm around her so Ash wouldn't be thrown against the railing. "Plus this way, you're kind of losing your ocean virginity to me."

"God, you're so bad." Ashley slapped at her shoulder, but she was laughing. "If anything, I'm losing my ocean virginity to Holly and Leo since they're paying for the trip."

"Who's losing their virginity to us?" Leo asked as the rest of the group joined them.

Ashley's earlier blush deepened to a dark pink. "No one."

"Um, since the sex talk is already starting, I've got one favor to ask," Holly said.

Ashley groaned. "We weren't talking about…that. Really." She nudged Sasha. "Tell them."

"We weren't talking about sex," Sasha said dutifully.

"Guys, I know this is a bachelorette party, but can we agree on no sex jokes, no strippers, no nipple-topped cupcakes, and no cocktail straws that are shaped like genitals?" Holly looked at each of her friends in turn, and Leo wrapped one arm around her in silent support. "I've attended enough bachelorette parties that made me uncomfortable. I don't want my own to be one of them."

"Damn, there go my weekend plans," Holly's cousin Nicole muttered with a teasing grin.

Sasha gave Holly an admiring glance, proud of her friend for standing up for what she needed. "We can do that, right, guys? No sex this weekend. Uh, I mean, no sex talk." *Shit.* Maybe she'd had one too many of those no-sex pep talks with her libido in the week leading up to this weekend.

"No problem for me," Holly's friend Meg said with a chuckle.

Her quiet queerplatonic partner nodded. Sasha hadn't heard her say more than "hello" since they had met at the airport.

The others murmured their agreement.

The boat came to a stop at the wooden dock. Sasha could understand Ashley's wide-eyed staring as they followed Leo and Holly off the boat. She felt as if she'd been transported to a tropical paradise. Coconut palm trees swayed in the warm breeze, the sun gleamed on the crystal clear water, and a white, sandy beach beckoned. No cars were allowed on the island, so nothing but the sound of the moored boats creaking and tinkling in the wind interrupted the peaceful sound of the waves.

"Ooh!" Jenny clapped her hands. "Let's go to the house and get changed. I can't wait to get to the beach."

They followed a path along the beach until Leo stopped and pointed. "This is it."

Despite knowing they would be twelve people once Lauren and Grace arrived, Sasha had somehow expected a cozy little cottage. Instead, a two-story house rose behind a white picket fence. The blue and white paint looked as if it had been freshly applied just for their visit. A wide porch seemed to wrap around the house, and another one stretched along the second floor.

Leo led them through the gate and up a short, palm-tree-flanked path.

When the front door swung open, Sasha caught sight of a wooden staircase that curved up to the second floor. Behind it, a fully equipped kitchen with blue cabinets ran almost the entire length of the house, ending in a sunlit dining room. French doors led out onto a huge patio with a large pool surrounded by tropical shrubbery and luxurious lounge chairs.

"Wow." Ashley twirled in a circle like Cinderella who'd been allowed to go to the ball for the first time. "I might not want to leave on Sunday."

"Wait till you see the view from the upstairs porch." Leo pointed at the stairs. "If you want to get settled and changed, go ahead. The master bedroom is ours, but other than that, pick whatever room you want."

That started a stampede to the stairs, with Cait and Lisa charging ahead of everyone else.

Sasha wasn't in a hurry. In a house this beautiful, she doubted there were any bad rooms. "Want me to take that upstairs for you?" she asked Ashley, pointing at her small suitcase.

"No, thanks. I'm coming up too." Ashley walked up the stairs ahead of her.

Sasha slid her hand along the intricately carved handrail. What an amazing house. She didn't want to think about how much staying for the weekend must be costing Leo and Holly.

By the time they made it upstairs, Jenny and Nicole, Lisa and Cait, and Meg and Jo had already picked rooms, leaving the two rooms at the end of the hall for Ashley and Sasha to choose from.

Ashley glanced into both rooms, then pointed to one of them. "This one is a bit smaller. I think we should take it and leave the other one for Grace and Lauren when they get here. They're probably used to big hotel suites."

In the past, Sasha had assumed that Ashley's consideration for others was just something she did to impress, but now she knew better. "Sure. I doubt we'll spend much time in our room anyway."

Their room was as beautiful as the rest of the house. It was painted in creamy white and soft blue, continuing the nautical theme from downstairs. The Florida sun shining in through the skylight made the polished hardwood floor gleam. French doors opened onto the porch, from which a white spiral staircase led down to the amazing pool Sasha had caught a glimpse of earlier, complete with rock waterfalls on both ends.

Then her gaze fell on the bed that sat with the headboard against the wall so they could see the ocean before they went to sleep. It was the only bed in the room.

Ashley stared at it too. "It's a king size. We can share, right?"

"Of course. No problem. We'll be fine. Pick whatever side you want, and I'll stay on mine." Sasha flashed a grin. "Unless, of course, you invite me over."

"Hey, no sex jokes this weekend, remember?"

"That wasn't a sex joke." Sasha gave her reply a teasing note, but deep down, she knew it really hadn't been much of a joke. If Ashley invited her over to her side of the bed, all her good intentions would fly right out the window; she knew that.

"I'll go get changed." Ashley unzipped her suitcase, selected a change of clothes, and walked past her toward the attached bathroom.

Sasha opened the French doors and enjoyed the view of the ocean for a moment, then dropped onto the bed and bounced up and down a few times. God, she would share not just a room, but a bed with Ashley tonight.

"Wow," came Ashley's voice through the closed bathroom door. "There's a huge walk-in shower in here. There's room enough for two! Can you imagine what Leo and Holly's master bathroom must look like?"

But Sasha's imagination was busy picturing Ashley and her in the shower together, the warm spray raining down on their naked bodies. "Stop. Just stop."

"Stop what?" Ashley walked out of the bathroom.

Jeez, she was fast. Definitely not a high-maintenance woman who needed hours in the bathroom.

Ashley rounded the bed, clad in cute, pink shorts and a white T-shirt with capped sleeves. Her waist-length hair was still falling onto her back, as if she had decided to let her hair down this weekend—literally.

"Um, bouncing on the bed," Sasha said. "Wouldn't want anyone downstairs to think there's an activity of another kind going on up here."

Ashley tossed the pair of jeans she had worn at her. "God, is that all you think of all day?"

"No." Sasha's teasing grin disappeared. While she definitely found Ashley attractive that way, it wasn't all she thought of. She found her appealing in a lot of ways that had nothing to do with sex—and that was part of the problem. Purely sexual attraction was so much easier to ignore than the emotional bond that was growing between them.

Ashley sat on the edge of the bed and looked down at Sasha, who was still stretched out spread eagle. "You okay?"

"Yeah. Just taking it all in." She swirled her finger around in a way that indicated the house and the island beyond.

Ashley slid farther up the bed, rolled onto her side, and propped up her head on one slender arm until she was facing Sasha. She looked like an excited teenager. "It's a lot to take in, isn't it?" She laughed. "I feel like I'm on my honeymoon or something."

"Nah. We're not the marrying kind, remember? So it can't be a honeymoon."

"Yeah. Right." Ashley looked at her for a moment longer, then gave her a light pat on the belly and climbed off the bed. "Come on. Get changed. The beach is calling."

As Sasha slipped off her long-sleeved shirt in the bathroom, she rested her fingertips on her belly, where Ashley had touched her, and looked at herself in the long mirror that took up half the wall above the sink. Was Ashley more touchy-feely here in Florida, or was she getting more comfortable touching her in general, instead of always fearfully holding herself back? God help her if it was the latter…not that the former would be easier to handle.

"You coming?" Ashley called through the door.

Sasha wrenched her gaze from the mirror and put on a pair of shorts and her *Keep calm and eat cupcakes* T-shirt over her swimsuit. An afternoon of exploring paradise with Ashley awaited her. Figuring out if things between them were changing could wait until later.

Just as they were about to leave the house for the beach, a knock sounded on the front door.

Leo went to open the door and returned with two women.

Ash would have known the shorter one anywhere. When Ash had been growing up, her mother had been a big fan of *Everything That Counts*, the sitcom that Grace Durand had starred in as a teenager, so that curvy figure and those famous cheekbones were unmistakable.

"Holy fucking unicorn," Meg whispered to Holly. "So it's true? You're really friends with Grace Durand?"

"She's just Grace this weekend, okay?" Holly whispered back. "So please don't ask her for an autograph or the latest Hollywood gossip."

Ash could imagine that Grace needed a break from the limelight and the constant acting—just as she did, only that her kind of acting wouldn't earn her any awards.

Grace and her wife exchanged warm hugs with Leo and Holly. Then, still smiling, Grace embraced everyone else too.

Wow. Ash squeezed her back, instantly taken by the actress's down-to-earth charm…and the heavenly scent of her perfume. Okay, maybe Sasha wasn't the only one with a bit of a teenage crush.

Sasha was the last one to be hugged. Grace's head tucked neatly beneath her chin, so Ash could see the expression on Sasha's face. She looked so much like a starstruck teenager with wobbly knees that Ash had to laugh.

She met the gaze of Grace's wife, who watched them through horn-rimmed glasses, an affectionate smile curling up her lips. "Hi." She stuck out her hand. "I'm Lauren."

Ash shook her hand, returning the pleasantly firm grip with equal pressure.

"I thought you'd already be here by the time we arrived," Leo said.

Lauren groaned. "Our flight was a little late, and getting through the airport was hell."

"Really?" Ash asked. When their plane had landed, the airport hadn't seemed all that crowded.

"There's always people who recognize that beautiful face, even with a hat and sunglasses, especially now that it has barely been a month since she won her Oscar." Lauren beamed with pride. "It took a while before we could make our escape."

Holly nudged her fiancée. "Why didn't you get ambushed by fans?"

Leo shrugged. "I hid behind Sasha whenever someone looked my way. Plus I've been mostly out of the limelight, with just a handful of concerts and no world tours for the past year and a half. There are more interesting celebrities to follow than a semi-retired pop singer."

"I beg to differ." Holly softly kissed her, and Ash realized that it was no longer weird to see the only two women she'd ever kissed be affectionate with each other.

Nicole pinched her cousin. "Hey, I thought you said no sexual stuff this weekend?"

Grace made good use of her acting skills to give them a horrified look. "No sex? Leo failed to mention that when she invited us."

Everyone laughed.

Sasha remembered only one family vacation with both of her parents before her mother had left them. It had been a weekend in Key West, so strolling along the beach now brought up some half-forgotten memories. To her surprise, most of them were good ones.

She remembered walking through the shallow waves at the shoreline to find seashells, the way Ashley was doing now, and getting more and more disappointed when she couldn't find any—until her mother had secretly sprinkled some she had bought at a shop along the beach for her to find.

Now she understood why her mother had done it.

Ashley waded through the water several steps ahead. Sometimes, she walked farther out until she was knee-deep in water, apparently not minding that some of the incoming waves were drenching the very bottom of her shorts. Then she came back to shore, bent over, and peered through the crystal clear water, but every time she reached down, she came up with nothing but a broken sea urchin or a piece of sea glass, never a shell.

"You won't find a lot of shells here," Sasha called to her. "At least not intact ones. Most of them break up over the reef before they make it to shore."

Ashley sent her a smile before continuing her search. "I'll find one."

Grace and Lauren, walking hand in hand, caught up with Sasha.

"You should take her snorkeling," Lauren said. "She'll find a lot more. Maybe even see a sea turtle."

Yeah, maybe she should. Sasha could easily imagine the wonder on Ashley's face as she swam through a school of colorful fish.

Ashley let out a cry that sent Sasha's pulse racing.

Water splashing everywhere, Sasha rushed over to her. "What is it? Did you step on something? Are you bleeding? Show me!"

But Ashley wasn't clutching her foot or her hand—she was holding out a seashell. "I found one! Look. It looks like a tiny wedding cake, don't you think?"

Sasha took it from her and examined it. The shell was round and about an inch in diameter. With a bit of imagination, it did indeed resemble a multi-tiered wedding cake with icing decorations.

"Yeah, it kind of does. Just don't try to take a bite." She handed it back, and Ashley resumed her search for shells, while Sasha walked back to Grace and Lauren. "What do you know? Ash found a shell, and now she's on a mission to find more. We'll probably have to drag her away from the beach at nightfall."

Grace chuckled. "She's cute."

Sasha had been watching Ashley, fascinated by the beads of water glittering on her bare arms. "Huh?"

"Your girlfriend." Grace nodded toward Ashley. "She's cute. First time at the beach?"

Sasha turned toward her. "No. I mean, yes, it is, but she's not my girlfriend."

"Oh. Sorry. Lauren always tells me I have no gaydar whatsoever." Grace lightly bumped her wife's shoulder. "I should know better than to assume everyone's gay, just because we're at a bachelorette weekend for two women."

"Well, your gaydar isn't completely wrong—in my case," Sasha added quickly. It wasn't her place to out Ashley, especially since Holly's sisters-in-law and her cousin were from Fair Oaks.

"Oh, so you are gay?"

Sasha shrugged. "Pansexual probably fits me best, but I'm not into labels."

"I see." Grace smiled softly and studied Sasha with eyes the exact color as the ocean. "But you are into her." She glanced over at Ashley.

Having this conversation with Grace Durand was surreal, but at the same time, she was so far removed from Sasha's life that it was easy to talk to her. There was no point in denying it. "It's complicated."

Lauren laughed. "When is it ever not when a woman is involved?"

"Hey, speak for yourself," Grace said. "I'm very uncomplicated."

"Oh yeah. Falling in love with the very straight star of hetero romance movies…who was also my client. My *married* client. That wasn't complicated at all."

"About-to-be-divorced and not-so-straight-after-all client," Grace said. "Although I don't like labels for myself either."

The media did, though. Sasha remembered that the tabloids had written sensational headlines about Grace Durand's lesbian relationship and had hounded the couple for months after Grace had first revealed that she was with a woman.

Sasha couldn't imagine what she must have been through. Even coming out in a small, conservative town like Fair Oaks was nothing compared to coming out to the entire world.

"Sasha, look!" Ashley rushed up to them. For a moment, she looked as if she was about to jump into Sasha's arms, but then she stopped herself and toned down her excitement. "I found another one." She held it out to her.

This time, it was a brown and white sea snail shell as thick as Sasha's thumb.

"I think this one is called a tulip shell," Lauren said.

Since it was shaped like a closed tulip, the name fit.

Ashley placed it on her palm next to the one she had found earlier. "A cake shell and a flower shell." She grinned up at Sasha. "Kind of fitting, isn't it?"

Sasha smiled back. "Yeah, it is." Inwardly, she cursed Leo and Holly. Why couldn't they have invited them to a mani-pedi party or a night out in Kansas City? This romantic island getaway was killing her.

Ash's sandcastle crumbled for the third time. "Oops. Good thing I'm a florist, not an architect."

Meg put her shovel down and looked at her with an amused shake of her head. "You know, I think the trick to building a sandcastle is to actually look at what you're doing."

Ash stared down at her pile of sand. "I am."

"Oh, then maybe you're cross-eyed. I could have sworn you were looking at Sasha the entire time."

"What? No!"

Meg slid her sunglasses to the tip of her nose and gave her an *oh-please* look.

Her irreverent but friendly personality reminded Ash a lot of Melissa— or of Melissa before she'd become withdrawn and brooding. "Okay, maybe I was. It's just good to see her relax for once, you know?" Ash said as casually as possible. Friends worried about the well-being of friends too, right? "She's working a lot at home, so I'm glad she's getting some R & R this weekend."

Meg chuckled. "If she were any more relaxed, she'd be comatose."

"True." Ash looked over at Sasha again.

Sasha had stretched out her long body on a beach towel, her sunglasses slid back onto her head and her eyes closed, while she was chatting with Jo.

Ash smiled. If anyone could make the taciturn Jo talk, it was Sasha.

"Let's make this a little more interesting." Meg waved at her partner. "Hey, Jo. Are you up for a sandcastle building contest? These two," she pointed from Ash to Sasha, "against the two of us?"

Jo immediately got up and trotted over. "Sure. I'm in."

Sasha leaned up on one arm. "How did I get involved in this?"

"Well, someone's got to help Ashley. Because this one," Meg wrapped one arm around Jo, "lived in Cancún until she was six. Prime sandcastle building years," she added with a toothy grin.

Uh-oh. Ash exchanged an alarmed gaze with Sasha. "Come on, Sasha. You can't let me go down alone."

"No one's going down. At least not without a fight." Sasha got up, put her sunglasses on, and drew her braid through the back of her baseball cap. She looked fierce, like a warrior getting ready for battle. "For a real contest, we need a prize. What does the winner get?"

"Are you crazy?" Ash mouthed at her.

Sasha patted her arm in an I-know-what-I'm-doing gesture. "So?"

"Hmm…" Meg ran her hand through her carefully spiked hair. "How about the losers make cocktails for the rest of us tonight?"

"Sounds good to me," Sasha said. "So, how do we do this? First ones to finish their castle win?"

Meg shook her head. "When it comes to sandcastles, beauty wins over speed. The pair who has the most beautiful castle in…let's say half an hour wins."

"Who's going to judge which one is more beautiful?" Sasha asked.

Meg pointed to Holly, Leo, and the rest of the group, who were lounging on beach towels or splashing each other in the shallow water. "We'll let them vote."

"All right."

"Ready?" Meg held up three fingers. "Three, two, one… Go!"

Ash's heart pounded even though it was just a fun contest. She started to pile up sand.

"No," Sasha called. "Follow my lead." She sprinted to the waterline and shoveled damp sand into a bucket. "We need wet sand. Dry sand doesn't hold its shape."

That would explain why Ash's castles had all collapsed.

Even though Ash had never built a sandcastle with another person before, they worked together like a well-oiled machine—Ash lugging over bucket after bucket of wet sand, which Sasha then packed down firmly with her hands and feet before pouring water over it.

They took their time building a good foundation and then used the buckets to shape two medieval towers.

Time and again, Ash's gaze was drawn to Sasha's nimble fingers as she shaved away sand in thin layers, forming arched doorways, little windows, and a crenelated wall around the castle. The way she smoothed her fingers along the outer wall looked almost like a caress.

Ash averted her gaze and focused on creating a little watchtower on top of the wall.

"Ooh, good thinking." Sasha formed a watchtower of her own on the other side of the castle. "Can you put your hand here for a moment?" She patted the sand outside of the wall.

When Ash put her hand down, Sasha piled wet sand on it and gently pressed down.

Ash shivered at the touch.

"Was the sand cold?" Sasha asked.

Ash nodded, even though she had no idea if it was. Her focus was on Sasha's hands, not on the sand.

Sasha put another layer on top and patted it down with both hands. "Okay. Now carefully pull out."

Was it just her, or did that sound like something someone would say during sex? Not that Ash had a lot of experience with sexual situations. The only woman she had ever slept with was Holly. It was probably just her imagination. Keeping her fingers together, she withdrew and stared down at the newest addition to their castle. "Oh! It's a drawbridge!" She sent Sasha an admiring look. "God, you're so good at this. If I didn't know any better, I'd think you'd grown up at the beach too. Your sand-castling skills are exceptional."

Sasha laughed. "I wish. But this is a lot like making a cake and then decorating it."

"I never saw it that way, but you're right."

"Time's up," Meg called from where they were building their own castle.

Sasha helped Ash up, and they stepped away from their creation.

Ash hadn't paid any attention to their competition's castle while they had built their own. Now she looked over.

It was good. Certainly better than anything Ash could have built on her own. But it didn't have any of the creative details Sasha had added, like the drawbridge or the watchtowers on the castle walls.

"Wow. I don't think we need the jury after all," Meg said with a laugh. "Guess we're making the cocktails tonight."

Sasha and Ash high-fived each other.

"I think I'll head back to the house now. I need a shower." Sasha had worked up a sweat while she'd packed down the sand, and the skin on her arms was gleaming where it wasn't covered in a thin layer of sand. She tugged on one leg of her shorts and squirmed. "I've got sand in some pretty uncomfortable places. You coming, Ash?"

"Oh yeah. Um, I mean, yes, I'm pretty itchy and sweaty too." Before Ash followed her to the house, she grabbed the waterproof disposable camera that Holly had handed out to everyone before they'd gotten on the boat and snapped a photo of the castle. But she knew she would never forget this day even without a picture.

Jo slid an orange slice onto the edge of the highball glass, then slid it over to Meg, who added a cherry on a stick and presented the cocktail with a playful bow. "One fairly won cocktail."

Sasha captured the straw with her lips and took a sip. The fruity cocktail had quite a kick. She tasted peach schnapps, cranberry, and orange juice, and if she wasn't mistaken, there was vodka in there too. "Oh wow. What's this?"

"A Cuddles on the Beach," Meg said.

Sasha laughed. "A…what?"

Meg grinned. "No sex this weekend, remember? So it can't be a Sex on the Beach. You're getting a Cuddles on the Beach."

Sasha took another sip. "Fine with me. Cuddles are great."

"Do you know what Ashley wants?" Meg looked around. "Where is she? I haven't seen her since dinner."

Sasha hadn't either. "Maybe she needed a minute to herself. If you make her a cocktail, I'll find her."

"I'll just make her the same," Jo said. "Ashley looks like a woman who'd appreciate a good cuddle session."

"Um…" Sasha didn't want to be thinking about cuddling with Ashley. Not when she had to sleep in the same bed with her tonight. But as always, her imagination didn't care about what she wanted. It showed her in vivid detail what it might feel like to have Ashley cuddle up to her and rest her face against Sasha's chest. For a second, it felt so real that Sasha could almost feel her warmth and smell her perfume. She had always thought that Opium was too bold, too spicy to fit Ashley, but now she was growing to like it.

Sasha fished one of the ice cubes from her cocktail and popped it into her mouth. Maybe it would help her cool down.

When Jo slid Ashley's cocktail over to her, Sasha took it and carried both glasses inside. The open floor plan of the beach house instantly revealed that no one was downstairs. Everyone but Ashley was outside, lounging around the pool.

Carefully watching the cocktail glasses so she wouldn't spill their contents, Sasha went upstairs to see if Ashley had withdrawn to their room. But it was empty and so was the bathroom.

Weird. Concern began to stir in her belly. She turned to go back downstairs and request some help in finding Ashley, but then a hunch made her pause. A second set of winding stairs, much narrower than the first, led up to the roof.

Following her instincts, Sasha climbed the wooden stairs and found herself on a small, square platform perched on the roof.

Somehow, she wasn't surprised to find Ashley standing at the white railing. She stood with her back to Sasha and gazed out over the ocean. The sun was slowly dipping toward the horizon, and the sunset cast a warm, orange-and-pink glow on Ashley, making her look like a creature from a fairy tale—ethereally beautiful and vulnerable at the same time.

Sasha's breath caught. The urge to walk up behind Ashley and take her into her arms gripped her so strongly that she had already taken a step toward her before she became fully aware of it.

Ashley turned and didn't seem surprised to see her. She gestured toward the orange ball sinking into the ocean. "Makes me wish I was a painter," she said quietly, as if speaking any louder would interrupt the peacefulness of the sunset.

Sasha's hands itched to have her watercolor pencils too, but rather to capture Ashley's features in the soft, amber light. She stepped closer until she stood at the railing next to Ashley. "Cuddles on the Beach?"

"Um…"

Laughter bubbled up, nearly making Sasha spill the cocktails. "It's not an offer. It's the name of the cocktail." She held the glass out to her.

Ashley took it, holding the highball glass with both hands, and took a sip. She sucked in air through her teeth. "Wow. That's pretty strong. I'd better stop after one, or I might jump up on a table and do some dirty dancing, and Holly requested a PG weekend."

Sasha bit the inside of her cheek so she wouldn't comment.

They leaned against the railing next to each other, their elbows brushing, as they sipped their cocktails and watched the sun set.

"Do you know why this," Sasha indicated the platform, "is called a widow's walk?"

"No idea." Ashley turned toward her and leaned her hip against the railing. "Tell me."

"Apparently, it's because in the past, wives came up here to wait for their husbands' return from the sea."

"Then why is it called a widow's walk, not a wife's walk?" Ashley asked.

Sasha swirled the ice cubes around in her glass. "Because some of them waited in vain. The ocean took the lives of many of the whalers and fishermen."

"How depressing," Ashley mumbled. She turned back toward the railing and gazed across the water. "But I guess if you have to live the rest of your life alone, there are worse places than here." An aura of sadness settled over Ashley like a heavy cloak.

Something was going on with her; Sasha could sense it. Was she thinking about her own life? But before Sasha could ask, Ashley shook off whatever was going through her mind and smiled.

"Look at that. Isn't it beautiful?" Below them, the setting sun tinged the ocean with golden, orange, and crimson colors.

"Very beautiful," Sasha murmured.

Slowly, the orange hues gave way to a purplish blue, then a dark navy, until only a band of light remained on the horizon. As if the darkness had triggered a switch, the pool lights came on, as did the lights illuminating the pathways through the lush tropical garden with its banana and key lime trees. It looked magical from above.

Even once their glasses were empty, neither of them moved to rejoin the others. Sasha had enjoyed the day with her friends and getting to know new people, but sharing a few quiet moments with just Ashley was even more special.

Ashley shivered and rubbed her arms.

Now that the sun had set, the temperature cooled down quickly.

Sasha untied her hoodie from around her waist and held it out to her.

"Are you sure you don't need it?" Ashley asked. "Won't you get cold?"

"Nah. In my family, everyone's naturally hot-blooded. My aunt says it's because the bakery ovens are part of our DNA." She gave the hoodie an inviting shake. "Come on. Wouldn't want to have to go back home and tell your parents I let you freeze to death."

Ashley chuckled. "In Florida? Not likely."

"Still." Sasha pulled the sweatshirt over Ashley's head and helped guide her hands though the correct holes.

The hoodie came down to mid-thigh on Ashley, looking like a dress, and the sleeves covered her hands. She snuggled into it and curled her fingers into the fabric, as if to soak up Sasha's body heat.

God. How could her old sweatshirt look so damn sexy? It felt incredibly intimate to see Ashley wearing her clothes.

Ashley looked down at herself and giggled. "I probably look ridiculous."

"Nah. You look—" Sasha stopped herself before she could say *sexy*. "Um, adorable. Like a little girl playing dress-up in her mom's clothes." Okay, that had been the last thought on her mind, but Ashley didn't need to know that.

Ashley grunted as if she didn't like that comparison, but now it was too late to take it back. Finally, she slid her hands into the pouch of the hoodie and looked down at the illuminated pool. "Do you like it here?"

"Yeah," Sasha said. "Very much so. You?"

Ashley nodded. "Me too. I always thought I liked staying home best, but this... I could see myself staying here for a couple of weeks."

"Or months," Sasha added with a laugh.

Ashley laughed with her. "Or months." Then she sobered. "I feel different here."

Sasha tried to see her face, but it was too dark to make out her expression. "Good different?"

"I think so. I feel...I don't know...freer. At least when it's just us."

Wow. That was quite a statement from someone like Ashley, who probably never felt completely free and uninhibited. Sasha didn't know what to say.

Before she could think of something, Ashley let her gaze slide over the lights glittering on the ocean one last time, then turned away. "We should probably go back downstairs before someone reports us missing."

Sasha picked up their empty glasses and followed her downstairs. Only when Meg gave them a curious glance did she realize that Ashley was still wearing her hoodie.

"Hey, there you are," Meg said. Thankfully, neither she nor Jo commented on the hoodie. "More Cuddles on the Beach?"

Laughing, Sasha held out their glasses. "Sure."

Sasha took her hair out of its braid, slid beneath the covers, and folded her arms behind her head as she listened to the noises of Ashley brushing her teeth in the bathroom.

"Jesus," Ashley called through the closed door, "those were some potent Cuddles. I actually feel a little buzzed."

Sasha chuckled. "Lightweight."

Ashley hadn't drunk that much, but since one beer at Johnny's was usually her limit, she probably felt the alcohol more. Another reason not to start anything tonight—not that Sasha had planned to.

The bathroom door opened, and Ashley stepped out, wearing a gray sleep shirt that reached her knees.

Sasha tried not to stare at her bare legs as Ashley walked toward the bed and climbed in on her side. She turned off the lamp on her bedside table, throwing the room into near darkness.

The light from the pool below provided a faint glow that still allowed Sasha to make out Ashley's shape beneath the covers next to her.

"Good night," Ashley said.

"Night," Sasha answered. "Sweet dreams." She had a feeling she wouldn't sleep anytime soon. Despite the long day at the beach, with plenty of fresh air and activity, she was wide-awake. Her body buzzed with the awareness of having Ashley so close.

Ashley lay without moving, but Sasha sensed that she was also awake.

In the stillness of the room, she could almost hear the gears in Ashley's head turning.

"You know," Ashley whispered so quietly that Sasha had to lift her head off the pillow to hear her, "I've been thinking about what I said earlier. About liking it here. I really do, but being here also makes me kind of sad."

Sasha longed to see the expression on Ashley's face, but she knew Ashley would stop talking if she turned on the light. "I think I sensed that. Want to talk about it? I won't judge, no matter what it is."

"I know." Sheets rustled as Ashley rolled over to face Sasha. "I guess it makes me realize how much I'm missing out on in life. I've never seen the ocean before, never built a sandcastle, never—"

"Never what?" Sasha asked in a whisper when Ashley didn't finish.

Ashley sighed. "Never been held all night. Never…done a lot of things."

Sasha ached for her. Ashley might be the darling of town, popular with pretty much everyone, but in a way, she was still lonely. Hiding a big part of herself cut her off from people. She reached out across the empty space between them and stroked Ashley's arm, hoping like hell that it really was her arm and not some other body part that she'd mistaken it for in the near darkness. "It's never too late to experience new things, Ash. Just because you haven't had them so far doesn't mean it has to stay that way. You deserve to have it all. You just need to have the courage to reach for what you want."

Ashley said nothing for what felt like several minutes. She breathed as if she was in the middle of a fierce struggle—and maybe she was. Finally, she cleared her throat. "Would you…?"

Sasha held her breath. What was she asking? But she already knew the answer would be yes, no matter what Ashley wanted.

Ashley slid a little closer. "W-would you…?" Again, she seemed unable to get it out.

"This?" Praying that she hadn't misinterpreted things, Sasha bridged the remaining space between them and pulled Ashley into her arms.

Ashley went very still, but only for a heartbeat. Then she melted into Sasha with a sigh that nearly sounded like a sob and buried her face against her chest, exactly the way Sasha had imagined earlier.

No, she corrected herself, better. Much, much better than she'd imagined. Ashley's body was soft and warm against her own, and they fit together as if they had done this a thousand times before.

"Is this okay?" Ashley asked, still whispering. "I don't want you to think I'm being a tease or playing with your emotions or—"

Sasha lightly touched Ashley's cheek with the back of her fingers. "It's okay. Better than okay, actually." All day, she'd been a bit worried about not being able to control her libido with Ashley so close, but right now, it wasn't that hard. While she was still aware of the pull between them, it was much more of a struggle not to bend her head and press a tender kiss to the top of her head.

Ashley let out a long breath and cuddled even closer, if that was at all possible. Her arm went around Sasha's waist, and she fisted her hand into the material of her T-shirt as if she wanted to hold on forever.

Sasha rested one hand on Ashley's shoulder. She fanned out her fingers to soak up as much of this experience as she possibly could, knowing it might be the only time she got to hold Ashley like this. She trailed her other hand up and down her back in long, soothing strokes, careful not to venture too far down. This was about comfort, nothing else.

Finally, Ashley gave a little sigh. "Thank you. That was nice."

When she started to pull away, Sasha put her hand on Ashley's hip and held on. "All night. That's what you said you wanted: to be held all night. Right?"

Ashley sniffed as if she was fighting back tears. "Y-you don't have to."

"I want to."

"Really?" Longing vibrated in Ashley's voice.

God, what had made her so insecure about this kind of human contact? "Of course." Sasha trailed her hand along Ashley's back. "I like holding you."

Ashley exhaled shakily and put her arm back around Sasha's waist. "I like it too," she whispered. "It feels wonderful. But can you sleep with me so close?"

"Sure." It didn't matter. Who needed sleep if they could hold Ashley? Maybe she was torturing herself with things she could never have, things she had always told herself she didn't want, but right now, Sasha didn't care. She gently guided Ashley's head back to that perfect spot on her shoulder. "Sleep."

Ashley settled back down. "Thank you, Sasha." She softly squeezed her hip. "Sweet dreams." Within minutes, her deep, rhythmic breathing indicated that she'd fallen asleep.

Sasha tucked the light duvet more tightly around Ashley to protect her from the ocean breeze coming in from the open French doors.

Ashley made a contented, little sound.

Getting to hold her while she slept felt like a wonderful privilege, yet at the same time a little voice in the back of her head screamed a warning. Letting herself get close to Ashley, physically and emotionally, would only lead to heartbreak. *What on earth are you doing?*

The darkness held no answers.

She draped her arm over Ashley's back and closed her eyes.

Chapter 16

Ash woke from the most pleasant dream she'd had in years—only to find that it wasn't a dream at all. She was lying in Sasha's arms, where she'd slept all night. If anything, she had moved even closer and was now half on top of her. Her head rested on Sasha's muscular shoulder, her arm was around Sasha's waist, and her hair spilled over Sasha's chest like a blanket.

Sasha was sprawled on her back, her body completely open to her, with no defenses up at all. She might come across as confident and strong to everyone else—and she certainly was both, but Ash knew that she also had a heart as soft as her buttercream frosting.

You shouldn't have asked her to hold you. You're leading her on. She knew this couldn't go anywhere, no matter how much she wished things were different. Having to live in the closet would kill someone like Sasha, and it would certainly kill whatever affection Sasha had for her. Ash had seen what a life of hiding had done to Holly, and she didn't have the energy to live through that again. Sasha deserved so much more.

Slowly, Ash eased out of Sasha's arms. Her body protested, wanting that warm contact back, but she forced herself to keep moving and tiptoed to the bathroom. When she reached the door, she couldn't resist one last glance back.

Sasha slept on peacefully. The first rays of sunlight touched her face, giving it a golden glow. Ash clutched the doorframe and drank in the sight of her—Sasha's broad forehead, her strong nose, her expressive lips. God, she was beautiful. She had gotten a little color yesterday, and Ash longed to smooth her fingers over the hint of red on her cheeks.

A low noise came from downstairs, and Ash finally tore herself away and ducked into the bathroom.

When she returned, dressed in shorts, a T-shirt, and flip-flops, Sasha was still sleeping, her arms now wrapped around Ash's pillow as if she was searching for her.

An almost physical pull tugged on Ash. She wanted nothing more than to crawl back into bed and into Sasha's embrace, but she firmly told herself that she'd had the one night of being held she had wanted. Now it was time to face reality.

Not allowing herself to look back again, she tiptoed to the door, opened it, and stepped into the hall.

Her senses were still focused on how it had felt to be in Sasha's arms, so it took her until she reached the bottom of the stairs to realize she wasn't just imagining the scent of cinnamon wafting through the house.

In the kitchen, someone was making cinnamon pancakes.

The aroma immediately catapulted her back to where she had burrowed her nose into Sasha's soft T-shirt.

She had expected to find Holly or maybe Jenny behind the stove, but instead, it was Grace who was expertly flipping a pancake. She was wearing a Boston University T-shirt that was too big for her, constantly sliding down one shoulder. It was wrinkled as if she'd slept in it.

Wow. Grace Durand was making breakfast in her sleep attire.

This weekend was proving to be miraculous in many ways.

Ash had always assumed that it was mostly film makeup and carefully calculated camera angles that made actresses look so good in movies, and maybe that was true for some of them, but Grace was beautiful in her wrinkled sleep shirt and without a hint of makeup.

She couldn't help comparing her to Sasha, though. While she appreciated the actress's graceful beauty, it was Sasha's sturdy body and the strong planes of her face that stirred her more deeply.

Stop thinking of her. You're only torturing yourself. Ash walked up to the counter separating the kitchen from the living area.

Grace looked up from the pan. "Good morning. I thought I'd let our hostesses sleep a little longer and make breakfast for everyone who wants it. Did the scent lure you downstairs?"

"No. I'm just not used to sleeping in." A glance at the clock on the wall showed that it was a quarter to eight; that was almost considered sleeping in for a florist—and certainly for a baker.

"I know what you mean. I just wrapped up shooting in New York, and I'm so used to early call times that I was wide-awake by five." Grace pointed at the stairs with her spatula. "Sasha still asleep?"

Ash nodded and hoped she wasn't blushing. Grace couldn't know she had spent the night using Sasha as her personal pillow, so there was nothing to be embarrassed about.

Footfalls sounded on the stairs.

Ash held her breath, not sure how to face Sasha after last night.

But luckily, it was Lauren who appeared at the bottom of the stairs. She strode into the kitchen as if she had an innate sense that told her where her wife had disappeared to. She stepped up behind her and slid her arms around Grace, who was still making pancakes. "Morning." She whispered a kiss on the rim of Grace's ear that made a visible shiver run through her wife.

Grace leaned back into her and let go of the spatula to cover Lauren's arms around her with her own.

Ash knew she should politely look away, but her gaze was drawn to them like a magnet to an anvil. God, she wanted what they had so much that it was almost like a physical ache. After sleeping cuddled up to Sasha all night, she'd had a taste of what she had been missing all her life, and that was almost worse than never having had it at all.

Lauren finally let go of Grace and turned toward Ash as if only now becoming aware of her presence. "Oh, hi. Sorry I didn't see you there." She gave an embarrassed laugh and climbed onto a barstool at the counter to watch her wife cook. "With Grace being on location so much, I get tunnel vision when she's around."

"Oh, you don't have to apologize." Ash sent them a warm smile. "I understand completely. If I had a girlfriend, I'd..." Then she realized her slip and hastily added, "Not that I would ever..." But the lie that usually came so smoothly didn't cross her lips so easily anymore. As much as she wanted to, she couldn't tell them that she was straight and would, of course, never have—or want—a girlfriend.

Oh God. This was scary. What had happened to her usual smoothness when it came to lies like that? Why was she suddenly unable to say the words?

"Good morning." Of course, Sasha chose that moment to make an appearance downstairs. She was dressed in the typical Florida uniform of shorts and a T-shirt but still looked adorably rumpled, her hair unbraided and sleep-mussed, as if she hadn't taken the time to do more than run her fingers through it. Her gaze brushed Lauren, paused on Grace for a second, and then zeroed in on Ash. "Sleep well?" She searched Ash's face with an intensity that belied the casual question.

Her mouth dry, Ash nodded. "Very. You?" Was Sasha feeling okay with what had happened between them, or did she feel weird this morning?

A soft smile played around Sasha's lips. "Me too. Best night's sleep I've had in a long time."

Ash reined in the beaming smile that wanted to spread across her face. Just because Sasha seemed okay with her practically sleeping on top of her didn't mean it would ever be repeated.

"It's the ocean air," Lauren said, oblivious to the subtext of their conversation.

Yeah, sure. Just the ocean air. Ash wished she could believe it. She hoped things would go back to normal once she got back home, or she would be in deep, deep trouble.

Grace Durand looked smoking hot in a bikini. But to Sasha's surprise, she hadn't thrown more than a fleeting glance in Grace's direction all afternoon.

She was much too busy watching Ashley float in the pool and dip her head beneath the spray of the artificial mini-waterfall. In a blue one-piece bathing suit, she looked every bit as hot as Grace in Sasha's opinion. But that wasn't why she was watching her.

She would have paid good money to know what was going on in Ashley's head.

Last night, she had revealed her needs to Sasha and made herself vulnerable, but now, in broad daylight, she had withdrawn, swimming and talking flowers with Jo—who, as it turned out, was a landscape designer—instead of searching Sasha out to talk about last night.

Maybe she shouldn't have been surprised to wake up alone, but after the intimacy of holding Ashley all night, it had felt like a bucket of ice-cold water being dumped over her head. This was what she had to look forward to if she didn't pull away.

Holly knelt next to Sasha's lounge chair and touched her shoulder. "You okay?"

Sasha slid up her sunglasses, which had provided a convenient cover so no one would notice she was watching Ashley. She pasted on her most convincing grin and pointed at where she was stretched out by the pool, enjoying a tamer version of last night's Cuddles on the Beach. "Does this look like I'm suffering?"

"No, but you've been a little quiet all day...and so has Ash." Holly glanced toward the pool. "You two aren't fighting, are you?"

"Definitely not." She squeezed Holly's hand, which lay on her shoulder. Despite Holly's touch, she could still feel Ashley's head resting there. "Don't worry. We're both having a marvelous time."

"Will you tell me later, when we're at home?" Holly asked.

Sasha sighed. She should have known Holly would see right through her. Unlike Ashley, she'd never been a good liar—but then again, if Holly had noticed something off with Ashley too, maybe she wasn't so good at lying after all. "I could use someone to talk to, but I'm not sure I can—or should." No way would she betray Ashley's trust by telling anyone, even Holly, about the vulnerability in Ashley's voice as she had asked to be held. "And just for the record, we really are having a marvelous time."

Holly rubbed Sasha's shoulder. "Good. Then I hope you'll enjoy what we have planned for tonight too. We're going to have a picnic and a bonfire on the beach."

Sasha's stomach rumbled, making Holly laugh.

"Guess you'd better get your mermaid out of the pool before you starve." Holly got up. "If you change your mind about wanting to talk..."

"I know where to find you." Sasha gave her a nod. "Thanks, Holly."

When Holly walked away and told the rest of the group about the picnic, Sasha's gaze returned to Ashley—then snapped back to Holly. Wait a minute! Had Holly just called Ashley *her* mermaid?

Ashley let out a long moan—a sound that went straight to Sasha's core. She shifted on the blanket she and Ashley sat on.

"Oh God," Ashley said. "Someone please take those conch fritters away from me."

"With pleasure." Sasha reached over to take the last fritter, but Ashley playfully batted her hand away, popped it into her mouth, and proceeded to lick bits of the spicy dipping sauce off her fingers.

Jesus. This woman would be the death of her. Now Sasha was the one who moaned. She quickly clutched her stomach and pretended it was because of the two hogfish sandwiches she had devoured.

"Oh, does that mean you two don't want any of the key lime cupcakes I've got?" Leo held up the basket of treats with a devilish grin.

"Well…" Ashley looked over at Sasha. "Want to share one?"

"What? Ashley Gaines wants to try a cupcake other than vanilla, and it's not one of mine? Should I be insulted?" Beneath the joking, she sent Ashley an imploring gaze. Was Ashley ready to leave her well-trodden paths when it came to things other than cupcakes too?

"No," Ashley said quickly. "Your cupcakes are the best ever. But key lime is a Florida thing, and when in Rome…"

So Ashley was ready to try new things, but only while they were in Florida. Sasha suppressed a sigh. She would miss this side of Ashley when they returned home—the side that leaned in to Sasha while they sat at the bonfire, resting against her shoulder, apparently without even realizing.

The dry wood crackled and popped. Sparks shot into the night sky and then trailed down slowly.

Sasha ate her half of the cupcake and stretched her legs to the side to dig her toes into the still warm sand. Ashley's shoulder warmed her from the other side.

"They're good," Ashley said around a mouthful of cupcake. "But I'm really looking forward to trying the cake at the wedding."

"Ooh, me too." Grace sighed. "Cake is my secret vice."

"Not-so-secret vice," Lauren corrected with a chuckle. "It was all over the tabloids when they caught you with a piece of chocolate cake on the set of *Lucky*, remember?"

Ashley looked from Grace to Leo, a wrinkle forming on her forehead. "How will you manage to keep the press away from the wedding, especially with Grace being there? If they think Grace eating a piece of cake is newsworthy, they'll be all over the wedding."

"Oh, don't worry about that." Lauren flashed them her best James Bond grin. "Operation Decoy is firmly in place."

"Operation Decoy?" Sasha asked.

"Lauren used to be my PR agent, and she managed to keep the press away from her and Grace's wedding, so I asked her for help in keeping our special day private," Leo said. "I want to give Holly the wedding of her dreams, away from the paparazzi and the glitzy persona of Jenna Blake."

Holly leaned over and kissed Leo's cheek.

"As soon as we leave here, someone will leak it to the press that Jenna Blake just spent the weekend in Florida to check out a location for her wedding," Lauren said. "The paparazzi will swarm all over the Keys, trying to find the place. No one will connect a pop star's glitzy nuptials with a tiny town in Missouri. Once they find out, it'll be too late."

"Thanks again, Lauren. I really owe you." Leo finished her Cuban sandwich, wiped her hands on her shorts, and pulled her guitar from its battered case.

Sasha traded a surprised gaze with Ashley. She knew Leo didn't normally share her music with anyone but Holly, at least not outside of concerts. She had played at the bar for Sasha's birthday, but that had been in public, where she could put on her Jenna Blake mask. This was different.

The others stopped chatting as she strummed a few chords, then launched into an instrumental piece Sasha didn't recognize. Maybe Leo had made it up on the spot. It certainly fit the atmosphere of this tropical setting, soothing yet lively.

Ashley leaned in to Sasha more heavily as the last notes of the song faded away. Was this bringing up memories of the time when she'd been in a band with Leo, playing the keyboard and providing background vocals? Sasha fought the urge to wrap an arm around her to comfort her.

Leo transitioned seamlessly into the next song, and Sasha recognized this one. It was a love song from Leo's latest album, the one she had written in Fair Oaks and produced on her own. This time, Leo added her voice to the sound of the guitar, and everyone listened, spellbound.

After singing a few more songs for her small audience, Leo reached for the case to put the guitar away, but Holly covered her hand with her own. "One more, please."

Leo kissed her softly. "Your wish is my command."

Lauren laughed. "I can see that you don't need my advice on how to make a marriage work. You already know that a happy wife means a happy life."

The others added a bit of gentle teasing too.

Leo just smiled, her gaze still on Holly. "Any requests?"

Holly shook her head. "You pick. I love all of your songs."

Leo trailed her fingers over the neck of the guitar for what seemed like a long time, as if she couldn't make up her mind. When the opening chords finally rang out across the beach, Sasha sucked in a breath.

It was the only song on Leo's latest album she had never played in public. "Three Things" was about her complicated relationship with her late father, at least that was what Sasha had thought when she had first heard it. Why had she chosen to play this one now?

But instead of launching into the song, Leo repeated the instrumental intro and looked across the fire at Ashley. "This one was really meant to be a duet, so I need someone to help me out. Ash? Do you happen to know the lyrics?"

Ashley stiffened against Sasha's side. "Um, yes, I do, but I can't sing it with you. I haven't been up on a stage for over fifteen years."

"This is a beach, Ash, not a stage," Leo said. "You're among friends. No one will judge if you're a little rusty."

The others murmured their agreement.

Sasha softly squeezed her shoulder. "I know you can do this."

Ashley leaned more heavily into her as if needing the support not to run away. Finally, she nodded and breathed an almost inaudible, "Okay."

"Great." Leo repeated the intro a third time and then started to sing. Her voice was beautiful and expressive, transporting the raw emotions of the song perfectly.

Then she nodded at Ashley to join in for the second verse.

Sasha held her breath.

Ashley's first line came out a bit shaky, but as she sang on, she either gained confidence or she forgot she had an audience. The fire threw flickering shadows across her features, revealing the myriad of emotions that darted across her face. By the time they started the third verse, joy was the most prominent one. She swayed softly to the rhythm of Leo's guitar, her entire body fully immersed in the music.

Sasha had heard Leo perform with other pop stars, but to her, this duet was her most beautiful by far.

Ashley's sweet tones complemented Leo's rich voice with its smoky edge perfectly. Of course, she couldn't keep up with Leo's incredible range—and she didn't try to. They weren't competing vocally but rather encouraging each other to let their voices soar into the night air.

As they took turns with the lyrics, the song seemed to become a conversation. Their voices mingled for the chorus, and they looked at each other across the fire as they sang about forgiveness and letting go of the past.

Sasha listened breathlessly. She had a feeling the song was no longer about Leo and her father but about Leo and Ashley and their complicated and, at times, hurtful history with each other.

When the last notes of the song faded away, silence settled over the beach, interrupted only by the steady murmur of the ocean waves.

Uncharacteristically, it was Jo who first spoke. "Wow. That was very nice."

Sasha stared at her. It had been way more than *very nice*. Didn't she understand how special their duet had been? But then again, Jo had no idea what music—and Leo's friendship—had once meant to Ashley. This was about so much more than singing a song with a friend while sitting around a bonfire. It was about forgiveness and about Ashley reclaiming a part of her that she had given up a long time ago.

Ashley slumped against her as if the effort of singing the song had drained her of the strength to sit up on her own.

Sasha could no longer stop herself from wrapping an arm around her. "It was beautiful," she said very quietly. *You are beautiful.* She bit her lip before she could say it out loud.

Ashley gave her a grateful look. She didn't pull away from the loose embrace, despite Lisa, Cait, and Jenny watching from the other side of the fire.

"See? It all came back to you quickly," Leo said. "We should do this again sometime."

Ashley nodded, and since they were touching all along their length, Sasha could hear her rapid swallow. She tightened her arm around her.

Finally, Leo put her guitar away and stood. "Well, on that note, I think I'll turn in now. All the food and the ocean air are making me sleepy. Thank you all for the great evening and for taking the time out of your busy lives to come to Florida with us. Having you here made this weekend truly special. Holly and I had a wonderful time—not just because of this magical place, but mainly because of you guys."

"A big thank-you from me too," Holly added. "I think I speak for Leo and me when I say that we are both very grateful to have you in our lives, and we look forward to also sharing our wedding day with you too." She smiled as everyone returned her sentiment. "Sleep well. Oh, just a reminder: our flight is at noon, so we should leave here around nine."

The fire had burned down while Leo had entertained her friends with her songs, and now they carefully shoveled sand over the gleaming embers.

Sasha stood too and smoothed a bit of sand off her shorts. She and Ashley worked together to fold their blanket and gather the remnants of their picnic.

As if by unspoken agreement, they hung back as everyone else strolled along the boardwalk to the house.

"I think I need a moment alone before I join them," Ashley said.

"Sure." Sasha pointed at where the others had disappeared. "Do you want me to—?"

"No." Ashley grasped her arm and then didn't let go. "Please stay. I didn't mean *alone* alone. Do you mind if we walk along the beach for a while?"

"Not at all." Sasha draped the blanket across Ashley's shoulders so she wouldn't get cold in the ocean breeze and then set them off along the shoreline, with the gently lapping waves a few yards to their right.

Ashley kept her hand on Sasha's arm as they walked. It felt a bit like an old-fashioned courting couple out for a midnight stroll, and Sasha decided that for a few minutes she would allow herself to indulge in the illusion that that was what they were—a couple.

"That was incredible," she said after a while and pointed back to where the fire had been. "I mean, I heard you and Leo sing together back when we were in school, but this just blew me away."

Ashley laughed giddily. "Really? God, I was so rusty. I must have listened to her album a thousand times, but I was so nervous that I think I got the lyrics wrong at least twice."

"It doesn't matter," Sasha said. "You both put so much emotion into every line, it was as if you were talking to each other—really talking for the first time in years."

Ashley stopped walking and stared at her in the near darkness. "You got all of that? That's exactly what it felt like to me too! Do you think Leo picked that song on purpose, to let me know she has forgiven me?"

"I'm sure she did. She's got seven albums under her belt. She could have chosen any of her other songs."

Ashley exhaled. "I'm glad. I mean, Holly said they'd decided to not hold on to any bad feelings and that she wanted to work on getting our friendship back, and they invited me along for the dress shopping and the bachelorette weekend, but I was never quite sure if they really wanted me there or whether Leo's mom convinced them because it would look strange to leave me out."

"They want you here." *And so do I.* Sasha held back from voicing that second sentence, though.

They strolled along the shoreline for another few minutes in amiable silence. Sasha didn't try to make conversation since she knew Ashley needed some space to let it all sink in.

Finally, Ashley squeezed Sasha's arm. "It's getting late. We should head back."

Sasha suppressed a sigh. They still had a few hours tomorrow morning, but their magical weekend in the Florida Keys was undeniably coming to an end, and she couldn't help wondering how things between them would be once they were back home. Ashley for sure wouldn't put her hand on her arm while they strolled along the creek. Reluctantly, she steered them back toward the beach house.

As if neither of them wanted the evening to end, they took the long way around instead of walking through the house. They wandered through the lush garden that was lit with solar-powered lamps, and Ashley pointed out the names of the tropical plants that grew there: birds of paradise, hibiscus, and bromeliads.

Sasha couldn't help smiling. "You're such a flower geek."

"Oh, do I hear the pot calling the kettle black, Ms. There's-a-little-too-much-sugar-in-these-cupcakes?"

Sasha chuckled. Yeah, admittedly, she had said that when she had tried the key lime cupcakes earlier. "Okay, maybe we're both geeks."

"Yeah, I think we're evenly matched."

In this romantic fairy garden, the words seemed to linger between them and take on a deeper meaning. Was it just her, or did Ashley feel it too?

But it didn't matter, she reminded herself. Tomorrow, they would go home, and things would go back to normal—whatever normal between them would look like.

She trudged up the stairs behind Ashley. They both smelled of wood smoke and ocean air, so Sasha escaped to the bathroom to unbraid her hair and take a shower.

Once she was done, it was Ashley's turn.

Sasha lay in bed, waiting for her. Would Ashley want to be held tonight too, or had that been strictly a one-time thing? Sasha didn't know what she should wish for. Another night with Ashley in her arms would be pure masochism. She needed some distance, not more intimacy. But she knew if Ashley asked, she wouldn't say no.

Damn. When had she gotten so weak? Just two months ago, she had been independent, easygoing Sasha, who wasn't looking to be tied down. And now…

A gasp from the bathroom interrupted her thoughts. She jumped up and hurried to the bathroom. "Ash?" she called through the door. "You okay?"

"Oh, yeah, yeah. I rubbed the towel across my back and discovered that I got a little sunburned." Ashley sucked in an audible breath. "Okay, a lot sunburned, actually. At least it feels like it."

Sasha winced in sympathy. "You should put some after-sun lotion on it. There's some next to the sink."

"Um, like I said, it's on my back. I can't reach."

"Oh." Sasha stared at the bathroom door between them. Should she offer to help? Just the thought of touching Ashley's bare back and smoothing lotion over her soft skin made her feel as if she had a sunburn too. *Bad idea. Really, really bad idea.* But instead of backing away, she heard herself say, "Want me to do it?"

For several seconds, she heard only silence, then Ashley said, "That would be, um, nice of you."

Nice. That was the last word Sasha would use to describe herself right now. Nervous, confused, eager—yes. But not nice. "Yeah, sure. No problem."

It wasn't a problem, right? She could do this. Put some lotion on Ashley without letting her hands—or her eyes—wander, go to bed, and sleep.

"Okay, I'm coming in. Are you decent?"

A nervous giggle came from the other side of the door. "Well, as decent as I can be while still allowing you to put lotion on my back."

Trying not to picture Ashley's state of dress…or undress, Sasha reached for the doorknob. Her palms were damp, so she quickly wiped them on her boxers. Slowly, she pushed the door open.

Ashley stood at the sink, her back to Sasha—her very naked back. She was wearing only a pair of panties, clutching her sleep shirt to her chest.

Sasha's gaze zeroed in on the bare skin on display. God, she so much wanted to run her fingers across it and soothe the hurt away.

"Um, does it look bad?" Ashley asked.

Bad? No, it looks beautiful. Sasha stopped herself from saying it. She tore her gaze away from Ashley's back and met her gaze in the mirror above the sink. "No. But it is a bit sunburned."

Slowly, Sasha stepped closer. The narrow space between them seemed to buzz with electricity. She swallowed and gently brushed Ashley's hair over her shoulder so it wouldn't get in the way.

Ashley held very, very still. Was she even breathing?

Sasha's fingers were a little unsteady as she reached for the bottle of after-sun lotion and squeezed a bit of it into her palm. She rubbed it between her hands to warm it, then hovered her fingers over Ashley's back before slowly lowering them.

Ashley sucked in a breath. A visible shiver went through her.

Instantly, Sasha stilled her fingers. "Am I hurting you?"

Ashley shook her head. "It was just, um, cold for a second."

"Okay. But tell me if I do hurt you." Tenderly, she smoothed her hands over Ashley's back, from her neck to her hips. Her skin was warm beneath her fingers and so incredibly soft. She longed to caress every inch of it and slide her hands to her sides, where it might be even softer, and then to her front. Jesus, this was insane. When her need became too strong, she recapped the bottle of lotion and turned away under the pretense of washing her hands at the sink, hoping some cold water would help regain her composure.

"Is it starting to feel better?" she asked over her shoulder to cover the awkward silence.

Ashley didn't answer.

Sasha shut off the water, reached for a towel, and turned.

Ashley was still standing in the middle of the bathroom, clutching the sleep shirt to her chest instead of sliding it back on.

"Ash? Hey, you okay?" Gently, she touched one slightly sunburned shoulder and guided her around so she could see her face.

A storm of emotions darkened Ashley's eyes. She reached out and gripped the fabric of Sasha's T-shirt with one fist. "No," she whispered. "I'm not okay. Not at all."

Sasha lifted one hand and cradled Ashley's face. "What's wr—?"

Ashley gave a desperate tug on Sasha's shirt. Then her lips were on Sasha's.

Oh holy...! Whatever fuses had held Sasha back blew in a spark of desire. She slid her hands along Ashley's smooth, lotion-covered back and drew her closer as she returned the kiss with equal passion.

Their tongues slid against each other. Ashley tasted of key lime cupcake, but on her, it didn't taste too sweet at all.

Ashley buried her fingers in Sasha's hair. The sleep shirt dropped to the floor.

Sasha groaned into her mouth when Ashley's bare breasts pressed against her.

Drunk with need, they tumbled against the sink.

Ashley flinched when the cold porcelain met her skin, but she didn't break the kiss.

Sasha slid her hands between the sink and Ashley to protect her from the hard edge. She pressed their hips together, wanting to feel more of her. God, this was so hot…and maybe something Ashley would regret in the morning. It took all of her willpower to offer her an out. "Ash," she whispered against her mouth in between little nips. "If we don't stop now, I'm not sure we'll be able to."

"Then let's not." Ashley tugged her back into another kiss.

Jesus. Sasha gave up her attempts to rein herself in and kissed her back, hard and demanding. If Ashley wanted her, at least for this one night, she would take whatever she could get. "Bed," she breathed against Ashley's lips, "now."

Somehow, they made it to the bedroom, still kissing. Next to the bed, they paused, and Sasha broke the kiss.

Ash shivered without Sasha's heat against her. The inch of space between them allowed doubts to intrude. *Oh God, what are we doing?*

But then Sasha lifted her T-shirt up over her head, revealing strong shoulders, smooth skin, and firm breasts. She stood in front of Ash in just her boxer shorts and looked her in the eyes, not shy of her nakedness at all.

Not that she had reason to be. She was striking. Ash wanted to cup those beautiful breasts, caress her entire body, crawl inside of her until the world receded.

Holding her gaze, Sasha stripped off her boxer shorts.

Ash's mouth went dry as she took her in. With trembling fingers, she followed her example and pushed her panties down her legs. She resisted the urge to cover herself with her hands.

Sasha reached out and trailed a single finger down the curve of Ash's hip. "God," she whispered, sounding almost as if she were saying a prayer. "You're sexy as hell."

It was a word Ash had never associated with herself before, but the heat flaring in Sasha's eyes left no doubt that she meant it.

Sasha stepped closer. A field of energy seemed to surround her, making Ash's body buzz. One hand in the small of her back and the other on her hip, Sasha guided her down onto the bed. She followed her down but braced herself on her hands and knees, not yet allowing their bodies to come into contact.

The sheets were cool against Ash's back, and the ocean breeze brushed along her overheated body because neither of them had taken the time to close the French doors. She shivered.

"Are you okay on your back?" Sasha asked.

Ash stared up at her without comprehension.

"Because of your sunburn," Sasha added.

Sunburn? Ash almost laughed. Her entire body was on fire, and it had nothing to do with being sunburned and everything to do with the woman hovering over her. She wanted so many things—wanted to touch Sasha everywhere, from the bold angles of her face to the shapely curve of her calves, until Sasha came undone beneath her hands. Most of all, she wanted to feel Sasha against her, so she reached up, gripped her hips, and softly tugged her down.

When their bare bodies came into contact, Ash gasped. Sasha's weight on her, the solid firmness of her body, and her soft skin against her own felt better than she could have dreamed up even in her most daring fantasies. Her entire body shook with nerves and desire.

"God, Ash, you feel so good. Incredible."

Ash couldn't answer; she could barely even think—and maybe that was a good thing. If she had stopped to think about it, she probably would have tried to run.

Sasha lowered her head and kissed her, and Ash stopped caring that this was probably a bad idea.

For an unknown amount of time, she lost herself in the warmth of Sasha's mouth.

Sasha kissed her with intensity, as if she were trying to make her come with just a kiss—and Ash wasn't so sure she wouldn't succeed eventually.

As their bodies started to move against each other, she groaned into Sasha's mouth, their moans mingling.

Finally, Sasha broke the kiss and stared down at her with a hungry gaze. "God, I want you."

Need surged through Ash so fiercely it almost scared her. No one had ever said those words to her. *I love you*, yes, but not *I want you*. Even now, a tiny part of her couldn't quite trust them. "You really do...don't you?"

"Oh yeah. Why's that so hard to believe?"

Cheeks heating, Ash shrugged.

"If you can't trust my words, maybe you can trust this." Sasha took Ash's hand and drew it down, between them, to the wetness between her legs. "Does this feel like I don't want you?" Her voice was raspy.

"Oh my God." Ash's head started to spin as she moved her fingers experimentally.

Sasha sucked in a sharp breath. "Fuck! Not yet." She pulled Ash's hand away, guided it to the side, and pressed it onto the mattress. "I want to touch you first. Every single inch of you."

A shiver went through Ash, and she left her hands where they were, as if shackled to the bed. Her body felt too heavy for her to move anyway, as Sasha brushed her hair to the side and kissed a trail down the side of her sensitive neck.

Sasha playfully nipped her shoulder, then nibbled her collarbone.

Goose bumps rippled across Ash's chest. She helplessly gripped the sheet with both hands, completely unprepared for her body's intense response to Sasha.

When Sasha reached the hollow of her throat, she dipped her tongue into it and tasted her skin. Her hand followed the path of her mouth. She caressed, teased, and explored as if she needed to know every inch of her, as she had promised. Each touch ignited fires across Ash's skin.

She quivered beneath Sasha's hands.

"Hey," Sasha whispered against her skin. "Breathe."

Ash exhaled and then gulped in a lungful of air, only now realizing that she'd held her breath.

Sasha stroked her cheek, her belly, the curve of her hip, taking her time, until Ash relaxed into the experience.

Then new tension shot through her as Sasha filled her hands with Ash's breasts and lightly rasped her thumbs over her already-erect nipples.

Ash's mind went blank. She cried out and covered Sasha's hands with her own, holding them tightly against her breasts.

"Ssh." Sasha covered her mouth with her own. "You have to be quiet, or the others will hear us."

Oh Jesus. Ash tensed. How could she have forgotten the others even for a second?

"Oh damn. Now you're thinking about them. Let's see if I can..." Sasha slid down the bed and ran the tip of her tongue along the curve of her breast, making each circle smaller and smaller. Then her warm breath fluttered across one aching nipple.

Ash's body ached with need. "Sasha," she whispered.

Sasha answered the unspoken plea by lowering her head and taking one hard nipple into her mouth.

"Oh that...yes!" She gripped the back of Sasha's head, tightening her fingers in her hair to hold her there, afraid that this incredible sensation would stop as soon as she let go.

"Don't worry," Sasha murmured, her breath bathing Ash's wet nipple with every word. "I won't stop. Not until you've had enough."

Ash didn't think that would ever happen. She shoved away the thought and focused on the feeling of Sasha's hot mouth on her.

Sasha switched to the other breast and flicked her tongue over the neglected nipple, then gently sucked on it.

Ash gasped out her name. God, this was like nothing she'd ever experienced. It wasn't only what Sasha was doing with her mouth and her hands, although that was incredible, but mainly the intense need behind each touch.

Sasha caught her other nipple between her thumb and forefinger and rolled it gently.

The double sensation slammed into Ash, making her bite down on her bottom lip, and yet it wasn't enough. Her hips rocked against Sasha's strong thigh in search of some friction.

"Slow down." Sasha lifted her mouth away from her breast and trailed her hand up and down her side. "I want to savor this. Savor you." But the hungry fierceness in her gaze only sharpened the edge of Ash's desire.

"I can't." Ash crushed her body to Sasha's. "Please."

"It's okay." Sasha kissed her again while she slid her hand down Ash's body, leaving a trail of fire.

Ash's stomach muscles tightened in anticipation. A needy sound escaped her. She no longer recognized her own voice.

Above her, Sasha's eyes blazed with passion as she dipped one finger into her wetness.

The first touch was like a bolt of heat, making Ash's nerve endings sizzle.

Sasha echoed her moan. "God, this is hot. You are hot."

Ash was beyond words. She clutched at Sasha with both hands. Her hips surged up to meet Sasha's finger.

Sasha stroked her gently, keeping her caresses light and slow.

But Ash didn't want her to hold back. She finally wanted to experience it all. "More." She panted through a dry mouth, almost panicked with want now.

Keeping her gaze locked on to Ash's, Sasha slid into her with two fingers.

The sensation made Ash gasp. She arched up, needing to feel her even deeper.

Sasha stilled for a moment, then started to move. The heel of her palm pressed against Ash's clit with every thrust.

Ash met her stroke for stroke. A roaring sound started in her ears, and pressure coiled deep in her belly. She raked the nails of one hand across the tight muscles of Sasha's back, while she brought her other hand to her mouth and bit her knuckles to stifle her cries.

Sasha buried her face against Ash's neck and rasped her teeth over her skin.

She did something with her fingers that made pleasure rip through Ash. Her eyes rolled back in her head, and lights burst behind her tightly closed lids. She bit down on her knuckles again and arched up against Sasha one last time before collapsing back onto the bed.

Her body pulsed for what seemed like a long time. As much as she wanted to put her hand on Sasha's shoulder and stroke her in silent gratitude, she couldn't move. Her limbs were heavy with languid pleasure.

Sasha stilled her hand and placed gentle kisses all over Ash's neck and face as she carefully withdrew her fingers.

Another shudder went through Ash. She wanted to grip Sasha's wrist and hold her hand against her for a little longer, but she didn't.

Then the soft kisses stopped. Sasha froze above her. An expression of panic replaced the passion on her face. "Ash," she whispered. "Oh my God, what's wrong? I didn't hurt you, did I?"

"H-hurt me?" Ash gasped out, still breathless.

Sasha touched her cheek. "You're crying."

"Crying?" Ash lifted her hand to her face and felt the wetness against her fingertips. How could she be crying at a moment like this—one of the most perfect in her life? But maybe that was it: It had been almost too perfect, making her feel too much.

While the aftershocks slowly stopped quivering through her body, the onslaught of her emotions didn't. It was as if her release had broken a dam that had held back her feelings for too long. Once she had started, she couldn't stop crying, although she couldn't pinpoint why exactly. A torrent of emotions—joy, gratefulness, fear, regret, and loneliness—roared through her, the flood too forceful to linger on any of them.

Finally, she gave up on trying to control herself. She buried her face against Sasha's shoulder and let her tears wet her skin.

"Ash," Sasha said urgently. She cupped her face with one hand and tipped it up so Ash would look at her. "What is it?" She leaned down and kissed a teardrop from the corner of Ash's eye.

The gesture was so tender that Ash almost burst into renewed tears. She tried to control her breathing.

Slowly, the stream of emotions trickled off. Ash heaved a shuddering sigh. *God, what was that?* She forced a reassuring smile to her lips, knowing she was probably scaring Sasha. "It was just a little intense and overwhelming—in a good way. A very good way."

"Are you sure that's all it is?" Sasha gently brushed the last of the tears away with her thumb.

Ash nodded. She didn't want to spoil this incredible experience by overanalyzing it. There'd be time for that tomorrow. Tonight, she just wanted to feel, not think. She reached for Sasha, pulled her down more tightly, and kissed her.

Sasha's lips tasted salty—or maybe it was her own. It no longer mattered as she poured everything she was feeling into the kiss.

Sasha moaned into her mouth. Her hips restlessly shifted against Ash's.

Ash pushed against her shoulder, urging her to roll over, and Sasha did without hesitation. She looked up at Ash with a completely open expression.

Wow. Ash reveled in that kind of trust and in the power she held over Sasha, but at the same time, it was also a little scary. She swallowed heavily. "I'm probably not very good at this. I hope I'll be able to...you know?"

"Trust me." Sasha chuckled roughly. "That won't be a problem at all. Just watching you come nearly got me there a few moments ago."

Ash's breath caught. Heat shot into her cheeks, but it wasn't all embarrassment. Knowing that she turned Sasha on gave her the courage to ignore her fears and to follow her instincts.

As she gazed down at Sasha, her breath caught. God, she was beautiful. Or maybe that was too weak a word to describe her. Sasha's skin glowed with a light sheen of perspiration. Without even thinking about it, Ash slid her hand down the valley between Sasha's breasts to see if her skin was as soft as it looked.

It was. She stroked down Sasha's belly, fascinated by the ripple of muscles beneath her touch. Without pausing her caresses, she ducked her head to taste her skin. She nibbled on her neck, inspired by what Sasha had done to her earlier.

Sasha instantly tilted her head back to give her room to work. Her pulse pounded wildly against Ash's lips, again confirming her ability to excite her.

Ash mapped out the long planes of Sasha's body with her hands and her mouth. Every now and then, she glanced up at Sasha's face, seeking confirmation that what she was doing was okay.

Each time, Sasha looked back at her with a heated gaze. "Anything," Sasha rasped as if sensing Ash's lingering insecurity. "You can do anything you want."

Ash wanted so much that she doubted she could do it all, even if they locked themselves in this room for an entire week. She didn't dare to try the one thing she wanted more than anything else—to taste Sasha—but with Sasha stretched out beneath her, open to her touch, there were plenty of other things she could do.

She pressed her lips to her strong shoulder and kissed a path down her chest, pausing every now and then to taste her salty-sweet skin.

The encouraging little noises that escaped Sasha made her grow bolder by the second. When she reached her breast, she cradled it in one hand. It fit perfectly into her palm, as if it had been made just for her touch.

She massaged it carefully, her gaze on Sasha's face.

Sasha's eyelids fluttered as if she was struggling not to close her eyes. "Mm, that feels so good."

"*You* feel so good." Ash rubbed her fingertip across the nipple, which hardened at her touch. She couldn't resist any longer. Bracing herself on her forearms, she slid down in bed and closed her lips around the tempting nipple.

Sasha groaned deep in her throat. Her hips bucked, and her damp heat slid against Ash's belly.

They both moaned.

Ash pressed down to feel it again, dizzy with the desire to bring Sasha pleasure, but the angle wasn't ideal.

Sasha's nipple popped out of her mouth as Ash rolled to the side so she was half next to Sasha instead of fully on top. That gave her the chance to explore even more of her, and she immediately took advantage. She slid her hand down Sasha's belly and traced the muscles in her thigh with her fingertips.

Sasha spread her legs in silent invitation. Her cheeks were flushed, and the need gleaming in her eyes went straight to Ash's head like strong wine.

Emboldened by the very clear signals Sasha's body was sending, she trailed her fingers up one silky-smooth inner thigh and into her wetness.

"Jesus," Sasha hissed out at the very first touch.

Ash's gaze flickered up to her face. "Still okay?"

"Okay?" A strangled laugh tore from Sasha's chest. Her voice was rough with desire. "It's perfect."

"It is?" Ash moved her finger a little. "Or would you rather I do this?" She slid lower, circled her entrance, and dipped just the tip of her finger inside. There she paused and gave her a questioning look.

A string of curses fell from Sasha's lips. "God, yes." As if she couldn't wait for Ash to initiate her next move, she reached down and pressed Ash's hand against her entrance, guiding her inside.

Oh my God! The sensation of Sasha enveloping her finger was the most incredible thing she'd ever felt. She clenched her own thighs together against the rush of arousal hitting her. For now, she wanted to focus just on Sasha. Slowly, she started to move her finger.

"Two," Sasha groaned out after a moment. "Use two."

Ash's head spun. She pulled out and pushed back in with two fingers, hoping she wasn't too clumsy because of her limited experience or because of the unbridled desire making her hands shake.

Sasha wasn't complaining at all. Her strong body arched up against Ash, and they started to move together.

Amazingly fast, Ash found a rhythm that made Sasha gasp and moan with every thrust. When Sasha started to move faster, Ash followed suit and tried to keep up.

Sasha's fingers dug into Ash's hip, and a husky groan rose from her chest.

The erotic sound sent shivers down Ash's body. Seeing Sasha lost in the throes of passion was the most mind-blowing thing she'd ever seen. She tried to heighten the experience for her by rubbing her clit while she touched her, but she knew she wasn't very coordinated.

It didn't seem to matter. Sasha surged up to meet her. "Yes! Just like… oh God!" Her eyes fell closed.

Ash reached up with her free hand and touched her cheek. "Open your eyes. Look at me. Please." She needed to see this—every last, amazing second of it—and she needed Sasha to see her too.

Sasha's eyes fluttered open immediately, and their gazes connected. The pleasure in her eyes—and knowing that she was causing it—sent a thrill directly to Ash's core.

God, she never wanted this to end.

But all too soon, Sasha's body went taut beneath her. She flung up her arm and pressed the back of her hand to her mouth, but a long moan still rang out.

Sasha's muscles contracted around her fingers, drawing her even deeper.

Ash held her breath in wonder. She stilled her fingers but didn't pull back, not wanting their incredible connection to end.

Sasha lay without moving; only her chest heaved in a fast rhythm as she tried to catch her breath. She had kept her eyes open through it all, and now they were hazy with pleasure. Her hair spilled onto her shoulders in a tousled tangle, and she looked wild and completely satisfied at the same time.

Ash couldn't help herself. She had to kiss her. Their sweat-dampened skin slid against each other, setting off renewed sparks in Ash, as she moved up her body and pressed her mouth to Sasha's.

Instantly, Sasha came to life. She wrapped both arms around Ash, deepened the kiss, and rolled them around so she was on top again.

Ash's fingers slid out, and they both groaned.

"Probably not very good at this?" Sasha repeated what Ash had said earlier. She playfully bit her earlobe. "If you were any better at it, I'd be dead…but what a way to go."

Her praise brought a flush to Ash's skin. She'd been praised for a lot of things in her life, but never for her skills in the bedroom.

Sasha captured her mouth again but then gentled the kiss. She cradled Ash's face in both hands and studied her with a concerned gaze. "About earlier, when you were crying… Want to talk about it?"

Ash quickly shook her head. Talking would lead to thinking, and that would ruin everything. She wasn't ready for reason to intrude into this magical night. "Can we talk tomorrow?"

"Sure." The serious expression in Sasha's eyes was replaced with a sexy devilish glint. "I can think of a thing or two we could do instead." She slid her hand down Ash's body.

Moaning, Ash drew Sasha to her for a deep kiss and stopped thinking for the rest of the night.

Chapter 17

THE FIRST LIGHT OF DAWN filtering into the room woke Ash. Goose bumps had formed on her chest in the cool breeze coming in through the open French doors, but her back and a strip of skin on her belly were toasty warm.

Ash peeked over her shoulder.

Sasha was holding her from behind, with not an inch of space between them. Her arm was around Ash's belly, and the wiry hair between her legs tickled Ash's butt.

Ash lay in her arms, caught between the urge to run and the desire to turn and kiss her awake so they could spend their last hour on the island making love again.

Making love? Ash stiffened. No. Not love. It couldn't be that. She was just overwhelmed with the brand-new experience of being desired and being allowed to desire without restrictions. Without a doubt, this had been the best sex of her life. Not that there was a lot of competition.

But deep down, Ash knew she was lying to herself. She knew this had not been just sex. Not even just great sex. The way Sasha had wiped away her tears and then, later, had held her as they had fallen asleep around four in the morning…

Why did Sasha have to be so sweet? That had made everything even more confusing. What was she supposed to do now?

Ash pressed her fisted hand to her mouth.

Her knuckles stung. Almost grateful for the distraction from a pain that went so much deeper, she gazed at her hand.

Four fading bite marks were still carved into her skin from when she'd bitten down on her knuckles so she wouldn't cry out in ecstasy. The tiny marks reflected exactly how she felt: marked by this incredible experience.

But she knew they would soon fade completely. By tomorrow, they would be gone—and so would her time with Sasha.

A wave of sadness clutched her so fiercely that Ash couldn't breathe.

All those emotions were too much for her. She needed to get out of here so she could think clearly. Gently, careful not to wake her, she lifted Sasha's arm from around her hip and slid out of bed.

Sasha mumbled something that sounded like a protest but didn't wake.

Ash walked around the room, looking for her clothes. God, her entire body ached as if she'd done the most intense workout of her life. She blushed at the thought of how they'd spent the night. They hadn't stopped for hours, both insatiable. She hadn't known it could be like that.

After a minute, she found a pair of shorts and put them on, then grabbed the nearest T-shirt. When she slipped it over her head, she realized it was Sasha's. She had pulled it off and discarded it on the bedside table last night. Sasha's scent clung to it, making her inhale deeply.

God, this was crazy. She was standing here, sniffing Sasha's shirt. She gave herself a mental kick and fled to the door.

Her first thought was to go down to the beach and hide out there until it was time to leave, but that wouldn't be fair to Sasha. She had promised they would talk this morning, so she couldn't go far.

Clanking sounds came from the kitchen. Someone was up and making breakfast, but Ash wasn't up for company.

The stairs up to the widow's walk promised solitude, and Ash rushed toward it as if it were a lifeboat on a sinking ship.

Sasha woke up shivering. She wasn't surprised when she reached out and found only cold sheets instead of Ashley's warm body. Waking up alone after a night in Ashley's arms was starting to become a familiar experience, and that set off every alarm in her head.

God, why was she doing this to herself? She should have known this would happen.

She rubbed her face and groaned as she caught Ashley's scent clinging to her fingers. Quickly, she dropped her hands to the bed and stared at the ceiling, trying to come to grips with the situation.

Okay, so they had slept together. It shouldn't have been such a big deal. A month ago, when she and Ashley had talked about relationships in the bakery, Sasha had said that she wouldn't mind having pizza again at some point—and now she had. Pizza wasn't usually a let's-hang-around-for-breakfast thing. So why was Ashley's absence this morning upsetting her so much?

If she was honest with herself, she knew the answer. This hadn't been a college fling or a few hours of fun with a virtual stranger. Last night had meant something to her; she just hadn't figured out what exactly.

The way Ashley had trembled beneath her, vulnerable and insecure, had touched her as deeply as her growing abandon as the night continued on.

While she wasn't sure what it all meant, she knew she wasn't ready to walk away and pretend it hadn't happened.

She swung her legs out of bed. Wow. She'd used some muscles last night that hadn't seen any action in some time.

Flashes of their night together followed her as she walked around the room to find her clothes. Her T-shirt was nowhere to be found. She ducked into the bathroom, but it wasn't there either. Only Ashley's sleep shirt lay abandoned on the floor.

Sasha washed her hands and her face. Then she picked up Ashley's sleep shirt and pressed it to her nose. *What are you doing?* God, this was getting ridiculous.

She folded the shirt and set it on the bathroom counter before getting a new T-shirt out of her bag. Where had the other one disappeared to? Had Ashley taken it?

The thought of Ashley wearing her T-shirt was sexy beyond words, and it gave her hope because she knew Ashley wouldn't go far if she wasn't properly dressed.

She might have run, but at least she hadn't run far.

When Sasha opened the door, the scent of coffee trailed up the stairs.

Was Ashley down there, making coffee, maybe even intending to bring it upstairs and crawl back into bed with her?

But when Sasha entered the kitchen, it wasn't Ashley behind the counter; it was Meg. Her spiky hair stuck up in all directions.

"Good morning." Sasha tried to look around inconspicuously.

There was no trace of Ashley anywhere.

"Morning." Meg yawned and slid a mug of coffee toward her. "You look tired. Did they keep you up too?"

"They?" Sasha took an eager sip of coffee, even though it was almost too hot to drink.

"I think it was Grace and Lauren. They went at it like rabbits for half of the night." Meg grinned. "Good thing Holly just requested that no one *talk* about sex, not that no one *have* sex."

Sasha nearly spat her mouthful of coffee across the counter. She hoped to hell she wasn't giving them away by blushing. Had they really been that loud? She hadn't thought so, but then again, Ashley had made her lose control a time or two. "Could I have another mug for Ashley? She, um, couldn't sleep all night either, so she could use the caffeine."

"Sure." Meg poured another mug. "Looks like Grace and Lauren kept up everyone."

Sasha didn't answer. She added milk and the amount of sugar Ashley liked, then fled back upstairs with both mugs. She had a feeling she knew where Ashley had gone. As she had suspected, she found her—and the missing T-shirt—on the widow's walk.

Once again, Ashley was staring out across the ocean. She had her arms wrapped around herself and huddled into the too-big T-shirt to ward off the early-morning chill.

Sasha wanted to walk up behind her and wrap her arms around her to provide some warmth but didn't know if that kind of touch was welcome, even after last night. Maybe especially after last night.

Ashley turned as if sensing her presence and gave her a smile that was strangely shy, considering they had spent most of the night exploring each other's body. "Morning."

"Good morning." Sasha held out one of the mugs. "I brought you some coffee." Okay, that was obvious, but she suddenly found herself a little tongue-tied, not sure what to expect from Ashley now. Would she want to pretend nothing had happened?

"Thank you." Ashley took the mug from her.

Their fingers touched, sending a tingle of sensation through Sasha's body. If she had thought one night was enough to get Ashley out of her system, that theory was definitely proven wrong. If anything, the pull between them had gotten stronger.

They stood side by side at the railing, watching the waves come in at the beach and sipping their drinks, as they had two days ago. But their time on the island had changed a lot between them, so this felt very different.

Sasha peeked over at Ashley and caught her looking at her out of the corner of her eye. God, this was silly. One of them had to act like an adult, or they would go home without having talked about last night. She turned to fully face Ashley, and after a moment of hesitation, Ashley did the same.

To Sasha's surprise, Ashley was the first one to speak. "I wasn't running from you." After a beat, she added, "Well, not much anyway. I just needed some space to think."

Sasha gave a nod of acknowledgment. "So, what are you thinking?"

Ashley stared into her coffee and trailed her thumb along the rim of the mug. "I don't know. I've never done anything like last night before. Just kissed someone totally out of the blue and..." She shook her head. "I'm sorry if I blindsided you."

Sasha held up one hand to stop her words. "Didn't I already prove to you last night that I wanted it to happen too?"

A pink tinge spread over Ashley's cheeks. "Yes, you did. But I admit I surprised myself." She let out a chuckle that sounded nervous. "Isn't it normally the bride who's supposed to do crazy things and have one last one-night stand during the bachelorette party?"

"One-night stand?" Sasha repeated. The words tasted more bitter than the coffee. She put her mug down. "Is that what it was for you?"

"Yes. No. I..." Ashley breathed in and out several times as if gathering her strength. "It didn't feel like a one-night stand," she finally said in a whisper.

The bitter taste in Sasha's mouth disappeared. "So we both agree that it wasn't just a quick bite of pizza that was good in the moment, but easily forgotten."

"It was more than pizza." A myriad of emotions glittered in Ashley's eyes. "But it can't be steak, Sasha. What happened between us...it will always be special to me, but it doesn't change my situation at home. I can't live my life as an outsider, and I can't lose my parents."

Sasha had known that Ashley would say something like that, but it still hurt. "So what happened in Florida, stays in Florida. That's what you're saying, right?"

Ashley hung her head. She put her half-finished mug of coffee down too. "I wish things were different, but I can't make you any promises that I know I won't be able to keep."

"No, I guess you can't." Sasha sighed. She couldn't blame Ashley for not wanting to leap out of the closet after one night of passionate sex. She had known who Ashley was and what kind of baggage she came with when she'd taken her to bed. But all of these reasonable thoughts couldn't stop the sadness that settled down on her like a dark cloud. "So this," she waved her hand at them, the house, and the beach, "is it? That's all we can ever have?"

"I think it has to be." Ashley looked her in the eyes, then glanced away. "I'm sorry, Sasha. I never meant to—"

Sasha surprised them both by bridging the space between them with one long step, crushing Ashley's body to hers, and kissing her. She had meant it to be a demanding kiss, one that would imprint her on Ashley's mind and make her realize what she was turning her back on, but as soon as their lips met, the kiss gentled.

Ashley didn't protest or push her away. She tangled her fingers in Sasha's hair and kissed her back.

It wasn't a passionate kiss or a seductive one. Even though they would fly home together, this felt like a kiss goodbye.

When it ended, Ashley leaned her forehead against Sasha's shoulder, and Sasha held her close. They stood that way, listening to the murmur of the ocean and each other's heartbeat, until it was time to get ready to leave.

Sasha hugged her tightly, and Ashley clung to her with unexpected strength.

"We won't lose our friendship once we're back home, will we?" Ashley whispered. "It might be a little selfish, but I don't want to give you up completely."

Maybe it would have been better to sever all ties once and for all, but was that really even possible in a small town like Fair Oaks? They would run into each other constantly.

Besides, she didn't want to lose Ashley for good either. "I hope not." Sasha forced a grin. "But we should probably give up the food fight kisses and sleeping in the same bed."

Ashley's laughter almost sounded like a sob. "And applying lotion to each other's backs."

"That too." Sasha nodded, but it felt as if they would be giving up much more than just these things. She gave Ashley one last gentle squeeze and then let go. "Come on. We need to hurry, or we'll miss our flight."

"I have to admit that at the moment, I really wouldn't c—" Ashley cut herself off.

"Really wouldn't what?"

Ashley shook her head. "Nothing."

"Oh, before we go downstairs, I think there's one more thing you need to know," Sasha said as they picked up their mugs. "Meg heard us."

"Heard us doing w—? Oh!" Ashley blushed so fiercely that her face looked as if it had gotten sunburned too. A second later, she turned very pale. "Shit! Did she tell the others?"

Sasha took the mug from her because Ashley was trembling so much that she nearly dropped it. "Calm down. She thinks it was Grace and Lauren, and I didn't correct her."

Ashley blew out a breath. "Thank God."

Sasha bit her lip. Ashley's relief hurt. Intellectually, she understood that Ashley's panic at the thought of someone finding out about them had nothing to do with her and everything to do with Ashley's fear of being outed, but her heart didn't care. *Yeah, and that's why Ashley is right. It's better to end it here and now. Trying to make things work with her would only end in heartache.*

But it didn't feel that way at all. Everything in her screamed that this was wrong.

Neither of them said anything else as they walked down the stairs and packed their bags. Maybe there wasn't anything left to say.

Chapter 18

Mrs. Beasley prattled on and on while Ash arranged white tea roses, white Stargazer lilies, and yellow stephanotis into a bouquet.

Ash nodded and hummed her agreement in all the right places, but her attention wasn't on the conversation or even on the bouquet. Her mind hadn't been on work since she'd gotten back from Florida three days ago.

Well, she was thinking about flowers…kind of.

The lilies made her think of the lily dust Sasha had gotten all over her shirt six weeks ago—and the way she had touched Sasha's breast with the tape. That, of course, led to her remembering the caresses she had bestowed upon Sasha's breasts Saturday night. A flush warmed her body.

"…can you believe it?" Mrs. Beasley stared at her, clearly expecting an answer.

Oh damn. She really needed to pay attention to one of her most important customers. Keeping her fingers crossed, she took a wild guess from Mrs. Beasley's tone and her usual favorite topic—complaining about someone else's perceived inappropriate behavior. "That's really quite scandalous."

Mrs. Beasley nodded. "It is. I don't know what she was thinking, wearing a miniskirt to church! Her poor mother was mortified."

Phew. That had been a lucky guess. Ash tried to keep her mind on what she was doing as she tied the bouquet and wrapped it in tissue paper.

Mrs. Beasley took the bouquet from her and pierced Ash with an imploring gaze. "Is everything all right, dear? You look a little flushed. You aren't coming down with something, are you?"

"Oh, no, I'm fine." Ash's hands automatically went to her cheeks, which warmed even more at being caught daydreaming about Sasha's breasts. "It's probably just a bit of leftover sunburn from the beach."

"Oh, that's right. You went to Hawaii with Leontyne and Holly, didn't you?"

"Florida," Ash said and could have slapped herself for mentioning it.

"I don't know what they were thinking." It seemed to be Mrs. Beasley's favorite phrase today. "Flaunting their money like that."

For a second, Ash considered letting it go. She needed to choose her battles wisely where Mrs. Beasley was concerned. In the past, she might have just meekly nodded. But now she couldn't. The need to defend her friends nearly made the words burst out of her. "They really weren't. All they wanted was to spend a relaxing weekend with their friends, and I found it quite generous that they paid for everything since most of us couldn't have gone otherwise."

Mrs. Beasley stared at her, probably not used to Ash—or most other people—disagreeing with her. "Well, then they should have gone to a less expensive, local place, like everyone else."

"I'm sure they would have, but many of the places in Missouri still aren't too eager to celebrate a wedding between two women. So they had no choice but to take their business elsewhere."

It wasn't quite true, but at least it shut Mrs. Beasley up for a moment.

"I heard about the country club canceling on them," Mrs. Beasley finally said.

Heard about it—or had she encouraged her friends from the country club to give the ballroom to a heterosexual couple instead? Ash wouldn't put it past her.

"It's unfortunate for them, but I guess it's everyone's right to pick what kind of customers they want to have," Mrs. Beasley continued.

"Actually," Ash said, surprising herself, "it might turn out to be much more unfortunate for the country club than for Leo and Holly."

A frown dug deep groves into Mrs. Beasley's forehead. "What do you mean?"

"How do you think it's going to look for them when the press gets wind of them canceling on Jenna Blake because she's gay? A reputation for discriminating against customers is never good for any business." Ash gave her a pleasant smile. "But I'm sure you and your husband would never think of doing something like that since you've always been clever businesspeople."

Mrs. Beasley let out a huff. "Of course we are." Bouquet in hand, she slapped a bill down on the counter, whirled around, and strode from the shop.

The door fell closed behind her with a loud jangle.

Brooke stuck her head out of the back room, where she had hidden when Mrs. Beasley had approached the shop. "That was awesome!"

Ash wasn't so sure. Even if she had won the argument this time, Mrs. Beasley had ways to get back at her if she aggravated her too much. "Will you be okay taking over the shop for twenty minutes? I need some air."

"Are you stopping by the bakery?" Brooke asked with a hopeful expression.

"I might," Ash said as casually as she could, as if her heart weren't beating faster at the mere mention of the bakery. "I'll bring you back something sweet if I do."

At least now she had an excuse to drop by Slice of Heaven and see how Sasha was doing.

She took off her florist's apron, nearly getting tangled in the strings in her haste to get out of the shop. *God, you're hopeless.* She wondered how long it would take until she got back to normal—or if she ever would.

Key limes had been impossible to find anywhere in town. Sasha had grumbled about it all morning. Finally, she had substituted Persian limes and experimented with the amount of sugar until she got it just right.

She tried a bit of the lime buttercream before spooning it into her piping bag. *Oh yum.* The tart yet sweet taste instantly transported her back to the Florida beach, where she'd shared a key lime cupcake with Ashley.

Okay, maybe making these cupcakes hadn't been such a good idea after all. She was supposed to forget about everything that had happened in Florida, not obsess over it like some masochistic fool.

Come on. Get it over with and get them out of your sight. She grabbed the pastry bag full of lime frosting and piped a swirl onto the first cupcake.

Aunt Mae stuck her head through the swinging doors. Her eyes widened. "Oh wow. Looks like Florida really left a lasting impression on you."

"Just because I'm making lime cupcakes doesn't mean I'm thinking of Florida," Sasha protested.

Aunt Mae let her gaze trail over the cupcakes that covered every available surface in the kitchen. "Maybe I'd believe that if you hadn't made so many."

Sasha sighed. She had indeed gone a little overboard in her attempt to lose herself in work and forget about Ashley. They would probably end up selling lime cupcakes at half price to get rid of them all.

"If it's any consolation, I think she's still thinking about whatever happened too," her aunt said. "When she came in and you weren't behind the counter, she looked as if someone had just snatched up the last cupcake right from under her nose."

"Ashley?" Sasha blurted out. The pastry bag slipped, and she accidentally turned one of the cupcakes into a lime buttercream volcano when she squeezed too hard. "She was here?" Ashley hadn't come in since they had gotten back from Florida.

"Still is. We're out of espresso chocolate chip cookies, so I told her I'd check to see if the new batch is done. Is it?"

"Yeah." Sasha pointed at the cookies, which were cooling on one of the racks hidden among the flood of cupcakes.

Aunt Mae put a couple of the cookies into a bakery box and held it out to Sasha. "Why don't you take them out to her?"

"Me?" Sasha shook her head. "I'm not done with the cupcakes."

Aunt Mae took the piping bag from her and pressed the bakery box into her hands. "I'll finish up here. Maybe take her a couple of lime cupcakes too. God knows we have enough of them."

Sasha shook her head. If Ashley saw the lime cupcakes, she would know Sasha was still thinking about their time in Florida. She was supposed to go back to being good buddy Sasha, so that was what she would do. Too bad that it was proving to be much harder than she had expected. "Um, no. I want to sprinkle some graham cracker crumbles and lime zest over the frosting before I sell them."

"Oh, I can do that and then take some out to her," her aunt said.

"No, no, that's not necessary," Sasha said quickly. "You know Ashley doesn't like anything but vanilla cupcakes."

Aunt Mae studied her through narrowed eyes. "If I didn't know any better, I'd say you're—"

"Um, I'd better take these out to her." Sasha held up the box of cookies and backed through the swinging doors before her aunt could voice whatever she'd been about to say.

But her sigh of relief at her escape had been premature. She had jumped out of the frying pan, into the fire, because Ashley was standing at the counter, waiting for her cookies.

Their weekend in the sun had lightened her hair to a pale blonde, and her sunburn had turned into a golden tan.

God. Why did she have to look more attractive than ever? That so wasn't fair. How was she supposed to forget how soft Ashley's skin had felt beneath her hands when Ash looked like this?

Sasha brushed her hand down her apron to remove any crumbs or specks of flour. She tried to channel her new acquaintance, Oscar-winning actress Grace Durand, as she walked up to her. "Hey, Ash," she said as casually as possible.

Ashley turned. For a moment, Sasha thought she saw an expression of longing in her eyes, but then Ashley smiled her girl-next-door grin and the impression faded. "Hi. Brooke sent me over for some cookies."

Was it just Brooke who'd missed her treats? "Here they are." Sasha held up the box. "Fresh out of the oven."

They both sounded so normal, like a baker and her customer, even though there was no one else in the bakery right now who could have overheard them.

"Thank you." Ashley took the box from her, overly careful not to let their fingers brush in the process.

For some reason, that made Sasha feel a little better. So Ashley was struggling with getting back into friends mode too. After all, if she didn't feel a thing for her anymore, why would she avoid touching her?

Ashley shuffled her feet.

"So," they both said at the same time.

Sasha waved her hand in invitation. "Go ahead."

"No, you go ahead."

Sasha shook her head at them both. She longed to have the easy familiarity of their time in Florida back. If she focused, she could still feel

Ashley lean in to her as they had sat beside each other at the bonfire. "Jesus, this is awkward."

"Yeah." Ashley rubbed her neck with her free hand. "How's your week going?"

"Fine," Sasha said. "How's yours?"

"Fine too."

They looked at each other.

"Are you really fine?" Sasha asked.

Ashley made a sound that could indicate yes or no. "Getting there. I know we were gone for only forty-eight hours, but it's weird to be back."

Sasha could have hugged her for being honest. Since Ashley hadn't been by all week, she had assumed that Ashley was hiding out in her shop, avoiding her. But it seemed Ashley wasn't shutting her out, at least not completely. "Yeah, I know what you mean. I—"

Aunt Mae burst through the swinging doors. "Ah. You're still here. Good." She headed straight for Ashley and piled another box onto the first one. "Here, have some free key lime cupcakes. Sasha made too many."

Oh great. Sasha sent her a death glare, which her aunt ignored.

A tiny smile tugged on Ashley's lips. "Key lime cupcakes, hmm?"

"Actually, they aren't key lime, just regular lime," Sasha mumbled.

"I know you usually prefer vanilla cupcakes," Aunt Mae said to Ashley.

"I'll make an exception for these," Ashley said.

An exception—like their night in Florida had been an exception. Sasha suppressed a sigh. It would take some time for the memory to fade.

"Brooke isn't picky anyway," Ashley added. "She'll eat whatever you put in front of her." She paused, and her eyes widened. "Um, that's not to say that a more discerning person wouldn't enjoy your cupcakes. They're great, so thank you."

Sasha bit back a smile. Ashley was cute when she got flustered.

"I'd better take these back to Brooke before she starts gnawing on some tulips." Ashley's gaze went to the door, then back to Sasha. "Will I see you at Johnny's on Saturday?"

Truth be told, Sasha had planned on skipping their Saturday night outings with the gang for a couple of weeks, until she felt able to look at Ashley across the table and not think of how it had felt to kiss her or caress her. But now that Ashley was looking at her with an expectant gaze, no excuse came to mind. Or maybe she didn't want to make up one. "Um, yeah, sure. I'll be there."

"Great." Ashley handed her a bill, again careful not to let their fingers touch, and waved off any change. "See you Saturday, then."

Sasha considered it a victory when she managed not to watch her retreating back. She turned toward her aunt. "Didn't I tell you not to bring her any lime cupcakes?"

"And I would have honored your request if you had given me more than just a bullshit excuse. It's pretty obvious that Ashley is over her vanilla phase."

Sasha started coughing. *Oh, get your mind out of the gutter. She didn't mean it like that.*

Aunt Mae studied her with a knowing look. "Let me guess... You and Ashley had a decidedly non-vanilla weekend in Florida. You had some fruity cocktails and then stumbled into bed with each other."

"We had a couple of cocktails, but nothing happened that night," Sasha said, hoping her aunt wouldn't notice the qualifier.

"Ooh! *That* night!" Aunt Mae did a little victory dance. "So you slept with her the second night! I knew it!"

Sasha said nothing. She had never lied to her aunt, and she wouldn't start now, not even to cover for Ashley.

"So, what happens now? Are you two dating?"

Sasha looked at her aunt's delighted smile. Maybe if everyone in town reacted like that, Ashley would be more open to the idea instead of hiding in the closet. "No. It was a one-time thing. Ashley isn't ready to come out. I don't think she'll ever be."

"Oh, honey." Aunt Mae hugged her tightly. "I'm so sorry." She held her at arm's length and studied her. "You really like her, don't you?"

"Yeah. I always thought it was only a little crush, and it was, up until we started spending more time together. But now..." Sasha sighed. "I think I could be falling in love with her."

Aunt Mae stared at her, and Sasha was equally shocked by what had just come out of her mouth. Love? That hadn't crossed her mind before, had it? She had thought about what it would be like to keep seeing Ashley, to date her...but love was a whole other ballgame.

Shit. Sasha rubbed her chest. Her entire life, she had carefully avoided any heartache by keeping her relationships light and fun, and now a woman she wasn't even in a relationship with was coming close to breaking her heart.

Aunt Mae gave her another hug. "If she doesn't think you're worth the risk of coming out, she doesn't deserve you. Don't worry, honey. You'll meet someone else who'll recognize what a catch you are."

Fat chance of that. There weren't that many new people moving to Fair Oaks. Even if there had been, her libido—and maybe her heart—were firmly stuck on Ashley.

The bell above the door jingled, and Derek entered.

"Hi, Sasha." He tipped an imaginary hat. "Hi, Mrs. Peterson. I thought I'd get some sugary treats for Ashley."

What the hell? Since when did Derek buy treats for Ashley? It wasn't as if they were dating…were they? Had Ashley given in and agreed to date him to re-establish her cover as a supposedly straight woman? Sasha gritted her teeth, but she knew she couldn't refuse to sell him anything.

"What did you have in mind?" she asked as professionally as possible.

Derek scratched his neck and peered at the baked goods behind the glass. "I have no idea what she likes."

Yeah, buddy, that's right. But I do. Sasha knew it was silly. She was behaving like a dog defending its bone, when it wasn't her bone to defend at all. But no way in hell would she help him woo Ashley by telling him her favorite treats.

"Something to cheer her up, I guess. Her mom said she's been kind of down this week." He flashed a grin. "Probably misses the Florida sunshine. Who can blame her? I bet it was great. Wasn't it, Sasha?"

Sasha bit the inside of her cheek. "Yeah, it was."

"Oh, we have just the thing for you." Aunt Mae gave her a conspiratorial grin. "Sasha made a batch of key lime cupcakes."

This time, Sasha abstained from pointing out that they weren't key lime. Admittedly, she took a certain satisfaction from knowing he'd bring Ashley a treat that would remind Ash of her.

Derek chuckled. "Seems like Ashley isn't the only one who misses the Florida sunshine."

"Yes, Sasha misses it terribly too," Aunt Mae said. "She's been moping around since she got back."

Sasha sent her a warning glare.

"I'll get them for you, Derek." Aunt Mae bustled past them into the kitchen.

When she had disappeared through the swinging doors, Derek leaned against the counter. "You and Ash are friends, right?"

Where was he going with this? Sasha nodded carefully. "Guess you could say that."

"So, you would know if she were dating anyone. I mean, her parents say she's not, but...well, people don't always tell their parents everything."

That was certainly true for Ashley. "I don't think she's looking to date anyone right now."

"So she's not with anyone? Great."

Sasha stared at him. That was what he took from what she'd just said?

Aunt Mae returned with a box of cupcakes.

"Thank you." Derek took the box from her. "What do I owe you?"

Sasha quoted the full price. No way would she give away free treats to the competition.

He paid and left the bakery with a skip in his step.

Aunt Mae watched him go and chuckled. "I hope Brooke likes the lime cupcakes. I think she'll be eating a lot of them today."

Ash was late meeting the gang on Saturday. Normally, she might have debated whether it was worth hurrying to the bar or if she should skip this week, but she didn't want Sasha to think she was avoiding her.

Truth be told, she had also been looking forward to seeing her all week. Since their entire group was going to Johnny's, no one would think anything of it.

She burst into the bar and headed straight for the corner table, where her friends were sitting.

Her gaze immediately zeroed in on Sasha.

God, she looked good. For once, her hair wasn't braided but tumbled onto her strong shoulders in carefree waves. Ash vividly remembered how it had felt to bury her fingers in it a week ago. Sasha had rolled up the sleeves of her button-down, revealing forearms that were tanned from their time in Florida.

Sasha looked up as if sensing her approach, and their gazes connected. A smile lit up Sasha's face.

Ash had to rein in her answering smile so no one would think she was too eager to see Sasha. She waved at the rest of the group. "Sorry I'm late, guys. I had to go out to my folks. My dad started planting the corn today, and my mom caught a bad cold, so I took them a tuna casserole."

"No problem. You are just in time for the interesting part," Jenny said. "Holly and Leo had the photos developed."

"Photos?" Ash repeated.

"The ones from the disposable cameras they gave us last weekend."

Derek jumped up from his end of the horseshoe-shaped booth and gestured for Ash to slide in between him and Holly.

Ash threw a longing glance toward Sasha's side of the table, but there was no way she could tell him she'd rather sit next to Sasha.

Cait had joined them tonight too, so it was a tight fit, and Derek's knee pressed against hers.

Ash tried to inconspicuously move her leg away.

He waved over the waitress. "Put whatever Ashley's having on my tab."

Shit. He had already bought her cupcakes this week. Obviously, he was trying to woo her with food and drink. Should she just accept not to cause any public drama?

But she knew it would only lead to problems in the long run, and she had promised herself not to play that game anymore. While she couldn't date whom she wanted, she also wouldn't make some poor guy unhappy by stringing him along.

Sasha looked as if she was ready to come to her rescue, so Ash quickly said, "I really appreciate the offer, Derek, but I'm fine paying for my beer."

Derek lifted both hands, palm out. "Whatever you want."

Travis laughed and reached across the table to slap his shoulder. "See? I told you, man. You're barking up the wrong tree."

"Shut up," Derek said. "Her wanting to pay for her own drink just means she's a modern, emancipated woman, not that she's…whatever you keep saying she is."

Her cheeks burning, Ash forced herself to look him in the eyes. "And as a modern, emancipated woman, I don't appreciate being talked about like I'm not sitting right here."

"Wow," someone mumbled.

Sasha threw her a surprised look. Then a grin curled up her lips.

Ash was equally surprised by what she had just said. That happened a lot lately, and part of it was Sasha's influence.

Derek ducked his head. "Um, sorry. You're right."

"So," the waitress said, looking back and forth between them. "What do you want me to bring you?"

Ash peered up at her. "A Bud Light, please."

When the waitress walked away, Holly lifted her stack of photos. "Want to see them?"

"Grace Durand in a bikini?" Travis grinned. "Hell, yes!"

"Sorry, Trav," Leo said. "No one took any photos of Grace. She's in the limelight so much that she asked us to not bother her with a camera for that one weekend."

That was a lie. Grace hadn't asked for any special treatment; Ash knew that. But she loved the way Leo was protecting the privacy of her famous friend.

Travis pretended to pout until Jenny elbowed him in the ribs.

They passed the photos around the table, and Ash oohed and aahed along with everyone else. The photos had turned out great. Snapshots of the beach, the great food, and them all having a wonderful time brought back a lot of good memories of last weekend.

A few of the photos were of Sasha and her—high-fiving each other after winning the sandcastle competition, sipping their second cocktail, and sharing a cupcake.

Of course, the most special moments of that weekend hadn't been captured on camera. Ash hid her red cheeks behind the beer bottle the waitress had just brought her and took a big sip.

Then someone handed her the next picture.

A drop of beer dribbled down Ash's chin as she nearly spat out the entire mouthful.

The photo had been taken at the beach, during the evening of the bonfire. Even though the fire provided the only light for the camera, the details were still clear enough. She and Sasha were sharing a blanket, and they had turned toward each other so their knees were touching. Sparks from the fire had lit up their features—or maybe it was the way they were looking at each other, as if no one else existed on the island…or the entire state of Florida.

Oh God. Ash's skin felt as if she were sitting next to a fire again.

This wasn't how two friends looked at each other. It had to be pretty obvious to anyone who threw even a fleeting glance at the picture. If she passed on that photo, everyone would know how she felt about Sasha.

How do you feel about her? a little voice in the back of her mind asked.

She silenced it immediately. She had avoided thinking about it too deeply all week, and now wasn't the time to do it. One panic attack at a time was enough.

Sasha gave her a questioning gaze from across the table. "Everything okay? There isn't a bikini photo of Grace after all, is there?"

"Gimme, gimme." Travis waved his hands.

"No. No one's wearing a bikini in this one." Ash wanted to slide the photo into her purse, but now everyone's attention was on her, so there was no way to make it disappear. With trembling hands, she passed the photo on to Cait across the table.

Cait looked at it for several moments as if she didn't recognize the people in the photo.

And maybe she really didn't. Ash had barely recognized herself that night.

"Oh, that was right after Ash sang with Leo, I think," Cait finally said. "So much emotion in that song."

Ash started to breathe again. Wow. She had gotten lucky. Cait had attributed the emotion that was obvious on their faces to the song.

Sasha was the next one to get the photo. She looked at it for what seemed like a very long time, then passed it on to Lisa without saying anything.

What was she thinking? What had she seen on Ash's face?

While the others exclaimed over a photo of the sunset over the ocean, Sasha and Ash looked at each other across the table.

"Jeez," Sasha mouthed at her, a stunned look on her face. "Did you see…?"

Should she pretend not to know what Sasha was talking about? It crossed her mind for a second, but she immediately decided against it. Sasha deserved better than such childish games. She nodded and pressed her beer bottle against her forehead.

We're screwed. So screwed. This thing between them was so much more than pizza. The picture screamed it loud and clear. It had the potential to be a steak dinner that would be satisfying for life—if only Ash had the courage to order it.

God, she wanted to. She really did. But was she ready to deal with the consequences? People would be staring, whispering, making ugly comments behind her back. The mere thought of it made her skin itch as if she was breaking out into hives. But there was another, a new voice in the back of her mind too, whispering that not everyone would react that way. Sasha's aunt hadn't. And maybe being with Sasha would be worth all the stares and comments.

Ash barely registered any of the other photos or the conversation around the table. She felt Sasha's concerned gaze on her several times but was glad when she didn't ask. Her thoughts were a jumbled mess, so she wouldn't have been able to explain them to anyone, not even Sasha.

As always, Ash and Sasha were the first ones to leave the bar. Since their friends knew they had to get up early most days, no one seemed to think anything of them leaving together.

Just when Ash thought they would make their escape and could finally talk, Derek hurried after them. "Wait up, Ash. I'll walk you to your car."

Sasha whirled around to him, blocking the door with her broad shoulders. "This is Fair Oaks, Derek, not the Bronx," she said with an uncharacteristic sharpness. "She doesn't need anyone to walk her to her car."

Ash put her hand on Sasha's forearm. The muscles beneath her fingers were tense.

"It's okay, Ash. I know she's right," Derek said. "Looks like I'm really putting my foot in it with you ladies tonight. I swear I'm not a patronizing ass who thinks women aren't capable of fending for themselves." He gave Sasha a wry grin. "I know any mugger would be more likely to run from you than from me anyway. It's just..." His cheeks colored. "I'm trying to find a moment alone with Ash."

Sasha opened the door and walked out, her long legs quickly putting some distance between them.

All of Ash's instincts told her to run after her, but under Derek's attentive gaze, she forced herself to follow slowly.

As Sasha approached Ash's SUV, parked along the curb, she slowed and then turned toward them.

Ash sent her a pleading gaze, silently begging her not to leave her alone with Derek.

But she knew she couldn't avoid it forever. A silent standoff between Derek and Sasha, with each one waiting for the other to leave, would look pretty suspicious to anyone passing by.

"Good night," Sasha finally said. "See you next week."

"Night, Sasha." Ash couldn't help watching her until her tall shape disappeared in the near darkness down the street.

"So," Derek said, "did you like the cupcakes?"

Ash bit her lip. Brooke had eaten them all. Ash was experiencing enough flashbacks to Florida as it was; the last thing she needed was anything else that made her think of Sasha. "I always do. Sasha's cupcakes are the best."

"So I heard. I haven't actually tried them yet. I mean, of course I had her aunt's before I left, but not Sasha's."

"You definitely should."

"Maybe we could get together and you could introduce me to your favorites," Derek said.

Ash watched him in the glow of the streetlight. "Are you, um, asking me out on a date?"

"Yes." He looked her in the eyes. "Yes, I am. So, what do you say? Will you go have coffee and cupcakes with me?"

Ash wished she could just jump into her car and speed away. But she would have to face this situation once and for all. "I think you're a really nice guy, Derek—"

He groaned. "I'm about to get friend-zoned, right?"

"Um, yeah. Sorry, Derek. I really like you, but not that way."

He stared at the pockmarked sidewalk, then lifted his gaze to hers again. "Is it because you're gay?"

The direct question hit Ash like a punch to the diaphragm. A wave of panic surged through her, not just because he had asked but mainly because for one crazy second, she thought she might answer yes.

Are you out of your mind? He'd tell his mother, and she would tell Mom and the entire rest of town!

"You're right—about you really stepping into it today," she finally told him. "Honestly, it comes across as pretty arrogant if you think any woman who's rejecting you has to be gay."

"That's not what I…" Derek scrubbed his hand across his face. "Sorry. I guess I let Travis's comments get to me."

Ash unlocked her SUV and opened the driver's side door.

"I really am sorry, Ash," Derek said.

She climbed in. "It's okay," she said, even though at the moment, nothing in her life felt okay. "See you next week." She closed the door and started the engine with trembling fingers, her only thought on making a quick getaway.

As she sped past the bakery, her foot lifted off the gas on its own volition.

No. Taking refuge in Sasha's arms would defeat the purpose. She couldn't have her cake and eat it too—or, in her case, have her baker and stay in the closet.

Chapter 19

"ARE YOU SURE THAT'S A good idea?" Aunt Mae asked as Sasha arranged her sugar flowers in a box the Thursday evening before the wedding. "I thought you wanted to spend less time around Ashley for a while?"

"I did." Sasha hadn't seen that much of Ashley in the nearly four weeks since the bachelorette weekend, partly because they were both working nearly around the clock, first because of Easter and now to get ready for the wedding and then Mother's Day the week after. "This is work, not pleasure."

"Uh-huh. Then why don't you have me or Tammy run the sugar flowers over to the flower shop? It's not like you don't have enough to do in the bakery two days before the wedding."

"Because...um..."

Aunt Mae walked over and put her hand on Sasha's arm. "I don't mean to nag you, honey. I just don't want you to get hurt."

Sasha flashed her a smile that she thought was pretty convincing. "Don't worry. I'm a lot like you. I need a relationship about as much as I need a third nostril."

Aunt Mae gently pinched Sasha's nose. "Liar."

"Ouch." Sasha rubbed her nose. "Seriously, Auntie Mae. I'm a big girl. I'll be fine."

"You'd better be, or I'll take Ashley over my knee."

The mental image made Sasha snort with laughter. God, she had needed that. "I'll tell Ashley you said so."

She tucked the box under her arm and walked down Main Street. It was after seven in the evening, but as she approached the flower shop, she wasn't surprised to see Ashley still behind the counter, working on something.

Seeing her always gave Sasha a little jolt that was part happiness, part longing, and this time wasn't any different.

At the jingle of the bell above the door, Ashley looked up. A genuine smile lit up her face. "Hey, stranger. I didn't think I'd see you before Saturday. How's the wedding cake coming?"

"Great. I baked it today, so I'll have all day tomorrow to decorate." Sasha walked up to the counter. "I thought I'd bring you the gum paste flowers you wanted and see if you needed any help with whatever you're doing."

Ashley stared at her. "Seriously? You want to help me after the long workday you've had and the even longer one you'll be having tomorrow?"

Sasha shrugged as casually as possible. "I promised I'd come over and play florist sometime if you baked cupcakes with me—and you did, so…" The memory of how that adventure had ended swept over her. *Oh no*, she told herself sternly. *You won't end up on the floor, kissing her, this time.*

"I'll make the boutonnieres, the corsages, and the bridal bouquets tomorrow, but if you want to help me with some centerpieces for the tables at the reception…"

"Sure." Sasha opened the box she was carrying. "Do you want to use some of these?"

"Not a good idea since I need to spray down my flowers with water to keep them fresh. I thought we could use the gum paste flowers to decorate the cake table." Ashley peeked into the box, then tenderly lifted out one of the Peruvian lilies and cradled it in her palm. "Oh wow. Sasha, these are fantastic. Like pieces of art. They look so real!"

Sasha laughed, stoked with Ashley's praise. "Yeah. And the best thing is that they won't get any pollen on Holly's and Leo's wedding outfits." The memory of the pollen Ashley had removed from her shirt made heat pool low in Sasha's belly.

Ashley cleared her throat as if she was thinking about the same thing. "Okay, then let's get started. We need to be in bed early. Um, not the same bed, obviously."

Sasha chuckled hoarsely. "Obviously." She watched Ashley prepare the flowers—remove leaves and trim the end of the stems.

"Why don't I do the roses, and you do the alstroemeria?" Ashley suggested. "That way, you don't have to deal with thorns. I wouldn't want anything to happen to your fingers."

Sasha tried not to read anything into Ashley's interest in her fingers. "Um, sure."

They worked together without saying much, each focused on her task. Once they had prepped all the flowers, Ashley started to arrange the centerpiece, first inserting fern into the green foam, then roses and Peruvian lilies.

Sasha watched Ashley's nimble fingers with fascination. They were covered in little nicks and scratches, and she wanted to place a healing kiss on each of them.

"What?" Ashley asked, not looking up from her work.

"Nothing." Sasha averted her gaze and searched for something to say. "I noticed Derek wasn't all over you like a bee on honey the last two Saturdays. Did you tell him to take a hike?"

"Um, I was a little more polite than that, but yeah, I made it clear that I have no interest in him."

The satisfaction Sasha felt was probably way out of proportion. "How did he take it?"

Ashley filled in the gaps in the arrangement with some greenery that had tiny, white flowers. "He wasn't happy."

"I can imagine," Sasha murmured. "You're a hard woman to get over."

She tried to insert humor into her tone, but Ashley must have heard something else too because she looked up from the glass cylinder vase she was inserting into the center of her creation.

Sasha squirmed. "What?" she asked, hoping Ashley would answer "nothing" too.

"Um, you have a pink streak on your jaw."

"Oh. That's probably some of the edible petal dust I used to color the gum paste flowers." Sasha rubbed her palm over her jaw. "Gone?"

"No. You're making it worse. Let me." Ashley wiped her hands on her apron and leaned across the counter. Slowly, she reached up and trailed her fingertips along Sasha's jaw.

It felt like a tender caress…and it didn't stop. Either it was the most stubborn streak of color ever, or Ashley had forgotten what she had set out to do. Not that Sasha was complaining. She held very still and stared into Ashley's nougat-colored eyes.

Ashley's face was moving closer—or maybe it was Sasha who was leaning toward her.

Sasha shuddered as Ashley's breath warmed her lips. This was crazy. This was… Without a conscious decision, she wrapped her arms around Ashley to tug her closer and bridge the remaining inch between them.

Ashley didn't resist.

Just as their lips were about to meet, the front door opened with a loud jingle.

They jumped apart.

"Hi, Ashley." It was Betty Mullen, the owner of the hair salon next door. "I saw that you're still working and thought I'd drop by to remind you of your appointment tomorrow."

"Oh, right." Ashley pretended to be busy with the centerpiece but didn't pull it off at all. Her voice trembled. "Midnight, right? Um, I mean, noon, of course."

Betty gave her a strange look but then nodded. "Yes. You said you only have time during lunch."

"Yeah, sorry. I'm very busy with the wedding and all."

"Then I won't keep you and your new assistant." With a smile and a wave, Betty ducked out of the shop.

Ashley slumped against the counter. "Oh my God. She almost…" She covered her face with her hands and then dropped them. "Do you think she saw?"

"No. I'm sure she didn't, or she would have reacted differently."

"Right," Ashley said but started to pace anyway.

Sasha wanted to embrace her to calm her, but she knew it would probably have the opposite effect. "Would it really have been so bad if she'd seen us together?" she asked, her voice a near whisper.

Ashley stopped pacing and reached out as if to touch her arm but then pulled back before her hand could make contact. "It's not about you, Sasha. I'm proud to be your friend."

"Friend." A headache started to throb behind Sasha's temples, and she reached up to massage it away. "We tried to be friends, Ash. It's not working. Friends don't look at each other the way we looked at each other in that photo. They don't kiss each other the way we were about to."

"I'm not denying that," Ashley murmured.

"Yeah, not as long as we're alone. But you do as soon as someone else is around. You act as if the world would end if anyone found out about us." The words were painful, but she knew she had to say them—to herself and to Ashley. "I can't keep doing this to myself. This back-and-forth we've been doing isn't healthy for either of us. If you can't be all in, I have to be all out."

Her heartbeat thrummed in her ears as she waited for Ashley's reply. A part of her hoped Ashley would declare herself all in, even though she knew better.

Ashley just hung her head.

The pain in Sasha's head spread to her chest. "You know what? I think I'd better go. I have a very early day tomorrow."

"Sasha!" Ashley called after her. "Please, wait! I…"

Sasha didn't wait around to hear what she had to say. It wouldn't be the words she longed to hear anyway.

Chapter 20

Ash had tossed and turned all night, unable to settle down. Sasha's words rang through her head, and she couldn't forget the expression on her face right before she'd walked out.

In the few minutes that she did sleep, she dreamed she was walking into the bakery stark naked and declared her love for Sasha in front of everyone, including Mrs. Beasley.

Someone shouted, "disgusting," and threw a cupcake at her.

Even her former math teacher wrinkled her nose and leaned across the small café table to whisper something to her husband.

Ash's parents got up with stony expressions and walked out.

The hurtful comments still echoed in her ears as she jerked awake. After that, she gave up on sleep and decided to start her workday early.

When Brooke arrived several hours later, she had already done both bridal bouquets and was in the middle of prepping the flowers they would need for the boutonnieres and corsages.

Brooke got herself an apron and joined her at the workstation.

She had helped with boutonnieres once or twice before, but it had been a while, so Ash showed her how it was done. "Take one of the roses and cut the stem to the length you need—about four inches." She snipped off the end of her rose to demonstrate. "Don't cut off too much. You can always cut off more, but once it's gone, it's gone."

Like Sasha, her tired brain provided.

The thought slammed into her with the force of a tractor trailer.

Sasha was gone, and she had only herself to blame. She couldn't expect her to hang around, not even as friends, if she refused to deal with her fears.

"He loves you, he loves you not," Brooke commented with a laugh.

Ash pushed away her thoughts of Sasha and looked at her. "Um, what?"

Brooke swiped a strand of her hair—cherry red this month—out of her face and pointed at the workstation.

Ash glanced down. Without her realizing it, she had been plucking the petals off her poor rose and was now worrying the empty stem between her fingers. She dropped it as if she'd burned herself.

"So, what's the verdict?" Brooke grinned. "Does he love you? And more importantly, who is he?"

"There is no he," Ash said firmly, hoping to end the topic of her love life.

Brooke flashed a teasing smile. "Ooh! So it's a she?"

The blood drained from Ash's face. She wanted to rapidly shake her head, but her body was frozen. "I...I..."

Brooke's grin died away. Her kohl-rimmed eyes widened. "Holy fuck! I was just kidding, but it's true, isn't it? Wow, that's so...wow!" She whistled through her teeth and looked like someone who had gotten water in her ear because she couldn't stop shaking her head. "It's Sasha, isn't it?"

A new surge of adrenaline shot through Ash. Her first impulse was to deny it all, as she had any time Travis had brought up his suspicions about her and Holly. But she couldn't bring herself to say it. It would have been a betrayal of everything she and Sasha had shared. Her vocal cords refused to work, so she merely nodded.

"Yaass!" Brooke pumped her fist. "That's totally lit!"

Ash peeked over at her. "Um, translation? Is that good?"

Brooke chuckled. "Yeah! It's, like, cool. I just told Logan last night that I'm totally shipping you two."

"Shipping?" Ash felt as if her brain was too sleep-deprived to make sense of this conversation. "You're not talking about mailing a package, are you?"

Brooke roared with laughter. "No. It means I'm rooting for you and Sasha to get together."

"Oh." Ash's mind was spinning. Then a ripple of alarm skittered down her spine as her brain caught up with what Brooke had just said. "Wait! You talked to the Beasleys' son about us?" she squeaked out.

"Yeah," Brooke said in a why-wouldn't-I tone. "I just told him that I don't think Sasha keeps bringing us cupcakes because I love them."

Ash pulled out a stool from under the counter and dropped down on it. "You don't think he'll tell his parents?"

Brooke snorted. "He doesn't even talk to them half of the time. Why would he mention you?"

Yeah, why would he? Apparently, this wasn't a big deal for young people like Brooke. Ash suddenly wished she were their age and could start over. "So you're both fine with it...with me being...um, gay?"

Brooke didn't bat an eye. She trimmed the stem of another rose. "Of course. Sasha's great. Not as boring as Derek. So, you like her back, don't you?"

Ash stared down at the rose petals she had plucked off. "It's complicated."

Now it was Brooke's turn to ask: "Translation?"

Ash gave a tired smile and looked back up. "I do." *God help me, I really, really do.* "But we're not...together or anything, so please don't tell anyone, okay?"

"Okay, but it's really not a big deal."

"It is for some people in town," Ash said.

Brooke groaned. "Man, I can't wait till I have enough money to get out of this town."

Ash gave a teasing tug on a cherry red strand of hair. "As much as I'll be happy for you when you finally do, I'll kind of miss you."

"Oh, don't worry." A cheeky smile flashed across Brooke's face. "I'll be back for your wedding to Sasha."

"Brat!" Ash threw a snipped-off stem at her and marveled how normal all of this felt—as if it really didn't matter one bit that Sasha and she were both women.

Maybe it doesn't, that new voice in her head said.

Finally, Ash swiped the destroyed rose into the wastebasket and picked up a new one. "Come on. Let's get these roses wired. Those boutonnieres won't make themselves."

By noon, Ash was glad to escape the flower shop for her appointment at the beauty salon. Not only did she need a break from making boutonnieres and corsages, but maybe the gossip usually going on at Betty's shop would bring her back down to earth before she could start believing that a life with Sasha might be possible after all.

When she entered the beauty shop, her mom's friend Karen sat at the color station with her head full of highlight foils. She seemed to spend more time in there than she did at home, even now that she was a grandmother.

One of the hairdressers was blow-drying Jenny's hair.

Ash greeted them as Betty led her to one of the sinks in the back.

"Everything?" Karen shouted over the noise of the blow-dryer.

The hairdresser nodded. "Everything—including his boxers. They were strewn all over the lawn."

Betty draped a towel over Ash's shoulders and adjusted the temperature of the water. "Have you heard?" she asked while she shampooed Ash's hair. "Heather caught Barry cheating—in their own bed, no less. She threw all his stuff out on the front lawn."

"Good for her." Heather might not have gotten the hidden message in the carnations-and-snapdragons bouquet, but at least now she knew about Barry's affair. Ash's eyes fluttered shut as Betty's practiced fingers started to gently massage her scalp. For a moment, she allowed herself to imagine they were Sasha's fingers instead.

While Betty shampooed her hair and then rinsed out the suds, she and her employee continued to catch their clients up on everything that had happened in town this week. No wonder the beauty salon was nicknamed Gossip Central.

"So," Betty asked as she walked Ash over to the cutting station and wrapped a cape around her shoulders, "what are we doing today? Just taking off half an inch, as usual, or do you want something special for the wedding?"

At the mention of the wedding, Karen lowered the magazine she'd been flipping through. "Oh, that's right. You're going to the wedding. You're friends with the bride…um, the brides. Or is one of them called something else?" She laughed and shook her foil-wrapped head. "Doesn't a wedding like that get confusing sometimes?"

Even the hairdresser shut off the blow-dryer so she wouldn't miss Ash's answer.

Jenny rolled her eyes and opened her mouth, but Ash was done letting others answer for her.

"No," she said quietly but firmly. "Not at all. I just call them by their names."

"I think a wedding with two brides is great," Betty piped up. "Men's hair is always so boring at weddings. Not like you can do much with an inch of hair."

Her down-to-earth argument made Ash stare at her in the mirror.

"Plus I'll be able to say I've done Jenna Blake's hair for her wedding." Betty moved her fingers in a rectangle as if she was imagining putting up a certificate somewhere in the salon.

No one could argue with that, so the conversation moved back to Barry's affair.

Betty ran her fingers through Ash's waist-length hair. "So, the usual?" she asked again.

It was the same question Sasha always asked her whenever she entered the bakery to get cupcakes.

Ash started to nod and tell her to just snip off the split ends. But it didn't feel right. Instead, she found herself saying: "You know what? Let's try something different."

"Ooh! You've met someone!"

Immediately, everyone's attention was on her again.

Ash whirled around in her swivel chair. "Um, what?"

"Anyone who comes in here and wants something different either recently went through a breakup or they've met someone new," Betty said. "And I know it's not a breakup, so…"

"I'm doing this for me, not to appeal to anyone else." Ash shrugged beneath the cape. "I…I guess it's just time for a change."

"All right." Betty trailed her fingers through Ash's hair. "So, how big of a change are we talking?"

Without allowing herself to think about it, Ash indicated a point just above her shoulders.

"Wow. That's a lot."

"I know," Ash croaked past the lump in her throat.

"Are you sure?" Betty asked. "Your mother will have a heart attack."

"It's my hair. I'm sure," Ash said, even though she wasn't.

When the first thick strands fell to the floor, Ash held her breath, expecting a feeling of regret to sweep over her. Instead, she felt strangely light.

"Like this?" Betty held up a now shoulder-length strand.

Ash stared into the mirror. She couldn't yet imagine herself with shorter hair, but she told herself she'd get used to it. "Yes. Exactly like that."

It was after eight by the time Ash locked the flower shop behind her, but instead of driving straight home, she found herself at the cemetery. The sun was starting to set as she walked along the familiar concrete path to her sister's grave.

A fresh, colorful bouquet of peonies lay on the grave, indicating that their parents had recently been by. Since they had been Melissa's favorite flowers, their mother always grew them in her garden.

Ash sat cross-legged in the grass beside the grave, the way she'd sat on Melissa's bed when she'd been eleven and had needed someone to talk to. She reached out her hand and traced her sister's name and the words *never forgotten* with her fingertips. The solid granite tombstone was warm beneath her hand.

"Hi, Sis," she said, then was quiet for some time because she had no idea where to start. She hadn't done this in a while.

Finally, when the sun dipped toward the horizon, she whispered, "I've met someone. Well, not really met. I knew her all along, but somehow, I didn't really *see* her until a few months ago. It's Sasha—Mae Peterson's niece. She's funny and kind, and we, um, had an adult sleepover when we were in Florida, and now I think…I think I'm in love with her, and I don't know what to do."

She blurted it all out in a rush, then snapped her mouth shut and pressed her fingers to her lips.

Her words seemed to echo along the rows of graves.

In love with her… The mere thought of it sent tiny shocks through her body. But, at least to herself, Ash could admit that it was true. What she felt for Sasha was unlike anything she'd ever felt for anyone before. Even the love she'd felt for Leo and Holly felt like immature crushes in comparison.

"I think she feels the same, Missy. But she walked away, and this time it's for good—unless I do something big to get her back. If I want a life with her, I need to come out. But that could mean losing Mom and Dad." She rocked back and forth. Never had she missed her sister's hug more than she did right now. She wondered what Melissa would have said if she had been alive. Would she have accepted Ash's sexual orientation, or would she have shared their parents' conviction that it was wrong?

Ash didn't know since she hadn't been old enough to talk about adult topics like that with her sister. All the missed time together hurt.

Steps sounded somewhere behind her.

Ash gritted her teeth. Couldn't she find some peace anywhere in this town, not even in the cemetery? She turned her head to see who was disturbing her.

The sun stood so low now that she had to shield her eyes with her hand.

After a moment, she could make out Leo's slim figure. She held the bouquet of white lilies she had bought at the shop earlier today. Her steps faltered, but then she walked up to Ash. "Visiting Missy?" she asked, as if it was the most normal thing in the world to talk to your dead sister.

But then again, Leo had always understood what Melissa had meant to her. Ash nodded. "And you? Visiting your dad?"

"Yeah. With the wedding being tomorrow and all, I thought it might be nice to bring him some flowers too."

Ash couldn't imagine getting married and not having both of her parents there. But if she ever got married, it would be to a woman—and her parents would most likely refuse to come. A deep sadness gripped her at the thought.

Leo sat in the grass next to her. "Hey, you cut your hair!" She reached out as if to touch the shorter strands but then let her hand drop to her lap.

Ash bit her lip. It would take some time until they would be completely comfortable around each other again. Ash knew that, and she was willing to work on it.

"Yeah. I'm still not used to it." Ash ran her fingers through her shoulder-length hair. "My parents will probably have a heart attack when they see it."

Leo leaned back on her hands. "Do you like it?"

"I think I do."

"Then that's all that matters," Leo said. "The time when your parents got to choose your haircut for you is long gone."

Ash suppressed a sigh. If only it were that easy.

"I know what you're thinking. If anyone can understand what it's like to try to live up to your parents' expectations, it's me." Leo looked down the row of graves to where her father was buried. "Trust me, it doesn't work. You have to live your own life, Ash."

Ash eyed her with a slight curl of her lips. "Are we still talking about my hair?"

"We're talking about you and Sasha."

If she hadn't already been sitting down, Ash probably would have fallen as her knees turned into some wobbly substance. A tremor went through her. "Oh my God! First Brooke, now you! Does everyone in town know about us?"

"No, of course not. You're too good at that pretending-to-be-straight game." A hint of bitterness sounded in Leo's voice. "But I know you, and I know it wasn't Grace and Lauren keeping everyone awake in Florida, because they were the only ones who looked well-rested the next morning, while you and Sasha slept all the way home."

A wave of heat shot up Ash's neck. She buried her face against her knees. How was she supposed to look any of them in the eyes ever again?

Leo chuckled and patted her back. "Don't worry. I don't think anyone else suspects. Well, Holly, of course, but she just wants you to be happy."

"Happy," Ash repeated to herself as if it were a word in a foreign language.

They were both quiet for a while.

Finally, when her face had cooled down a little, Ash lifted her head from her knees and peeked over at her old friend.

Leo was studying her with an intense gaze. "So you're still not planning to come out? You'll just do to Sasha what you did to Holly? Damn, Ash, I thought you learned your lesson."

"I did," Ash said quickly, not wanting her to think she would string Sasha along.

"So you will come out to everyone?"

Ash stared at the inscription on her sister's headstone as if the answer was written there. "I...I don't know. This wasn't supposed to happen. I wasn't supposed to be with anyone…to fall in love ever again." The last words were barely more than a whisper.

A mild smile curled Leo's lips. "And I wasn't supposed to fall in love with a small-town nurse and decide to stay after fighting so hard to escape Fair Oaks, yet it still happened—and I'm happy it did. Don't you think you'll one day feel the same, even though it's hard now?"

"I want to…I want to believe it so much, but…" Ash sent her a look of despair. "How can I be sure?"

"You can't. And you certainly won't get any answers from the dead, Ash," Leo said quietly. "You have to talk to the living."

"I don't think I'll like what my parents have to say."

"Maybe, maybe not. But they might surprise you. I never thought my mother would come to accept me either, but now she's over at our house, nearly dizzy with excitement because Holly and I are getting married tomorrow." It wasn't just the light of the setting sun that made her appear to glow.

"I'm truly happy for you," Ash said, meaning it, "but it took her fifteen years to get to that point, and I'm not sure my parents would get there at all."

"So you're going to put your life on hold until they're gone?" Leo asked.

Ash flinched. "No, of course not. I have a life."

"Looks to me like you have what I had before I came home—a career, not a life," Leo said. "If you want a life, you have to open yourself up to love and all the risks that come with that. Yeah, you might disappoint some people—maybe even lose some, but there'll always be people who won't care and who'll support you."

Ash sighed. "I know you're right. I know it here." She tapped her head. "But…"

"No buts. I know it's scary, but you can't live a lie. You have to be yourself. Not Melissa's little sister. Not Tom and Donna's daughter. Just Ashley." Leo got up and let her hand linger on Ash's shoulder for a moment. "See you tomorrow at the ceremony."

As Leo walked over to her father's grave, Ash sat frozen next to Melissa's headstone. Leo's words echoed through her mind. *You have to be yourself.*

She was never more herself than when she was with Sasha; she knew that without a doubt.

Could she really do this—open herself up to love, all risks be damned?

Chapter 21

THE WEATHER WAS PERFECT FOR an outdoor wedding. The afternoon sun gleamed on the gurgling water of the creek, but it wasn't so hot that the strings of flowers Ashley had draped along the railings of the bridge would wither. Ashley had even pinned boutonnieres to the suits of the four security guards Leo had hired in case any uninvited guests or members of the press showed up.

Everything looked beautiful—but most of all Ashley did.

Sasha had chosen to sit in the last row of folding chairs that had been set up along the creek so she could duck out after the vows to make sure the caterers didn't ruin the cake.

Ashley had stayed in the back too, probably so she could dash off and put the last touches to the flower decorations in the barn.

While everyone else craned their necks to catch a glimpse of the brides, Sasha's gaze was drawn to Ashley instead.

God, she looked incredible in her summer dress and modestly heeled sandals—and she had cut off her hair! Her once waist-length mane now barely brushed her shoulders. No longer dragged down by its own weight, it had a natural wave to it that made her look even sexier. The new haircut transformed her face from nice girl next door to a stunning woman who stood up for what she wanted.

Don't let it fool you, Sasha told herself. Even with a new look, Ashley was still the same person who did what was expected of her instead of what she wanted.

But Ashley's dress kept drawing her gaze. It wasn't just the keyhole cutout in the back that had allowed her to catch a glimpse of the bare skin beneath earlier. What had caught her interest even more was the dress's color. It was a perfect match for the purple bow tie Ashley had picked for her. What did her choice of dress mean? Was it merely a coincidence? Sasha didn't think so. Ashley worked with colors, after all. She knew they had meaning. Was Ashley trying to tell her something, or was Sasha reading too much into it?

She hadn't found an answer yet when a flute and a guitar player started playing a piece of classical music.

Leo and Holly walked down the makeshift aisle created by the rows of folding chairs.

Sasha liked that they had chosen to walk down the aisle together instead of one of them being given away. She flashed her friends a smile as they passed. They both looked great, Holly in her traditional wedding dress and Leo in a custom-tailored, ivory pantsuit. They held hands, and each carried an identical bridal bouquet in her free hand. When they reached the edge of the creek, where the officiant waited, they gave the flowers to their mothers to hold so they could join hands.

As they started to say their wedding vows, Sasha kept glancing at Ashley, who watched the ceremony with tears in her eyes. Were they happy ones for their friends? Sasha thought she saw a sad longing on Ashley's face too.

Ashley looked over at her.

Sasha quickly turned her head and directed her attention back to the couple's vows.

"I promise to love and appreciate you just the way you are—which will be easy because you're perfect in my eyes," Leo said to Holly. "I promise to make you laugh as often as possible, to love your family as if they're my own, and to always let you win at Xbox."

Sasha chuckled because she knew that Leo had never won a single game.

Leo looked deeply into Holly's eyes as she continued. "I promise to be your best friend, your sidekick in all adventures of life, and the person you can always rely on. No matter what life might throw at us, you'll always have my heart."

Then it was Holly's turn to say her vows. "I promise to love you for who you are, not for who the public sees you as, to support you in whatever you do, to always be honest with you, and to never watch *Central Precinct* without you."

Leo laughed through the tears in her eyes and kissed her hand. "You'd better not."

Holly smiled. Her voice was choked with emotion as she continued, but she spoke without hesitation and never looked away from Leo. "Most of all, I promise to be your best friend, your biggest fan, and your partner for life."

Sasha listened with a lump in her throat. For someone who had declared to not want steak only a few months ago, she suddenly wanted someone to make the same promises to her—and not just anyone. She peeked over at Ashley, who was looking at her too.

When their eyes met, they both glanced away.

The officiant waited until Holly and Leo had exchanged rings and then gave them a nod. "With the power vested in me by the state of Missouri, I declare you married. You may both kiss your bride."

A cheer echoed around the creek as Leo and Holly exchanged a gentle kiss.

Sasha watched them for a moment, allowing herself a few seconds to bask in their joy, before she rose and hurried to her car.

She caught glimpses of Ashley's SUV in the rearview mirror as she drove. Knowing they would soon be alone and forced to interact sent a jolt through her that was part dread, part excitement.

Just be professional, and you'll be fine, she told herself. She was there as Sasha, the baker, and Ashley was just a florist she worked with.

But no matter how often she repeated it, her heart didn't believe it for a second.

She parked next to the barn and got out.

The big double doors were folded back and adorned with the same flowers Ashley had used for the bridal bouquets. Wooden barrels with more flowers flanked the entrance, and above it hung a sign that said *Welcome to Holly & Leo's wedding.*

How had Ashley gotten her parents to allow all of this?

The caterers had set up their tables beneath a tent next to the barn. Sasha would check in with them in a second, but first she wanted to see the inside of the barn.

She paused at the entrance and looked around.

Wow.

The barn didn't look like a farm structure anymore. The tractor parts and other equipment had been removed. Round tables had been covered with festive linens, each one decorated with one of Ashley's beautiful centerpieces.

White drapes were strung tent-like between the high rafters. Lanterns cast a warm glow over the tables. Strings of twinkling fairy lights were twined around the beams and wooden support columns, creating an intimate, magical atmosphere.

Great. Just what she didn't need: being alone with Ashley in such a romantic setting.

She felt more than heard Ashley walk up behind her. Her breath caught in anticipation of Ashley touching her shoulder, her arm, or any part of her in greeting, but she didn't. It was ridiculous how disappointed she felt. *You need to stay away, remember?*

"Do you like it?" Ashley asked, her voice low.

Sasha turned toward her. "It looks incredible. And so do you." The words slipped out before she could censor herself. But it was true. Up close, Ashley was even more beautiful. She was also wearing a new perfume—something lighter, more floral, with just a hint of a sensual aroma. Sasha wanted to bury her face against Ashley's neck and inhale the intoxicating scent. "Uh, I mean, the new haircut looks good on you."

Ashley blushed and fingered the now shoulder-length strands. "Thank you."

With every second Sasha spent around Ashley, her resolution to stay away from her was melting faster than vanilla ice cream on hot apple pie. "Um, excuse me. I think I'd better go check on the cake before everyone arrives."

"I'll come with you," Ashley said. "I put the sugar flowers on each table in the barn, but I haven't put any on the cake table yet because I wanted to wait until the cake was all set up."

They walked toward the tent next to the barn, with Sasha automatically matching her strides to Ashley's, ready to reach out a hand to steady her should she step into a pothole in her sandals.

But Ashley walked sure-footedly, reminding Sasha that she'd grown up here.

When they ducked into the tent, the wedding cake was on a small table by itself.

"Wow," Ashley murmured.

Sasha looked at her creation too. It was covered in a smooth, ivory fondant that matched the color of Holly's dress and Leo's pantsuit. She had chosen not to set the top tier into the center of the tier below but had put it more toward the back, creating a ledge for the cascade of gum paste flowers that trailed down the cake. "You like it?" she couldn't help asking.

"Like?" Ashley laughed. "Heck, it makes me want to get married just to get a cake like this!"

Sasha bit her lip so she wouldn't offer to make her one. "Nah. You're not the marrying kind, remember?"

Ashley sighed. "Right." She squeezed past Sasha and started to arrange the gum paste flowers Sasha had made around the cake, framing it perfectly.

When she was done, she stepped back, and they stood side by side, looking at their creations like two proud parents.

"Sasha, I—"

Several other cars pulled into the yard. Car doors banged, and the voices of the mothers of the brides came closer.

"I'd better go," Ashley said. "I've already caught Sharon rearranging the flowers in the barrels twice this morning."

Sasha's gaze followed her as she rushed from the tent. God, it would be a long day.

The wedding reception went off without a hitch. Lauren's Operation Decoy had been a total success—no paparazzi had found them—and the food had been delicious.

Ash sat with Jenny, Travis, and the rest of the gang—and that, of course, meant Sasha too. She wondered if Leo and Holly had arranged it that way on purpose. Were they trying to play matchmaker?

But she and Sasha needed more than a little nudge from their friends. Ash knew it was all on her.

One of Holly's brothers rose and tapped his fork to his glass to give a speech that ended with him welcoming Leo into the family.

Ash took a big sip of champagne, but it didn't help to remove the lump from her throat. If only her own family were half as accepting as Holly's and Leo's. Her parents hadn't even come to the reception, even though Leo and Holly had made sure to invite them.

Sasha leaned toward her. "You okay?" she asked so quietly that no one else could hear.

Ash just nodded because she didn't trust herself to speak without her voice trembling. Besides, she didn't want to tarnish this happy day with thoughts of her parents and their lack of acceptance should she ever come out.

"Could I have your attention, everyone?" the DJ's voice came through speakers set up in the back of the barn, where the makeshift dance floor was. "It's time to cut the cake."

A wrinkle formed on Sasha's forehead as she watched the caterers roll in the three-tiered wedding cake.

Ash put her hand on Sasha's arm to calm her worries.

Leo and Holly walked up to Sasha's masterful creation.

"Cut from the bottom tier," Sasha told them.

Holly smiled at her before taking hold of the cake knife. Leo wrapped her arms around her from behind and placed her hands over Holly's to support the weight of the knife. Together, they cut through the fondant and lifted a piece of cake onto a plate.

Flashes went off as guests and the professional photographer took pictures of the moment.

Leo sliced off a bit of cake with her fork.

Holly watched her warily. "You're not going to smash Sasha's beautiful cake into my face, are you?"

"Wait and see." Leo grinned. She moved the fork toward Holly's lips but then pulled it back at the last second, teasing her, before finally popping proffered morsel into her mouth.

"God. This is delicious," Holly mumbled around a forkful of cake.

Next to Ash, Sasha finally relaxed. A proud smile made her look even more stunning.

Holly sliced off a piece of her own.

"Behave," Leo said.

Grinning, Holly picked it up with her hand and smeared it all over Leo's face.

Laughter rippled through the barn.

"I knew you would do that!" Buttercream dribbled down Leo's chin, but she was laughing as she grabbed what was left of the slice of cake and returned the favor.

Leo's mother handed them napkins, and they cleaned each other's face with such tenderness that Ash had to look away, feeling as if she were intruding into a private moment.

Her gaze met Sasha's, and they shared a smile at their friends' happiness.

The caterers interrupted their eye contact as they began to hand out cake to the guests.

At her first forkful, Ash let out a moan. "God, Sasha. You outdid yourself. It tastes as good as it looks, and that's saying something."

Sasha beamed.

Soon, the DJ's voice came through the speakers again. "Ladies and gentlemen, it's time for the brides' first dance as a married couple."

"Holly's Song"—which Leo had written about her feelings for Holly—began to play as Leo and Holly walked to the dance floor and began to dance.

Ash slid sideways on her chair, folded her arms over the back of it, put her chin on top, and watched her friends. God, they looked so good together. They seemed to have forgotten that they had an audience, seeing only each other, as they floated across the dance floor.

When the first dance was over, the brides danced with their mothers, then switched so each was dancing with her mother-in-law. Finally, everyone swarmed onto the dance floor.

Jenny dragged her husband up from his chair and waved at Sasha and Ash. "Come on, guys. Let's have some fun!"

Sasha shook her head. "Wouldn't be much fun for the poor person I'd be dancing with. I've been known to maim my partner's toes. I'm a terrible dancer."

Ash couldn't believe that Sasha would be terrible at anything, but she was secretly glad not to remain behind at the table by herself. They exchanged awkward glances.

"Um, I think I'll get myself a little more of your delicious cake," Ash said.

But before she could get up, Leo and Holly came over. Leo's bow tie dangled undone around her neck as if she'd gotten too hot on the dance floor. She blocked Ash's escape route and extended her hand. "May I have this dance?"

Ash stared at her. They had danced with each other as teenagers, to practice for the prom, but never as adults. She had never danced with any woman as an adult because she'd been afraid to give herself away. "Um, what are you doing?"

"Asking a friend to dance," Leo said easily. She wiggled the fingers of her extended hand. "Come on. Stop overthinking it. Look, even our mothers are dancing together, and no one gives a damn."

Ash glanced toward the dance floor.

Leo was right. The mothers of the brides were dancing and laughing with each other, and no one was paying them any attention.

Holly was already pulling Sasha to the dance floor, ignoring her warnings that she was about to have her toes crushed.

You're being silly, Ash told herself. Just because she was about to dance with another woman didn't mean a red L for lesbian would be tattooed on her forehead. She put her slightly sweaty hand in Leo's and followed her to the dance floor.

The DJ was playing a fast-paced, fun number that didn't require them to dance close, putting Ash at ease. Soon, she was even enjoying herself and moving to Leo's undeniable sense of rhythm.

Leo led her around the dance floor, closer to where Holly was dancing with Sasha.

Sasha hadn't lied. Her dancing was awkward, but in such a cute way that Ash had to smile.

Even though the song wasn't yet drawing to a close, Leo let go of Ash's hand and tapped Sasha's shoulder. "May I cut in and dance with my wife?"

"Oh, sure." Sasha immediately released her awkward but gentle grip on Holly.

When Holly and Leo danced away, Sasha and Ash were left behind in the middle of the dance floor, staring at each other.

Sasha glanced after them. "Why do I get the feeling they set us up?"

"Because I'm sure they did," Ash murmured.

"Well, we don't have to dance together just because they tricked us into it," Sasha offered. "If you're not comfortable dancing with me, you can always tell them you didn't want to have your toes crushed."

Ash hesitated. Sasha had given her an easy way out—but did she want it?

She looked around. All around them, couples were dancing and having a good time. Holly's brothers were spinning their wives around, and even Travis was trying to keep up with Jenny. Grace was dancing with her hands slung around Lauren's neck, looking deeply into her eyes, even though the song was really too fast for it.

A few people were staring, but the expressions on their faces said they were in awe of being in the presence of such a famous actress. No one seemed to be disapproving of two women dancing so close.

Ash wanted that closeness—and she wanted it with Sasha. She didn't want to sit back down and give her up for good. She wasn't entirely sure she was ready to deal with the consequences, but she'd think about that later. For now, she wanted this one dance in Sasha's arms.

When Sasha moved past her to lead the way off the dance floor, Ash grasped her hand with trembling fingers. "Stay."

Sasha turned back toward her, her eyes wide. "Are you sure?"

Every muscle in Ash's body was so tense that she felt as if she were stuck in a corset that restricted her breathing. She nodded.

"Your toes might end up regretting it," Sasha murmured. "I'm really a horrible dancer."

Sasha's words when she had talked Ash into baking cupcakes with her flashed through Ash's mind. "You just have to follow my lead, and it'll turn out great."

Sasha chuckled. "You're quoting me. Guess I'll have to dance with you, then."

But just as they started to move together, the song ended and the next number started. This one wasn't a fast beat that two friends could hop around to and have some fun. It was a slow love ballad that immediately had the couples move closer to each other.

Ash was pretty sure Holly and Leo had arranged that too. But it didn't matter now. She had decided to do this, and she was determined not to back out. Her mouth went dry as she rested her hand on Sasha's strong shoulder.

Sasha's muscles were tense beneath her fingers. Was she scared of trampling on her toes, or was she tense for another reason?

"Do you want this?" Ash asked in a whisper.

Sasha looked into her eyes as if trying to find out if she was talking about the dancing or something more. Ash wasn't even sure what she'd meant. "Yes," Sasha whispered back. She entwined their fingers and rested her other hand in the small of Ash's back.

God, it felt so right—like coming home. Ash realized how much she'd missed that little touch. Again, something Sasha had said ran through her mind: *Sometimes, you just have to trust your heart if it tells you it's right.*

"Um, if you're leading, shouldn't we do this the other way around?" Sasha lightly squeezed her fingers and nodded at Ash's hand on her shoulder.

"Oh. Right." Ash's cheeks flamed. "Sorry. I'm not used to dancing with women." Plus she liked Sasha's hand exactly where it was. She tried to switch positions, but Sasha didn't let go.

"You know what?" Sasha said. "This is our dance, so we get to make the rules. Let's dance like this."

"Okay." Her hands still shook as she guided Sasha into the rhythm of the music. She felt as if everyone was staring at them, but she tried not to glance left or right to check if it was true. For now, she would tell herself it was just her imagination.

A sharp pain shot through her bare toes as if to provide a distraction. "Ouch."

Sasha winced along with her and caressed Ash's back as if soothing away the pain. "Shit. I'm really sorry." She gave her a sheepish smile. "I warned you your toes would be in danger."

Ash wasn't worried about her toes. If anything, it was her heart that was in danger. "It's okay. At least if I'm worried about my toes, I might forget to worry about people staring at us."

"If they are, it's only because they feel sorry for you—or because you look really good in this dress. Relax, okay?" Sasha spread her fingers across Ash's back in a protective gesture.

"Okay." Ash exhaled against the smooth fabric of Sasha's shirt and tried to focus just on Sasha and their dance. She wasn't used to leading, but since they were merely swaying together and shuffling their feet to the slow beat, there wasn't much to it. Soon, she forgot to think about where to step or which way to turn. Even the people around them started to fade away.

Ash barely even heard the music anymore. The thudding of her heartbeat was much louder.

Their bodies seemed to mold themselves to each other, such a perfect fit despite their differences in height and build. Every inch of her prickled with awareness at Sasha's closeness. The hem of her dress flared about her as they danced, the soft fabric tickling her oversensitized skin. The warmth of Sasha's hand in the small of her back seemed to sear into her even through the fabric of her dress. Sasha's strong thigh brushed hers, and the gentle press of Sasha's breasts against hers made heat pool low in her belly.

The intoxicating scent of cinnamon and just Sasha made her want to press even closer. The lanterns and fairy lights above them threw a succession of light and shadow across Sasha's face, and Ash longed to trace those strong features and caress her soft skin. She could feel Sasha's warm breath on her cheek. If she turned her head a little, their lips would be nearly touching.

Sasha turned her head.

Their gazes locked. The intensity of their connection and the heat in Sasha's eyes stole the air from Ash's lungs. She trembled against her.

Sasha held her even closer. Their feet were either perfectly in sync, or they had stopped moving. Ash didn't care which it was.

The last notes of the song faded away, and couples jostled them as they walked past to leave the dance floor.

No, everything in Ash screamed out. She wasn't ready to give up this connection.

Neither of them let go. They stood in the middle of the dance floor, their bodies still pressed together, and stared into each other's eyes.

Finally, it was Sasha who broke away first. "Ash…" It sounded like a groan. "I think we'd better sit down before we do something in public you might end up regretting." She led her off the dance floor, still holding on to Ash's hand as if she wasn't even aware of it.

Dazed, Ash followed her back to their table.

Jenny and Travis were already there, staring at them.

"Holy moly, you two!" Jenny fanned herself with both hands. "What was that?"

"Ash took pity on me and suffered through my horrible dancing," Sasha said.

Jenny rolled her eyes. "That did not look horrible…or like dancing. It looked like you two were about to tear each other's clothes off in the middle of the dance floor any second!"

Heat seared through Ash's cheeks. "N-no, w-we…I…" She snapped her mouth shut. There was no way to explain this without lying and denying what Sasha meant to her—and she didn't want to do that anymore.

"Hey, we don't mind." Travis flashed them a grin. "Right, Jenn?" He wiggled his fingers at the rest of the gang. "Especially since you all owe me twenty bucks. I told you there's something going on between these two."

Chris shook his head. "I didn't bet against it, so I owe you zilch."

"Ignore them," Jenny said. "But Travis is right. We really don't mind. In fact, we're happy for you." Her reassuring smile faded. "Your parents might not be, though. They stormed out of here as if they'd seen a ghost."

Shards of ice seemed to stab Ash's chest. "What? My parents were here? They…they saw…us?" *Oh my God, oh my God, oh my God!* The world started to spin around her, and only Sasha's grip on her hand kept her on her feet.

Sasha rubbed Ash's fingers, which had gone cold. "Do you want me to talk to them? I could tell them…whatever you want me to."

Sasha would lie for her; Ash knew that. It was tempting—really tempting—to have Sasha be the knight in a bow tie who would make it all go away, but Ash knew as much as it scared her, she had to face her parents. No one else could do this for her. She squeezed Sasha's hand. "Thanks, but I think I need to do this on my own." Not that she knew exactly what she would say or do.

With obvious hesitation, Sasha let go of her hand and gave her an encouraging nod. "I'll be right here, okay? No matter what."

Ash nodded, afraid her teeth would chatter if she spoke. After one last glance back at Sasha, she rushed out of the barn on wobbly legs.

Shit. Sasha sank onto her chair and stared toward the barn entrance. It had gotten dark outside, so she couldn't watch Ashley cross the yard. Her mind was spinning like dough in a bread machine. What the hell had just happened?

Ashley had slow-danced with her in front of pretty much everyone they knew…and now she was running after her parents, probably to make up an excuse about it. Or would she dare to come out to them?

Travis gave her a friendly punch to the shoulder, as if she were one of the guys now. "So, you and Ashley, huh?" He waggled his eyebrows.

Sasha was so tense that her muscles felt as if they were about to snap. She had no patience for Travis's comments right now. "Grow up, Trav. Not everything in life is about sex."

"Oh, come on. After the way you two just looked at each other, you still expect me to believe that there's nothing between you?" Travis snorted. "Yeah, sure."

"I never said that." But what they had—what she wanted to have with Ashley—was about so much more. When she had looked into Ashley's eyes on the dance floor, the connection between them had made her forget everything else, and now that it had been torn away, her chest ached with the sudden emptiness.

"So Travis was actually right for once," Jenny said. "Ashley really likes women, doesn't she?"

Sasha didn't answer. Her attention was on the open barn doors and the darkness beyond. Was Ashley talking to her parents right now? If she was, what was she telling them?

"Duh." Travis nudged his wife. "She likes Sasha, most of all."

"Why didn't Ash ever tell us?" Jenny asked. "We're her friends. Did she really think we would ostracize her?"

Sasha shrugged. "You'll have to ask Ashley about that. She can speak for herself. Now you'll have to excuse me, guys. I need to…" She gestured toward the door and stood. But before she could make her escape, Leo's mother grabbed her arm.

"Oh, no, no, you can't leave now, dear. It's time for the bouquet toss."

Sasha groaned. She hated that silly, outdated ritual. Why were people still assuming every single woman must be desperate to find a husband—or a wife? "I thought Holly and Leo didn't want to do that?"

Leo's mother shrugged. "Beth and I talked them into it."

"Well, I'm sure someone else will be delighted to catch one of the bouquets, but I'm not superstitious and I really need to—"

"In a minute, dear. It won't take long, especially since they won't be doing a garter toss."

Sasha threw one last glance to the doors before she gave up and let herself be dragged to the group of unmarried women who had gathered on the dance floor.

Leo and Holly stood with their backs toward the crowd, their bouquets at the ready.

Sighing, Sasha tried to hide in the back of the group, but that wasn't easy to do when you were six feet tall. Well, at least she wouldn't get caught in the frenzy and could get out of there as soon as this silliness was over. She ignored the chiding gaze Leo's mother sent her.

"Three, two, one," Holly and Leo counted together before tossing the bouquets over their shoulders.

Both arced high into the air, and dozens of eager hands reached for them as they descended. Sasha was the only one who didn't even raise her arms.

One bouquet headed straight for her.

Oh shit. She sidestepped quickly, but that brought her into the path of the other bouquet, which bounced off the outstretched hands of another woman and sailed directly into Sasha's arms.

She stared down at the flowers as if they were a grenade.

Holly's cousin laughed at her. "So much for you not being the marrying kind."

Ash must have crossed the yard a few thousand times in her life, but the distance had never seemed so long and yet so short at the same time.

Her cheeks were still flushed from dancing with Sasha, and the cool night air made her shiver. Or maybe she was trembling with fear. Her heart hammered so loudly that she could no longer hear the music from the reception.

There was light in the kitchen. Normally, the lights in her parents' house always seemed inviting, but now it felt as if she was walking toward sure doom. Ash was only too aware that this might very well be the last time she set foot inside the house she'd grown up in.

With damp hands, she knocked on the back door. She didn't want to give her parents a heart attack on top of everything else.

When no immediate reply came, she entered. "Mom? Dad? It's me."

Her mother was sitting at the kitchen table with her head in her hands, while her father paced in front of the sink.

The sight sent a stab of pain through Ash. She'd seen her parents like this far too often in the months after Melissa's death. Was Ash being gay really equivalent to Melissa killing herself for them?

Her mother looked up with tears in her eyes. That was a much too familiar sight too. "Oh my God!" She jumped up, rushed around the table, and touched Ash's hair with trembling fingers. "I didn't even see this earlier! What did you do to your beautiful hair?"

Red-faced, her father stopped his pacing. "Do you really think her hair is what's important right now?" He towered over Ash and stabbed his finger in the direction of the barn. "What on earth was that?"

"I-I…I was dancing."

"With another woman?" her mother squeaked out.

Ash stared down at the tile that had been chipped ever since she'd dropped a mug on it when she'd been six. She knew she was at a crossroad now. She could tell them it had been completely innocent, just a harmless dance at the request of the brides. Her parents were probably so desperate to cling to the thought of her as straight that they'd believe it, if she lied convincingly enough. Or she could tell them the truth and come out to them—and possibly lose them for good.

She glanced over her shoulder toward the barn, where Sasha was waiting. *No matter what,* she'd said. Ash squared her shoulders and braced herself for the worst. A thousand thoughts tumbled through her brain as she searched for a way to make her parents understand and accept her. Finally, what came out of her mouth was, "I'm gay."

Her father's face took on an even deeper shade of red. His teeth ground against each other so loudly that Ash could hear it.

Her mother shook her head repeatedly. "W-why would you say that?"

"Because it's true." Ash's voice shook, but she forced herself to repeat it. "I'm gay."

"No, you're not," her mother said, still shaking her head. "You're just confused or—"

"I'm not a teenager, Mom. This isn't something that I just discovered about myself. I've known it for fifteen years."

Her mother gasped. "F-fifteen years? You kept this from us that long?"

Ash lowered her head at the hurt in her mother's voice. "I didn't want to, but I was too afraid to tell you."

"But we could have helped you to…to overcome this!"

"There's nothing to overcome." Ash lifted her head and made eye contact, hoping to reach her parents. "This is who I am."

"No, it's not. It can't be." Her father started pacing again, back and forth like a caged animal. "We didn't raise you to be…" He couldn't even get the word out, as if saying it would make it true. "…like that."

"Raised me?" Ash shook her head. "That's not how it works, Dad. You can't raise someone to be straight. You either are, or you aren't. And as much as I've tried to pretend otherwise, I'm not."

Her mother began to sob. "How could you do this to us after everything we've been through?"

A wave of frustration and despair surged through Ash, nearly making her break down in tears too. Were they even listening to her? "I'm not doing anything to you. Don't you understand? This has nothing to do with you. I've tried so hard to be the way you wanted me to be. I've tried to be the perfect daughter for you. I've tried to be straight, like Missy. I did everything I could not to cause you more pain. But I can't do it anymore. I just can't."

"So you're planning on making this public?" Her mother groaned into her hands. "Oh my God, Ashley! Can you imagine what people will say?"

"Yeah, Mom. I can imagine it very well." Ash's voice was rough with bitterness. "I've heard what they said about Leo and Holly, and I don't have Leo's celebrity status to protect me. I know it'll be tough, especially at first. That's why I need your support now more than ever."

Her mother gripped Ash's hands with both of hers and squeezed almost painfully tight. "Why does anyone have to know? You're risking your reputation and your business! Mrs. Beasley will try to get her husband and her Bible study group to boycott your shop."

"I know, Mom. But I can't go on like this, always pretending. It's killing me inside."

Her father flinched at the word *killing*.

"Not like that," Ash said quickly. "You never have to worry about me harming myself. I wouldn't do that. I meant that it's breaking me apart." She pressed one hand to her chest as if to make sure it wouldn't burst open. "Do you have any idea what it's been doing to me, always having to lie and hide a part of myself? I tried to convince myself that I could still have a fulfilling life, and I wasn't exactly unhappy for a while, but now…"

"Now?" her mother prompted quietly.

At least she seemed to be listening now. "Do you remember what Dad said a few months ago? That I'd find someone and fall in love, probably when I least expected it?"

Her mother nodded reluctantly.

"I think it's happened," Ash whispered.

"You're in love…with Sasha Peterson?" Her mother sounded as if she couldn't imagine it any more than she could picture a spaceship full of tentacled aliens landing on earth.

Ash held her gaze, even though it was difficult after years of hiding. "Yes, I am." She sniffled. "She's wonderful, Mom."

"I don't doubt that, honey. She seems very nice. I have absolutely nothing against you being her friend. But if she were your…" Her mother waved her hand as if she didn't even have a word for what Sasha could be to Ash. "That's not something your father and I can support."

The tears that had burned in Ash's eyes finally spilled over. She tried to wipe them away, but they were coming too fast. While their reaction wasn't a surprise, it still hurt to actually hear the words and to face that kind of loss again. "What does that mean? You're just going…" A sob rose up her throat, and she could barely get out the rest of the sentence. "…cut me out of your lives?"

Her gaze darted from her mother to her father, who had both hands fisted in his graying hair as if wanting to tear it out by the roots.

Her mother sank onto her chair and buried her face against her arms. Her sobbing filled the silence.

Her father walked over to her and put a hand on his wife's heaving shoulder. When he looked up, there were tears in his eyes too, and that shook Ash to her core.

She'd seen her father cry only once—the day Melissa had died.

Her throat burned. She could no longer speak. She stared at him, waiting for the inevitable. There wasn't a doubt in her mind that he'd order her out of his house and tell her to never return.

His Adam's apple jumped as he swallowed several times. "I'm not gonna lie. I don't like this...you being..." He waved his hand, apparently unable to even say the word *gay*. "I'm not sure I will ever be able to accept it. But to cut you out of our lives?" He roughly shook his head. "I could no more do that than cut out my own heart. I lost one daughter. I won't lose another, no matter what."

No matter what. He had unknowingly echoed Sasha's words. Hope flickered in Ash. "Y-you won't," she choked out. "I don't want to lose you either."

Her mother jumped up and nearly tackled Ash in a desperate embrace. Her body shook in Ash's arms.

Her father walked over and put his arms around both of them. They stood clinging to each other in the middle of the kitchen for quite some time.

"I just want to be happy," Ash sobbed against her mother's shoulder.

"I want you to be happy too, honey. That's all I ever wanted." Her mother pulled back a little to brush the tears off Ash's face. "But why does it have to be with...with another woman?"

"I don't know why, Mom. It's just the way I am, and it's not something I can change. God knows I tried."

Her father heaved a sigh. "I can't pretend I like it—or promise I won't break some noses if I hear people around town talk about you."

It wasn't exactly warm-hearted acceptance, but at least he was ready to defend her to the town gossips. His protectiveness soothed Ash's raw emotions, even though she didn't want him to break any noses. "Thanks, Dad, but I think I'm old enough to defend my own honor."

He cleared his throat. "You'll always be my little girl, no matter how old you get," he said, his voice rough with emotion.

Ash struggled against a fresh bout of tears.

Her mother trailed her fingers through Ash's hair as if trying to get used to the new length. "What you said earlier...about you trying to be like your sister... I never wanted you to be like Missy or to replace her," she said in a whisper. "No one could ever replace Missy, but that doesn't mean we love you one bit less than we loved her. You know that, don't you?"

Ash nodded, the lump in her throat preventing her from speaking. But maybe she had needed to hear it anyway. She squeezed both of her parents one last time and then let go. "I think I'd better get back to the wedding." She gestured toward the barn. "I kind of ran out of there when Jenny told me you'd come in. Were you looking for me?"

"No, we…we wanted to extend our congratulations to your friends. We might not agree with their, um, lifestyle, but…" Her mother shrugged. "Well, it's the neighborly thing to do, especially since we're letting them use our barn. Will you tell them for us?"

Ash nodded. Her parents might not be passionate supporters of LGBTQ people, but they were trying in their own way.

Her parents walked her to the back door.

"You'll be coming for lunch tomorrow, right?" her mother asked. "I thought I'd be making a tater tot casserole for the three of us."

The three of us, Ash mentally repeated. The message was clear: The invitation had been extended just to her, not to Sasha, even though her parents now probably assumed they were a couple.

They had a long road ahead of them as a family, but at least they hadn't cut her out of their lives. Maybe someday her mother would make tater tot casserole for four.

Okay, now she was getting ahead of herself. She hadn't even talked to Sasha—really talked to her—since Sasha had told her she couldn't do that back-and-forth anymore and had walked out on her two days ago.

She hugged her parents, who both held on for longer than they usually did. As she stepped out into the yard, they stood at the open door and watched her as if she were an explorer setting out to sail across unchartered, shark-infested waters.

Once Ash had reached the darkness away from the house, where her parents could no longer see her, she paused and stared up into the sky. It was filled with stars.

The night air was cool on her bare arms since she'd run out of the barn without the cardigan sweater she had draped over the back of her chair earlier. But Ash barely felt the cold. A strange lightness came over her, as if a cloak had been placed on her shoulders that made her invincible. She knew that feeling would fade. By tomorrow, the talk buzzing around town would probably hurt like hell, but for now, she'd enjoy this feeling of vast relief.

Sasha leaned against the barn's doorframe and stared out into the darkness, trying to make out any movement. Would Ashley even be coming back?

Of course she will, she told herself firmly. She wanted to believe that Ashley wasn't like her mother, who'd left for good, but those old fears were hard to shake completely, especially after waking up alone twice in Florida.

"Hey."

A soft touch to her shoulder made her turn.

Holly stood in front of her.

"Hey," Sasha said. Since she'd been busy with last-minute preparations for the wedding, she hadn't had much of a chance to talk to her best friend all day. "Have I told you what a wonderful ceremony it was and how beautiful you look?"

"Thank you. You look pretty dapper yourself." Holly tugged on Sasha's bow tie. "I couldn't help noticing that it's the same color as Ash's dress."

"Um, yeah." Sasha shifted her weight. For a moment, she thought about telling Holly it was probably just a coincidence, but that didn't feel right. Deep down, she knew it was so much more, and she had promised Holly she would tell her if there was ever something interesting going on in her love life. She had brushed Holly off in Florida, but now it was time to make good on that promise. "Remember when I promised to let you know if I ever get involved with someone new? Um, well, I have something to tell you. I think you might have already figured it out, but I wanted you to hear it from me."

Holly smiled. "Thanks for telling me. So, what exactly *is* going on between you and Ash?"

A sigh escaped Sasha. "I'll tell you when I know. Just two days ago, she didn't stop me when I told her I can't play that hiding game anymore and walked out, but today, she danced with me in front of half the town."

"That surprised the hell out of me. I didn't think she'd do it, even with that little nudge Leo and I gave her." Holly looked up into her eyes. "I hope that wasn't a mistake. I don't want to contribute to you getting hurt."

Sasha squeezed Holly's arm. "Don't worry. I'm a big girl."

"A big girl with a soft heart," Holly said. "I normally wouldn't have gotten involved, but there's something about the two of you together… The Ash that spent the bachelorette weekend with us and the one who danced with you tonight, that's not the Ash who tiptoed out of my house in the middle of the night and refused to be seen out in public together too often, even as friends."

The thought of Ashley and Holly as a couple made Sasha's stomach tighten with jealousy. At the same time, the idea of them together was so unreal that she almost couldn't imagine it. "I think she's grown a lot since then," she said softly. "I just don't know if it's enough to—"

"To what?" Holly prompted when Sasha trailed off.

"To choose me…us over the safety of hiding herself away in her hermetically sealed closet."

"I have a feeling it's not so hermetically sealed anymore."

"Holly," Beth called from inside of the barn before Holly could say more. "The Mitchells are getting ready to leave. Can you come and say goodbye?"

Holly glanced over her shoulder. "Sorry. Bride duty is calling."

"It's okay. Go."

Holly gave her a short hug. "Just for the record, she'd be stupid not to choose you."

"Well, she let you go too, so…"

"Yeah, but that turned out to be for the better," Holly said. "Ash and I were never destined to be more than friends, but I think she and you would actually be good for each other."

Sasha had only ever considered carefree, spontaneous people a good fit for herself before now, but she had to agree. Someone as responsible and thoughtful as Ashley balanced her well. She could only hope Ashley would come to the same realization.

The reception was still in full swing as Ash crossed the yard, even though it felt as if a lifetime had passed since she'd left the wedding.

As she got closer, she made out a tall, shadowy figure standing at the entrance, like a silent guard. The lanterns from inside the barn backlit the powerful frame, creating a halo effect around their head and strong shoulders. The person's face was obscured in shadows.

It could have been anyone—one of the wedding guests who'd stepped out for a breath of fresh air or one of the security guards—but Ash had no doubt who it was.

"Sasha?"

"I'm here," Sasha replied immediately. Her voice, soothing and steady, was like a lifeline that drew Ash to her with two more long steps.

They both half-turned so that the light from the barn was hitting their profiles and they could see each other.

"Ash!" Sasha sucked in a breath and dropped the bouquet that had been tucked beneath her arm. "Have you been crying?"

"It's okay." Ash rubbed her face with one hand.

"No, it's not." Sasha wrapped the cardigan sweater she must have taken from the back of Ash's chair around Ash's shoulders and tenderly brushed away the tears with her thumbs. "What happened?"

"I came out to my parents." Even as she said it, Ash could hardly believe it. She hadn't thought this day would ever come—nor had she believed she'd still have a family afterward.

Sasha froze. "Wow! That's... Wow." Still cradling her face, she studied Ash in the dim light. "I take it they didn't react too well?"

"Yes and no. There was a lot of crying and denial. It was a huge shock for them, and I don't think they're going to join PFLAG anytime soon. I was so sure I was going to lose them as soon as I told them."

"But you didn't?"

"No. I didn't." Ash's voice vibrated with joy, and she didn't try to control it. "They're struggling. I think it'll take them a long time to really accept it. But they said they still love me. Maybe it's not much compared to your aunt, but it's much more than I ever expected from them."

"God, I'm so happy for you!" Sasha grasped her around the waist, literally swept her off her feet, and twirled her around.

Laughter bubbled up from Ash's chest, loud and unrestrained. For once in her life, she didn't care who heard it. Her arms went around Sasha's neck, holding on as the world tilted around her. "Put me down," she called but was still laughing.

Sasha complied, gently setting Ash on her feet.

The feeling of sliding down Sasha's solid body sent shivers through Ash that had nothing to do with the cool night air.

With Sasha's warm hands on her hips and Ash's arms still around Sasha's neck, they paused and stared at each other.

Ash couldn't tell who moved first. It didn't matter.

They came together in a kiss that set Ash's world spinning again. She clung to Sasha as their tongues slid against each other, caressing, reconnecting.

When they finally broke the kiss, Ash felt as if every bone in her body had melted.

"Want to get out of here?" Sasha whispered against her lips, her voice rough and breathless.

Ash wanted nothing more than to finally be alone with her. "Yeah. Let's go say goodbye to Leo and Holly and the gang."

Without another word, Sasha picked up the bouquet she'd dropped earlier and placed her free hand in the small of Ash's back.

"Um, Sasha?" Ash asked as Sasha guided her back into the barn. "Why do you have a bridal bouquet?"

Sasha chuckled. "Because I didn't move out of the way quickly enough."

Main Street lay in silence as Ash parked her SUV in front of the bakery and jumped out.

Sasha had already parked her own car and was waiting at the bottom of the stairs leading up to her apartment.

Ash took several eager steps toward her, then glanced back. Her steps faltered. If she had interpreted the heated look in Sasha's eyes correctly, she would be staying the night. It was what she wanted too.

But that meant her car would be out here until morning, for the entire town to see. Her stomach tightened.

When Ash reached her, Sasha made no move to lead her upstairs. She looked her in the eyes as if knowing exactly what was going through her mind. "Are you sure about this...about us?" she asked quietly. "For the first time in my life, I can imagine having a real relationship with someone—with you, Ash. But I can't be in this alone. As much as I want you right now, we're not doing this unless you tell me I won't wake up tomorrow morning and find you gone." Her gaze was open and vulnerable. Sasha was putting herself out there, taking a leap of faith by trusting in Ash's word, even though she'd run from her before.

Ash's heart clutched. She knew how scary this had to be for Sasha. "You won't. I'll be here. Right here with you." She pulled her down and kissed her as if to seal the deal, telling herself she didn't care if any of Sasha's neighbors saw them. She was out now, and she wanted to live her life—wanted to live it with Sasha, even though it was probably too soon to say so.

Sasha pulled her closer with one hand in the small of her back and deepened the kiss.

Desire sparked in Ash's belly. With a gasp, she broke the kiss, took Sasha's hand, and pulled her up the stairs.

Sasha's normally steady hands shook as she unlocked the door. Then, as soon as she finally had it open, she kicked it shut behind them and pressed Ash against the wall next to it.

The way Sasha kissed her neck made Ash weak in the knees. For the first time in her life, she considered just dropping the flowers Sasha carried onto the first available surface, without putting them in water. But maybe slowing things down would be good. She wanted to remember this night for the rest of her life, not have it end in a frenzy of messy passion.

"Water," she whispered, but it came out sounding more like a moan as Sasha nibbled the sensitive spot below her ear.

Sasha lifted her lips off Ash's skin. "Hmm? You thirsty?"

"No." The only need she felt was that for Sasha. "The flowers are."

"Oh." Sasha stared at the bouquet in her hand as if she had forgotten she was still holding it. Then she strode over to her kitchenette and opened a cupboard.

Ash drank in the confident way in which she moved. Then she blinked as she realized the thing Sasha was filling with water wasn't a jug or a measuring cup. "You bought a vase."

Sasha smiled. "Looks like I'm spending too much time with a certain florist."

"Not possible."

Sasha put the flowers into the water and blindly set the vase down on the nearest surface. Her intense gaze was on Ash. "No?"

"No. I want to spend more time with you." Ash had rarely voiced her wants so openly, but her courage was immediately rewarded by the smile spreading over Sasha's face.

"I want that too. Starting with spending the next twenty-four hours in bed with you."

"Twenty-four hours?" Ash squeaked out. She'd never spent that much time in bed with anyone.

Sasha nodded fiercely. "At least. Is there a problem with that?"

"Um, well…" Ash could hardly think, especially not of a reason to ever leave Sasha's arms. "Uh, I'm supposed to have lunch with my parents tomorrow."

"You could call them and tell them you're passed out from pleasure and can't move," Sasha suggested.

Her words and the heat in her eyes sent a bolt of desire straight to Ash's core. "I think we should stop talking about my parents."

"Or stop talking period." Sasha kissed her, hot and possessive. Without breaking the kiss, she maneuvered her backward, through the door to the bedroom and turned on the light.

Somehow, Ash's cardigan dropped to the floor, and the heat of Sasha's hand radiated through the thin fabric of her dress.

"How does this dress…?" Sasha murmured against her lips. Her hands swept up and down Ash's back, then grazed the outer curves of her breasts, making her shiver. "Zipper?"

Ash struggled to remember. "No. There's a button."

Sasha found it. Then her lips were back on Ash's.

They broke the kiss just long enough for Sasha to pull the dress over Ash's head. Sasha even managed to unclasp Ash's bra while kissing her.

Ash tried to take off her sandals, but one of the straps got tangled and refused to cooperate.

Sasha knelt, opened the tiny buckles, and slid the sandals off her feet.

Now Ash was naked except for her panties, while Sasha was still fully dressed. With anyone else, it would have made her feel much too vulnerable, but she trusted Sasha with her body and her heart.

Still kneeling, Sasha peered up at Ash, her gaze full of admiration, then whispered a kiss onto her belly, right above the edge of her panties.

Ash's breath caught.

Slowly, keeping eye contact, Sasha hooked her fingers into the sides of Ash's panties and tugged them down over her hips. She leaned forward again and pressed a soft kiss to the curls at the juncture of Ash's thighs.

A breathless little gasp escaped Ash. She had to grip Sasha's shoulders with both hands so she wouldn't sink to the floor.

When Sasha got to her feet, she slid up Ash's body, leaving a trail of hot kisses until she reached her lips again. "God, you feel so good." Sasha trailed her hands along her bare back and over her hips, pressing her closer.

"I want to feel you too."

When Sasha reached for the buttons of her shirt, Ash nudged her fingers aside. "Let me."

Even though she was taller and stronger, Sasha allowed Ash to push her backward. When the backs of her legs collided with the bed, she sank down on the edge of it.

Ash stepped between her legs and undid the bow tie but left it dangling around her neck for now. Slowly, she slid the suspenders off her strong shoulders. God, undressing a woman in a men's suit was incredibly hot, especially since she vividly remembered every detail of the female body she'd find underneath.

Sasha held still and watched her with an expression that made Ash's skin tingle.

Ash's fingers shook with need as she knelt between Sasha's thighs and tugged the hem of the shirt from Sasha's dress pants. She slid the tie out from behind the shirt's collar and opened the first button, then another. After each one, she paused to kiss every bit of skin she'd just laid bare. It felt as if she were unwrapping a much-anticipated gift. Finally, the shirt was completely unbuttoned, revealing a tantalizing glimpse of the inner curve of her breasts, nestled into a surprisingly lacy bra.

"God," Ash whispered against Sasha's skin. "You look like a model."

Sasha barked out a startled laugh. "Me? I'm not exactly tiny."

"That's what makes you so beautiful. I'd buy whatever you'd model."

"You'd drown in it," Sasha said, her voice husky.

"I wouldn't buy it for me. I'd enjoy dressing you in it—and then slowly taking it off you." *Wow.* Ash barely recognized herself. She'd never talked like this to anyone.

But Sasha's groan and the passion in her eyes revealed that she thought it was hot.

Despite all her talk about undressing Sasha, Ash paused. She wanted to look at her like this for a moment. After she had enjoyed the view for a while, she pulled the hair tie from Sasha's braid, separated the strands, and ran her fingers through her soft hair. "I've wanted to do this for a while."

Sasha leaned her head into the caresses. "Really?"

"Mm-hmm. And this." Ash slipped her hands inside the unbuttoned shirt and cupped Sasha's breasts through her bra.

"Oh God." Sasha swayed backward and gently grasped Ash's shoulders with both hands as if she needed to hold on so she wouldn't collapse onto the bed. Her fingers slid restlessly over the nape of Ash's neck, sending shivers through her.

Ash leaned forward and pressed her lips to the slope of her left breast. Sasha's heartbeat thudded beneath her mouth.

Somehow, this felt very different from their night in Florida—just as good, but even more intimate. Ash hadn't thought that possible.

Through the silky material of the bra, she stroked her thumbs over Sasha's rock-hard nipples and delighted in the drawn-out moan that pulled from Sasha's chest. Slowly, she pushed the shirt over her shoulders and down her arms until the cuffs caught at her wrists, basically tying her hands to her sides.

Erotic possibilities danced through Ash's mind. She'd never been one to experiment, but the thought of Sasha writhing helplessly beneath her made her gasp for breath.

But not tonight. Tonight, she wanted both of them free to touch.

She removed the cuff links, set them on the bedside table, and slid the sleeves off Sasha's wrists.

Sasha's hands were on her the second they were freed. She tangled her fingers in Ash's hair and guided her mouth to hers for a passionate kiss.

Ash could feel Sasha's heat pressing against her belly through the fabric of her pants. She moaned into their kiss. Suddenly, she couldn't wait to feel more of her against her. She reached around Sasha and managed to unhook her bra with only minimal fumbling.

The bra straps slid down Sasha's arms, revealing firm breasts and creamy skin that Ash immediately wanted to taste. She reached between them, eager to have every obstacle separating them gone. With trembling fingers, she unbuckled Sasha's belt and unbuttoned her dress pants. The rasp of the zipper as she drew it down was louder than the sound of her elevated breathing.

Sasha kicked off her shoes and somehow managed to get rid of her socks. She let herself fall back onto the bed and arched her hips off it so Ash could tug off her pants and the pair of lacy panties she wore beneath.

God, sexy panties beneath a men's suit… It was as unexpected as it was hot.

Then Sasha lay naked before her, legs dangling off the bed. The sight of Sasha's body, powerful yet vulnerable at the same time, robbed Ash of breath. Still kneeling before her, Ash put both hands on Sasha's thighs so she wouldn't topple over. "Sasha," she whispered. "I…I want…"

"Anything," Sasha answered without hesitation. "Anything you want. Just tell me."

A mix of embarrassment and desire warmed Ash's cheeks. "I want to make love to you." She struggled to hold Sasha's gaze and added more quietly, "With my mouth."

Sasha shuddered as if Ash were already touching her. "God, yes. I want that too."

"But I…I've never done that before." Embarrassment won out for a second, and she stared at the sheets next to Sasha's head.

"You…wow. Never?"

Still not looking at her, Ash shook her head.

Sasha sat up. She took both of Ash's hands and tugged her onto the bed until they were lying side by side, not yet touching. She trailed her fingertips over Ash's flushed cheek. "You don't have to."

Ash flicked her gaze to Sasha's face. "I want to. I wanted to in Florida, but I wasn't sure you'd let me."

"Let you?" Sasha let out a disbelieving laugh. "Just the thought of you… Jesus!" She kissed her with so much passion that Ash felt as if she'd catch on fire. "But I'm still glad we waited," she murmured when they came up for air. "Because now that it won't just be a quick slice of pizza, it's going to be so much better."

Ash's embarrassment retreated. Sasha talked so openly about her wants and needs that she dared to do the same. She cupped Sasha's face between her hands. "It's not going to be quick at all. I want to kiss and caress and taste every inch of you."

A long groan wrenched from Sasha's throat. "God, you're going to kill me, aren't you?"

"No. I'm going to love you." The words hung between them, more meaningful than Ash had intended, but she refused to take them back—or to linger on what they meant. That could wait until later. Much later.

She urged Sasha onto her back, leaned over her on one elbow, and kissed her slowly. God, this might be her favorite thing in the whole world.

Sasha moaned into her mouth and pulled her down more fully until their bodies touched all along their lengths, bare skin against bare skin.

Ash gasped for breath and then used the moment her lips left Sasha's to slide a little lower and press her mouth to her throat. So lovely. She nuzzled the side of her neck, then tried an experimental lick.

Sasha's hands came up, and she raked her fingers through Ash's hair, just stroking, not stopping or guiding her. She seemed content to let Ash explore at her own pace, and Ash took full advantage.

She trailed her lips over the arc of her ribs, smiling as Sasha squirmed, and then nibbled the undersides of her breasts. Gently, she kissed each nipple, which immediately hardened against her lips. Beautiful. She could spend a lifetime worshipping Sasha's breasts. Experimentally, she flattened her tongue and swiped it across the taut nipple.

Sasha arched her back, pressing herself against Ash's mouth.

With a freedom she'd never had before, Ash tested her reaction to quick flicks, languid circles, and gentle nips.

Sasha seemed to like it all. Her breathing grew rough, and she pressed Ash against herself with both hands.

Ash placed one last kiss on Sasha's breast before sliding down her body. She trailed lingering kisses down Sasha's quivering stomach, alternating with licks and nibbles. Her taste, her scent, the softness of her skin, and the low sounds coming from Sasha made Ash's senses come alive.

Sasha restlessly stroked Ash's shoulders. When Ash kissed the curve of her hip, Sasha bucked beneath her and let out a long groan. "God, you're making me crazy."

Ash lifted her head and looked up into Sasha's flushed face.

Their gazes locked, Sasha's full of smoldering desire. She lay before Ash, completely open, willing to trust her with her body—and maybe her heart. Naked need darted across her face. Need for Ash.

The sight took her breath away. She hadn't thought it possible to feel such a mix of tenderness and burning desire at the same time.

When Ash slid even lower, Sasha parted her legs farther, opening herself to Ash's touch.

Ash nestled herself between her strong legs and pressed her cheek to the inside of Sasha's thigh.

God, how silky her skin was. She rubbed her face against it like a cat and pressed a soft kiss to the pale skin where Sasha's hip and leg met.

A shudder ran through Sasha's body.

Ash touched the neatly trimmed dark curls with trembling fingers and parted her gently.

The musky scent of Sasha's arousal drifted up, and Ash inhaled it deeply. She held herself very still for several seconds, hovering over Sasha. *Oh my God. I can't believe I'm about to—*

"Please." Sasha twitched and writhed beneath her. "Ash…"

The desperate plea in her tone swept away the last of Ash's hesitation. She wanted to give Sasha everything she needed.

She slid one hand up onto Sasha's stomach, anchoring them both, then lowered her head and touched her tongue to Sasha's swollen folds.

Sasha groaned deep in her throat and lifted her hips toward Ash's mouth.

Ash stroked her, first tentatively, then, encouraged by Sasha's gasps and moans, more boldly.

It felt so good to be able to give Sasha pleasure. She dipped deeper into Sasha's wetness. The salty-sweet taste of her went straight to her head like a delicious wine.

"God, Ash. Oh, that's so good." Sasha slid one leg over Ash's shoulder and cupped the back of her head with one hand, pressing her closer.

With that, Ash let go of her insecurities and experimentally rolled her tongue over the tip of Sasha's clit.

"Ah!" Sasha bucked against her mouth. Her legs wrapped around Ash more tightly.

Ash reached up with her free hand, blindly found Sasha's fingers, and entwined them with her own as she continued to caress her with her lips and her tongue.

All too soon, Sasha's thighs started to tremble against her. "Ash. Ashley."

Ash looked up, needing to connect with her. The sight before her made her head swim. She'd never seen anything more beautiful.

Sasha's head thrashed against the pillow. Her cheeks were flushed, and her lips parted as she gasped for breath. Her eyes were open, watching Ash move between her legs.

The look of total abandon on Sasha's face sent a rush of desire to Ash's core. She loved the way Sasha wasn't afraid to give herself over to pleasure.

Caressing Sasha's heaving belly with one hand, Ash lowered her head back down and closed her lips over Sasha's clit.

A raw cry resembling Ash's name tore from Sasha's chest. Her fingers tightened in her hair, and her belly muscles contracted beneath Ash's palm as she came against her mouth.

Ash held very still and tenderly stroked her belly until Sasha's legs relaxed and her grip on Ash's hair gentled to a caress.

"Jesus, Ash," Sasha whispered, her voice hoarse from panting. She tugged on the hand that was still entwined with her own. "Come up here."

After one last gentle kiss to Sasha's sensitive flesh, Ash eased her lips away, wiped her mouth, and slid up Sasha's body until she was in her arms.

Sasha cradled her face between her palms with a tenderness that nearly made Ash cry. "You really are going to kill me if this is what your very first time is like."

"Really?" Ash's cheeks flushed, more with pride than with embarrassment.

"Really." A devilish glint entered Sasha's dark eyes. "Well, if you still aren't sure how good you just made me feel, how about I do the same to you and then we compare notes?" Without waiting for Ash's reply, Sasha rolled them around until she was on top. "Okay?"

"Okay," Ash breathed out.

Then Sasha's lips were on hers, and all Ash could do was hang on and try not to come on the spot as Sasha kissed her and caressed her, reverently and yet full of urgency at the same time.

She worshipped Ash's breasts for what seemed like an eternity—massaging, nibbling, sucking—until Ash was a quivering, moaning bundle of need. Her skin burned everywhere Sasha touched. She rubbed herself against Sasha's muscular thigh. "Can you…touch me? Please."

"Touch you where?" Sasha asked with a smile. "Here?" She kissed her breast once more, then a spot just above Ash's belly button. "Here?"

Ash weakly lifted her head off the bed. "Yes. No."

"No? Then maybe…here?" Sasha slid down her body. She gently nudged Ash's legs apart with her broad shoulders. Her hair tickled the sensitive skin of Ash's inner thighs, nearly driving her mad with anticipation.

Ash had a feeling Sasha had wanted to continue her teasing by kissing her thigh, but Sasha sucked in a breath and seemed to forget her little game. Her nostrils flared, and she let out a hum of appreciation that sent warm breath across Ash's damp heat.

She shuddered and groaned helplessly.

Eyes blazing, Sasha looked back up at her, then dipped her head. Her warm tongue swirled through Ash's wetness.

The pleasure was so intense that Ash cried out. She clamped her teeth onto her bottom lip to hold back the loud moans rising up her throat.

"No," Sasha said fiercely. "Don't hold back. I want to hear you."

When she closed her mouth over Ash and slid two fingers into her at the same time, holding back wasn't an option anyway. With a strangled gasp, Ash arched up against her and clutched at Sasha's hair, her shoulders, anything she could reach.

Sasha matched the rhythm of Ash's hips with her fingers and her mouth.

Much too soon, tension uncoiled from deep inside of her. Her legs shook uncontrollably. Her senses blurred, and her entire world was reduced to the pleasure caused by Sasha. She bucked her hips against Sasha one final time, then shouted out her name as her entire body seemed to melt into one pulsating ball of ecstasy.

Sasha stayed with her, letting her ride it out as Ash continued to shudder and quake against her. When the tremors finally stopped, she carefully withdrew and slid up Ash's body.

Ash swallowed against a dry throat. She lifted her arms, which felt heavy with pleasure, and tightly wrapped them around Sasha.

Lovingly, Sasha kissed her shoulder, her neck, her forehead. She took Ash's face between her big hands and caressed her cheeks with her thumbs. "Again?"

Ash groaned, half enthusiasm, half protest. "Oh God. I might need a moment to recover first. That was pretty intense."

Sasha laughed, but her gaze was concerned. "No, I mean, you're crying again."

Dazed, Ash reached up and touched her face.

Sasha brought Ash's hand to her lips and kissed the dampness off her fingertips. "Are you okay?"

"Yes. More than okay. I don't know why this keeps happening. I promise it won't always—"

Sasha kissed her, slowly and deeply.

Tasting herself on Sasha's lips made new heat rush through Ash.

"Don't apologize," Sasha said fiercely. "I want you to feel everything when we're together. No hiding, no holding back."

Ash kissed her back. "I don't think I could hold anything back with you, even if I wanted—and I don't."

"Good." Sasha rolled onto her back, drew Ash half on top of her, pulled the blanket up over both of them, and turned off the light.

Ash cuddled close. She slid her leg across Sasha's thighs and laid her head on what was quickly becoming her favorite spot on her shoulder. Every inch of her body felt languid, and she knew that, for the first time, no doubts, regrets, or concerns would keep her awake after a night of passion.

Sasha's heartbeat settled into a calming rhythm beneath her ear, and the soothing caresses along Ash's back slowed and then stopped.

Sleep tugged at Ash's eyelids too, but she fought it, because as content as she felt, there was something clawing at her chest that needed to come out. "Sasha?" she whispered into the darkness.

"Hmm?"

"Um, would it be very cliché of me to tell you that I think I love you?"

The peaceful breathing beneath her ear stopped and was then replaced by a startled gasp. Sasha darted her hand around until she found the light switch. When the light flared on, she stared up at Ash with wide eyes.

Oh shit. Ash stared back. Sasha clearly hadn't been ready to hear that. "I mean, I know it's probably too soon and not very original to say it right after we...you know, but..."

Sasha smiled. "Well, then I'm just as unoriginal, because I love you too."

"You...you do?"

"Yeah." Sasha looked deeply into her eyes, radiating so much love that Ash nearly teared up again. "I've probably been in love with you since Florida—that first night, not the second—but I didn't want to admit it, even to myself."

"I think it was even sooner than that for me," Ash admitted with a smile. Now that she could look back at it without fear, it was easy to recognize.

Sasha caressed her back with long strokes. "When?"

"When we made cupcakes together and then got into that food fight. I'd never done anything so crazy before. And then that kiss…" Ash let out a little moan. "I don't think I'll ever be able to eat a cupcake again without thinking about it."

"Hmm. I don't have any cupcakes in the house right now, and that might be a problem because you," Sasha rolled them over and captured Ash's mouth in a deep, heartfelt kiss, "are going to miss breakfast."

"I am?" Ash gasped out, her hips already rocking against Sasha's thigh.

Sasha nodded and leaned down to nibble her throat. "And possibly lunch."

That was the last thing either of them said for quite some time, with the exception of "oh God," breathless gasps of each other's name, and whispered words of love.

Chapter 22

Sunlight filtered through Sasha's closed lids. She blinked open her eyes and realized she was on her side, facing the bedside table, where the alarm clock showed it was eleven o'clock. *Wow.* She hadn't slept that late since culinary school.

Her gaze fell on the empty spot in bed beside her.

Sasha tensed.

Then she felt the warmth against her back.

They had changed positions while they had slept, and now Ashley was cuddled up to her from behind, her leg tucked between Sasha's and her face pressed between her shoulder blades.

Relief flowed through Sasha. She exhaled sharply and only now realized how worried she'd still been, even after Ashley's declaration of love and her promise to stay. Apparently, the fear of being left sat deeper than she'd thought, but she trusted them to work through it together.

"Morning," Ashley mumbled behind her and sleepily pressed her lips to Sasha's back.

Sasha turned in her arms and kissed her. "Good morning. Hmm, I love waking up with you."

Ashley looked her in the eyes, and Sasha could tell Ashley sensed the deeper meaning behind her words. "I promised."

"You did." Sasha caressed her cheek, and Ashley leaned her face into the touch, her eyes fluttering closed. "But that doesn't mean it's going to be easy for you. People will talk, and I know that will bring up a lot of painful memories for you. If you'd rather not make it public yet…"

"Thank you." Ashley took Sasha's face between both hands and kissed her tenderly. "I know what that offer cost you. But I don't think it's how we should do this. It's not going to work anyway. Half of the guests at the wedding probably saw us kiss in front of the barn last night, and Brooke already guessed days ago."

"Wow. She did?" Sasha would have loved to have been a fly on the wall during that conversation. "How did she react?"

"She said she's shipping us, whatever that means."

Sasha chuckled. "She's a woman of taste. I'm shipping us too." Then she sobered and studied Ashley's face. "Are you okay with that? People finding out, I mean."

Ashley leaned her head against Sasha's shoulder and sighed. Her warm breath fanned over Sasha's skin, making her shiver pleasantly. "It's going to be hard for me. Not being able to hide that part of me that I've kept hidden for so long. It feels like suddenly everyone can see me naked."

"No." Sasha trailed her hand down Ashley's bare side. "Only I get that privilege."

Ashley smiled. The worry lines on her forehead disappeared. "Are we feeling a little possessive?" she asked, her tone teasing.

"Maybe a little." Sasha held her thumb and index finger a fraction of an inch apart. "Is that okay?"

"Yeah. Because I don't want anyone else to see you naked either."

Sasha kissed her. "Don't worry. The two of us are having steak, and no one else is invited to dinner. And if you want to dine in private for a while, that's fine with me."

"Like I said, I'm not sure that's even an option anymore. By Monday, half of Fair Oaks will probably know. I'll get used to it. I just…"

"What?" Sasha trailed her fingers through the hair at Ashley's temple. "Talk to me, please."

"I'm worried about Mrs. Beasley. Everyone else could hurt my feelings, but she could really hurt my shop. What if she convinces her husband and her friends to get their flowers elsewhere?"

Sasha grimly shook her head. "Your flower shop is the best one in town."

Ashley's lips curved up into a small smile. "It's the only one in town."

"Yeah, well, it would be the best even if it wasn't the only one," Sasha said with conviction. "And I'm not just saying that because I'm biased.

Yes, you might lose some customers, but I think you'll keep most. People like going with what they know. Plus you have friends. Leo's mother is in the choir, and Holly's mom has helped every pet owner in town at some point. I also know a little bakery who'd love to do some fun promotions with you—buy a bouquet, get a cupcake free or something like that. The possibilities are endless."

"Endless, hmm?" Ashley looked at her with so much tenderness that Sasha's chest swelled. "Have I told you how much I love you?"

"Not in the last," Sasha glanced at the alarm clock, "five hours."

"How negligent of me. Can't have that." Ashley kissed both corners of Sasha's mouth, then nibbled her lips. "I love you."

"I love you too." Hearing the words—and saying them—still made Sasha's heart sing, and she didn't think that would change anytime soon, if ever.

Their lips met in a long kiss.

"You are right," Ashley said when the kiss ended. "I'll be fine, no matter what. Even if things are tough for a while, we'll think of something."

"I like the sound of that," Sasha said softly. "We."

"That's how I want to handle things from now on. Together. That's why it's not just up to me to decide how we'll handle people. What do you want?"

Sasha thought about it. "You know I'm not the type to make a huge public declaration either. Why don't we play it by ear and just do whatever feels right at any given moment?"

Ashley smiled and cuddled closer. "Hmm. Do what feels right. Sounds good to me. Because this," she let her hands wander over Sasha's bare back, "feels very right."

"Yes," Sasha breathed out as Ashley's leg slipped between hers, "yes, it does. But I think you need to call your parents first and tell them you'll be missing lunch."

Ashley lifted her head and stared across Sasha at the alarm clock. "Oh shit. I didn't realize it was so late. Sasha, I'm so sorry. There's nothing I want more than to stay in bed with you all day, but my parents are really struggling with my sexual orientation, and if I skip lunch because of you, it's not going to help them accept it—or you."

As much as Sasha wanted to ignore the rest of the world and keep Ashley in her arms for the entire weekend, she knew Ashley was right. She threw back the covers and swung her legs out of bed.

"You don't have to get up," Ashley said.

"I do. Because I'm going to introduce you to the pleasures of a quickie in the shower."

Ashley jumped out of bed with a speed that made Sasha laugh.

Early on Monday morning, Ash sang along with one of Leo's songs on the radio all the way to the farm. Twice, a yawn interrupted her enthusiastic singing.

After two nights with little sleep and getting up at four a.m. this morning, when Sasha's alarm clock had gone off, she was tired, but at the same time, she felt more alive than ever.

Maybe she could keep up her good mood by slipping in and out of the barn without her parents noticing.

Lunch with them yesterday had been tense, with her parents going out of their way to avoid mentioning Sasha, the wedding, or Ash's coming-out. Apparently, they had decided that the way to handle her sexual orientation was to ignore it.

Ash had let them get away with it—for now. But in the future, she would try to weave Sasha into the conversation whenever she could. Not that it would be difficult since Sasha was pretty much all she was thinking of right now.

The sun was just rising over the horizon when she parked her car in front of the barn and began gathering her centerpieces and containers left over from the wedding.

The catering tent was gone, and so were the white drapes and the strings of fairy lights.

Ash stood at the entrance of the barn and stared inside, almost unable to believe that this had been the magical place where she'd worked up the courage to dance with Sasha.

A gum paste alstroemeria rested on the barrel next to the barn doors. Ash picked it up and lifted it to her nose, then laughed at herself. Of course it didn't have a scent, no matter how real it looked.

But then her nose detected a hint of cinnamon.

Mmm. Ash closed her eyes and inhaled deeply.

"Good morning," her mother's voice from behind her made her jerk.

Ash turned and automatically hid the gum paste flower behind her back. Then, when she noticed what she was doing, she withdrew her hand and returned it to the front. No more hiding. "Morning, Mom. You're up early."

Her mother gave her a puzzled look. "You know we keep farmer's hours. But what brings you out here so early?"

Keeping baker's hours, Ash nearly answered, but despite her resolution to not hide anymore, she didn't want to rub it in her mother's face where she'd spent the night…or rather the last two nights. "I thought I'd get my stuff before work so Dad can have the barn back."

Her mother nodded and helped her get the flower arrangements to the car. They worked in silence until all the centerpieces were stowed in the back of the SUV. Ash missed the easy chatter they normally kept up. It would probably be a while before things between them returned to normal. But at least her mother was trying.

Ash carefully set the gum paste alstroemeria in a safe corner of the trunk.

"It's beautiful," her mother said quietly.

"Sasha made it."

"I know." Her mother's expression was stony.

Ash swung the hatch closed and shuffled her feet. "Is it okay if I take Casper with me now? Thanks for offering to take him all weekend, by the way."

"Of course. We always love having him." Her mother sighed and added, "Since he's going to be our only grandchild."

Ash bit her lip, totally unprepared for that topic. She had never allowed herself to think about kids, and she had no idea if Sasha would want any, so she pretended she hadn't heard her mother's mumbled words.

Silence settled over them as they crossed the yard and entered the house. Ash was glad for Casper's excited whining when he saw her. She greeted him, then looked around for his leash.

Her mother leaned against the sink and watched her every move, as if comparing what she saw to the Ashley she had thought she knew. "Do you want to stay for breakfast? Your father and I already ate, but I still have a bit of leftover tater tot casserole from yesterday."

Ash's stomach let out an enthusiastic growl, answering for her. She pressed her hand to her belly and fought a blush as she remembered what had made her skip breakfast. "Thank you. I'd like that."

She sat at her customary place at the table and dug into the casserole while her mother nursed a cup of coffee and watched her.

Neither of them said anything beyond "This is great" until Ash had cleared her plate.

It was only when Ash rinsed her plate and put it into the dishwasher that her mother said softly, "You look good. Different, but good."

Ash kept her back to her to hide the blush climbing up her throat. Could her mother really see a change in her? Ash certainly felt different.

When she slowly turned, her mother ran her fingers through Ash's hair, as she'd done when Ash had been a little girl.

Oh. She means my hair. She self-consciously fingered the shorter strands. "Thank you. I like it."

"Well, I'll admit I liked your hair better when it was longer."

"You'll get used to it," Ash said.

Her mother studied her for several seconds, then she sighed. "I suppose I will." She walked Ash to the door and kissed her cheek.

Ash could feel her gaze following her all the way to the car. With Casper in the passenger seat, she drove back into town and steered down Main Street. When she passed the bakery, she couldn't resist and stopped the car. "Casper, stay. I'm gonna get us a treat."

Her real treat, of course, was getting to see Sasha.

As she crossed the street, she could see her behind the counter, selling her delicious baked goods to several early-morning customers. Ash's heart skipped a beat at the sight of her.

She drank in Sasha's tall form, her confident stance, her easy laugh, and the way she didn't slouch even though her height made her stand out in the crowd.

Before she could even pull open the door, Sasha looked up, and their gazes connected through the glass.

A broad smile crinkled the corners of Sasha's eyes.

The person in front of the counter turned, probably to see who had made Sasha smile that way.

Oh shit. It was Mr. Beasley, of all people. Ash swallowed down the lump in her throat and forced herself to pull the door open.

There was a line in front of the counter, typical for a Monday morning, and Ash felt as if everyone was watching her as she got in line. Cindy Kaufman, the choir leader, leaned across one of the small tables to whisper something to a friend of hers.

This was starting to resemble one of Ash's nightmares.

She squared her shoulders and kept her gaze on Sasha, watching her nimble fingers as she slid donuts and cupcakes into boxes.

"Morning, Ashley." Mr. Beasley stopped next to her on his way out the door, a bakery box in his hands. "The flowers looked wonderful."

"Oh, you mean Mr. Kamp's funeral on Wednesday."

"No. I meant the wedding." Mr. Beasley pointed over his shoulder. "Sasha just showed me some photos on her phone. The centerpieces looked wonderful, and so did the bouquet she caught. Looks like our Sasha is going to be the next to marry."

Heat rushed up Ash's neck until even her ears burned.

Mr. Beasley patted her arm and lifted the bakery box. "I'd better get these home." The bell jangled as the door closed behind him.

Ash stared after him. Did he know about Sasha and her? No, impossible. If he had known, he wouldn't have commented on Sasha being the next to marry so casually, would he? But at the very least, he didn't seem to hold it against her that she'd done the flowers for a same-sex wedding, and that was encouraging.

Breathing a little more freely, she waited her turn to step up to the counter.

"Hi." She looked up into Sasha's warm brown eyes, and the tenderness in them made her forget what she'd been about to order.

Luckily, Sasha's aunt waved the two people in line behind Ash over to her side of the counter so that they could talk for a minute.

"Let me guess," Sasha said. "Two espresso chocolate chip cookies, one Beagle Bite, and one vanilla cupcake with strawberry buttercream frosting. You're in luck."

Ash smiled. "I know. I'm a lucky woman."

They stared into each other's eyes.

Sasha cleared her throat. "Um, I meant because I made the vanilla cupcakes the daily special, so you get fifty cents off." She gestured up to the blackboard above the counter.

"Hmm, too bad, because I don't want one."

"You don't?"

"No," Ash said. "Not today."

"Wow. Ashley Gaines is finally trying one of my non-vanilla cupcakes." Sasha pressed a hand to her chest. The expression on her face was comical for the sake of the other customers, but her eyes revealed that it had a deeper meaning for her too. "So, which one do you want?"

"I thought I'd get a Sweet Kiss."

"I thought you already did," Sasha whispered so softly that only Ash could hear.

Ash's cheeks grew warm again. She'd gotten all kinds of kisses this morning, from sweet to hot. "Yeah, but I need one more."

Sasha flashed her a smile that made Ash's belly tumble. "Just one?"

"For starters."

Chuckling, Sasha slid a chocolate cupcake with salted caramel frosting into the box with Brooke's cookies and pressed another one into Ash's hand. "Eat one right here. I want to see the look on your face when you take the first bite."

Ash peeled back the paper liner and took a bite. Chocolate and caramel burst on her taste buds, making her moan.

Heat flickered in Sasha's eyes. "Good?" she asked, her voice husky.

"Oh yeah," Ash replied around a mouthful of cupcake. She chewed and swallowed. "I think it's love at first bite."

"Is it?"

"Mm-hmm."

Ash wanted to put money on the counter, but Sasha waved her away. "It's on the house."

"Hey, Ash." Travis walked up to the counter behind her, interrupting their eye contact. "Are you done flirting? Because there are other people who want to get some Sweet Kisses before work too, you know?"

Then get your own baker, Ash nearly answered. She put the rest of the cupcake into the box with the other treats and then hesitated, knowing she wouldn't get another chance to talk to Sasha all day. With Mother's Day coming up, it would be a busy week for both of them.

Her gaze darted to Sasha's eyes, then her lips. Should she...?

Do whatever feels right at any given moment, Sasha had said. And this felt right, so Ash ignored the prickle of unease that told her people were watching, leaned across the counter, and placed the shortest, softest of kisses on Sasha's lips.

Then, cheeks flaming, she turned and walked out, not stopping to see if anyone was staring at her in disgust.

"Wow," she heard Travis mumble behind her, "guess my Sweet Kiss isn't going to resemble hers."

"Nope," Sasha replied. Her tone was stunned, yet elated. "That kind of Sweet Kiss is reserved for Ashley from now on."

Then the door closed behind Ash, and she dared to turn around for one last glance back.

Her gaze met Sasha's, and when Sasha smiled at her, Ash no longer cared how anyone else was looking at her.

If you enjoyed *Not the Marrying Kind,* check out Jae's romance novel *Perfect Rhythm,* the book in which Holly and Leo met and fell in love.

About Jae

Jae grew up amidst the vineyards of southern Germany. She spent her childhood with her nose buried in a book, earning her the nickname "professor." The writing bug bit her at the age of eleven. Since 2006, she has been writing mostly in English.

She used to work as a psychologist but gave up her day job in December 2013 to become a full-time writer and a part-time editor. As far as she's concerned, it's the best job in the world.

When she's not writing, she likes to spend her time reading, indulging her ice cream and office supply addictions, and watching way too many crime shows.

CONNECT WITH JAE
Website: www.jae-fiction.com
E-Mail: jae@jae-fiction.com

Other Books from Ylva Publishing

www.ylva-publishing.com

Perfect Rhythm
(Fair Oaks Series – Book 1)
Jae

ISBN: 978-3-95533-862-6
Length: 298 pages (107,000 words)

Pop star Leontyne Blake is over love and women falling for her image. When she heads home to be near her sick father, she meets small-town nurse Holly, an asexual woman who has no interest in dating, sex, or Leo's fame. Can their tentative friendship develop into something more despite their diverse expectations?

A lesbian romance about finding the perfect rhythm between two very different people.

A Curious Woman
Jess Lea

ISBN: 978-3-96324-160-4
Length: 283 pages (100,000 words)

Bess has moved to a coastal town where she has a job at a hip gallery, some territorial chickens, and a lot of self-help books. She's also at war with Margaret, who runs the local museum with an iron fist. When they're both implicated in a senseless murder, can they work together to expose the truth?

A funny, fabulous, cozy mystery filled with quirkiness and a sweet serve of lesbian romance.

Major Surgery
Lola Keeley

ISBN: 978-3-96324-145-1
Length: 198 pages (69,000 words)

Surgeon and department head Veronica has life perfectly ordered...until the arrival of a new Head of Trauma. Cassie is a brash ex-army surgeon, all action and sharp edges, not interested in rules or playing nice with icy Veronica. However when they're forced to work together to uncover a scandal, things get a little heated in surprising ways.

A lesbian romance about cutting to the heart of matters.

Hooked on You
Jenn Matthews

ISBN: 978-3-96324-133-8
Length: 281 pages (98,000 pages)

Anna has it all — great kids, boyfriend, good teaching job. Except she's so bored. Perhaps a new hobby's in order? Something...crafty?

Divorced mother and veteran Ollie has been through the wars. To relax, she runs a quirky crochet class in her English craft shop. Enter one attractive, feisty new student. A shame she's straight.

A quirky lesbian romance about love never being quite where you expect.

Made in the
USA
Columbia, SC

Made in the
USA
Columbia, SC